ABEL'S ISLAND

ABEL'S ISLAND · *William Steig*

A Sunburst Book / *Farrar, Straus and Giroux*

For Jeanne

ABEL'S ISLAND

◦ 1 ◦

Early in August 1907, the first year of their marriage, Abel and Amanda went to picnic in the woods some distance from the town where they lived. The sky was overcast, but Abel didn't think it would be so inconsiderate as to rain when he and his lovely wife were in the mood for an outing.

They enjoyed a pleasant lunch in the sunless woods, sharing delicate sandwiches of pot cheese and watercress, along with hard-boiled quail egg, onions, olives, and black caviar. They toasted each other, and everything else, with a bright champagne which was kept cool in a bucket of ice. Then they played a jolly game of croquet, laughing without much reason, and they continued laughing as they relaxed on a carpet of moss.

When this happy nonsense got boring, Amanda crawled under a fern to read and Abel went off by himself for a bit. Roaming among the trees, admiring the verdure, he saw a crowd of daisies clustered above him, like gigantic stars, and decided to cut one down and present his wife with a pretty parasol.

He was already smiling at the little joke he would make as he held it over her head. He chose a perfect daisy and, using his handkerchief to avoid being soiled by the sap, carefully cut through the stem with his penknife.

The daisy over his shoulder, he sallied back toward his wife, very pleased with himself. It grew windy rather suddenly, and some rain fell, wherever it could through the foliage. It was hard to hold on to the flower.

His wife was under the fern exactly where he'd left her, absorbed in the life of her book. "I have something for you," he said, lifting the tip of the fern. Amanda looked up at him with large, puzzled eyes, as if a page of words had unaccountably turned into her husband. A sharp gust of wind tore the daisy from his grasp.

"It's raining," Amanda observed.

"Indeed it is!" said Abel indignantly as the rain fell

harder. It flailed down while they tried to gather their
things. They huddled under Abel's jacket, he offended
at the thoughtless weather, she worried, both hoping
the downpour would soon let up. It didn't. It grew
worse.

Tired of waiting, and of wondering where all that
water came from, they decided to make a break for it.
With the jacket over them, they headed for home, leaving their picnic behind, but they could make little

progress against the wind. There was some angry thunder and dazzling flares of lightning near and far. "Dear one," cried Abel, "we must find shelter! Anywhere!" They stopped bucking the wind and ran skeltering with it, in dismay.

Clinging together, they ran, or were blown, through the woods, and eventually came up against a great, rocky cliff that shimmered in the pounding rain. They could be blown no farther.

The shelter they'd been seeking was very close. "Up here!" some voices called. "Up here!" Abel and Amanda looked up. Not far above them was the opening of a cave from which various furry faces peered out. They clambered together up into the cave, greatly relieved and panting for breath.

° 2 °

The cave was full of chattering animals who'd been lucky enough to find this haven. There were several mice that Abel and Amanda knew, and a family of toads they had once met at a carnival; all the rest were strangers. A weasel was off by himself in a corner, saying his prayers over and over.

Abel and Amanda were welcomed by all, and congratulations passed around. The storm raged as if it had lost its mind completely. The damp occupants of the

cave stood close together in the vaulted entrance like
actors who had played their parts and could now watch
the rest of the show from the wings. The storm was turning into a full-fledged, screaming hurricane. Huge trees
were bent by furious blasts of wind, branches broke,
thunder volleyed, and crazy shafts of lightning zigzagged
in the dark, steamy sky.

Abel and Amanda stood in the forefront of the group,
entranced by the fearsome drama. Amanda craned forward to watch an oak topple, when suddenly the wind
tore from her neck the scarf of gauze she was wearing,
and this airy web of stuff flew like a ghost from the
mouth of the cave. Abel gawked in horror, as if Amanda
herself had been rudely snatched away.

He dashed out impulsively. To no avail, Amanda tried
to stop him. "Abelard!" she screamed. She always used
his full name when she thought he was acting foolish.
He slid, unheeding, down the slope of rock.

The scarf hooked onto a bramble, from which he
retrieved it, but when he tried to climb back with his
trophy, the wind walloped and sent him spinning like
weightless tumbleweed, his sweetheart's scarf in his paw.
Helpless, unable even to struggle, he tucked in his head
and was whirled along, shocked and bewildered.

Heaven knows how far he was hustled in this manner,
or how many rocks he caromed off on his way. He did
no thinking. He only knew it was dark and windy and
wet, and that he was being knocked about in a world

that had lost its manners, in a direction, as far as he could tell, not north, south, east, or west, but whatever way the wind had a mind to go; and all he could do was wait and learn what its whims were.

Its whim was to fling him against a huge nail, where he fastened with all his strength. The nail was stuck in a fragment of board that had once been part of a large animal's house, and the fragment of board was embedded in a gully full of gravel. Abel clung to the nail and to Amanda's scarf, fighting the wind, whose force seemed to increase when he stopped riding with it.

The torrent of wet air tearing past made breathing difficult. Abel stuffed Amanda's scarf into his inner pocket and buried his head under his blazer. He soon found himself haunch-deep in a swelling stream. Rain had filled the gully and a heavy flow of muddy water loosened his board from its gravel mooring. He went sailing along, spinning this way and that, drilled with a trillion bullets of rain. Whatever happened no longer surprised him. It was all as familiar as one's very worst dreams.

It was definitely night now. He could see nothing, not his own paw in front of his face, but he knew he was moving swiftly upon his board. Soon he sensed he was in a river. In the immense darkness he could hear only wind and, all around him, rain falling into water.

A new sound slowly emerged, the murmur of roiling foam. His boat was moving toward it, and it rose to a turbulent roar. Then, with no advance notice, the boat tilted vertically and shot downward on what he was sure was a waterfall. Plunged deep in the water below, he fought against drowning; then, still hugging his nail, he rose slowly into a maelstrom of churning river, gasping for indrafts of air. Never had he been subjected to such rude treatment. How long could it last? How long, he wondered, could he abide it?

As if to answer that question, his craft shot forward again and he was pitched, jerked, and bandied about by the writhing, charging stream. His boat capsized, then righted itself and began turning over and over; each time his exasperated head bobbed up, he gasped for his possibly final breath. His fortitude amazed him.

Suddenly, thump! He was no longer moving. His craft had struck an unyielding mass and stuck in it. He had no idea, in the blackness, where in the world he was—it was any wet, windy where. He could feel the heavy water hurrying past him, tugging at his clothes. Drenched, cold, exhausted, he still held on to his nail, but the water pressing him against it allowed him to ease his grip, and it was a relief.

The wind still screamed, the rain still pelted, the river still raged, but he felt in some sort of harbor. Momentarily moored, wherever it was, he was able to wonder about Amanda. She was surely safe in the cave, among friends. She would be worrying about him, of course, but he would be getting back to her as soon as

he could. This was the weirdest experience of his life. He could never forget it. Never forget it . . . never forget . . . But for the moment he did. Merciful sleep shrouded his senses.

He slept curled around the rusty nail, wind and rain drubbing his tired young body.

Abel slept for fourteen hours. When his eyes opened, he was startled to find he was not where he ought to be; that is, in bed with his wife, Amanda. There was no wife; there were no walls. There was only a dazzling brightness in a landscape such as he had never seen. It was midafternoon.

As always after a hurricane, the atmosphere was crystal clear. He was now able to see his boat, the piece of board with the rusty nail that had probably saved his life. It was lodged in the uppermost branches of a tree that was mainly submerged in the river. Above was an endless cerulean blue. Below, water flowed swiftly, sparkling like champagne in the sun. The water was all around him, but some distance to his left, and some distance to his right, more trees stuck up out of the water, and beyond the trees on both sides the ground rose into wooded hills. Turning around, he saw behind him the waterfall over which he had plunged.

His tree seemed to be in the middle of the river. There was no doubt he was on an island. The rain must have ended shortly after he fell asleep, and during that time the flood had crested. It had already subsided some, or else he would not be as far above the water as he was. He would be able to descend to solid ground when the river fell farther.

He stood up, stretching, and winced; all his muscles ached. He had to sit down again. He wished Amanda was with him, or, better yet, he with her. As far as he could tell, apart from the trees, he was the only living thing between the horizons. He let out his loudest "Halloo-oo-oo-oo," then listened. There was no response, not even an echo.

The state of his clothes disturbed him. Damp and lumpy, they no longer had style. That would be corrected as soon as possible. He stared into the distance and speculated. "They're all wondering where I am, of course. Many I don't even know are wondering. It's certainly gotten around that Abelard Hassam di Chirico Flint, of the Mossville Flints, is missing."

It was distressing to consider the misery and anxiety his absence was causing those who cared. Search parties were surely out, but they wouldn't be anywhere near him. How could they even begin to guess what had happened: that, by freak chance, rain had formed a rivulet around a sort of boat he had boarded accidentally, that the rivulet, swelling, had taken him into a stream, the

stream had carried him into a river, the river had rushed him over a waterfall, and that he was now where he was, on his boat at the top of a tree, on an island, in whatever river this was.

When the water subsided, he would descend and go home—and what a story he'd have to tell! Meanwhile, he wished he had something to eat—a mushroom omelet, for example, with buttered garlic toast. Being hungry in addition to being marooned like this was really a bit too much. Absent-mindedly, he nibbled at a twig on his branch. Ah, cherry birch! One of his favorite flavors. The familiar taste made him feel a little more at home on his roost in the middle of nowhere.

He munched on the bark of a tender green shoot, his cheek filled with the pulp and the juice. He was eating. He sat there, vaguely smug, convinced that he had the strength, the courage, and the intelligence to survive. His eyes glazed over and he returned to sleep.

∘ 4 ∘

Abel awoke early in the morning, a new mouse after his second spell of healing slumber. Stretching felt good. It struck him that his landscape had changed. There were trees in his vicinity, all around him. His boat had been stopped by a towering one near the river's edge.

Looking below, he saw that his tree towered not only

because it was tall but because it stood on a rocky prominence. The water had returned to its proper level. In many places the grass was flattened, half buried in silt and gravel. Otherwise, it seemed a normal world.

He climbed to the very top of his tree and made a survey. He was indeed on an island. He could see the waterfall and river above; he was on one side of the island, by one fork of the river, and through the trees he could make out the fork on the opposite side; way below, he could see where the two forks rejoined. No one was anywhere visible.

It was time to be getting home. He started descending the birch, and in another moment he was grinning like an idiot. He was climbing down a tree he had never climbed up! Amanda would enjoy hearing about this. She had a sense of humor almost as sharp as his.

How good to be standing on solid earth again. He did some quick knee bends and ran around the tree just for the joy of the free movement. Then he sat on a stone, his elbows on his knees, and looked up and down the river. Perhaps by now they had managed to figure out what had happened to him and would be turning up in a boat, or something, after all. He waited, and to keep himself amused, he hummed snatches of his favorite cantata and imagined how he would narrate his adventures. He would be quite matter-of-fact, especially about the parts where he had shown courage and endurance; he would leave the staring and gasping to his audience.

No one turned up and Abel realized he'd been expecting too much. They'd never look for him here. Well, he would have to cross the river, one way or another. He ran to the other side of the island; perhaps the river was narrower there. It was wider. He ran back. He removed his shoes and socks, rolled up his trousers, and waded into the water to try the current.

No, it would be impossible to reach the far shore by swimming, even though he was a competent swimmer. The rush of water was much too strong. He'd be dashed against a rock, or dragged under and drowned.

He needed a boat of some sort. How about his board and nail? Perhaps he could do something with that. He climbed his tree, dislodged the board, and followed it down when it fell to the ground. He stood over it muttering to himself, thoughtfully fingering a filament of his mustache. How could he navigate this crude piece of wood? With a rudder! If he held the rudder at an acute angle, the boat would gradually work its way to the opposite shore. That would be bending the power of the stream to his own ends.

With a stick he scratched a diagram in the sand. It was a long rectangle, the river, crossed by a long diagonal, the course his boat would take. He should eventually land on the other side, much farther downstream. He was pleased with the way his mind was working.

He managed to tear a flat strip of wood from a nearby log and with his pearl-handled penknife whittled a shapely handle. The nail would help him keep the rudder firmly in position. Now he put on his shoes and socks, arranged his clothes as neatly as he could, and edged his boat into the water. It was really much too long since he'd seen Amanda. Since their wedding they had not been apart for as much as a day.

He got aboard, pushed off from the shore with his rudder, and quickly braced it against the nail, holding the handle firmly in his paws. The rudder worked! He was moving away from the bank. Then the boat reached the powerful current farther out. It began to bobble and buck. Abel's rudder shuddered in his paws, though he used all his strength to hold it steady. His knees bobbled and bucked with the boat as it sped along, snaking its way in the writhing grooves of the stream. It pitched left, then right, then the rudder was wrenched from his grasp; and now he was no longer a helmsman but a stunned passenger on a bit of flotsam at the mercy of the rampaging water.

His boat skedaddled up to a rock, hit it catty-cornered, and spun, and Abel was suddenly in the water, without his boat, borne along like a limp rag.

By good fortune, instead of being carried past the island and down the river, he was able to catch hold of a low-hanging streamer of weeping willow and pull himself ashore. The whole ordeal had lasted just a minute.

He ambled back to his starting point near the cherry birch, his toes turned awkwardly in. The mess of wet clothes he wore added to his sense of ineptitude and shame; he was used to their being dry and pressed. Where had he erred, he wondered. He should have bound the rudder to the nail, of course. He had been too hasty in his preparations, and he had underestimated the force of the rapids.

He would have to design and build a real boat, not a raft like the piece of board that had just quit his company. Perhaps it should be a sailboat; his jacket might serve as a sail. The rudder this time would be firmly secured through a hole in the stern.

The sailboat so clearly envisioned, some confidence returned. He felt a bit proud, even in his wet pants. He found a piece of driftwood, somewhat disgusting since it had been gnawed and bored and channeled by lower forms of life. But he couldn't afford to be overly sensitive now. He dragged the driftwood to the edge of the water. It would be the bottom of his boat. He washed his paws.

Next he peeled three large sections of bark from a dead tree, and shaped them for the sides by bending and breaking them on the straight edge of a rock. He collected a great deal of tough grass and fashioned lengths of rope by tying the ends together. When he thought he had enough of this rope, he began cutting grooves in the driftwood.

It was slow work with the small penknife. Not thinking, he fell to using his teeth. What? He drew back for a moment, in revulsion. Then he continued to gnaw away. He had never before gnawed on anything but food. But the grooves were done in no time, and he didn't honestly mind the taste of the somewhat decayed wood.

He fitted the bark into the grooves and then went to work lashing everything together, going round and round with the rope, and over and under, until his boat could hardly be seen for what it really was under all the lashings. Now he gathered a heap of soft grass and, with stone and stick for hammer and chisel, tamped it into all the crevices to prevent leakage.

He was pleased with his ingenuity. He had never

built a boat before; in fact, though he was a married mouse, he had never built anything, or done a day's work. However, he had watched others working, so ideas came to him readily. When he finished his caulking, he made a mast with a crosspiece, or boom, out of branches.

The mast was inserted among the numerous lashings and fastened with more. He made a rudder like the first, put it through a hole in the stern as he had planned, and surveyed the completed boat. Considering the crude materials and the lack of tools, he had to admit it was a fine piece of work. Too bad the bright day was his only witness.

Before dressing the mast with his jacket, where it hung like a scarecrow's slack raiment, he removed from the inner pocket Amanda's scarf, the bit of beloved gauze that accounted for his being where he was. He kissed the piece of fluff and tucked it inside his shirt.

A favorable breeze was drifting across the island toward the shore opposite. It seemed a good omen. He looked back in a farewell glance at this remote part of the world's geography that had given him shelter for two nights. Then he shoved his ship into the water and leaped aboard, grabbing the tail of his coat with one paw, the rudder with the other.

Boat number two fared worse than the first. The stream was too swift and the breeze too light for the sail to be effective. The boat swung around despite the rudder, hit a rock, and shattered. Luckily, Abel was pitched into a pebbled shallow and managed to scramble ashore, where he stood and watched his jacket and the wreck of his ship go the way of the river.

Wringing his clothes, he made his way back to the birch, which had become his center of operations. He resented the stream and meant to best it.

Abel grimly decided that in his next effort he would not count on a rudder; rudders were too dependent on the behavior of wayward water. Nor would he count on a sail, because wind was fickle. He would rely only on the strength of his own two arms. He had seen water striders, those insects that support themselves in swift streams on long legs kept wide apart. He would build a sort of water strider, a catamaran, and row it.

Excited by this new idea, he quickly put together a catamaran of crisscross sticks in the form of a pyramid, tying the sticks together wherever they crossed. Next, using that remarkable, newly discovered tool, his rodent teeth, he made two long oars, or sweeps, which he placed in notches he had gnawed out for oarlocks. In a sporting spirit, he tied his handkerchief to the top of a pole as a pennant.

Convinced he had finally solved the problem of conquering the stream, he launched his craft and climbed into the captain's seat with his oars. The moment they touched the water, they were wrenched from his grasp, and the river took over once more. Once more he foundered on a rock, and once more barely managed to

scramble back up on the island.

He was beginning to feel he owed his wife, and the whole world, an explanation. He wished he could let them all know what was delaying him.

He sat on a stone, staining it with his wetness. He pulled at his snout and chewed his lips. He was beginning to comprehend the awkwardness of his position.

He was marooned on an island, nowhere near civilization, as far as he could tell; and if he was going to get off, it must be by his own devices. But he was obviously not going to cross that river in any boat he could put together out of the available materials.

He had worked so quickly that it was still only mid-afternoon. He returned to the birch, thoughtfully munching on mushrooms along the way. He knew which ones were safe. He had studied mushrooms in Souris's *Botany* at home, and he and Amanda had picked them in the forest. He was hungrier than he had realized.

Abel posed this question to himself: Other than by swimming or on boats, how *do* rivers get crossed? By tunnels and bridges, of course. Could he tunnel under that river with his paws, his penknife, and a homemade wooden shovel perhaps; no pickax, no crowbar, no wheelbarrow or wagon, not even a pail to carry out the earth and rocks?

He would have to start far back from the shore, so as not to have to carry the diggings out of too vertical a shaft; and he would have to burrow way down deep where it was almost as hard as rock, if indeed it wasn't rock itself. And how could he be sure he was tunneling well under the riverbed? What if the river flooded his tunnel, or if the tunnel simply collapsed on him? What a way that would be for the descendant of an ancient and noble family to die! Pressed out of existence in mundane mud, and no one even knowing what had happened to him, or where. Only he himself would know, and just

for a second at that. The tunnel idea was out.

He would have to construct a bridge of some sort. He was intelligent and had imagination. Something would surely occur to him. The situation was by no means hopeless. However, he was clearly not leaving the island that day. He decided to explore it.

His birch was situated near the upper end, which he had already hastily crossed. He now carefully walked its length. It was a typical piece of the temperate zone, with familiar kinds of rocks, trees, bushes, brambles, grass, and other plants. It was gravelly near the water, rockiest at the lower end, and, from a mouse's point of view, hilly. Abel estimated the island to be about 12,000 tails long, 5,000 wide.

What most felt like home in this strange place full of familiar objects was the birch. He had already slept in it twice. Returning there, he heard birdsong and saw birds, but they showed no interest in him, and he felt no hope of communicating with them. They were wild, and he civilized. He knew that certain pigeons could be taught to carry messages. He had heard the woeful sounds of a mourning dove, but that was the wrong kind of pigeon.

Though he was having a most extraordinary experience, Abel was bored. It was not an adventure of his choosing. It was being foisted on him, and that he resented. He even began to dislike his friends back home for lacking the powers of logic to puzzle out where he was so they could come to his rescue. He wished to be in his own home, with his loving wife, surrounded by the books he liked to browse in, by his paintings and his elegant possessions, dressed in neat modish clothes, comfortable in a stuffed chair. He wouldn't even mind being bored *there,* staring at the patterns in the wallpaper. He was fed up with the stupid, pointless island.

But the stupid island was where he was going to spend this night, at least, in soiled clothes that were beginning to smell fusty. What if he had to stay longer than this night? Food would be no problem. The island abounded with edible plants, many of which he recognized from illustrations in his encyclopedia. And there were insects he could eat if it came to a choice of that or starving. He could continue to sleep in the birch, where, if not completely protected, he had the advantage of a high redoubt, the upper hand in case of a conflict.

For dinner he ate wild carrots, carefully scraped with his knife. Then, with his paws folded across his belly, where the nourishment was being extracted from the carrots, he sat under his birch in the opal glow of the waning day and took stock of his resources. He had a shirt, trousers, socks, shoes, underwear, a necktie, and suspenders. His jacket had gone with the smashed sailboat, his handkerchief with the catamaran. In his pockets he had the stub of a pencil, a small scratch pad, quite damp, a few coins, the keys to his house, and his penknife.

And of course there was Amanda's scarf. He pressed it to his face. In spite of all the washings it had been through, its threads still held Amanda's dear scent. Abel fought off a wave of self-pity. Only when he considered the unhappiness he was causing Amanda, his family, his friends, did he finally allow himself some hot tears. Despair was darkening his spirit. Deep down, where truth dwells, he wasn't at all sure he'd be getting off the island soon.

He rested against his tree and gazed at the river just being itself, burbling along. The river was where it

ought to be; Abel wasn't. He felt out of place. When it grew dark, he climbed to the top of his tree and lay down in the crook of a branch, hugging Amanda's scarf.

He was suddenly thrilled to see his private, personal star arise in the east. This was a particular star his nanny had chosen for him when he was a child. As a child, he would sometimes talk to this star, but only·when he was his most serious, real self, and not being any sort of a show-off or clown. As he grew up, the practice had somehow worn off.

He looked up at his old friend as if to say, "You see my predicament."

The star seemed to respond, "I see."

Abel next put the question: "What shall I do?"

The star seemed to answer, "You will do what you will do." For some reason this reply strengthened Abel's belief in himself. Sleep gently enfolded him. The constellations proceeded across the hushed heavens as if tiptoeing past the dreaming mouse on his high branch.

Abel dreamed of Amanda—odd, unfinished dreams. As the new day dawned, he dreamed he was falling. There was nothing to get hold of in the awesome void, and he plummeted toward unthinkable pain on the hard ground. Was he really dreaming? Yes. But he was also really falling. Dream and reality were the same. He hit a leafy branch which broke his fall and he landed in deep grass and was awake. It sickened him to see the river in the pale, early light.

° 6 °

Was it just an accident that he was here on this uninhabited island? Abel began to wonder. Was he being singled out for some reason; was he being tested? If so, why? Didn't it prove his worth that such a one as Amanda loved him?

Did it? Why *did* Amanda love him? He wasn't all that handsome, was he? And he had no particular accomplishments. What sort of mouse was he? Wasn't he really a snob, and a fop, and frivolous on serious occasions, as she had once told him during a quarrel? He had acted silly even at his own wedding, grinning during the solemnities, clowning when cutting the cake. What made him act that way when he did?

Full of such questions, he went to wash his face in the river that kept him captive, and drank some of its water. It was foolish, he realized, to harbor a grudge toward this river. It had no grudge against him. It happened to be where it was; it had probably been there for eons.

He found a bush of ripe raspberries and ate his fill for breakfast. This was his third morning on the island. Carefully cracking the few seeds that remained in his mouth, he thought again about a bridge. He decided he could make one of rope, a single floating strand on which he could pull himself across. It would have to be strong enough so the current wouldn't tear it, and light enough so he could sling it across to the other side. He would tie a stone on one end and try to make it catch in some bushes he'd picked out on the far shore.

This time he proceeded methodically, not in nervous haste. He went first to defecate, behind a rock, though no one was watching. Then he cut long blades of tough crab grass, and sat cross-legged on the ground tearing the grass lengthwise so that each blade became many strands. He worked this way for hours and he enjoyed the absorbing task.

When he felt he had enough, he proceeded to braid and weave the long fibers to form a continuous rope. Occasionally he would encircle the rope with a few strands of grass and tie a firm knot to prevent unraveling. He was doing the kind of thing he had often, leaning on his cane, watched others do.

Noon passed. His thoughts concerned only rope—its making and how he would use it. But as the rope grew, Amanda, who was always somewhere in his mind, came forward. What was she thinking, he wondered.

No doubt they had searched for him in a large area around the cave, dreading to find him injured, or dead. But what did they make of not finding him at all? Had they gone after him right away? The hurricane would have prevented them from getting very far. He was certain Amanda had to be restrained from risking her life to aid him. They must have spent a sleepless night inside the cave and started looking early in the morning when the storm was over. By now the whole town was certainly looking; his powerful father would have seen to that. They might look pretty far. But this far? Never!

How frantic Amanda must be! But so much greater her joy when she had him back again.

It was evening when he'd woven enough rope to span the river. He had it neatly coiled on the ground in a large ring. It would be wise to wait for morning, though, before crossing over. If he crossed now, he'd have to sleep on the other side, where he'd be less at home than he was here. And he was tired.

He ate the seed from the grass he'd worked with; it was scattered all around him. He drank at the river and then, for diversion, wandered toward the interior of the island, chewing on fragrant raspberries as he wandered. In a pleasant place, open yet sheltered by overhanging boughs, the hollow bole of a dead tree lay on the ground. He entered.

Recalling his fall from the birch, he felt this log would afford a safer night's lodging. He went to work carting out some of the rot. The log had limbs which were also hollowed by decay. It amounted to a house with several wings. No beast of prey could fit into that log, or reach beak, talon, fang, or claw deep enough to get at Abel where he planned to sleep. As for snakes, there were stones with which to close the entrance when he went in.

He lay on his back for a while, Amanda's scarf held with both paws to his breast. Having worked all day,

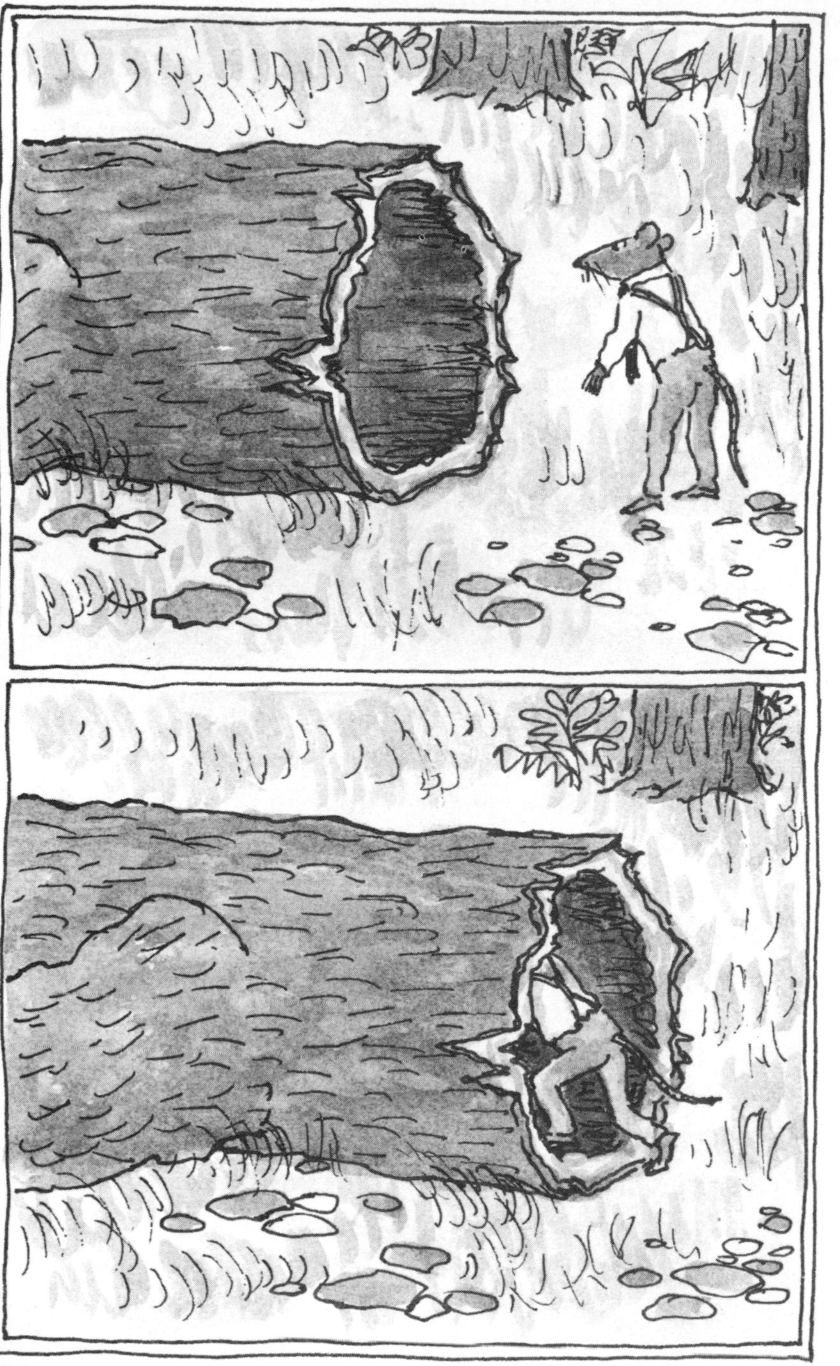

seriously and well, he was warmed with a proper self-regard. He had provided food and shelter for himself, and woven a rope which would be his bridge to freedom, home, and love.

He spent that night in the log, eager for the morning. He believed he could shoot his rope across the river by using his suspenders as a slingshot.

○ 7 ○

At sunrise Abel was at the river, where he washed, had breakfast, and got to work on his bridge. He set up his suspenders as a slingshot, fastening one end to a stout bush. Then he arranged his rope in a few long, loose loops that would straighten out easily as it arched over the gap. He tied one end to a stone and the other to the bush, made a pocket in the suspenders to hold the stone, and was ready for his shot.

Grasping the stone in its pocket and leaning backward, he pulled mightily, stretching the suspenders as far as the elastic would allow, and aimed his bridge, or life line, in the direction of the bushes on the opposite shore. Fervently hoping for success, he released his hold.

The stone, with the rope trailing it, made a small parabola in the air, and the line, as if with a sigh, fell limply into the river only ninety tails away. He quickly hauled it in. A bit of faith still remaining, he set up his machinery and tried again, using a lighter stone. The result was even more disappointing. The rope was wet now, and heavy.

Abel tried swinging the stone around and around above his head with a gradually lengthening line and then releasing it like a bola. This simpler method

worked better than the suspenders, but not enough better to matter. He pulled in the rope and sat beside it,
clutching his head in his paws.

The stubbornness of his character stood him now in
good stead. He refused to consider himself defeated. A
few minutes of gloomy pondering produced a new idea:
a bridge of steppingstones. Why hadn't he thought of
this simple scheme before? He would make piles of
stones, using each pile as a step to build the next one,
until he'd made enough to walk, or hop, his way across
the river.

He spent the rest of the day amassing a huge heap of
pebbles and rocks, going farther and farther afield to
find them. By sundown he was so exhausted he lay down
in his log without having eaten, and fell asleep before
the birds had finished making their final evening statements.

The next morning, after wolfing a big breakfast, he
stood in water up to his neck, building the first step.
He viewed it with satisfaction. He realized that the steps
would have to be close together, because he could make
only a short leap carrying a heavy weight. He managed
a second and a third step, and that was all.

The would-be fourth step, which was started in swifter
water, never formed, because the current carried away
the largest rocks Abel could handle. It was a hopeless
project. The middle of the river, if ever he could reach
it, was surely very deep, and even if the rocks held, the

amount required to make a single step would be more than he could find on the island or carry in what remained of his life.

He would keep thinking. It was his family tradition never to give up but to keep gnawing away until problems were solved. For the time being, however, he had run out of ideas. He began to develop an obstinate patience.

In the next few days he discovered additional sources of nourishment: groundnuts, mulberries, wild mustard, wild onions, new kinds of mushrooms, spearmint, peppermint, and milkweed. His former days of reading helped him identify these plants. He made a hammock of grass fibers and swung himself in it by pulling on a rope, swaying from side to side like seaweed on the rolling sea, full of vacant wonder. He was stunned with his own solitude, his own silence.

Every night he slept in the log. It had become half hotel, half home. But he still regarded the birch as the focal point of his comings and goings. He would often climb it to scan the surroundings and sit there chewing on a twig.

By the end of the month of August he knew he was an inhabitant of the island, whether he liked it or not. It was where he lived, just as a prison is where a prisoner lives. He thought constantly of Amanda. He thought of his parents, his brothers, sisters, friends. He knew they were grieving and he was moved by their grief. He, at least, knew he was alive. They didn't. What was Amanda doing? How did her days drag out? Did she still write poetry? Was she able to eat, to sleep, to enjoy her existence in any way?

Her image was in his mind, as clear as life sometimes, and he smiled with wistful tenderness, remembering her ways. Amanda was dreamy. It often seemed she was dreaming the real world around her, the things that were actually happening. She could dream Abel when he was right there by her side. Abel loved this dreaminess in her. He loved her dreamy eyes.

Wherever he went about the island, he wore Amanda's scarf around his neck, the ends tied in a knot. He would not leave it in the log.

∘8∘

It was September when Abel evolved another scheme for getting home. He would catapult himself across the stream. With his clothes stuffed full of grass for a cushioned landing, using a small stump as a winch, he tried with a rope to bend a sapling down to the ground so it could fling him over the water. But he managed to bend it only two and a half tails. That was all the wood yielded to his strength. So this scheme, too, miscarried.

A few days later he succeeded in making fire. He had

learned about the primitive methods in school, but he had never tried for himself. After a series of failures, he finally found the right kind of stick to twirl in the right piece of dry wood, and the right kind of tinder to flare with the first flame. His fires were as magical to him as they had been to his prehistoric ancestors.

He first used his fires for smoke beacons, to attract the attention of some civilized being who might just possibly be among the trees on the far shores. When he had a fire burning, he would partially cover it with damp leaves so that it sent up a thick white smoke.

He learned to roast his seeds by placing them on rocks close to the fire. Later he was able to cook various vegetables, flavored with wild garlic or onions, in pots made of a reddish clay from the lower end of the island. The clay was baked hard in prolonged, intense firing.

He also made paper-thin bowls of this clay, and from time to time he would float one down the river with a note in it, and a flower or sprig of grass sticking out to attract notice. One of his notes:

*Whoever finds this: Please forward it to my wife,
Amanda di Chirico Flint, 89 Bank Street, Mossville.*

DEAREST ANGEL—I am ALIVE! I am alone on an island,
marooned, somewhere above where this note will be
found, God willing. There is a tall cherry birch on the
northern end of the island. The island is about 12,000
tails long and is below a waterfall. Do not worry, but
send help.

My utmost and entire love,

ABEL

*Whoever finds this, please send help too. I will be able
to give a substantial reward.*

Sometimes Abel would climb to the top of his birch,
or some other tree, and wave his white shirt up and
down, and back and forth, for many minutes, hoping
that someone would make a miraculous appearance, return his signal, and come to the rescue. There was no
point in yelling; the river was too noisy for his halloos
to carry.

During the equinoctial rains, he spent the whole of a
dismal day indoors, listening to the unceasing downpour
on the outside of his log, watching it through his door
and through portholes he had made—the infinite pall
of falling rain, the sagging, wet vegetation, the drops
dripping from everything as if counting themselves, the
runnels and pools, the misty distances—and feeling an
ancient melancholy.

Rain caused one to reflect on the shadowed, more poignant parts of life—the inescapable sorrows, the speechless longings, the disappointments, the regrets, the cold miseries. It also allowed one the leisure to ponder questions unasked in the bustle of brighter days; and if one were snug under a sound roof, as Abel was, one felt somehow mothered, though mothers were nowhere around, and absolved of responsibilities. Abel had to cherish his dry log.

At night, when it cleared up, he went out in the wet grass and watched a young moon vanishing behind clouds and reappearing, over and over, like a swimmer out on the sea. Then he went inside the log, barred the entrance, and lay down with Amanda's scarf.

Drugged with the aroma of rotting wood, he lost consciousness. There was a din of crickets outside, and the pauseless roar of the river, and the stately world was illumined with pearly moonlight; but inside the log it was dark and hushed, like a crypt.

The castaway dreamed all night of Amanda. They were together again, in their home. But their home was not 89 Bank Street, in Mossville; it was a garden, something like the island, and full of flowers. What was marvelous about this otherwise ordinary dream was that Abel *knew* he was dreaming and was certain that his wife was dreaming the very same dream at the same time, so that they were as close to each other as they'd ever been in the solid world.

∘ 9 ∘

The feeling that he could visit Amanda in dreams haunted Abel. Perhaps he could reach her during his waking hours as well. He began sending her "mind messages." Sitting in the crotch of his favorite branch on the birch, he would project his thoughts, feelings, questions, yearnings, in what he considered the direction of his home. Sometimes he felt that Amanda could "hear" these messages and was responding with loving messages of her own. This feeling elated him.

He became convinced he could fly to his wife through the air, or glide, like a flying squirrel. He made a glider by stretching a catalpa leaf across two sticks, attached it to his back, and climbed to the top of his birch. From there he flung himself into the void, arms outstretched, aiming for the far shore. Instead of the soaring ride he had anticipated, he made a slow, graceful half circle, heels over head, and thudded down on his back in the grass. He lay there for several hours, brokenhearted and dazed with pain.

When body and spirits recovered, he took to climbing his birch again. One day, when he was winding his way upward, around and around the trunk, it seemed to him that the tree was somehow aware of his ascending spiral, and that it enjoyed his delicate scurryings, just as he enjoyed the rugged toughness and sensible architecture

of the tree. He felt the tree knew his feelings, though no words could pass between them.

He believed in his "visits" with Amanda; he had his birch, and his star, and the conviction grew in him that the earth and the sky knew he was there and also felt friendly; so he was not really alone, and not really entirely lonely. At times he'd be overcome by sudden ecstasy and prance about on high rocks, or skip along the limbs of trees, shouting meaningless syllables. He was, after all, in the prime of his life.

Late in September, when he woke up mornings, he would see rime on the ground. That and the nip in the air made him worry about the coming of winter. What if he was still there? In his tours of the island he had found acorns and hickory nuts and also wild sunflowers full of seed. He began storing these in his log.

Living in the heart of nature, he began to realize how much was going on in the seeming stillness. Plants grew and bore fruit, branches proliferated, buds became flowers, clouds formed in ever-new ways and patterns, colors changed. He felt a strong need to participate in the designing and arranging of things. The red clay from which he had fashioned pots and dishes inspired him to try his hand at making something just for its own sake, something beautiful.

He made a life-size statue of Amanda. Though it didn't really resemble her, it did look like a female mouse. He was amazed at what he had wrought. Good or bad, it was sculpture. It was art. He tried again and again, profiting from his mistakes, and finally he felt he had a likeness of his wife real enough to embrace.

Next he made statues of his dear, indulgent mother, from whose wealth his own income came, and of his various sisters and brothers, and he stood them all outside his log where he could see them from the windows.

Another day he did his father. Him he carved in tough wood, fiercely gnawing the forms out with his teeth. He stood back often to study the results of his gnawing, and

at last felt he had captured the proud, stern, aloof, strong, honest look of his male parent. He stood this statue next to that of his mother.

Abel had not been keeping track of the days, but the color of the leaves was being transformed from green to various yellows, burning golds, flaming reds, and he realized it was October. He gathered masses of fluff from the seed pods of milkweed to keep him warm in his log.

With threads of grass, he wove mats for his floor, and curtains for his windows to keep out drafts, and he tacked these curtains up with thorns. Later he made shutters out of bark.

He relayed the news of his doings to Amanda, sure that his airborne messages reached her. He added to his winter store of food, at what he thought was her urging, and meanwhile he kept dining on what remained available outdoors. At night, from its eminence, his star shone down on him with proud approval.

When the trees were in the full flame of autumn's fire, Abel wandered aimlessly over the island until the sight of the high color had him glowing inwardly with sensations of yellow, orange, and red. He pressed the juice from elderberries he had garnered earlier in the month and stored it in clay pots to let it turn to wine. His paws and shirt were stained with purple, but he no longer cared about his appearance.

In gray November, when the dry leaves huddled in drifts on the ground, he made a remarkable discovery. He thought he had thoroughly explored the island. He hadn't. Near the lower end, by the eastern shore, he found a huge watch with a chain, and an enormous book. The watch was as large as a dining table to accommodate three mice. The book was four tails long, three wide, and almost a tail thick. There was a stone on top of it, and it was the stone, no doubt, and the lay of the ground, that had kept it from being washed away in the flood.

Judging by its condition, the book had been there some time and had seen several changes of weather in addition to the flood. The cloth binding was puffed into blisters and wrinkled; the title, *Sons and Daughters,* was

faded and hard to discern. Some large creature had been on the island, perhaps picnicking, and had gone away forgetting the book and the watch. Probably the stone had been placed on the book to keep it from blowing open.

Abel's heart raced. The island was known to civilized

creatures and would be visited again! He would have to leave signs all about to make his presence known. Meanwhile, he was curious about the book. With great effort he rolled away the stone, which was larger than himself, and pried the stiff cover open.

The pages were buckled and water-stained, but the type was clear enough. He managed to separate the title page from page 1, and began reading, pacing from side to side on the printed lines. The book opened with the description of a masquerade ball. The characters were bears, which, like other large animals, had always fascinated Abel. It was wonderful to have a long book to entertain him and keep him company. He decided to read a chapter each day.

He closed the book and carefully buried it under a heap of leaves to prevent further damage by sun and rain. Then, with the end of the chain slung over his shoulder, he began hauling the watch to his house. It was heavy, but the smooth platinum of the case slid over the dry fallen leaves and made the hauling not too hard.

Early next morning Abel raced back to the book, removed the leaves, and took up reading where he had left off. The masked ball was a happy affair, even though there was talk among the guests of possible war. The

main character was a captain in his country's army. He was snout over claws in love with a beautiful young lady bear with whom he danced a couple of waltzes. Abel had to laugh over one of the bears, who was masquerading as a mouse. What he read made him wistful for his normal life, but he still enjoyed reading.

After hopping from side to side eagerly devouring the words, he forced himself to stop at the close of the chapter. He re-covered the book with the leaves and went home.

There, in case the bears who had left the book behind, or anyone else, should turn up, Abel made clay tablets like this:

and baked them in his fire.

The next day the signs were placed in well-chosen parts of the island, leaning against trees or stones, with the arrow always pointing to his home, the log. He had to drag the tablets along the ground with a rope, they were so large. He noted that there were thin wafers of ice along the shore, and for a moment he had excited visions of a frozen river that could be crossed by walking; but he quickly remembered that such swiftly flowing water could not freeze.

He was curious to know if the watch would run. Some prodding and shoving with a pole in the grooves of the stem-winder made it turn round a dozen times. The watch began to tick. The sounds he had become accustomed to, the roaring and gurgling of the river, the wailing and whining of the wind, the pattering and dripping of rain, the chirruping of birds and the chirring of insects, had natural, irregular rhythms, which were very soothing, but the steady, mechanical tempo of the watch gave him something he had been wanting in this wild place. It and the book helped him feel connected to the civilized world he'd come from. He had no use for the time the watch could tell, but he needed the ticking.

Abel led a busy life. He had used up the pages of his scratch pad floating messages down the river, but he still occasionally sent up smoke signals, and once in a while, futile as it seemed, he would climb a tree and wave his stained and tattered shirt. He had his book to read and think about, there was the winding of the watch to be attended to, he kept working at sculpture, and of course he had his practical needs to provide for.

Abel also kept busy taking it easy. Only when taking it easy, he'd learned, could one properly do one's wondering. One night while he was resting under the stars and enjoying the noise of the river and of the November wind, a winged shadow suddenly hung over him, black-

ing out the stars at which he'd been gazing. Instinct brought him to his feet and sent him diving into a crevice between two rocks.

In mute terror he crouched in the crevice while the owl, with grappling talons, tried to fish him out. It stood on the rock and poked in, while Abel made himself smaller and smaller and receded farther and farther into the seam. Then the poking stopped and the owl scrabbled about on the rock, staring into the night with unfathoming eyes. It took off at last and perched in a tree.

Abel could see the dark shape of the owl in the branches above, and the vibrating stars beyond. Where had this trespasser come from? Why? Had it perhaps seen Abel's signals? He'd been astounded by the stillness with which it had dropped from the sky. There'd been no beat, no ruffle, of wings. This was bone-chilling, to be approached so noiselessly by a winged assassin.

Abel's star was up there among the others. It seemed to say, "I see you both." Abel broke from his sanctuary and dashed for the log. The owl was right behind him. Abel ran as fast as his thin, terrified legs would take him.

He gasped when the owl seized him. He was snatched and rushed aloft, sick with fear, into the ominous air. He had the wit, and just enough strength, to pull out his penknife, open the blade, and frantically slash at the owl's horny toes.

With a screech the owl released him, and Abel fell

with no fear at all of falling. He scrambled with awkward haste to his house, plunged in, and barred the entrance with stones. The next moment he felt the owl land on the hollow log and his innards quivered. Abel crouched motionless in a corner. He could hear the owl shuffle about right above him, a single tail away.

As the night advanced, terror turned to resentment. The mouse considered battling the owl with his knife, putting out his stupid eyes with a pointed pole, setting fire to his feathers with a torch. Indignant and unfearing, he fell asleep.

In the morning, caution returned. He peered from his windows, craning his head upward, and made sure there was no dealer of death on his roof. Most of that day he spent in his bed of milkweed fluff, and ventured out only in the late afternoon, carrying over his shoulder a long pole, his open knife tied to the end.

After his encounter with the owl, he was extremely wary for a long time, even in full daylight, when owls are expected to sleep.

∘11∘

In late November, Abel was on his way home from the book, mulling over a chapter he had just read. The bears were going to war, against bears from another country. They were going even though, on both sides, everyone wanted peace. This was something to think about, with so much time to think.

The sky was gray. Nature looked its drabbest. Abel thought he saw snowflakes, not falling, just wandering about in the air. Then there were more and he felt a few melt on his head. That winter was coming he had known all along, but here was more evidence and it made him uneasy. Was he as prepared as he ought to be? There was an owl around too, with nasty intentions, and that added to his uneasiness. The environment didn't seem altogether friendly.

In the dead grass he saw a gray-brown feather. Certain that it could only be the owl's, he took it home. There he poked the quill into the soft, rotting wood of his floor, where it stood erect, a sort of talisman. He owned something of the owl's, from his very body, but the owl had nothing of his. This gave him a sense of advantage, at least for the moment.

He found himself uttering an incantation at the
feather, not knowing where the words came from:

> Foul owl, ugly you,
> You'll never get me,
> Whatever you do.
> You cannot hurt me,
> You cannot kill,
> You're in my power,
> I have your quill!

He felt he was casting a spell on the detested bird of prey that would paralyze its evil force. After this, out in his yard in the light, descending snow, Abel addressed Amanda's statue as if it were she herself. "Amanda," he said, "I am safe." Then he went indoors and worked at making himself a winter cape, with hood. He wove two layers of cloth from the fine filaments of grass, and sandwiched in between the two layers some of the milkweed fluff he'd stored in his log.

Still full of forebodings of a hard winter, he foraged about for what he was sure was the last edible stuff on the island: various seeds, dry berries, mushrooms. He crammed his rooms full of these viands. Perhaps it was more than he would need to see the winter through, but he had no way of knowing. Anyway, his abundant store eased his misgivings.

Engrossed one day in these practical chores, he was shocked to see the owl again, up on a branch in a tree near his house. It was asleep, but its erect posture, like that of a sentinel of hell, its eyes, which even shut seemed to stare, the tight grasp of its talons on the bough, and the bloody sunset in the sky behind it, filled poor Abel with wintry dread. He hurried home, his heart tripping. What should he do? Could he possibly kill the obnoxious creature while it slept, so it would die as if in a dream? How? With a rock on the end of a rope? With fire? With a burning javelin of wood?

So many birds had gone south. Why not the owl?

Was an owl really a bird? What an odd, unheavenly bird! Abel, back in his log, knelt in prayer and asked a question he had asked before, though never so urgently: Why did God make owls, snakes, cats, foxes, fleas, and other such loathsome, abominable creatures? He felt there had to be a reason.

In December, Abel began talking to himself. He had done it before, but only internally. Now he spoke out loud, and the sound of his own voice vibrating in his body felt vital. Addressing himself by name, he would give advice, or ask questions and answer them. Sometimes he argued back and forth, Abel with Abel, and even got quite angry when he disagreed with his own opinions. He often found himself hard to convince.

He talked aloud to Amanda too, addressing her statue. He assured her that he would see her again, and the others he loved. There was no question he'd be getting off the island, though as yet he had no idea how. He was patient; that is, he considered himself patient. Because what other love-longing, wife-craving, homesick creature would remain so pacingly calm, so nervously resolute, so crazily sane, as long as Abel had?

The first real snowfall was a tail deep. Abel made himself snowshoes and went to his book with a homemade shovel in one arm, his spear in the other. He dug the book out of the snow and read Chapter XIX.

By Chapter XIX, the bear war was at its worst; many had been killed or wounded. It made Abel wonder about civilization. But, come to think of it, the owl, who was not civilized, was pretty warlike too. The hero, Captain Burin, was writing home from the battlefield to the one he had waltzed with in the first chapter, the one he loved. It was also winter in the story, and a drunken sergeant was saying things that were foolish and wise and funny—he wished he were hibernating instead of warring. Some of his statements made Abel roll around on the page, his cloudy breath exploding in spasms of laughter.

It was hard to cover the book when he finished his reading for the day, because the leaves stuck together in frozen sheets. His paws got icy cold. At home, he had to drink some of his wine to dispel the chill in his bones.

On his way home from Chapter XXI, he had a perilous encounter with the owl. But he wasn't caught off guard. Whenever the spear was in his paw, the owl was on his mind, as he, apparently, was always on the mind of the owl. Each one kept a sharp eye out—the would-be killer, and the intended victim.

Hoping to catch Abel napping, the owl swept down from an old decayed tree—it seemed at home in rotten trees—but Abel had his spear at the ready the moment the owl reached him. The owl swerved off as Abel thrust at it, and pretended to fly away defeated, but immediately it swooped down again. This time Abel slashed sideways and thrust viciously upward, and he could feel the point of his knife penetrate the owl's flesh, though the owl made no sound.

It only winced, and fending off the spear with one claw, it ripped off Abel's cape with the other. In a fit of fear and rage, Abel thrust again and again, desperately, without plan. His fury so upset and bewildered the owl that it flew upward and roosted on a dead limb of the tree, staring down in disbelief.

Instead of making off while he had the advantage, Abel cocked his spear and challenged the owl to descend and fight. The owl continued to stare.

"Coward!" Abel screamed, the veins swelling on his neck. "Come down and do battle—bird, reptile, fiend, or whatever kind of villain you are!" If the owl was offended at Abel's insults, it didn't show that it was. Solemnly, it blinked and stared.

"Down with unsightly devils! Down with evil of any sort!" Abel yelled, and with all his might he foolishly flung his spear at the bird of prey. It struck the branch where the owl stood, and fell to the ground. As Abel ran to retrieve his weapon, the owl dived. Abel dodged and raced around the trunk of the tree. The owl couldn't fly in circles any faster than Abel could run, so there was always the tree between them. The chase went on and on, sometimes reversing direction.

This mad carrousel so offended the owl's ancient sense of decorum that it grew confused and crashed into the tree. It had to go off somewhere to sit in a huff, unruffle its feathers, and regain its ruthless composure. Abel grabbed his spear and cape and scampered home.

By now, Abel owned three of the owl's feathers—he was quite sure they were the owl's. Without waiting to catch breath after his heroic skirmish, he began uttering, over these detested feathers, the most horrible imprecations imaginable.

Heaven forfend that the owl should have suffered a fraction of what Abel wished it. Abel wished that its feathers would turn to lead so it could fall on its head from the world's tallest tree, that its beak would rot and become useless even for eating mush, that it should be blind as a bat and fly into a dragon's flaming mouth, that it should sink in quicksand mixed with broken bottles, very slowly, to prolong its suffering, and much more of the same sort.

December grew steadily colder. Abel began tearing margins from the pages of his book and using this paper to fill the chinks in his doorway whenever the stones were set in place. Even so, the cold lanced through, especially when it was windy.

Abel spent most of January and February, and part of March, indoors. In January there was a great blizzard. The snow descended from the bleary sky in thick, heavy curtains, through a long night. Curled up in his bed, Abel listened despondently to the howling and yowling, the lashing and whistling of the wind.

His log was buried deep, and though a dim light penetrated the snow, almost none got in through the tightly shuttered windows. Even by day, he had to probe his way around. Fortunately, some air filtered through the tightly packed crystals.

Hardly knowing day from night, Abel slept and kept no schedule, and the days came and left, uncounted. His chief occupation when awake was finding his food

in the groping dark of his storerooms and eating it, which was a sort of tiresome ritual, a solemn munching. Otherwise, he yawned, oh how he yawned, turned over time and again, thrashed around, ever so much, scratched, over and over, pushed the shells of acorns, hickory nuts, and sunflower seeds out of his way, and thought of nothing.

Meanwhile, the sun, and occasional thaws, kept lowering the level of the snow, so that eventually Abel had the thrill of seeing the light that had long been denied him slice through the edge of a wind-struck shutter. He woke up one day and there it was—things were visible!

"Abel," he shouted, "do you hear me? I can see!" He flung the shutter open. How beautiful everything looked after the prolonged darkness. How unspeakably beautiful even the shells on the floor. How vividly actual and therefore marvelous!

Abel opened his doorway and let the light flood in. The day seemed confident of its own splendor. The icicles hanging in the open entrance glittered. One was as big as Abel himself. He ate, and drank cold water from a clay pot. Then he shoved the great accumulation of shells out of his house and went to stand before Amanda's statue, which was chest-deep in snow.

"Dear heart, I love you," he exclaimed. "What a lovely day! It's February, isn't it? I need to be moving." He flexed his arms, bent backward and forward, and felt foolish before his wife. He didn't know what to say.

He put on his snowshoes, got his shovel and spear, and went to read his book. Captain Burin had been wounded, he remembered. Was he going to live or not? He was going to live; his wounds were healing, thank God. And spring was coming. The talk of spring filled Abel with unbearable longing. How deeply one felt when alone!

It *was* February, as Abel had surmised, and now winter really took hold. January had been only the prelude. Abel came in from his book one afternoon, unable to keep his body from shaking. His teeth chattered and clacked, and nothing would make his frigid shuddering stop. His snout ran, his eyes teared and grew dim, his head pounded and pained.

It was a time when even the most stalwart of mice would wish to be an infant again in his mother's warm embrace. He tottered about, shivering, and stuffed every open chink as well as he could with his palsied paws, until no light came through anywhere. The only source of warmth was his own heat-hungry body.

How wonderful a fire would be, but if he made one, he realized, he could burn himself out of his home, or anyway use up the oxygen. He donned his entire wardrobe, got all his mats together, all the paper he had torn from the novel, whatever milkweed fluff he could find in his storerooms, and half sitting, half reclining against a wall, he quilted himself all around with these paddings and buried his face in Amanda's scarf. Gradually his shivering subsided and his tired muscles relaxed. He tucked his head under his coverings and his breath helped warm his body.

Thus began another long month of sad sequestration inside the log. Whenever Abel was convinced it couldn't get any colder, it got still colder. The wind tore wildly around the world, whipping up the snow in mountainous drifts, breaking frozen branches off trees, sending icicles clattering to the glassy ground. Abel listened and it lasted so long he stopped hearing it. But still it went on.

He was sick. He was weak; merely to turn over took great effort; and he was wretched. One day he found himself wondering, with dull resentment, why Amanda hadn't tied her scarf on better, so that he wouldn't have had to chase it out of the cave. If she were less dreamy, more attentive to reality, if she had tied her scarf on tighter, he would now, this moment, be at home, wearing his velvet jacket and satin-lined pantofles, ensconced in an easy chair among plump pillows, reading a good book, or perhaps merely looking out his window at the snow. There'd be a fire in the fireplace, lentil soup with an onion in it simmering on the stove, Amanda would be at her escritoire correcting a poem, or better still, she'd be in his lap covering him with warm kisses. The cold and the wind outside would only set off the indoor coziness.

But he wasn't at home, nowhere near it. He thought of his loved ones, his faraway friends. Amanda was his mate, yes, and would always be. His parents, sisters, brothers, and friends would always be his parents, sisters, brothers, and friends, but his feeling for them all had become shadowy. How could he go on having warm, alive feelings for merely remembered beings? Living was more than remembering, imagining. He wanted the

real Amanda at his side, and he tried to reach out to her. His messages, it seemed, could not travel through the icy air.

He became somnolent in his cold cocoon. In his moments of dim-eyed wakefulness he had no idea how much time had passed since he was last awake—whether an hour, a day, or a week. He was cold, but he knew he was as warm as he could get. The water in his clay pot was frozen solid. His mind was frozen. It began to seem it had always been winter and that there was nothing else, just a vague awareness to make note of the fact. The universe was a dreary place, asleep, cold all the way to infinity, and the wind was a separate thing, not part of the winter, but a lost, unloved soul, screaming and moaning and rushing about looking for a place to rest and reckon up its woes.

Somewhere out there, in the night sky—and it could only be night—were the glittering stars, and among them his, the one he had always known. This star, his, millions of miles away, was yet closer than Amanda, because if he had the will and the strength to get up, uncover his window, and look out, he could see it. He knew, therefore, that it existed. But as for Amanda, father, mother, sisters, brothers, aunts, uncles, cousins, friends, and the rest of society and the animal kingdom, he had to believe they were there, and it was hard to have this faith. As far as he really knew, he himself was the only, lonely, living thing that existed, and in his coma of coldness, he was not so sure of that.

°14°

Sometime in March, Abel felt he was thawing out. More wakeful than he'd been, he realized that winter had become less cold, and he bestirred himself to be up and around. He went outside feeling weak, but as he moved about under the wide, blue sky, breathing the clear air and exercising his limbs, he grew stronger.

There were two crocuses in the snow, sure harbingers of spring. Enlivened by this miracle, the dainty flowers braving the cold, he bustled about outside his log, setting things in order. He wound his watch, listened in rapture to its steady ticking, and went to read his book, really more to be back in his old routine than for the sake of reading.

The sun seemed full of plans, less bored with the world than it had been, less aloof. But after a pleasant day, it turned terribly cold again at night, and Abel crawled back under all his coverings, disappointed. Yet the very next morning it was again spring.

Snow melted, revealing the earth. The river, swollen with freshets from the thawing, was swifter than ever, exultantly rushing along. Abel finished reading his book in a few more visits and he was glad to be finished, because what was happening around him was a lot more exciting than any book. Now he liked to lie in the warm sun on the open patches of ground and be part of the world's awakening.

He visited the birch, sat in his favorite roost, and admired the birch's buds as one admires a friend's babies. At night he found his star in the sky and was happy— in case the star had missed him—to show he was still alive. All this time of burgeoning life and joy, he hadn't failed to carry his spear and watch out for the owl. He never saw it, and concluded that it must have gone away, if it hadn't died during the deadly cold months.

Of course Abel took to communing again with Amanda, and by April he was rather sure they were in touch with each other. By then there were many bright birds about, setting up house in the north after their sea-

son in the south, expressing delight at being back. Fresh grass pushed through the old, dead stubble, buds embroidered the trees. Abel saw his whole world suffused with green.

When the flowers appeared in May, he went crazy. Violets, dandelions, pinks, forget-me-nots bedecked the island. Abel ate grass and young violet greens, fresh food with the juice of life. He drank large draughts of his wine and ran about everywhere like a wild animal, shouting and yodeling. How it would surprise his

family to see him now! A group of geese passed overhead, honking. He waved a greeting. They passed on.
At times he felt he had no need of others.

He bathed in the fresh cold water at the river's edge
and lay on his back under the sun, trying to fathom the
firmament. One day, as he was sunning this way, with
wine in his belly, who should come huffing and puffing
and staggering out of the stream but an obese, elderly
frog. Drunk as he was, Abel wondered if he was seeing
things. But the frog began to talk.

"Ho! Wow! Whoosh! Whoa! Goshamighty! I never thought I'd make it." He flung himself down on the bank, flopped over on his back, legs and arms outstretched, and spluttered some disconnected words.

Overjoyed at hearing civilized speech again, Abel ran over to the recumbent frog and looked down at him, beaming with candid delight.

The frog blinked. "Hi!" he said. "Wow! Did I have a time with that river! And that waterfall! I thought I'd drown!"

"What happened?" asked Abel. The frog sat up. Abel sat down beside him. Having come from the busy world of society, the frog was less surprised to see Abel than Abel was to see him.

"Gower Glackens is the name," said the frog. "Who might you be? Where am I?"

"On an island," Abel answered. "You are talking to Abelard Hassam di Chirico Flint—for short, Abel."

"Pleased to meet you," said Gower, extending a cold, clammy hand. Abel had never enjoyed shaking hands with his frog friends, but he enjoyed grasping Gower's. "Imagine someone my age, with all my years of experience, letting himself get into that kind of water! Spring fever, I guess. I'm always a little batty after lying in the cold mud all winter. The sun made me think I could navigate anything. The river can't handle all those freshets pouring in. It goes wild. Where is this, anyway? Is there a town here? A post office? Any boats?"

"No," said Abel. "There's only me. I'm sorry."

"Don't be sorry," said Gower. "I'd rather find you than find no one. Why are you here?"

"I came the way you did," said Abel, "against my will." And for the next half hour he told his story.

"Wow!" said the frog when Abel was finished. "I was sure I was dead after that waterfall. I must have hit the bottom, filled my big mouth with sand. I didn't know where I was going after that. I just went. Gosh! My family must be worried. They're all asking, Where's Gramps?"

He told about his big family and where he came from. Abel had never heard of the place. And the frog had never heard of Mossville.

"Let's go to my house," Abel said. "It's over that way." He helped Gower to his feet and conducted him back to the log, where he gave him a big drink of wine.

Gower drank in glugging gulps. "I needed that," he said. Then he went into a trance. He squatted on the ground, as frogs do, blinked in what seemed to Abel a smug way, and remained motionless. Abel saw him as crude, but utterly charming.

He prodded him. "Gower?"

"Who? What? Where am I?" said Gower. "Oh, it's you." He did this often, as Abel was to learn.

·15·

They remained together till June and became fast friends. Gower said he would be leaving as soon as he regained his strength and the swiftness of the stream had sufficiently subsided. "I wish I could carry you off the island," he told Abel, "but I'll have enough trouble making it by myself. I'm not what I was in my mating days."

"You could carry a rope across for me," Abel said, and he outlined his original plan for a rope bridge.

"That doesn't make sense," said Gower. "Do you realize how far down the river I'll be when I hit the other side? That rope would have to be thousands of lily pads long. Having it attached to me, maybe catching on things and all, could give me a heart attack. I'm no tadpole, you know!"

"But you *will* come back with rescuers, won't you?" Abel asked.

"Sure as shooting," said Gower. "That'll be the first order of business."

"And you *will* get in touch with my wife, won't you? I'll give you her address."

"Wife?" said Gower.

"I've told you about her many times," said Abel. "That's her statue."

"Oh, yes," said Gower. "Of course. I remember." He was always forgetting things.

One day Abel started on a statue of his new friend. As he shaped the clay, they conversed. Abel learned that Gower played bass fiddle in a small orchestra whose specialty was country music, had great-grandchildren by the dozen, all of whom were musical, and was happy with his old wife, though they often quarreled and spent whole days sitting around in a huff, trying to remember what they were angry about.

Once Gower asked Abel what his trade or profession was. "I haven't found my vocation yet," Abel answered. "The only real work I've ever done has been here on this island."

"Holy bloater! What did you live on?" Gower wanted to know.

"My mother has provided for me," Abel answered. "I'm quite well off."

Gower grinned. "You sure don't look it," he commented, surveying Abel's frayed trousers and stained, tattered shirt.

"I usually dress better than this," said Abel, laughing. For a moment he was embarrassed, but then he wiped the clay off his paws with the tail of his shirt.

Abel talked about Amanda, about her poetry, her grace, her tendency to dream. He speculated on why *her* movements, *her* gestures, *her* voice, *her* way of dressing, were so much more charming and heart-winning than those of any other female mouse he had ever known, including his own dear mother and favorite sister. It puzzled him.

"It's the magic of love," burped Gower.

"Could you raise your chin a bit higher?" Abel asked.

Gower did not move. He was in one of his reptilian torpors again. There he crouched with heavy-lidded, unseeing eyes, not asleep, not awake, not dead, not alive, still as a stone, gyrating with the world.

Abel watched in wonder. Gower's eyelids lifted slightly and his tongue suddenly shot forward and nailed a fly, which he swallowed. This feat always impressed Abel, and disgusted him too.

"Could you raise your head a trifle?" he asked again.

It took a week to complete the statue. It was the best Abel had ever done, a perfect representation of stupefied repose. Every wart was lovingly modeled; the eyes bulged properly, the full throat with the delicate wrinkles of age was definitely Gower's. The fulsome belly, the haunches and feet, rested firmly on the ground. There was a vague smile on the broad mouth and in the lines of the closed eyelids that made the frog appear to be meditating on a homey universe.

Abel was so proud of his accomplishment he wished he could show it to Amanda that minute. "Well, what do you think of it?" he asked Gower.

"It's me all right," Gower said. "It's more me than what I see in the mirror. It's what I see when I imagine how I look. It's a work of art, that's what it is!"

Abel allowed the compliment to stand. Looking at his own opus, he saw no reason to pretend modesty.

"I think you've found your vocation," opined Gower.

Abel swallowed, then blushed. He had never thought along these lines.

°16°

Early one morning in the middle of June, Abel heard a knocking on his log and stepped outside. It was Gower, who'd been sleeping by the river. His manner seemed less than casual.

"What's up?" Abel inquired.

"I've been watching the water," said the frog. "It's not as rushy as it was." Actually, the river had returned to normal a week earlier, but Gower had been unusually meditative lately. "I think I can make it to the other side."

"Why so soon?" Abel asked, full of sudden foreboding. "We're just getting to know one another. Aren't you happy here? Have I offended you in any way?"

"I'm happy, all right," Gower glumped. "But I'm worried. I've been thinking of Gammer, my wife, and all the children, and their children and their children's children. They can't be getting on too well without me."

"How I hate to see you go," sighed Abel.

"I hate to go," allowed Gower.

"Then don't," said Abel.

"My family," said Gower.

"*I'm* your family," said Abel.

Gower's eyes bulged. "You're a mouse," he said.

"How about some breakfast?" asked Abel.

"No, thanks," said Gower. "I've been eating flies all morning. They're at their best today."

"You won't forget to come back with help, will you?" Abel pleaded. "And you will get in touch with Amanda? 89 Bank Street, Mossville."

"Don't worry," said Gower.

"Don't forget," said Abel.

"How could I?" said Gower. "It's the first thing I'll do after I get home and see my family." Then he went into his trance; his eyes rolled up under the lids as if he were storing a memory there for future use.

When his absent mind returned, they walked down to the water, both sad to be parting. "Knowing you, dear Gower, has been one of the most rewarding experiences of my life," said Abel.

"Ditto," said Gower. "Shucks, why grieve? It's only temporary. That's a great statue you made of me. It will be in a museum someday, I'll bet."

"Thank you," said Abel.

"I'll have to play my bull fiddle for you when we meet again."

"We *will* meet again, won't we?" said Abel. "You won't forget?"

"You bet," said Gower. He was standing on the bank of the river with bowed legs. "Farewell, my friend." He put a cold hand on Abel's shoulder.

"Farewell, good Gower," said Abel in a husky voice.

Gower dived. He disappeared under the water and in a while his head bobbed up, far out and downstream. He waved back with his webbed hand. Abel waved. And then Gower was off and swimming, a strong breast stroke, making lateral headway but also being carried downstream, until he disappeared, at least from sight.

Abel was certain the frog would make the other bank. He wished he could swim as well. He watched the empty river for a while, then walked back to his log in tears. He sat on a stone, looking with wet eyes at a blurred world at the statues, Amanda, Gower, and the others, at the daisies beyond the statues, at the tall, silent trees. He could not stand his own sorrow.

The watch ticked away without feeling. Abel got up, went to the cherry birch, and climbed up to his roost. He sat there all day, not thinking, numb.

At night his star appeared. "I'm lonesome," Abel said when he saw it.

"So am I," the star seemed to answer.

°17°

Summer progressed. While waiting for Gower Glackens's rescue crew, Abel kept busy, providing for himself, working at his art, doing whatever he could to be steadily occupied. He ate dandelion greens, birch bark, pigweed, wild onions, mushrooms, grass seed, watercress. He found he liked burdock root very much, and when the strawberries turned red, he had them on his breath all day.

He began to make sculptures of plants, and the more elaborate he made them, the more it distracted his mind. He took to drawing, with bits of charcoal, in the empty spaces on the pages of his bear novel, and he discovered he could color his drawings by rubbing them with flower petals.

He swam. He went on long, rambling walks. He kept his watch ticking. But all the time he never forgot he was waiting, waiting for his rescuers. Either Gower would bring them, or Amanda, or both. He waited for weeks. No one came.

Finally, he was achingly certain that Gower had forgotten him. He had surely succeeded in crossing the river, but somewhere along the watery way his memory of a mouse named Abel had leached out.

Abel looked at Gower's statue and had new insight into the mystical expression on his face. He realized that

if Gower was not drilled into remembering the everyday world, it became a dream that faded from mind as he dwelled on the ultimate reality beyond it. If he remembered his family, that was because a family is the one thing nobody can ever forget. Abel built fires to make smoke signals again and sent messages down the river on scraps from his book.

In the hugging heat of July he was struck with a new, most exciting possibility. For weeks it hadn't rained and the river looked a bit slower, a mite shallower. Could he, could he possibly, hope that the short dry spell would continue into a drawn-out drought? That the river would get low enough for him to risk swimming across? He would hope it, but he warned himself not to be too devastated if it didn't happen.

He climbed his cherry birch. He was still wearing Amanda's scarf. It was the only thing he wore that was not in shreds. He had had to discard his shoes and socks sometime ago. His necktie had been used to help hold up his hammock. He removed the scarf from his neck and let the birch feel its wispy softness. Then he fell to kissing it.

He had avoided dwelling too much on Amanda, even while waiting for rescuers. Now she occupied his mind constantly. He could see her beautiful black eyes vividly. Dreaminess and vivacity, what a wonderful combination of qualities! How much her brisk, graceful bustling had enlivened his idle days! How often, when he'd been lying on the sofa at home, wondering what to make of his life, her mere passing through the room had cheered him up. Even her scoldings he remembered with pleasure. She had only meant him well. His whole being ached to be with her.

He was glad the sun was so fierce and burning. He slept on the ground outside his log and was happy to wake every morning to a bright, torrid day. The first thing he did on waking was to look at the river. Its flow was clearly diminished. A few sand bars had become visible, and dry rocks showed that had previously been under water.

The island was still green in spite of the drought, and it was green on the opposite shores of the river. But, beyond, the green looked tarnished and the tops of the distant wooded hills were turning brown. That dying vegetation gladdened Abel's heart.

He woke one morning in August to find the sky dark with clouds. A few drops of rain had fallen and been quickly absorbed by the dry ground. Abel ran to the river and looked up and down its length. It's now or never, he decided.

He raced back to his yard and, addressing himself to Amanda's statue, declared, "I'm coming home!" Then, entering his log, he looked around as if to etch forever

in his memory this piece of dead tree that had been his haven. He lovingly caressed each of his sculptures. The ticking watch urged him not to tarry. He ran to the birch and pressed his face to its bark. The birch stood erect and encouraging.

He hurried to the river, to the tip of a small peninsula. For one moment he turned to stare back and was filled with sudden anguish. The island had been his home for a full year. It had given him sustenance, guidance, warmth, like a parent. Something important had happened there. How could he help loving it!

"Goodbye," he said. "I'll be back." And he waded into the water.

·18·

When the water was neck-high, Abel flung himself forward and started swimming. He was carried downstream, but he made progress across too. It was still, for him, a strong current, but not like before. He swam with great resolve. He didn't mind the water engulfing him now and then, filling and hurting his nostrils. He snorted bravely when it did. He was at last actually doing what for weeks he had been doing only in his imagination.

Fortunately, he was able to climb a rock after a while and rest there until his panting had subsided. He was a quarter of the way over! Now he confronted the most challenging, the deepest, part of the stream. He had to believe he would be able to reach another rock to rest on. Having come so far, he felt his confidence swell. He was wiry-strong after his rugged year in the wilds. The Abel who was leaving was in better fettle, in all ways, than the Abel who had arrived in a hurricane, desperately clinging to a nail.

He sucked his lungs full of air and threw himself into the water. Again he was carried downstream and again made crossways progress, stroking and kicking with power. He felt a minnow brush his leg and he exulted to be doing so well in the minnow's own medium. He kept swimming. But soon he was overwhelmed by the water's swiftness. It tore and tumbled and he was swung

around like someone dragged against his will into a reckless dance.

He stopped swimming, lay with his arms and legs outstretched, face to the heavens, and let himself be carried along for a while. With a sodden thump, he again found a rock. Blessed rock. He mounted it and rested on his back, his body heaving. It was very much as he had imagined it would be—difficult. But he was mastering the river, and he felt he was being guided. Hallelujah! Light rain began to fall. It didn't matter. Abel knew he was equal to the rest of his task. He dived once more. A dozen strokes and his feet were touching bottom! He was on a gravelly welt of raised river bed. He walked across it and, without hesitating, made his final, easy swim.

When at last he came out of the water and touched the shore he had been yearning toward for the whole round of a passing year, he experienced a burst of astounding joy. He lay on the longed-for ground, flooded with ecstatic feelings of triumph and well-being. Then he broke into uncontrollable laughter. He was a free mouse!

In a while he started upstream, walking along the bank, where no tall grass obstructed the way. His thoughts were full of the future, but they were also full of the past. He was imagining ahead to Amanda, and beyond her to his family, his friends, and a renewed life in society that would include productive work, his art;

but he was also remembering his year on the island, a unique and separate segment of his life that he was now glad he had gone through, though he was also glad it was over.

As to what was to come, he began to be disturbed by vague apprehensions. What was he really walking toward? Would Amanda be home? Had things changed during his year of exile? What if, believing him dead, she had married another? Many mice had been in love with her. Was she even alive? He had been in touch with her, but had he really been in touch? Or had he only imagined it?

After much walking, he arrived at a spot opposite his island. He saw it for the first time from a far perspective,

embracing its wholeness. No wonder he loved it; it was beautiful. Through the rain he saw his beloved birch and all the trees around it. These images would be his forever.

Having no wish to dally, he continued steadily northward. When he climbed the steep hill alongside the waterfall, he was amazed that he had traveled over this cataract when it was much mightier, and had survived. He had been through great ordeals, but here he was. Life surely meant him well. He kept walking.

If only the rain would end, if only for an hour. He felt the need to be dry. Eventually, he found shelter in a natural vault of jutting rock, lay down, and was instantly asleep.

When he woke, the moon was out and a cat was staring him in the face.

For a moment Abel was stiff with terror, then he scrambled to his feet, but before he could get away he was in the cat's mouth. He could feel her sharp teeth holding him firmly by the skin of his back

Now he was being trotted off somewhere in a very businesslike way, and there was no question about the nature of the business. His thoughts remained remarkably clear. Was this the culmination of all his plans, all

his yearning, all his work, all his waiting, for a long, long year? Would he *not* see Amanda again? His family? Not be at home again? Not be? Could life be so cruel?

The cat dropped him on the ground. He darted off like an arrow. The cat pounced, held him under a paw, and in another moment let go. Abel did nothing. He couldn't tell whether it was fear that held him, or sudden loss of hope, or whether he was playing dead out of long-forgotten instinct. It amounted to the same thing. He was motionless. The cat was motionless. They waited.

Then, swipe! She struck him, tossing him into the air with a cuff of her paw. At that, Abel was off and running, the cat after him. Again she snagged him in her teeth and again she let him go. Abel crouched, only his eyes moving. He was bleeding, yet he felt strangely detached now, curious about what the cat, or he himself, would do next.

The cat watched. She blinked. Was she bored? Abel felt she was being much too casual about his imminent end, as though it were only one of many she had contrived. He saw a tree a short way off and scampered wildly toward it. The cat allowed him a head start, perhaps to add interest to the chase. Abel fled up the tree in sudden streaks, going this way, that, under and over branches, around the trunk. The cat stayed close, but slipped once, while Abel kept going.

He made his wild way to the very top, to the slenderest branch that would support his weight. The cat couldn't follow that far. They rested. They could see each other

clearly in the moon's mellow light. Looking down from the safety of his position, Abel realized that the cat had to do what she did. She was being a cat. It was up to him to be the mouse.

And he was playing his part very well. A little smugness crept into his attitude. He seemed to be saying, "It's your move." Whether in response to this, or merely because she was tired of waiting, the cat leaped. Abel gripped his twig. It bent like a bow when she struck it, swung back, swayed, and shook in his grasp, and he could hear the cat drop, hitting branches as she fell, yowling and screaming in pain and amazement. He heard the thud as she struck the ground, and her crazy caterwauling as she shot off in utter confusion. The unruffled moon continued to shine.

Abel stayed in the tree and eventually slept. In the light of morning, taking his bearings, he was overjoyed to see Mt. Eunice to the northwest. The fire observatory was on the side visible to him, and at last he knew where he was. He had to travel northward with a bias to the east, and he would be in Mossville sooner or later—with luck, in less than a day. He would be seeing *her* again! He hustled down the tree and started homeward, half walking, half running.

By late afternoon he was on rocky ground cleft with ravines. It must have been one of these he was flushed down a year ago in the hurricane, because he arrived before long at the cliff with the cave where he and Amanda had taken shelter that day. He pressed on.

He was walking in the woods where he had picnicked with his wife. There were signs of last year's great storm. Broken branches lay on the ground, and uprooted trees with slabs of earth still attached to their bases. In the shade of the woods it was still quite green in spite of the drought.

Abel's heart pounded with his exertions and excitement. And with dreadful anxiety. Would Amanda be there, at home? Would she be happy to see him? At moments he was afraid he might even be unwelcome. It grew dark and he was glad of it. He had every reason to be in rags, but he didn't want to be seen that way. He didn't want to be seen in any way, not by anyone but Amanda. Later there would be time to see mother, father, family, and all the others.

He reached the edge of town at night. He was in Grover Park. The soft gas lamps were lighted. It was a hot night, and the park was full of townsfolk, outdoors after dinner to keep cool, strolling on the graveled walks, chatting on the benches, laughing, watching the children romp and frisk about. How wonderful, after the year alone in the woods, to see this model of civilized society, the town where he was born. He recognized many faces; he was back where he belonged. But he stayed in the shadows to avoid being seen.

Then, suddenly, whom should he see! She, herself, Amanda! Sitting on a stone bench in a perfectly everyday way.

How could he keep from rushing out and holding her dearness in his arms? He managed to restrain himself. There were others on the bench and on the walk. He had waited a year; he could wait a bit longer. Their reunion should be theirs alone. He hurried quietly home, avoiding any encounter.

Home! He grasped the graceful railing and bounded up the steps. He still had the keys in his ragged pants. He opened the door. It was all exactly as he had left it,

as he had remembered it so often during his exile. It was nothing like his hollow log.

Amanda's radiance was there. How good to see her things about. And his own—his books, his favorite chair. He went into the kitchen, looked in a pot on the stove, tasted the soup.

In the bedroom he looked around with anxious joy at the familiar objects. He washed, with scented soap. He donned his best silk shirt, his purple cravat, his brown velvet jacket with the braided lapels. These elegant clothes felt uncomfortable.

Now, smiling, he put Amanda's scarf on the taboret in the entrance hall where she could see it when she entered, then went into the parlor and lay down on the

plush sofa, his paws behind his head, his heart full of bold expectations. It seemed a long time before Amanda came home. At last he heard the door open and then a gasp and a cry.

"Abel! Oh, dear Abel! It's you! It's really, really you!" Amanda came rushing in and flung herself into Abel's arms. They covered each other with kisses.

When he was able to speak, Abel said, "I've brought you back your scarf."

GET A FULL YEAR MEMBERSHIP FOR ONLY $99!

Welcome to the National Association of Pizzeria Operators.
Please complete this membership application and join the world's #1 pizza team.

Annual Fee $~~200~~ $99

Membership Application

Date	Owner's Name			
Restaurant Name (DBA)				
Address:	City:		State:	Zip:
Phone:	Fax:		Email:	

Please Check ALL Program(s) in which you are interested:

❏ Bottled Beverage Program
❏ Health Smart™ Healthy Pizza Promo
❏ Payroll Processing
❏ Free Check Recovery

❏ Loss Recovery
❏ Discount Healthcare
❏ 401-K Account

Insurance Program
❏ General Liability
❏ Workers' Compensation
❏ Delivery Liability

Credit Card Services
❏ Loss Recovery
❏ Wireless Terminal
❏ Merchant Support 24/7

Would you care for a FREE Subscription?

❏ YES ❏ NO - Please start/continue my FREE Pizza Today subscription.

Which one of the following best describes your business and/or occupation (check one only):

01 ❏ Independent Operator
04 ❏ Chain Operator
07 ❏ Dealer/Distributor

02 ❏ Franchise Operator
06 ❏ Manufacturer/Supplier
99 ❏ Others Allied to the Field

Signature and date required to recieve a free subscription   Date

Would you like to Join NAPO?

❏ YES - Please enroll me in NAPO today!
Annual Fee $~~200~~ $99 - Payment method:
❏ Check - Make your check payable to NAPO
❏ Visa   ❏ MasterCard
❏ American Express   ❏ Discover

Name on Card

Signature

Card Number   Exp Date

Please return Membership Application to: National Association of Pizzeria Operators
908 South 8th Street, Suite 200, Louisville KY 40203 • Phone: 502-736-9530 • Fax: 502-736-9531

NATIONAL ASSOCIATION OF PIZZERIA OPERATORS

with foreword by Pete Lachapelle,
President and Publisher of *Pizza Today™ Magazine*

How to Open a Financially Successful

Pizza & Sub

Restaurant

Shri L. Henkel & Douglas R. Brown

**with
companion CD-ROM**

**The companion CD-ROM contains all forms from the book, PLUS a
pre-written, editable business plan in Microsoft® Word format.**

How to Open a Financially Successful Pizza & Sub Restaurant:
With Companion CD-ROM

Copyright © 2007 by Atlantic Publishing Group, Inc.
1210 SW 23rd Place • Ocala, Florida 34474 • 800-814-1132 • 352-622-5836–Fax
Web site: www.atlantic-pub.com • E-mail: sales@atlantic-pub.com
SAN Number: 268-1250

ISBN-10: 0-910627-80-0 • ISBN-13: 978-0-910627-80-1

Library of Congress Cataloging-in-Publication Data

Henkel, Shri L., 1965-
How to open a financially successful pizza & sub restaurant / Shri L. Henkel.
     p. cm.
  Includes index.
  ISBN-13: 978-0-910627-80-1 (alk. paper)
  ISBN-10: 0-910627-80-0
  1. Restaurant management. 2. Pizza industry--Management. 3. New business
enterprises--Management. I. Title.

  TX911.3.M27H45 2006
  647.95068--dc22

                         2006013809

EDITOR: Jackie Ness • jackie_ness@charter.net
PROOFREADER: Angela C. Adams • angela.c.adams@hotmail.com
ART DIRECTION, FRONT COVER & INTERIOR DESIGN: Meg Buchner • megadesn@mchsi.com
BOOK PRODUCTION DESIGN: Laura Siitari of Siitari by Design • www.siitaribydesign.com
Printed in the United States

Table of Contents

Foreword   13

Introduction   15

Chapter 1: Start Your Own Pizza and Sub Shop   17

Pizza History 18
Ways to Explore Your Passion 19
How Much Money Do You Need? 20
Is It for Me? 23
Learning the Ropes 26
Some of the Big Boys' Stories 27
Choose the Best Business Method for You 29

Chapter 2: Buying a Pizza and Sub Shop   35

Find Potential Pizza Shop Sites 35
Population and Demographics 39
Site Research 41
Competition 43
Evaluate the Real Estate Value 45
Valuing Other Assets 46
Reviewing the Books 50
Financing 51
Equity Funds 51
Borrowing Money 52
The Deal 55

Chapter 3: Writing a Business Plan 59

Five Keys of Success...60
What a Business Plan Includes 60
Business Plan—Description of the Business 62
Legal Business Forms...63
Products/Services...65
The Location 65
The Marketing Plan 66
Franchise Owners – Specifically 67
What Will You Serve and How Will You Serve It?..............68
Pricing...68
Advertising and Public Relations 69
The Management Plan 70
Specific Franchise Questions 72
The Financial Management Plan...72
Business Plan Resources 74

Chapter 4: How to Invest in a Franchise 75

Franchise Costs 76
Definition of Franchising 77
Finding a Franchise 78
Investigating Franchise Offerings...79
Additional Sources of Information 80
Advantages of Franchising 81
Disadvantages of Franchising..83
Minority Participation in Franchising.....................................85
Franchise Financing...85
Evaluating a Franchise Opportunity 85

Chapter 5: Starting Off 87

Governmental Requirements..87
State Registration 88
City Business License 89
Sales Tax..89

Health Department License..90

Fire Department Permit 90

Building and Construction Permit 91

Sign Permits 91

Zoning...91

State Liquor License 92

Internal Revenue Registration 93

Federal Identification Number (Employee Identification Number) ...93

State Tax Assistance 94

Chapter 6: Internal Bookkeeping   95

Budgeting 95

Accounting Software 96

Payroll...97

Taxes 99

Forms You May Need...100

General Tax Calendar 100

Tipped Employees 101

Handling Cash 101

Cash Handling...103

Chapter 7: Budgeting and Operational Management 109

Monthly Budgeting..110

Total Sales 111

Track Sales Growth..112

Sales Categories 112

Labor...113

Controllable Operational Costs 114

Services..114

Utilities 115

Fixed Operating Costs...116

General Operating Costs..116

Total Net Profit...118

Depreciation 118

Chapter 8: What to Serve   121

Pizza Marketing Quarterly Annual Report for 2005 121
Pizza Trends You Should Know 126
Specialty Items 136
Healthy Options 140
Food Allergies..143
Alcohol..144
Serving Alcohol 147
Beer 152

Chapter 9: Recipe Development and Production   159

Experimentation...160
Ask Employees for Help 161
Test Your Ideas 162
Set Production Standards 162
Shift Production Volume...163
Quality Standards...164
Acceptable Substitutions..164

Chapter 10: Recipes to Sample and Inspire New Creations 167

Pizza Dough Recipes 168
Pizza Sauces...174
Pizza Sauce Toppings...178
Appetizers and Miscellaneous 178
Pizza Recipes 182
Miscellaneous Entrée Recipes 189
Sub Recipes 199
Desserts..203
Additional Recipe Resources..207

Chapter 11: Control Your Costs   209

Profits Don't Guarantee Success..210
Controlling Costs Works...210

Interpret the Numbers...212
Set Standards...215
Inventory and Product Management 216
Control Food and Beverage Costs 218
Check Average..219
Sales Analysis...220
Profit Analysis 220
Controlling Food Costs..220
Sales Mix...224
Pricing..226
Financial Analysis 228
Theft..228
Control Labor Costs...229
Scheduling 230
Prepared Beverages and Foods 233
Work Area Layout and Equipment Design 233
Creating Productivity 234

Chapter 12: Profitable Menu Planning   235

Menu Style..235
Formatting Your Menu...236
Daily Specials 237
Developing the Menu Selections 237
Limiting the Menu 239
Portion Control = Savings 240
Your Recipe File 241
Ordering Manual..242
Figure Menu Prices...242
Preparing Your Menu 243
Menu Design 244
Menu Size and Cover 244
Menu Content 245
Price Placement..248
Arrangement of Text...249
Menu Psychology 249
Menu Layout...249

Graphic Elements..251
Printing Your Menu Production 251
Menu Design Dos and Don'ts 252
Truth and Accuracy in the Menu......................................252
Disclaimers...254
Nutritional Claims 254
Menu Design Help..255

Chapter 13: Your Staff 257

Cook...257
Prep Cook..258
Manager...258
Dishwasher...259
Delivery Personnel..259
Front Counter 259
Job Descriptions 260

Chapter 14: Successful Employee Relations and Labor Cost Control 273

The Value (and Cost) of Employees....................................273
Hiring Pizzeria Employees 276
Key Points for Conducting Employment Interviews.......278
Unlawful Pre-Employment Questions 279
Things to Look for in Potential Employees.......................281
The Final Selection and Decision 283
Rejecting Applicants...284
Employee Handbook/Personnel Policy 284
Personnel File..287
Training..287
Orientation and Instruction...288
Outside Help in Training 289
Outside Help: Speakers and Subjects.................................290
Scheduling 290
Evaluating Performance..292
The Decision to Terminate an Employee...........................294

Chapter 15: Equipping Your Pizza and Sub Shop   297

Create an Equipment Budget 298
Used Equipment...299
Leasing Your Equipment 301
Make Wise Purchases 302
What Quality Level?...305
Service Contracts...306
Equipment Records..306
Pizzeria-Specific Equipment, Tools, and Supplies 307
Wash Up Afterwards..321
Computers – How to Use Them and Profit From Them 324

Chapter 16: Successful Kitchen Management   337

Purchasing...337
Receiving and Storing Supplies....................................340

Chapter 17: Public Areas   343

Outdoor Areas...344
Parking...345
First Impressions 345
Your Restrooms 347
Countertop Displays 348
Front Work Areas 349
Shelving..350
Dedicated Work Areas 350
Delivery Areas 351
Storage 352
Waste & Recycling 353
Last But Not Least – Your Office..................................354

Chapter 18: Marketing Your Business   357

Hiring Marketing Experts 357
You Can Do It Yourself..358

Guerilla Marketing...359

Advertising...361

Improving Your Skills..366

Utilize Your Computer in Another Way.................................366

Use E-Mail Effectively...367

Promote with Your Logo 369

Business Cards and Brochures 370

Should You Have a Web Site?..375

Coupons...381

Direct Mail...382

Packaging...383

Band Together 384

Market to Your Existing Customers.....................................385

Talk to Your Customers...385

Delight Your Guests 387

Public Relations...387

Charity for PR..391

Special Events..391

Maintain Employee Relations..393

The Other PR – Press Releases 394

Chapter 19: Carryout and Delivery 399

Carryout...399

Delivery 400

Delivery Equipment...404

Food Safety for Carryout and Delivery................................407

Chapter 20: Dining In 411

Create a Design Focal Point...411

Set the Mood 412

Table, Chair, Booths, and Bar Stool Options.......................412

Cover Your Floors..414

Looking Up – Selecting Ceilings 417

Let a Little Light Shine..418

Colors That Complement 420

A Little Artwork 420

Amusement 421

Serving 421

Self-Service Displays 421

Chapter 21: A Safe Work Environment   425

Agencies 425

First Aid and Safety 426

Fire 426

Accidents and Security 427

Kitchen Safety 428

Electrical Shock 431

Strains 431

Slipping and Falling 432

Choking 433

Exposure to Hazardous Chemicals 433

Good Ergonomics 434

The Air We Breathe 435

Chapter 22: The Essentials of Food Safety, HACCP, and Sanitation Practices   439

HACCP Defined 440

Why Should You Use HACCP? 441

Implementing HACCP 441

HACCP Procedures 444

Storage Options and Requirements 446

Preparing Food 451

Cooking 453

Serving and Holding 454

Cooling 457

Reheating 459

Clean Versus Sanitary 459

Sanitize Portable Equipment: 460

Sanitizing In-Place Equipment: 461

A First-Rate Facility 462

Ventilation 463

Restrooms 464

Cross-Contamination Concerns 464

Contributing to Foodborne Illness............................465

Personal Hygiene..469

Chapter 23: Leaving Your Business   475

Your Exit Plan 476

Pass Your Business On..477

Groom Your Replacement 477

Selling Your Business to Your Employees 478

Say Goodbye 479

Conclusion..480

Manufacturer's Reference   481

Resources 486

Index   487

Foreword

Many people dream of owning their own pizza and sub shop, but few actually make the leap into entrepreneurship. Starting a business, especially a restaurant, takes hard work, long hours, a willingness to sacrifice time with family and friends, and a passion to succeed. Even those entrepreneurs with the determination to succeed face daunting odds. Statistics show that between 90 and 95 percent of all new pizza shops fail in the first year with 90 percent failing in the second year; however, in the third year, the failure rate drops to an estimated 60 percent.

Opening a pizza shop requires much more than having a few out-of-this world recipes. All that needs to be done before ever serving a single customer—from purchasing the proper equipment and keeping track of inventory to hiring the best employees and setting prices—can be overwhelming, especially for first-time business owners.

During our 25 years in the industry, we've watched entrepreneurs come and go. One of the key ingredients to success is to understand exactly what must be done to build a successful pizza shop, and that takes time. First, you want to read as much as you can about the industry. *Pizza Today*™, the premier industry magazine, offers potential and current pizza shop owners valuable information, including all the latest industry news. Read it. You'll find it a valuable asset both during your research phase, as you continue to build your business, and once your pizza shop becomes a fixture in the community.

Come to the International Pizza Expo in Las Vegas. It's held every March and offers nearly 12,000 pizza professionals under one roof for the sole purpose of helping folks in the industry become more successful. There are over 60 seminars available on topics that range from marketing to production and menu expansion to personnel management. Talk with other pizza shop

owners to glean valuable advice from them – ask them what mistakes they made when they were starting out and what, in particular, helped propel them to success. Don't be afraid to ask a lot of questions. Talking with other pizza shop owners also allows you to network, an important tool for any business owner.

Make sure you read *How to Open a Financially Successful Pizza & Sub Restaurant* thoroughly because it is more than just a typical how-to book. Rather, it is a comprehensive guide that teaches entrepreneurs, like you, everything they'll need to know to make an informed decision about going into business for themselves, tips to increase their chances of success in this competitive industry, and a host of appetizer, pizza, and dessert recipes. Included with the book is a companion CD, complete with detailed checklists, recipes, and all the information a new business owner needs to effectively get started in the industry.

The research stage of starting a business takes time, but it could very well mean the difference between failure and success, so make time for it. Once you're ready, you'll move from research to beginning your business. It will undoubtedly be an exciting time, but remember to take heed of the mistakes you'll make. You will make mistakes; all business owners do, but make those mistakes work for you. Use them as learning tools, instead of allowing them to get you down.

Late at night when you're exhausted from a day of preparing for your opening, remember the rewards that will come with your success. You're embarking on a journey that many people, at best, only dream about. Enjoy it.

A fixture in the restaurant and publishing industries since 1979, Pete Lachapelle is currently President of Macfadden Protech LLC, a position he assumed in 2000. Responsible for the tradeshow division, Lachapelle manages the International Pizza Expo™, Pizza Today's Northeast Pizza Show™ and the National Association of Pizzeria Operators (NAPO). He's also the president and publisher of the industry's most-respected and well-read magazine, Pizza Today™.

Introduction

The aroma. Isn't that the first thing that attracted you to pizza? We enjoy the wonderful combination of cheese, tomato sauce, garlic, oregano, and the toppings of our choice. Imagine owning your own pizza and sub shop. You can learn to spin pizza dough and watch the shining eyes of children as they enjoy the show. Subs are simple, and there are many varieties. What could be better than owning a pizza and sub shop?

If you feel like that, this book is for you. I'll walk you through all the steps of buying and establishing a profitable pizza and sub shop. There are many factors to consider; and in this book and the accompanying CD, I'll help you make informed and educated decisions about whether you should own a pizza and sub shop.

There are calm pizza restaurants, and there are incredibly busy pizza shops. You can decide which business is suited to your personality and your abilities. We will discuss how to make a good decision and how to develop your business plan. This will keep you focused on the things that must be done to open a profitable pizza shop.

Every business must meet local and state requirements. These could include a local business license, acquiring tax identification numbers for payroll and sales tax, permits, insurance and so on. It is a long list, and each item is necessary. These details will be discussed in detail, to help you operate legally from the beginning.

We'll discuss how to decide whether to buy a pizza franchise or if you are better suited to run an independent pizza shop. Make the decision about what items you will serve. Once you have chosen your menu items, hire the right employees to work in your pizza shop. This book will explain how to write job descriptions, interview, hire, and train your team members.

You will equip your kitchen and a dining room, if you have one. There are ways to use décor and atmosphere to your benefit. We will develop a plan to set up your work areas and your areas for the public in the best way for your pizza shop.

The food and drink items on your menu will help you determine food costs, suppliers, prep work, and staff. The ingredients for your menu items must be purchased, maintained, rotated, and used in a timely manner. This will help you in the preparation of the recipes you plan to use in your pizza shop.

An important part of the process is marketing. No matter how wonderful your pizza shop is, you still need to attract customers. We will review strategies to bring customers to your shop and to increase your sales. Effective marketing is crucial to your success.

I worked for three years as a pizza shop assistant manager and then a store manager. For about twenty years, I've managed a wide variety of businesses. In the following pages I will share marketing strategies we used to increase our sales. We'll also review things I learned that are valuable when you manage a business and your team members. I'll share this and much more. Now, let's get started.

I compiled the resources listed in this book, and they are in a file on the accompanying CD. These resources are listed by the chapter where they were used. I hope they will be helpful in your research.

1

Start Your Own Pizza and Sub Shop

Running any restaurant is hard work, and a pizza and sub shop is no different. In 2003 H. G. Parsa, an associate professor of hospitality management at Ohio State University, showed the failure rate of restaurants was lower than people previously thought. The assumption was a 90 to 95 percent failure rate in the first year and 90 percent in the third year. However, his research revised those figures to 60 percent in the third year. Even the lower numbers are significant and shouldn't be ignored. I don't want to discourage you, but this will allow you to go into this business with your eyes open. That will give you a much better chance to succeed.

The old saying is that "anything you really want is worth working for". So if your dream is to open a pizza and sub shop, statistics like these won't stop you. They'll simply make you more resolved to be successful. Realizing your dream can be a rewarding endeavor—personally and professionally. But, achieving your dream takes more than your grandmother's secret recipe.

Your recipe for success includes a blend of passion, vision, risk-taking and business sense.

One of the first things you need in order to fulfill the dream of owning your own business is to create a solid vision on how you will accomplish your dream. Developing a solid vision will help you write your business plan and sell your concept to lenders and potential investors while communicating your vision to the multitude of people you will work with to make your dream a reality.

This understanding will help you make decisions when faced with compromises, budget concerns, and unexpected obstacles. The sections below will help you do the soul searching needed to solidify your vision.

Pizza History

Pizza made its first appearance in the early 1900s, when Italian immigrants first came to America. Italian immigrant Gennaro (or, Giovanni, depending on the source) Lombardi opened the first pizzeria in 1905 in the Little Italy section of New York City. By the 1930s, pizzerias had spread across the country. Something that contributed to the popularity of pizza was the soldiers returning from Italy during World War II.

Pizza is one of America's most popular foods. It is a convenient and enticing food that we eat at slumber parties, buy for work lunches, and many other events. What is a football game without a steaming pizza? College students can live on pizza for entire semesters. I had experience with this personally at the pizza shop I managed. It's astounding how much pizza college students eat. By the end of the 1990s, Americans were eating 350 slices of pizza per second, and children between three and 11-years-old said pizza was their favorite meal in 2000.

Pizza was made for Americans. It is convenient, covered in cheese and can

be eaten with your hands. By the late 1990s, pizza was one of our favorite foods. During this time, three pizza restaurants ranked among the top 11 restaurant chains in the United States: Pizza Hut ranked third; Domino's Pizza ranked ninth; and Little Caesars Pizza ranked eleventh.

Ways to Explore Your Passion

Can you see your dream pizza shop when you close your eyes? Is there a fleet of delivery trucks with your name on the door? Would you decorate with the colors of the Italian flag? Does the aroma of garlic and bubbling cheese tickle your nose?

Set aside some uninterrupted time to consider your personal and financial reasons for wanting to open a pizza shop. You may need to commit your energies and "nest egg," take on a partner or commit to a long-term loan. Keep in mind that you won't be profitable overnight—are you prepared for the financial and emotional investment?

Any time I consider a major move in my life, I like to create a list of the positives and negatives. Every venture has risk (negatives), but the positives for you should outweigh the negatives. This will help you get a clear picture of what is involved and help you to set realistic expectations. Then you will be better prepared to build, buy, or lease your facility, launch the new business and create a solid foundation to succeed and to turn a profit.

Now that you've given some thought to your idea, create a one-minute "elevator pitch". If you were in an elevator with a wealthy investor, could you describe your vision (and convince the person to invest) before you reach the 20th floor? A couple of things that will help you succeed with your pitch are to show your passion while emphasizing the tangible benefits. This is good practice because you will probably need to deal with a banker before your pizza shop opens.

How Much Money Do You Need?

The following worksheets, from the Small Business Administration, can help the potential pizza shop owner estimate the expense to get started. This list will help you estimate how much financing is needed to get your business started. Keep in mind that everything on this list might not apply to your business. It's best to estimate the monthly amounts for each item. You may need to make some phone calls to get some information.

(We will discuss these various items in more detail throughout the book.)

BUSINESS STARTUP COSTS	
Salary of Owner/Manager (if applicable)	
All Other Salaries and Wages	
Mortgage/Property Taxes	
Advertising	
Delivery Expenses	
Supplies	
Telephone	
Utilities	
Insurance	
Taxes, Including Social Security	
Interest	
Delivery Cars	
Gas and Car Maintenance	
Maintenance (Facilities/Equipment)	
Legal and Other Professional Fees	
Dues/Subscriptions	
Leases (Equipment/Furniture/Etc.)	
Inventory Purchases	
Miscellaneous	
One-Time Start-Up Costs	
Fixtures/Equipment/Furniture	

BUSINESS STARTUP COSTS	
Remodeling	
Installation of Fixtures/Equipment/Furniture	
Starting Inventory	
Deposits with Public Utilities	
Licenses and Permits	
Advertising and Promotion for Opening	
Accounts Receivable	
Cash Reserve/Operating Capital	
Other	
TOTAL	
*Your total amount will depend on how many months of preparation you want to allow for before actually beginning operations.	

Please see the accompanying CD to print a copy of this form for your use.

These are details about expenses you will face in the early months:

- **Take the time to investigate all the options.** There will be additional costs after the initial setup is complete. Include them in your calculations.

- **Your down payment should be a quarter of the sale price.** The amount of your down payment will affect the final price. The seller may agree to a lower sale price, if you offer a larger down payment and so on.

- **Many amounts may be prorated**, including: insurance, payroll, taxes, employee benefits, licensing fees, marketing expenses, etc.

- **Determine how much cash you have available** for initial purchases.

- **You may need to pay deposits for all utilities** even if you have existing residential accounts. Speak with the companies to determine the amounts.

- **Obtain all required licenses and permits.**

- **Legal fees for negotiation, contract review, and closing should be included.**

- **Figure the costs to meet building code violations.**

- **Equipment and utensils may need to be replaced or purchased.** Maintenance agreements for large purchases should be included.

- **Opening marketing costs need to be estimated** such as replacement of signs and any promotional coupons and incentives.

- **Your "doing business as" needs to be registered** at the courthouse.

- **Include any loan fees you will need to pay.**

- **Depending on the type of business entity you decide to establish, you will need an attorney** to draw up the necessary documents.

- **Your lender will require life and disability insurance** with the lender named as sole beneficiary. Sufficient property insurance will also be needed.

- **When you buy a franchise, you'll have additional fees to pay.** We will discuss this in more detail in Chapter 4.

- **Figure your labor costs to prepare for your opening.**

- **You may need to pay a restaurant consultant,** labor-relations specialists and computer consultants.

- **Since you are a new account, some creditors and vendors may require payment in full, up front.**

- **Don't forget to change the locks after the sale is finished.** You never know who might have a key.

- **Check security system prices.** Once you make a decision, you may need to transfer existing service or set up your own service.

- **It is advisable to have a contingency fund that will keep the business afloat for the first six months.** Many expenses will be higher in the beginning, including payroll since you should over hire and over schedule your employees. It's better to have too many people on staff instead of too few. Many businesses without a contingency fund will fail in the first few months.

Furniture, fixtures, and equipment will account for a decent amount of money. Your amounts will vary depending on the location and property you choose. The worksheet on page 24 will help you break down these costs in more detail.

Is It for Me?

Once you determine if your dream is financially viable, you must decide if it's right for your family. Can your family deal with you working until 3 or 4 a.m. on the weekends? Do you like to travel and take time off? If so, you need to understand that owning any type of restaurant is a seven-day-a-week job.

After talking with your family and getting their support, determine what important traits you bring to the venture. Do you love to cook? Can you deal with people in a positive way? Do you work well in a fast-paced environment? How are your marketing and sales skills? Do you prefer to write a check and let professionals handle the details, or do you want to be consulted on every detail? There are various skills a restaurant owner needs. The checklist on page 25 is a way to assess the traits you need.

FURNITURE / FIXTURES / EQUIPMENT					
Items Which May Be Needed	Amount If Paying In Full	Price	Down Payment	Amount of Each Install-ment	Amount Needed For Fur-niture, Fixtures & Equip-ment.
Cash Register					
Linens					
Storage Shelves					
Display Stands					
Shelves					
Tables					
Safe					
Computer					
Special Lighting					
Outside Sign					
Kitchen Equipment					
Dining Room Furniture					
Delivery Vehicles					
Total Furniture, Fixtures & Equipment					

Please see the accompanying CD to print a copy of this form for your use.

SKILL ASSESSMENT INVENTORY		
Entrepreneur/Managerial Qualities	**Qualified**	**Not Qualified**
I am good at resolving conflicts		
I enjoy working hard		
I am able to meet deadlines		
I am able to maintain a budget		
I am a self-starter		
I am a creative problem-solver		
I set clear goals		
I have the ability to follow through		
Organizational Qualities		
I'm good with figures		
I keep an updated calendar		
I have to-do lists		
I have the ability to prioritize tasks		
I am good at recordkeeping		
I have a good filing system		
Communication Skills		
I am good at giving instructions/ directions		
I am good at writing memos/letters/ reports		
I am a good listener		
I speak clearly, making sure people understand		
Customer Service Skills		
I don't get frustrated easily		
I don't lose my temper easily		
I am comfortable with enforcing rules or policies		

SKILL ASSESSMENT INVENTORY		
I like to solve problems		
I tolerate all people, no matter their race gender or religion		
Hospitality Skills		
I am friendly and open		
I like working with people		
I enjoy pleasing people		
I enjoy helping people get the information they need		
I am optimistic		
I like to entertain		
I like to cook		
TOTALS		

Please see the accompanying CD to print a copy of this form for your use.

How'd you do? If you possess the majority of these traits, you'll probably do fine as pizza and sub shop owner. This is only a partial list, and you might want to keep the list of things you should work on for future reference. Remember that you can save a lot of money by doing your own repairs and operating a profitable business.

Learning the Ropes

You must learn about a specific business before you decide to start your own. Domino's Pizza realizes this, and that is one reason a person must be a store manager for one year minimum before he can own a franchise.

I'm not saying you must work for Domino's, but you should work in a pizza shop and get to know the business inside and out. This is most effective if you work in a shop that is similar to the shop you have in mind. If you want

a sit-down restaurant, working in a carryout-and-delivery-only shop will be of limited help. It would be good to devote at least six months to this learning process before you'll be ready to start on your own.

Be honest about your other skills. Have you always had problems with math? You should consider a bookkeeping class at the local community college. Many business owners hire an accountant for the major issues, but you will save money if you handle the daily accounting.

Another good way to learn about the business is networking. Talk to pizza shop owners about their experiences. If you don't want to approach your potential competitors, do an online search to find pizzeria owners in other regions who might be willing to talk about their operations.

A great resource is *Pizza Today®*. It has 40,000 subscribers and contains articles that focus on marketing, training, menu development, safety, and business practices. You can also attend trade shows like the International Pizza Expo™, the Chicago Pizza Expo™, the New York Pizza Expo™, and the National Association of Pizzeria Operators (NAPO).

Membership in NAPO will provide you with:

- A direct mail database of 10,000 pizzeria operators
- Pizza Expo booth discount coupons
- A monthly newsletter
- NAPO Web site listing with hyperlink to your site
- Permission to use the NAPO logo in your advertising

Some of the Big Boys' Stories

Do you have doubts about whether you fit the pizza/sub shop owner profile? Following are background stories of some major pizza franchise owners:

Papa John

John Schnatter worked in a local pizza pub in Jeffersonville, Indiana, during high school. In 1984, he converted a broom closet in his father's tavern into a pizza shop. He had to sell his 1972 Camaro to purchase used equipment. The tavern customers bought his pizzas, and he expanded in 1985 by opening his first Papa John's restaurant.

Today Papa John's has almost 3,000 restaurants in 49 states and 20 international markets along with over 100 Perfect Pizza restaurants in the United Kingdom.

Buddy LaRosa

Buddy LaRosa began the Cincinnati pizza chain. Buddy was originally named Donald Sebastiano LaRosa, but was called "Buddy" by his uncles. He grew up in an Italian-America household, and he helped at his uncles' fruit-and-vegetable stand.

In the early 1950s, he came home from serving in the military, got married, and became a father. Around this time, he helped his mother and aunt sell pizza at church and realized this could become something bigger. The American public was just becoming familiar with pizza. Buddy borrowed his aunt's recipe and bought a pizza oven after he cashed in a $400 life insurance policy in 1954. He used some of the money to rent a small building near his uncles' fruit-and-vegetable stand.

Buddy's first eat-in restaurant, The Italian Inn, opened in 1961. He sold the first franchise to the bread deliveryman in 1967, sealing the deal with a handshake. His business expanded to 25 restaurants by 1980. LaRosa's branched into the pizza delivery business in 1984.

Domino's Pizza

In 1960 Tom Monaghan and his brother, James, started a pizza shop in Ypsilanti, Michigan. They chose the name Dominick's Pizza. With a $75 down payment and $500 they borrowed, they bought a store. James decided he wanted out about eight months later. He traded his share in Dominick's with Thomas for a used Volkswagen Beetle. Tom changed the name to Domino's Pizza and sold the first franchise within a few years. In 1978 the 200th Domino's franchise opened, and in the 1980s, the first international Domino's opened in Canada. Domino's now has over 7,875 stores throughout the world.

East of Chicago Pizza

East of Chicago Pizza Company began in 1990. At that time they had a single store in Willard, Ohio. It has grown to over 140 locations spread throughout Ohio, Indiana, Virginia, and Florida. These stores make their signature deep pan pizza dough fresh every day.

Scott Granneman opened his first pizza shop in 1982 in Greenwich, Ohio. The "Greenwich Pizza Barn" serves traditional thin crust pizza; but, he wanted to set himself apart from other pizza shops, so he created the deep pan crust that is served in the East of Chicago restaurants.

The company continued to expand, and opened their 100th store in 1998.

Choose the Best Business Method for You

There are three ways to launch into business for yourself:

1) Start from scratch.

2) Invest in a franchise.

3) Buy an existing pizza operation.

We will discuss the basics of buying a pizza and sub shop and how to invest along with the positive and negative aspects of each choice. Before you can secure financing, prepare a business plan, and we'll discuss how that should be done.

All three methods (scratch, franchise, existing) can be the basis for a successful business. There are emotional and psychological differences along with financial variations with each. Weigh the pros and cons for yourself personally before you decide which avenue to take. Consider your personality, your strengths and weaknesses, your expectations, and consider your potential customers' needs. These factors will help you determine which method is best for you.

Jump Starting a Business

One option is to purchase an existing business. This will open doors quickly. But, be sure you are ready to be in business right away. Also, there are reasons the business is for sale. Are they things you can fix or overcome?

There are some common reasons a business struggles. These things will cause you problems. Your first priority will be overcoming the existing problems:

- The location may be bad.

- The existing business may have a bad reputation.

- Their products may be overpriced.

It is possible you won't be able to find a business for sale. If you do find the business you want, make them an offer "they cannot refuse." First, you should do adequate research before you make an offer.

Quality franchise organizations have market restrictions and assigned

territories. The franchise you want might not be available in your area. Popular franchises often require higher investments and a great earning potential.

Starting from Scratch

Starting your pizza shop from scratch will allow you to choose every element of your pizza shop in order to create the business you have dreamed about!

This worksheet will help you determine the best approach for you to start a business that best suits you.

GOING INTO BUSINESS			
determine what will be involved in each method			
Factors	**Start From Scratch**	**Existing Business**	**Franchise**
Time			
Availability			
Time Before Opening			
Financial			
Cost			
Available Financing			
Investors			
Personal Worth			
Total Indebtedness			
Break-even Point			
Royalties & Fees			
Purchasing Restrictions			
Current Profitability			
Intangibles			
Goodwill			

GOING INTO BUSINESS			
determine what will be involved in each method			
Factors	**Start From Scratch**	**Existing Business**	**Franchise**
Historical Recognition			
Known vs. Unknown (obstacles to success or existing profitability)			
Reputation			
Convenience			
Exclusivity			
Assets			
Location			
Facility			
Equipment			
Existing Staff			
Customer Base			
Owner			
Independence			
Business Experience			
Food Service Experience			
Restaurant Experience			
Management Experience			
Owner Expectations			
Outside Expectations			
Training			
Support			
Market Share			
Marketing Support			
Product Mix			
Competition			

GOING INTO BUSINESS			
determine what will be involved in each method			
Factors	**Start From Scratch**	**Existing Business**	**Franchise**
Customer Needs			
Other (your personal list)			

Please see the accompanying CD to print a copy of this form for your use.

You have evaluated the method that is right for you; now it's time to move ahead.

STUDY YOUR OPTIONS

Complete all necessary research before deciding on a new venture. Know the costs associated with the business up front, the hours necessary to run it, employees needed, licensing issues, Health Board requirements, and expected profit margin. If you start out well-informed and knowledgeable, you will have a greater success rate.

Each type of business has different aspects to review. For instance, starting a mom and pop pizzeria will give you a one-on-one relationship with your customers and not cost as much in startup funds, but you will work long hours to make the company a success. No one will care about your restaurant the way you will.

A franchise will cost more in initial capital because of the required franchise fees, but if the franchise is already branded, you have a greater opportunity for success. A franchise will offer you training. They will have a tried and true formula in all areas of the business that will lead to your success. They've been there, made the mistakes and are now successful. Don't get me wrong—it will still be hard work, but the methods are already in place and that makes it easier for you.

My husband and I have grown several businesses. Some have been wildly successful; others have been a struggle, and still others have failed. With each business we learned something about ourselves, our goals as entrepreneurs, and building a business. But, the joy of owning a company, building it, and watching it grow is something that gives a proud sense of accomplishment. The best advice I could give you is to walk into this endeavor with your eyes wide open, gain as much knowledge as possible, and work hard to meet those goals. And hey—maybe one day the pizzeria that I visit will be yours!

— Melissa Alvarez, Entrepreneur

2

Buying a Pizza and Sub Shop

Before you decide whether to purchase an existing business, a franchise or to establish a new restaurant, you need sufficient market research. As you consider possibilities, evaluate what factors should be important in determining the best location for your business.

There are four main steps to market research. Your situation will determine how many of these steps are needed.

Find Potential Pizza Shop Sites

Before you begin your search, make a list of what you want to find, including:

- A rough idea of the sale price you want to pay.

- Terms you want for the purchase.

- Analyze how potential sellers came to their sales price.

- Decide what type of pizza shop you want to own.

- Remember that you will probably work 12 to 14 hours a day. Will you be happy in that pizza and sub shop 80 to 90 hours a week?

Most major decisions in life include some compromise. Create a list of the features you must have and items you are willing to trade off.

- **The best possible price** – There will usually be some compromise on the sales price. But, don't pay more than the estimated replacement cost of the pizza and sub shop.

- **Down payment** – The buyer may want 50 percent down, but you should expect to put at least 20 to 30 percent down. Be careful not to put too much money down and risk putting yourself in a financial bind.

- **Maximum future profits** – You are buying the pizza shop based on the current sales, but you hope for the highest possible return.

- **Limit chance of failure** – Statistics indicate that 20 percent of purchased established businesses fail while 80 percent of new businesses fail. Your results will depend on the quality of the business you are interested in buying.

- **Increased borrowing power** – Lenders usually prefer to finance a pizza shop that has proven it can show a profit.

- **Minimize tax liabilities** – Be aware of any tax consequences for the pizza shop you are buying. Check on the payroll tax situation. For example, when you buy a business, you inherit the

unemployment rate with the state. It would be good to hire an accountant.

When you consider buying an existing business, find out the seller's motivation. These are some of the most common motivations:

- **Owners who want to retire** – After years in business, some people want to sell the business and build their retirement fund.

- **Disillusioned owners** – Absentee owners often want to get out of the business when it starts doing poorly. If they had a great person running the business who quit, they might want to get out when they cannot find another qualified manager.

- **Owners with tax problems** – When the pizza shop owners have maximized all their tax benefits, they may choose to sell and reinvest in another business.

- **Other investment opportunities** – The pizza shop owners may have other investment possibilities, but need to sell their shops to fund their new ventures.

- **Distressed properties** – Be cautious about properties that need a lot of repairs or remodeling. The business may not generate income to pay for the work.

- **Distressed owners** – People with personal difficulties may not be in a position to handle a profitable pizza shop. It is very time consuming, and they might not be able to dedicate the time that is necessary. A partner may have left or died, thereby changing their situation and making it impossible to handle the business.

Decide where you want to locate your pizza shop. There is a wealth of information to help you evaluate a prospective area. This is also a good thing to do when you want to buy a shop in a familiar area.

National Research

You will need national research if you plan to open a business in a different area of the country. This would be the situation if you plan to relocate to an area with better weather or to a larger city. These are some resources to evaluate different areas:

According to *Forbes* magazine, the 25 best metro areas to start a business in 2005 were:

- Boise, Idaho
- Washington, DC
- Hunstville, Alabama
- Norfolk, Virginia
- Madison, Wisconsin
- Raleigh-Durham, North Carolina
- Albuquerque, New Mexico
- Fayetteville, Arkansas
- Atlanta, Georgia

The 10 best small metro areas were:

- Sioux Falls, South Dakota
- State College, Pennsylvania
- Bismarck, North Dakota
- Lincoln, Nebraska
- Iowa City, Iowa
- Rochester, Minnesota
- Fargo, North Dakota
- Rapid City, South Dakota
- Las Cruces, New Mexico
- Bloomington, Indiana

Market Area Research

"Market" is one way of referring to a city or a metropolitan statistical area (MSA). It is a term used to talk about census research. First, decide on a target city for your business. Then start looking at various parts of the city, and focus on the parts that would be good for your business. One tip from my pizza shop experience: Look closely at towns with colleges. You want to

be close to students.

Trade area research – Trade area refers to the area from which most of your customers will come.

Site research – After you have narrowed down your choices, it's time to look at the sites. Take pictures, make notes, and you will need to evaluate the various sites to determine the best site for your pizza and sub shop.

Population and Demographics

Population and demographics are factors to consider in choosing your location. Some of the best places to obtain the details you need would include: The United States Census Bureau (**www.census.gov**). The Census Bureau can supply important information about many factors. Pay special attention to statistics about the restaurant industry.

Demographics to evaluate include:

- Population density
- Age groups
- Employment statistics
- Personal income
- Ethnic populations

My favorite source for information is the local Chamber of Commerce. To contact a Chamber in another area, go to **www.chamberofcommerce. com** for contact information. You can get in touch with the state restaurant association and peers can assist you with economic and lifestyle patterns for your business research.

Your library and online sources can provide valuable information. There are trained research librarians who can help you. Some books you should check are:

Demographics USA (ZIP edition). Find out the market statistics in different

areas of the United States.

Lifestyle Market Analyst. Standard Rate & Data Service—look under "gourmet cooking/fine foods" and cross-reference market, lifestyle, and consumer.

Standard & Poor's Industry Surveys.

For additional data and statistics, visit the following sites online:

- **www.ameristat.com**
- **http://quickfacts.census.gov/qfd/index.html**
- **www.searchbug.com/reference/demographics.asp**
- **www.melissadata.com/Lookups/index.htm**

The American Community Survey – This is additional information from the supplemental census survey. This information includes demographic information by county and MSAs. An MSA is an area with at least one major city and includes the county or counties located within the MSA. This survey is replacing the Census Bureau's long survey. It provides full demographic information for communities each year, not every ten years.

Censtats – This Web site provides economic and demographic information that you can compare by county. The information is updated every two years.

County Business Patterns – Economic information is reported by industry and the statistics are updated each year. Statistics include the number of establishments, employment, and payroll for over 40,000 zip codes across the country. Metro Business Patterns provides the same data for MSAs.

American FactFinder – http://factfinder.census.gov lets you evaluate all sorts of United States' census data.

Check the accompanying CD for information about creating customer and competition surveys and learn more about the potential area for your pizza shop.

Site Research

You can use the following list to evaluate a potential business site:

- Downtown area
- Business district
- Colleges/universities
- Religious schools
- Hospitals
- Beaches/Ocean
- State parks
- Rivers
- Nature preserves
- Hotels

- Historical district
- Government offices
- Technical schools
- Military bases
- Major highway
- Lakes
- Sports arenas
- Mountains
- Zoo
- Shopping

There are specific lifestyle details that are critical for your pizza shop. Evaluate these specifics about any location you are considering:

- How many similar pizza shops are located in the area?
- Find sales volume. (Check business license for previous year.)
- Are there colleges or student housing in the area?
- Is there a high number of working mothers in the area?
- What is the population of the immediate area?
- Is the population increasing, stationary, or declining?
- Are the residents of all ages or old, middle-aged, or young?
- What is the average sales price and rental rates for area homes?
- What is the per capita income?
- Find the average family size.

- Is the building/location suitable for a food service establishment? Does it meet the zoning and parking ordinances? Think about natural barriers, such as hills and bridges, when considering environmental impact, accessibility and visibility for your business.

Pizza shops generally thrive near college campuses, because students love to eat pizza. Another good location is near working families. Mothers who work full time often need a quick option for dinner. Whether it's a long day at work, a Parent-Teacher meeting, the children's ballgame, or something else, your pizza shop can be a godsend for the working mothers and fathers in your neighborhood. Business areas are good locations for pizza shops. If you are located near a lot of businesses, you should really consider lunch specials for these offices and businesses.

When you go into an established pizza business, customize your offers to fit the surroundings. But, when you start a pizza shop at a new location, you can handpick the surroundings that would be best for your shop. My store was near a college campus with over 15,000 students and we targeted them with many types of advertising which we will discuss in more detail in Chapter 18.

PROPOSED LOCATION RATING	
Use this score sheet to rate the proposed location. Grade each: "A" = excellent, "B" = good, "C" = fair and "D" = poor.	
FACTOR	GRADE
1. Good location for your target market	
2. The products you need are readily available	
3. Evaluate local competition situation	
4. Proximity to area attractions	
5. Employee qualifications	

PROPOSED LOCATION RATING	
Use this score sheet to rate the proposed location. Grade each: "A" = excellent, "B" = good, "C" = fair and "D" = poor.	
FACTOR	**GRADE**
6. Local wages for employees	
7. Parking facilities	
8. Adequate utilities are available	
9. Traffic flow	
10. Taxation burden	
11. Quality police and fire protection	
12. Housing availability for employees	
13. Details about schools and community activities	
14. Is the building suitable for your business?	
15. Type and cost of building/business	
16. Are there possibilities for future expansion?	
17. Estimate of site suitability in 10 years	

Please see the accompanying CD to print a copy of this form for your use.

Competition

Never underestimate the value of knowing your competition. Make a list of the other pizza shops in your market. Which ones target the same population that you will? Find out what they are selling and their prices.

Take a detailed look at your competition when you narrow down your choices. The information you want can be hard to find. The best way to find information about your competition may be a visit to their establishments.

Be creative. One thing I did to study my competition was to order a pizza each Sunday. The box label had a number. By comparing the previous number,

I knew how many items were sold during the week. I lived a block behind my primary competition, and a couple of us would watch their delivery truck and make note of the supplies and dough trays that were returned and how many were delivered. These were various ways to verify the details we gathered. Since their computer system was just like ours, we could easily glean information from their labels and their dough was delivered in trays that were similar to ours. It's always good to have an idea of the product your competitor is serving and how much business they are doing.

Other sources of information on competition include the following ideas:

- **Telephone book** – Will give you the number and location of your competitors.

- **Chambers of commerce** – They have lists of local businesses. Verify whether it's a complete list, not just Chamber members.

- **Local newspapers** – Study the local advertisements and help wanted ads. There could also be a weekly entertainment section with information about local restaurants, their prices, and menus.

- **National Restaurant Association** – They provide by state, the number of establishments, projected sales, and the number of employees. This can be found at **www.restaurant.org/research/ state/index.cfm**.

Scouting the Competition

Mark the proposed location on a street map. You can determine how far to research, depending on how far you believe people will travel for your products.

Once you determine your target area, visit every business that serves pizzas and subs. Sample items from businesses that have similar menus or serve your target customer. If they have menus you can take, grab one. Be critical

and answer the following questions:

- What did and didn't work for you in their restaurant?
- Do they serve your target customer?
- If not, who do they serve?
- Do their customers seem to like the surroundings?
- How busy are they at peak times?
- What kind of presentation do they have for their menu items?
- How is the food?
- What does the plate presentation look like?
- Do they offer anything unique?
- What is their seating capacity?
- What is the atmosphere?
- When are their busy periods?

Evaluate the Real Estate Value

"Real estate" includes the land and any permanent improvements on the land. This includes utility connections, parking lots, buildings, etc. Many pizza shops are operated in leased buildings. There are three primary procedures to determine the value of a pizzeria: Market Approach, Cost Approach, and Income Approach.

Market Approach – The property value can be determined by comparing similar properties in similar areas. Market Approach isn't normally used to estimate the value of real estate. It would be used if the land is actually being sold. This can help you determine the value of the property.

Cost Approach – The property value is based on the replacement cost for everything on the property. This should be based on current purchase prices

for new equipment and building, etc. Any outdated equipment would be figured with the price for new, comparable equipment. Include all taxes, freight, and installation in your quotes, and factor in depreciation. This is not widely used to estimate the value of a restaurant's real estate, but it is used by insurance companies to process a claim.

Income Approach – This amount is based on future income.

Valuing Other Assets

The business includes everything the owner wants to sell. This can include furniture, fixtures, equipment, supplies, etc. The current owner may also have tax credits, customer mailing lists, and positive name recognition. To figure the price of a food service business, take 40 to 70 percent of the 12-month food and beverage sales. Typically, the seller starts at the high end while the prospective buyer starts at the low end.

In order to determine a realistic sale price, there are many factors to consider, including:

- **Profitability** – This has the greatest influence on the sale price of a pizza and sub shop and can be determined by examining the net operating amount and comparing it with the industry and regional standards for a pizza shop.

- **Existing Lease Terms and Conditions** – Investigate the time remaining on the lease and the monthly payments. Also be aware that some leases include common ground maintenance agreements. These can run into a sizable amount of money, and plan for those expenses. Some property owners will rework your lease if you are new, and the monthly payments will start lower and increase as you become more established. Try to negotiate nothing less than a five-year lease unless the price is too good to

turn down. Your lease and common area maintenance shouldn't exceed six to eight percent of the monthly food-and-beverage sales.

- **Business Track Record** – Check the sales records for the business. To be attractive to a buyer, the business needs an acceptable track record. To establish this record, the store should be at least a year old. You can use the past sales figures to project the future sales numbers. Verify whether you will need any highly skilled employees because this will impact your payroll projections. With a pizza and sub shop, this shouldn't be a big issue. Most people can learn to make a good pizza.

- **Franchise Affiliation** – When you consider purchasing a pizza shop that is part of a franchise, the sales price will increase. National franchise stores will cost more than regional franchises.

- **Contingent Liabilities** – Contingent liabilities is a big word to say that some things the previous owner did will impact your bottom line. One example would be coupons that were distributed by the previous owner. These will have a negative impact on your profit margin, but refusing to accept them would have a much bigger negative impact. Factor these things into the sale price.

- **Grandfather Clauses** – The previous owners could have been grandfathered in and didn't have to meet some fire, health, and safety codes. You will be expected to meet the codes, and you must factor these expenses into your plan. Grandfather clauses usually expire when a business changes hands. This would mean the seller or you could be required to bring the building up to code. You must discuss this with the seller to find an equitable agreement for both parties. The expenses could affect the sale of the business.

- **Goodwill** – Goodwill is the amount of money paid in excess of the book value of physical assets. This is how many investors consider goodwill:

  – Excess earnings caused by positive goodwill.

  – Deficient earnings caused by negative goodwill.

  The seller will want the buyer to pay more for the goodwill he established. It is in the interest of the buyer to downplay its value.

- **Terms, Conditions, and Price** – Sellers usually determine a sale price, terms, and conditions. They will pad those to give room for negotiation. An experienced business broker can help determine a sale price.

- **Terms** – These are the procedures the buyer uses to pay the seller. When the seller provides financing, you make a low down payment, and make payments over the next three to five years. Sellers like to collect a large down payment, but your financial advisor can help you determine an appropriate down payment. A large down payment could get you more agreeable terms from the seller. These are things to consider when you are negotiating a deal.

- **Conditions** – The buyer and seller can attach certain conditions to the sale contract. These can be included in a separate document or within the contract. These are some of the seller's concerns:

  – When can the sale be closed?

  – Must determine your access to the facility and staff.

  – Sellers can attach conditions to the existing contracts. The wording needs to be specific to avoid confusion and future problems.

- Establish conditions and penalties, if either party reneges on the deal.

- It's wise to hire an independent third party to oversee the paperwork.

- The buyer and seller need to agree to comply with all pertinent laws and statutes that apply to the transaction.

- Provide your personal and business financial records, and give permission for the seller to run your credit report.

- The seller needs to approve any additional financing you might secure. A promissory note will provide for the lender to foreclose if you default on the payments. Any other specific conditions for the business should be included.

- Give all details about any assumable contracts, loans, and leases that affect the business.

- You should have life and disability insurance that names the seller as beneficiary if you cannot repay the loan due to death or disability.

- If there are existing receivable accounts, there needs to be an agreement pertaining to the collection of these accounts. Who will collect these, and who will receive the funds?

- Take a physical inventory of all food, beverages, and supplies, and the value needs to be figured into the sale. It is a good idea to verify expiration dates on the items.

- The seller needs to sign a non-compete agreement which states he won't start or run a competing business nearby for a specific amount of time.

- You can include an agreement which gives the seller an option to buy the business back within a certain time period.

- The buyer may decide to hire the seller as an employee. The details need to be outlined and agreed upon.

- The seller may stay on as a consultant. If so, you need to agree, in writing, to the terms of your agreement and compensation for his services.

- Finally, include an agreement that the seller can back out without penalty if the buyer does not meet the conditions of the sale.

Reviewing the Books

People review and tour a business property when they consider buying. You look at the condition of the shop, the neighborhood, location of your competitors, and the customer base. This is a great start, but you also need to review the finances for the business. Review the cash flow, income, and current expenses. Many people can come to a business with fresh eyes and find ways to cut costs or reallocate money for their expenses. Use this information to project potential revenue.

You can hire a good accountant to review the pizza shop and see if it would be a good investment for you. The Small Business Development Centers (SBDC) offer free consulting services to businesses with less than 500 employees. You can contact a local SCORE chapter, which is made up of retired businesspeople who help other small business owners. Their Web site is: **www.score.org**.

Analyze balance sheets and income statements carefully. Balance sheets can reveal potential problem areas for the seller. You can learn a lot about the seller's management skills from the balance sheets. I've been in business

situations where a more qualified manager or owner made a huge difference in the profitability of the business. Remember that you base your offer on current income, but plan based on the potential profitability.

Financing

Most agreements are fairly typical. However, there are a couple of things that might cause problems. You need to qualify for financing and must get all of the necessary licenses and permits. If you don't qualify for a permit, it could be because you need to fix code violations. Get a complete list and collect estimates to have the needed work done.

You do have more control about financing issues. Keep in mind that many businesses fail because of insufficient or incorrect financing. Excessive debt is one of the most consistent reasons businesses fail, and your pizza shop is no different.

Atlantic Publishing offers a book titled *How to Get the Financing for Your Small Business: Innovative Solutions from the Experts Who Do It Every Day* (**www. atlantic-pub.com,** Item # HGF-01). Many business owners understand that insufficient financing can be a death blow to a new or struggling business. This book shows you ways to secure sufficient financing for your business. It delves into detailed valuations, proper funding projections, and illustrates the various types of financing options which could be available to you.

Equity Funds

Equity is capital that is at risk. This money is risked with no guarantee of a return. These are the most common types of equity financing techniques:

- **Personal equity** – This is funded entirely with personal equity or a combination of personal equity, lease and debt financing.

- **Partnerships** – Partners can invest together. These are active or silent partners.

- **Corporations** – Raising capital by selling stock to public or private investors.

- **Venture capital** – Professional investors or investment companies can be venture capitalists that want long-term financial gain. They might not be interested in the net profits of a new establishment. Pizza shops have high earning potential which can help you qualify for venture capital.

Borrowing Money

Many people believe that small business owners have a hard time borrowing money. That isn't necessarily true. We all know banks are in business to lend money. Prove that you are a good risk. One way to do this is by having a complete and accurate business plan. We will discuss the business plan in detail in Chapter 3.

Reviewing Your Loan Request

Lenders are most concerned with your ability to repay the loan. They will request a copy of your credit report. This information will be used with your business plan to evaluate your ability to repay the loan.

These are some of the issues lenders consider:

- How much of your own savings or equity are you investing in the pizza shop? Banks rarely loan 100 percent, so you will need to include some of your own money.

- How does your credit look? Do you have a steady work history?

How many letters of recommendation can you produce? These are important.

- Are you qualified to run a successful pizza and sub shop?

- Does your business plan show that you understand what is involved in operating a successful pizza shop?

- Will the business have sufficient cash flow to make the monthly payments?

Financing Options

SBA Financial Programs – The Small Business Administration (SBA) has various financing options for small businesses. These include long-term loans for machinery and equipment, working capital, a line of credit, or a micro-loan. Each of these options is discussed in detail on the SBA Web site at: **www.sba.gov.**

Friends and relatives – You may have friends or relatives who will give you an interest free or a low interest loan. Be sure to put all details in writing.

Banks and credit unions – The most common sources of funding are banks and credit unions. Loans are based on solid business proposals and your written business plan.

A bank and a banker – Borrowing money is a major commitment and shouldn't be taken lightly. Talk to friends and other business owners to find out which banks they borrowed money from and how their experiences went.

If you are in a new town, visit several banks and talk with the loan managers:

- Compare rates, services, and customer service.

- Was it difficult to get an appointment with the right person?

- Were they interested in you and your business?

- Did they explain their services and requirements adequately?

- Check their savings and checking plans as well.

- Is the bank convenient to your shop location?

- Do they have a safe place to make night deposits?

What the Banker Will Want from You

Banks are cautious when dealing with small businesses, and they require a lot of information. They will need to see how you intend to repay the loan. This might require several income sources, including:

- Sufficient collateral to secure the loan.

- Your signature and credit score may be enough.

- You may need a co-signer.

- Equity in real estate you own is a possibility.

- They will check your assets-to-debt ratio.

- Do you have a savings account?

- Do you have any investments, stocks, and bonds, etc.?

- Cash value on a life insurance policy.

Negotiating Your Loan

You have all the information together to make your presentation to the lender. You dress in a professional manner and have your business plan under your arm or in your briefcase. Everything is going according to plan, and then they ask you to have a seat. While you wait, doubts and concerns race through your mind. Get rid of this state of mind before the loan officer calls you into his office. It is up to you to convince him that you have a

thorough plan and that the bank should lend you the money you need. This is another reason you want a great business plan. It can speak even when you get tongue-tied.

This is a little tidbit that I will share with you. Loan rates and terms can be negotiable. Over half the business owners who apply for loans could get a lower rate if they just asked. The interest rate and the length of the loan can both be negotiable. Listen to the offer the loan officer makes then ask if it is negotiable. Don't ask after the final papers are signed.

Here are some tips on asking for a lower interest rate:

- Ask to make the length of the loan shorter. Keep in mind that a shorter loan term will make the payments higher.

- Increase the value of the collateral you offer.

Appraisal – Any lender will need to see an appraisal. The lender, real estate agent, or you can schedule the appraisal. A good source for locating an appraiser is: **www.appraisersource.com**.

Survey and Inspections – Inspections should be done before you make a firm offer. We discussed this earlier to determine if you will need to make any improvements to the property. You also need to get a survey of the property. This is an added expense, it but will verify there are no problems with the property in the deeds or with easements, etc. The survey and title search will uncover details that aren't obvious in a visual inspection. It will save you from potential problems. Study the survey and inspection reports carefully, and ask any questions before you make a final offer.

The Deal

Finalizing the deal may seem intimidating at first, but include everything that was discussed in writing. It is also good to anticipate problems at the last

minute. Real estate closings rarely go smoothly. Your business transaction is no different. A number of people, and many reports and commitments, need to come together at one time. When that many people are involved, there are usually problems and delays. Don't think you're the only one who has these problems. You aren't.

When you are ready to close, there can be a lot of people with you including you, the seller, both real estate agents, both attorneys, and your loan officer. They will be shoving papers at you to sign. It can be good to have a trusted friend with you who has been through this procedure before. The other people are familiar with it, but your head will be spinning. This is a normal reaction.

What If the Deal Breaks Down?

No matter how hard you work to finalize a deal, there may be times when it breaks down. One of the most common reasons for this is if your financing isn't approved. Do you have any alternatives when this happens? Here are a few:

- **Talk to the lender and find out, specifically, what happened.** Did you leave something off your business plan? Was any information missing on your application? You may be able to solve the problem with this banker.

- **What if your credit is the problem?** That isn't a quick fix, and you may lose the location. But, you should repair your credit if you plan to go into business. You can ask the loan officer for his advice on how to improve your credit rating.

- **Would your plan work with less money?** You can review your business plan and see where you can make adjustments. When you start a business, it is very likely you will have to tighten your personal financial belt for a time. Did you figure this into the

plan? It could make a difference in your expenses.

- **Talk to another banker.** Start with your first choice, but you may need to deal with your second or third choice. Don't settle for a bad deal, but look around for other comparable deals.

Closing the Sale

When your financing is arranged and you have agreed on all the details, sign a binding sales contract and transfer ownership. Many people can be involved in this process, including lawyers, accountants, lenders, real estate agents, family members, and so on. Be prepared because it can take 30 to 60 days to complete the ownership transfer.

WHAT KIND OF ADVERTISING?

When I received my culinary art degree, I recall my instructor telling budding future chefs, managers, and food service operators; "There is dough in dough". Meaning you can make a good living owning a Pizzeria or Submarine shop. But, my instructor went on to lecture, "before you work on your recipe for pizza sauce, to ensure you can pay the bills you need a complete business plan."

After 20 years of cooking and making money for others, I decided to open my own fast Mexican food restaurant. My business plan was rock solid. My research was University level quality. I spent hours in the local library and called many city agencies of the Huntington Beach California to ensure my success. But, mostly my business plan was my outline, or study guide, for success.

My businesses included my advertising plans. But, as one really starts their business, be it 900 or 20,000 square feet, you really don't know what type of advertising to do. My business plan included five or six methods of advertising I was going to perform. Radio, newspapers, coupon mailers, community events, door flyers, and more. I tracked my marketing (by the way, I have read advertising is telling customers you have something to sell, and marketing is reminding customers you are still open for business) and found out door flyers and community service (such as catering for City Council meetings) worked best for my business. I owed this to following my business plan.

— Rick Martinez, CEC, CCE, CFE
Rick4goblue@yahoo.com, Culinary Art Instructor Los Angeles Trade Technical College, Former founder, owner, operator of "Fiesta Grill and Catering" of Huntington Beach, CA

3

Writing a Business Plan

Every businessperson needs a thorough and workable plan and especially when you try to secure financing. A complete and professional business plan is a great way to prove you are serious about your pizza shop venture. There are various benefits for you. They include:

- Clearly explain your ideas and hopes for this business.

- Explain your vision to family, friends, and potential backers.

- Help you focus and provide a solid foundation for your pizza shop.

- Prepare you for the inevitable obstacles and pitfalls.

- It will help you get a realistic view of what you are facing.

- Are you ready to dedicate the hours needed to succeed?

- Can you get the pizza shop you want with the money you have?

- Are you ready to interview, hire, train, and manage employees?

- Is your family ready for the impact a pizza shop will have on your lives?

Five Keys of Success

Research the area where your pizza shop will be located. Then you will be able to identify the five keys to success. These are the things you bring to your customers that will help you be a success.

1. Does your area need a pizzeria? Is there a specific niche that isn't being served? How can you fill that void?

2. Will there be enough potential customers who will deal with your pizzeria? Is there a lot of competition? Will you spend a lot on advertising? Can the people in your area afford your rates?

3. Is your location convenient for your customers? Is the price good?

4. Can you find the supplies to produce the products your customers want? Have you done the research to know what they want?

5. How will you establish yourself from your competition? Are there enough qualified potential employees nearby?

You will need to do sufficient research to complete your business plan. It will require thought and effort, but it will pay off over time and with lenders. We'll discuss each point in the order on your business plan.

What a Business Plan Includes

The business plan is made up of four sections:

1. Describe your pizza and sub shop.
2. Outline how you will market your shop.
3. Explain your management plan.
4. Outline your financial management plan.

You can add some additional information within the plan, including an executive summary, documents to support your conclusions, and your financial projections for the pizza shop. This would include additions you plan to make and other changes.

Business Plan Contents

You can use this list to create your original business plan. It is advisable to update your plan throughout your first year. Update ideas that worked and ones that didn't work. These updates should reflect things you learn that will enable you to target your customers in a better way.

Each business needs short term and long term goals. If you open a pizza shop in a college town, you will also have different plans for the various school semesters. We'll discuss that more in Chapter 17.

Elements of a Business Plan

- Cover sheet
- Table of contents
- Marketing
- Operating procedures
- Business insurance
- Loan applications
- Break-even analysis
- Three-year summary
- Pro-forma cash flow
- Pro-forma income projections (profit and loss statements)
- Detail by quarters, second and third years

- Statement of purpose
- Description of business
- Competition
- Personnel
- Financial data
- Balance sheet
- Capital, equipment, supply list
- Detail by month, first year
- Supporting documents

- Assumptions upon which projections were based

- Tax returns of principals for the last three years

- Personal financial statement (all banks have these forms)

- In the case of a franchised business, a copy of the franchise contract and all supporting documents provided by the franchisor

- Copy of proposed lease or purchase agreement for building space

- Copy of licenses and other legal documents

- Copy of resumes of all principals

- Copies of letters of intent from suppliers, etc.

Check the accompanying CD to print a copy of this list.

Business Plan — Description of the Business

Give a detailed description of your business. Ask yourself, "What kind of pizza business do I want to be in?" Your answer needs to include your products, market, services, and a complete description of the things that make your pizzeria unique. Keep an open mind, and modify or revise your plan as needed.

Section 1 describes your business; Section 2 describes your products and services; and Section 3 explains your business location and why this location is desirable. These descriptions need to clearly identify your goals and objectives in order to explain your desire to be in business.

Your business description should explain:

- Will you be a sole proprietorship, partnership, or corporation?

- What licenses or permits are needed?

- Describe your business in less than 25 words. This will be your

business "tagline". Make it catchy and attention-grabbing.

- You will need this short description when you promote your business. Use it with potential vendors, suppliers, bankers, lenders and friends. Let others use your "tagline" to get the word out about your business.

- Explain your products and services. You can include a menu when it is completed. Include some ideas of daily or seasonal specials.

- Will your pizza business be a new, independent business, a buy out, an expansion, or a franchise?

- What will make your business profitable? What are your plans to expand the business?

- Give your hours of operation.

- Include details you learned from suppliers, bankers, other franchise owners, franchiser, publications, etc.

- Insert a cover sheet before you begin the description. It should include all contact information for you and any other principals within the company.

Legal Business Forms

Each business needs a business structure. Your choice will depend on how many principals are in the company. There are also tax and legal benefits to various types of businesses. We will discuss the main points in this chapter. More details on each structure are contained on the accompanying CD. Discuss the options with your attorney and accountant. They can explain the advantages and disadvantages of each. These factors impact decisions about your business.

Following are brief descriptions of the business entities:

- **Sole Proprietorship** – This is the easiest and least costly way of starting a business. You can establish a sole proprietorship by finding a location and opening for business. The attorney's fees are less than other business forms. The owner has absolute authority over all business decisions. However, with a sole proprietorship, you are personally liable when the business defaults on a loan or is involved in a legal dispute.

- **Partnership** – Two or more people that share ownership. The most common partnership types are general and limited. A general partnership only requires an oral agreement between the involved parties, but you should have a signed legal agreement. There will be some legal fees to draw up a partnership agreement, but the cost is lower than incorporating. A written agreement will help resolve disputes. You and your partner are responsible for one another's actions.

- **Corporation** – Business control is based on stock ownership. You can incorporate without an attorney, but you might need legal advice about which type of corporation is best for your situation. A corporation is more complicated and expensive to organize. Small corporations can be more informal, but you still have to keep accurate records. Corporate officers are liable to their stockholders for improper behavior.

- **Limited Liability Company (LLC)** – An LLC is not a corporation, but it offers similar advantages. Many small business owners and entrepreneurs prefer an LLC to have the limited liability protection along with the tax benefits of a sole proprietorship or a partnership. LLC's offer more flexibility in business management and organization.

Products/Services

What makes your products and services better than those of your competitors? Explain them from the customer's point of view. Successful business owners have a good idea of what their customers expect from them. Develop this skill to be truly successful. It is important to beat the competition.

- Explain what you are selling. Include your product listing and menu here (if appropriate).

- What does your product or service do for the customer? This is more than filling their stomach. Dig deeper, and explain how your product and service can help the customer.

- Which products and services are in demand?

- Why are your products different? What makes your pizza better? What need does it fill? This will include your USP (Unique Selling Position), which will be at the center of your marketing message.

The Location

Your location will play a critical role in your business' success or failure. You've heard the saying, "Location, Location, Location." Choose a location that will cater to your customers. Don't expect your customers to bend over backward to find you. Choose a location that is easy to find; it must also be safe and accessible. Answer these questions in your business plan:

- What is needed at your location?

- How much space do you need?

- Do you have room to expand?

- Have you researched all environmental or zoning issues?

- What is appealing about the neighborhood?

- What are the positive aspects of the building?

- Is it easily accessible and visible to passersby?

- Do you have adequate lighting for visibility and safety?

- Is the price within your financial plans?

- Take note of the other businesses near your location. Nearby businesses can benefit you.

The Marketing Plan

Marketing plays a critical role in the success of your pizza and sub shop. You have to market your business. A crucial part of the marketing equation is how well you know your customers. Do you understand what they want, and what they don't want, from your shop? When you have this information, you can create a marketing plan that will help you get their attention and bring them to your pizzeria.

Who Are Your Customers?

Identify your customers by their age, sex, income/educational level, and residence. Your first priority will be the customers who are most likely to buy pizza and subs from you. As you learn the area, you can revise your plan to include new potential customers.

A great way to develop a marketing plan is to first answer several thought-provoking questions. Use questions that make you think about all the details of your business. (If you plan to open a franchise, the company will have an established plan that you need to complete.)

Include your marketing plan within your business plan. Answer each of these questions:

- Define your target customers – in detail.

- Is your customer base growing? Staying steady? Or declining?

- Identify the condition of your share of the market.

- Can you expand your target markets?

- What techniques will you use to attract and increase your share of the market? How do you plan to promote your pizza shop?

- How does your pricing compare to your competition?

- It isn't necessary to be the cheapest, but the customer must see the value in your pizza and subs. That value can be increased by providing excellent service. Set yourself apart from your competitors in ways other than price.

- Know your competition. Eat at their establishments, study their menus, and have them deliver to your home; each of these things gives you insight into what they are doing well and how you can do better.

Franchise Owners – Specifically

- What part of the marketing is within your franchise area?
- Can you get assistance from the company for your franchise?

You need the answers to these questions:

- Name your closest competitors.

- Name any indirect competitors.

- Are their businesses staying steady, growing or decreasing?

- What ideas did you get from their businesses and advertising?

- Identify their strengths and weaknesses. How can you improve?

- What are the differences between their products and yours?

- Should you make changes to your menu to be up-to-date?

Create a file on each of your competitors. I insert copies of their menus, coupons, advertisements, and my own notes about their operation. When a customer mentions them, make a note and stick it in the file. Take out the information, and review it from time to time. If they change their menu, get a copy. It is also good to eat their food periodically. The quality can change, and you need to know if their quality decreases.

What Will You Serve and How Will You Serve It?

The items you offer every day are called your product mix. Beyond pizza, you may choose to have other "profit centers," including subs, popular Italian dishes, desserts, drinks, breadsticks, and salads.

Your business plan needs to explain what you will serve, how you will serve (carryout, delivery, or dine-in) and why this is the best plan for your pizza shop and your target customers.

Pricing

We discussed this above; you need to have a competitive price, but still maintain a profit. Learn the pricing your competitors are using and what they give the customer for that price. This will help you determine what you can charge.

Determine what type of pizzeria you want. This will have an effect on your prices. Will it be a family restaurant, or cater to a high-end crowd? Your service, food items, atmosphere, and clientele will impact the prices you can charge and how large your target market will be. Pricing possibilities include:

- **Food cost** – Fresh and organic ingredients are more expensive.

- **Competitive pricing** – Mid-range pricing will promote your value while still appealing to a wide demographic.

- **Pricing below competition** – Undercutting the competition will bring in customers and is a nice approach for your Grand Opening and special occasions. But, your quality, service, and overall value will keep them coming back for more.

- **Multiple pricing** – This is a wonderful price structure for pizza, and we used it in the shops where I worked. Charge a good price for the first pie then offer additional pies for $5.

- **Service components** – Your prices will also depend on what types of service you offer. Carryout is the most reasonable. Delivery has certain expenses involved, and dine-in will require extra staff and a dining area. Your prices need to reflect the costs involved. Carryout specials are common and cost effective.

- **Overhead costs** – Don't let your facility costs escalate your product pricing unreasonably. Sure, it's great to be located in the new strip mall, but how many $15 pizzas will you have to sell every month just to meet expenses?

Advertising and Public Relations

Promotion can make or break a business. It isn't enough to just have a

quality product. You have to get the word out to potential customers. I've worked with some business owners who felt a good business would promote itself. Sorry to say, that isn't how it works. You MUST promote your business. Word-of-mouth is wonderful, but you will need more than that, especially in the beginning. We will discuss specific marketing ideas in detail in Chapter 17.

Your marketing plan should include advertising copy, a company tagline, and a series of marketing plans. These can include coupons, yellow page ads, special offers, and so on. You make a wonderful, mouth-watering product, and it is good to use pictures of appetizing pizzas. I've always thought scratch and sniff coupons would be wonderful and effective.

If you buy a franchise, much of your marketing will be done for you on the corporate level. You might also need to get corporate approval of marketing you want to do for your particular pizzeria. When you are a new pizza shop owner, it is good to ask your corporate representatives for their thoughts about your marketing efforts.

Include a list of promotional activities you will use and estimated prices for each item. This will help you determine the marketing budget for your pizza shop. I like to talk with suppliers and others about co-op funds. (Some businesses will pay a portion of your marketing expenses when you use their name or logo in your ads. They need to approve advertisements before they are finalized.)

Keep in mind that your marketing plan is very critical, and give it the necessary attention. Successful marketing will help ensure the success of your pizza shop.

The Management Plan

When you think about owning a business, what comes to mind? Do

you envision yourself walking around the pizza shop with a white chef's hat and issuing orders to your employees? Being a good manager is very involved, and there are many books on that subject. But, some of these basics are commitment, dedication, persistence, and the know-how to make decisions. These decisions often need to be made in a moment. You also need to manage people and money. Each of these responsibilities involves a lot of work, patience, and ability. The management plan is the final part of the business plan that will enable you to start your pizza shop on a solid foundation.

Be brutally honest with yourself. What skills do you have, and what skills are you lacking? This is not the time to exaggerate your skills. Be honest, and make notes about the skills you need in the employees you hire. Potential team members should compliment you and will fill the voids in your abilities. This will give you a well-rounded crew who can handle the extensive responsibilities of running your pizza shop.

I like to create a team atmosphere within a business. Each employee should have specific responsibilities, and each person handles various portions of the work. Making employees responsible for something specific will help them feel like a contributing part of your crew.

These are the questions you need to answer in your management plan:

- Do you have the background and experience to run the business?
- How will you compensate for your shortcomings?
- Which employees will be part of the management team?
- What strengths and weaknesses do they bring to the job?
- How do these strengths and weaknesses compliment your skills?
- What duties will you assign them?
- Have you clearly outlined their responsibilities?
- What staff members do you need right away?

- How will you hire and train your new staff members?
- What salary and benefits will you offer?

Specific Franchise Questions

- Does their management package cover any of these issues?
- How will the corporate office offer you assistance?
- Will this assistance be ongoing?

If you purchase a franchise, you should include many specifics from their plans. This will help you see how their requirements will work into your plans. You must work their procedures into your plan. A representative for the franchise should help you manage the pizza shop. Take the chance to learn from the representative's experience.

The Financial Management Plan

Sound financial management will enable you to remain profitable. You must manage your finances in order to show a profit and to be successful. Keep in mind that you cannot operate at a loss and stay in business. Thousands of businesses fail each year because the finances are not managed.

A realistic budget is necessary to manage your finances. This will also help you determine the amount of money needed to open your pizza shop. The financial plan must include startup costs and your operating costs. Startup costs will be different from your weekly and monthly operating expenses.

Operating Budget

An operating budget will apply when you open your doors for business.

You will need to make decisions and set priorities about what to pay and when. Some spending may need to be postponed based on the money that is available. Include a "cushion" in your budget. There are always unexpected expenses, and you should set aside some money for problems. The operating budget in your financial plan should include enough money to cover your expenses for three to six months.

The financial plan should include information about:

- Pending loan applications
- Equipment value
- List of the value of supplies on hand
- Up-to-date balance sheet
- Your break-even analysis
- A profit and loss statement

Include an income statement and cash flow projections for the first three years. Break this down by month, quarter, and year in your report.

Figuring these financial projections will be complicated. Be accurate, and make adjustments as time passes. It won't do you any good to insert inflated income projections. This may temporarily impress lenders, but you will need to answer for the discrepancy. It can make you look unprofessional and unprepared. You can ask your financial advisor to help you with the financial section of your plan.

Ask these questions to figure how much startup money you will need:

- How much capital do you have?
- How much will a franchise cost?
- How much will your startup cost?
- How much do you need to stay open for business?

You also need to consider these questions:

- Have you determined sales and profit goals for your first year?

- What projections need to be in your business plan?

- Which inventory-control system will you use?

If you buy a franchise:

- Does the corporation set your sales and profit goals?

- What sales and profit margin are you expected to reach and maintain?

Explain how you established these projections. You might want to talk to your accountant and/or financial advisor. They can help you review your research and decide how the various reports should be organized. It is more cost effective to do the research and compile the basic numbers before you meet with the advisor. This person can also work with you to help you reach your goals.

Business Plan Resources

The accompanying CD has a pizza business plan template you can use to develop your plan. It is a word document, and you can insert the information specific to your pizza and sub shop. If you would like additional information, you can find a great business plan resource from Atlantic Publishing: *How to Write a Great Business Plan for Your Small Business in Sixty Minutes or Less* (**www.atlantic-pub.com**, Item # GBP-01).

There are many reasons to develop a thorough business plan. It can be time consuming to develop from scratch. This book has a CD that works with the book to help you create a complete and effective business plan. It will save you time and help you to create a business plan that will help you secure financing and to manage and market your pizza shop.

How to Invest in a Franchise

One way to get into the pizza shop business is by buying a franchise. We're all familiar with the big franchises. They include: Pizza Hut, Domino's, Papa John's, Little Caesar's, Cici's, and so on. Buying a franchise can help you start a step above independent pizza shop owners. You can have a business under an established name and product. The corporation will give you training and help managing your store. It may also offer financial assistance for qualified applicants.

This makes it sound like franchises are a totally positive experience, but let's take a look at the other side of the equation. You have less control over the menu, advertising, décor, uniforms, etc. Even though you own the business, you answer to the corporation. If something happens to the company, it will affect you in a positive or a negative way. Lastly, you must pay fees and share the profits.

There are conflicting viewpoints about the franchise market. Some believe it's saturated while others feel that competition is stiff. Papa John's was

started 27 years after Pizza Hut opened and 25 years after Domino's Pizza started to deliver. At this time, there are over 3,000 Papa John's stores. Each store I'm familiar with is thriving.

The big question is whether you think a franchise is right for you. The following questions will help you decide:

- Would you be happy with someone else's vision?

- How would you react if corporate support slacks after a few years?

- How does your family feel about you being part of a franchise?

Franchise Costs

Your franchise fee – You are buying an existing and established business plan. The fee can be several thousand dollars. This fee allows you to use the company name, and they will help you set up and run your business. They may help with finding a location, training you and your staff, and assisting with your marketing.

Costs involved in buying a franchise – Your startup costs can be less, but you also need to figure in the franchise fees. Are you willing to give up a measure of control in your pizza shop? There are established rules you will have to follow. Analyze what you really want and if that is a franchise. These are some of the fees you have to pay for a franchise:

- **Initial fee** – This might be added to the money you spend to set up your store. It's in addition to rent, building, remodeling, and buying equipment and inventory. There are licenses and insurance you must acquire before you can open. The corporation may charge a "grand opening" fee to promote your opening.

- **Ongoing royalties** – These royalties are a percentage of weekly or monthly gross sales. There could be a minimum royalty fee

just to use the franchise name. It's possible the corporation could stop giving you support, but you would still be required to pay royalties.

- **Advertising fees** – You may pay for a portion of the national or regional advertising that is done each month.

- **Business or operating licenses**

- **Real estate and leasehold improvements**

- **Training**

- **Legal fees**

- **Financial and accounting advice**

- **Insurance**

Review these fees with your accountant early in the process.

Definition of Franchising

Basically, franchising is a plan where individually-owned businesses are operated under the name and rules of a large chain. Products, trademark, and designs are standardized in the stores. A supplier (franchisor) sells the dealers (franchisee) the right to operate a business using the company's product, name, reputation, and selling techniques.

The franchise agreement (or contract) is generally for a specific geographic location. I know people who wanted to open a franchise in a certain area, but someone else owned the franchise rights for that area.

The franchisee pays a set sum of money (a franchise fee) and/or a percentage of gross sales and may be required to buy equipment and supplies from the franchisor. There could be any combination of these elements mentioned in the franchise contract.

Finding a Franchise

You can look into various franchise opportunities to see which one suits you. Some information can be found at **www.franchiseopportunities.com** and **www.franchisegator.com/pizza_franchise.html**. There may also be listings in your local newspaper's classified section. The companies may provide a lot of information to help their franchisees get started. The easiest way to learn more about a franchise is to search its Web site.

Attending a franchise exposition is another great way to get more information and compare the possibilities. Of course, the salespeople go to the expos for the purpose of selling franchises. Decide not to make any decisions at the expo. Go to ask questions and get information. This will give you a chance to review the details and take time to think about the choices without anyone pressuring you.

Research before you attend the expo. It is good to know your financial limitations before you attend. Have your relevant experience and goals firmly in mind. Take the opportunity to ask a lot of questions. Have a comprehensive list of your concerns and questions.

These are some possible questions you could ask:

- How long has the company been in business?
- Ask for background information about the company.
- How many franchise businesses does the company have?
- Where are their stores?
- Ask for a breakdown of all franchise fees and startup costs.
- How do the royalty fees work, and how long do you pay them?
- Are royalty fees a percentage of sales or a set fee?
- What business assistance does the franchise offer?

- What control do you have over the business?

You can usually register online to be pre-screened for a pizza franchise. This gives the franchisor an idea of your financial situation and qualifications to own a franchise. Once you pass the pre-screening process, the company could set up an interview. It is better to fill out the pre-screening questionnaire only when you have narrowed down your choices.

Investigating Franchise Offerings

You can request a copy of the franchisor's disclosure document. This is a document you should review carefully before making a final decision. The Federal Trade Commission requires that this be given to you 10 business days before you have to sign papers or pay any fees. This gives you time to review the document with your attorney to fully understand the details of the deal.

The disclosure document, also called the Uniform Franchise Offering Circular (UFOC), is supplied to pre-qualified franchisees. These documents are available online and are about 50 pages long and include many details.

Franchising for Dummies says that each UFOC includes these specifics:

- Franchisor name
- Business experience of key officials
- Litigation Record
- Bankruptcy Record
- Initial franchise fee
- Other fees
- Initial investment (franchise fee, signage, equipment, etc.)
- Any requirements about where to purchase products and services

- Franchisee's obligations

- Financing options

- Franchisor's obligations

- Territories (including exclusivity and growth options)

- Trademarks

- Patents, copyrights, and proprietary information

- Obligation to participate in operating the business

- Restriction on what franchisee may sell

- Contract renewal, termination and transfers, dispute resolution

- Earnings claims (estimates of what the franchise may earn)

- List of all franchise outlets (with contact names and numbers)

- Franchisor's audited financial statements

- Franchise agreements (contracts to sign to complete transaction)

- Receipt (signed proof that prospective franchisee received UFOC)

- Use of public figures (payment to celebrities or high-profile persons, and/or their investment into the system)

This will give you a comprehensive overview of the business, background, stability and what is expected of franchisees. Don't take these requirements lightly, because you will be bound by the rules if you buy the franchise.

Additional Sources of Information

Do your research before making any decisions about your pizza shop. This is especially important when you consider a franchise. Once you have a clear idea of what is involved, talk to additional resource people you trust.

- **Accountant** – Can review company financial records and earnings projections.

- **Lawyer** – Can help you understand the complicated franchise contract. (Finding problems after you sign can be impossible or expensive to fix.)

- **Financial institutions** – Can give objective thoughts on the franchise you are considering. They can review Dun and Bradstreet reports for more details.

- **Better Business Bureau** – Call the BBB for cities that have the company franchises, and find out about problems or complaints.

- **Federal Trade Commission** – The FTC has business guides that are helpful.

- Atlantic Publishing offers a book titled *The Franchise Handbook: A Complete Guide to All Aspects of Buying, Selling or Investing in a Franchise* (**www.atlantic-pub.com**, Item # TFH). This is a must-have book for any person who is considering buying a franchise. It delves into the advantages and disadvantages in complete detail. There are many things to consider and research before making a final decision. This book will help you make an educated decision. The book also includes a list of franchise opportunities, along with contact information.

Advantages of Franchising

A franchise allows you, the franchisee, to own and operate a business. Once you pay the franchise fee, the company gives you a system which was developed to use for your business. The franchisor allows you to use the company name and gives you some assistance with your business.

As we discussed earlier, the franchisor may help you find a location, provide some training, and will give some advice on the initial set up, management, marketing, and staffing for your restaurant. This assistance is not indefinite,

and you should take advantage of the help while it is available. Depending on the company, they may offer a monthly newsletter, toll-free phone number for assistance, and seminars.

Analyze the pros and cons. Franchising may make it easier to get established, but you will pay for the franchise benefits. You are required to give up a measure of control and will be contracted to the franchisor. Weigh each of these factors.

Franchising Allows Some "Luxuries"

- **Limited experience** – Draw on the franchisor's experience and know how.

- **Growth** – Name recognition can help you grow your business quicker. Association with a nationally recognized company can also help you when you talk with lenders and suppliers.

- **Consumer recognition** – You will have instant customers because people are familiar with the name and the products you will serve.

- **Tested design for facilities, layout, and displays** – The company uses standard designs and procedures in all their stores.

- **Chain buying power** – Your supplies may be more reasonable since you can buy chain-style equipment, supplies, promotional products, etc.

- **Business training and support** – The company can share proven business techniques. It's in their interest to train you the right way, to manage and promote the business. They can help you in all facets of the business.

- **National or regional promotion** – This promotion will help your business. The company can also help you with local advertising.

You shouldn't rely on the company's marketing efforts, do local promotion.

These "luxuries" will help you increase your sales and can significantly lower your chance of failure. It isn't foolproof, but will definitely give you a boost in the right direction, if you decide to become a franchisee.

Disadvantages of Franchising

Remember that you will have to follow the company rules. You will not be able to make the rules or all of the decisions. If you've dreamed of having your name on the signage, you won't want a franchise. These are some specific things that you have to accept with a franchise:

- You must follow their standardized procedures.

- You must carry their products whether they are profitable or not.

- You must follow their policies, which at times will help others and not you.

- You must share a portion of your gross sales with the franchisor. The amount you are required to pay has no relation to your profits.

- You could be required to buy specific items from the company with no regard to the amount they decide to charge.

- You could have restrictions about the prices you can charge. This could prevent you from competing in your local market.

Other items you may have limited control of include:

- Your store location may not be your decision.

- The franchisor has the authority to dictate all appearance standards for your pizza shop. They can also require you to remodel your shop—at your expense.

- The franchisor can set your hours of operation, and must approve your signs, uniforms, advertisements, and bookkeeping system.

- It is very possible the contract will be written to the franchisor's benefit. They can set high sales quotas, the ability to cancel your agreement for minor infringements, can limit ways for you to sell and recoup your investment; territory assignments can overlap and could hurt your sales. If you have a problem with the franchisor, they have far more power than you do in most cases.

- Anticipate the time it will take you to complete the required franchisor reports. The reports should be helpful to you, but can be very time consuming.

- Understand that big chains do have problems with consumers. If your franchisor had problems or a previous franchisee had issues, you could pay for that when you open. Some consumers will avoid any franchise when they have problems with another. They may blame you for things that were out of your control, but you need to know it could happen.

- You can lose your franchise for breaching the franchise contract. Keep in mind the contract is usually for 15 to 20 years, and it might not be renewed at that time. If you are renewed, the franchisor can change your royalty rate (possibly higher) or could require you to change the store's appearance.

Minority Participation in Franchising

Some companies have programs for minorities who want to go into business for themselves. One program requires only a 2 percent down payment. That could be very attractive to potential franchisees.

Another program involves a joint venture with a minority-owned business and an established franchising company. Both companies contribute an equal amount of money, but the minority owner is responsible for the day-to-day business operation.

Franchise Financing

More and more lenders are beginning to offer franchise financing. Lenders have discovered the potential for growth and stability in the franchise market. This gives a potential franchisee another financing option. The International Franchise Association (**www.franchise.org**) lists over 30 franchise lenders in the Franchise Opportunities Guide. The U.S. Small Business Administration (**www.sba.gov**) also works with banks with its guaranteed loan program to startup franchisees.

Evaluating a Franchise Opportunity

A franchise costs money, and the amount can vary dramatically. This is one of the reasons to evaluate the opportunity carefully. Franchising has attracted some people who will try to get the better of you. These people can only offer a name and some high priced equipment. In this situation, you will be abandoned once you pay them. Remember that you cannot get rich overnight, especially in the pizza business. It takes hard work and time.

Please see the Franchise Resource list on the accompanying CD

for agencies that can provide additional franchising information to help you make an educated decision.

Franchising programs have a definite place in our environment, and there are plenty of pizza shop franchises available. Many pizza shop owners might not be in business without this option. It allows people with limited money to have a larger presence in the marketplace. Franchisees have the opportunity to draw on the experience of people within the corporation.

But, you still need to understand that this does NOT guarantee success. You will still be the main person responsible for the daily operations and for the fees and loans for the business. You will still be required to invest your time and money. Review the positives and negatives of franchising, and thoroughly research a company, no matter what you may think you know about them, before signing a contract.

Starting Off

Iknow it's hard to take the time to plan, but proper planning is critical to your success. When you open your doors for the first customer, everything needs to be in place. Let's cover the important things needed to legally open and take a big step toward being ready to open.

Governmental Requirements

Become familiar with the local, state, and federal laws that affect you. These include zoning requirements, scheduling and passing inspections, and licenses to purchase. The U.S. Business Advisor's Web site, **www.business. gov**, offers a variety of information to help you, including:

- A business resource library

- The Small Business Administration's start-up advisor

- Online counseling

- Information on financial resources

- Links to laws affecting different industries

- Legal and regulatory information for small businesses

Other federal Web sites you will find useful:

- The Small Business Administration –
  www.sba.gov/advo/laws

- The IRS – **www.irs.gov/businesses/**

- The U.S. Department of Labor – **www.dol.gov/osbp/sbrefa/
  main.htm**. The elaws page has employment law assistance – **www.
  dol.gov/elaws**.

Check the Department of Development office for your state. They can provide a lot of information for new entrepreneurs. (This is the Web site for Ohio's 1st Stop Business Connection—**www.odod.state.oh.us/onestop/index.cfm**). This site will take you step-by-step through the creation of your business information kit. You can find forms, state regulations, and much more on the site. Contact your local Economic Development Center, the Chamber of Commerce, or the Small Business Development Center for more information. You can also contact the local Equal Employment Opportunity Commission (EEOC) office for information. Contact the U.S. EEOC at 800-669-4000, or log on to **www.eeoc.gov/contact.html** for a list of their field offices.

State Registration

Contact the Secretary of State's office in your state as soon as you know you want to start a business. Be prepared because each state has different regulations. They can give you details about the laws and they can help you

contact the local and county offices in your area. There is usually a state fee, but it should be under $100.

They will check to see if the business name you want is being used. You may also need to file and publish a fictitious name with the local newspaper. From time to time, renew the name to keep it legitimate.

While you are filling out forms, get copies of all information from the Department of Taxation for income tax on your payroll. There are forms, tax tables, filing requirements, and publications to explain everything. Payroll will include periodic federal and state deposits, along with federal and state unemployment deposits. Each has deadlines for filing, and the penalties and interest can add up quickly. It's best to be sure you understand the details before you hire your staff.

City Business License

Most cities and counties require that you purchase a business license. The fees are based on different amounts, and it's best to check with your local business license office for details. The zoning office will verify that your location meets local requirements. If you buy an existing business, this should be a simple process.

Sales Tax

Most states require a vendor's license when you collect sales tax. The taxes might be local, county, and state. Check the details on the State Department of Taxation Web site. The Web site is filled with useful information. Each state has its own requirements for food tax. Many states require you to post a deposit on bond against future taxes. The Revenue Agency can waive the deposit and require you to post a surety bond from your insurance company. This is usually 5 percent of the total bond amount. When you

buy food for your menu items, you can avoid sales tax on the amount, if you present your sales tax permit to the wholesaler. Research your state to be sure how the tax rules work.

Health Department License

All restaurants must have a food service license. In order to get this license, you need to contact your local or state Department of Health. It is good to make a personal visit to discuss the details with them early. Let them know you want to cooperate and comply with their regulations. The Health Department can, and will, shut you down if you fail to meet their regulations. This can be the kiss of death for a restaurant, so do everything possible to keep them satisfied.

Before you open, the Health Department will conduct an inspection. When you pass a thorough inspection, they will issue a license, and you can open. If the inspector finds problems, you have to correct them before you can open. During the year, the Health Department will do unannounced inspections. The inspector will complete a form during the inspection. When there are violations, you are required to fix them, and the inspector will return to ensure the changes were made.

Some states now require that the restaurant manager, and sometimes the whole staff, pass a health and sanitation program. ServSafe is the most common program. You can purchase the necessary products at **www. atlantic-pub.com** or call 800-541-1336. The program includes instructor guides, slides, answer sheets, manager training, food safety CDs, and other tools for the instructor.

Fire Department Permit

The fire department needs to issue an occupational permit before you can

open for business. Contact the fire department early, in person, and they can supply the information. The fire inspector will check the fire exits, fire extinguishers, smoke detectors, and the hood and sprinkler systems.

The inspector will evaluate the size of the building and the number of exits to determine the "capacity" for the restaurant. It is critical that you follow these guidelines, even if you have to turn customers away. Verify any other fire regulations that will impact you and your business.

Building and Construction Permit

Will you need to remodel the building? If so, acquire a building permit. A building permit can be obtained from the Building and Zoning office and is usually based on the cost of the renovations. The building inspector will need plans for the work you plan to do. When the permit is approved, post it within the building; and periodic inspections must be done during the work, and the work needs to pass the inspections. These inspections will include: footers, framing, insulation, electrical, plumbing, and so on. Check with your local authorities to verify the requirements in your area.

Sign Permits

Your area may have specific ordinances regarding the sort, location, lighting, and size of the sign that you can use. There are requirements about how high, how close to your business, and how close to the street your sign can be placed. Keep in mind that flashing neon isn't appropriate in every environment.

Zoning

The purpose of zoning requirements is to monitor what activities are

conducted in certain places. This helps to keep similar businesses and residences in the same neighborhoods. There are some exceptions, and sometimes you need to acquire a special permit for a business location. Zoning will also have an impact on your parking, sign usage, and the appearance of your business. If you decide to locate your business in a historic district, there will be strict restrictions which will affect you. There may be laws about the number of businesses that can be within a specific area. Check all of these details BEFORE you sign a contract. The local laws could change your plans, and you should confirm that before you are committed to a contract.

State Liquor License

Learn the state liquor laws if you plan to serve wine, beer, or liquor. This process needs to start early because the state liquor control board will do an extensive investigation. The prices for a liquor license vary greatly, and check the details and prices before you decide to serve alcohol. Some areas prohibit the sale of alcohol, and other areas do not have licenses available. If you are moving into a new area, to check the liquor laws before you make final menu and product decisions.

It is very critical to follow the laws to the letter when you obtain a license. Review the extensive laws to ensure you know what to do, and review them with anyone else in your pizza shop licensed to serve alcohol. If you break any of the liquor laws, you risk losing your license.

All employees need to understand the laws that gauge how you serve alcohol in your pizza shop. It's imperative to train all employees, and you can create a test to ensure they understand the laws. Unfortunately, your employees may grow slack, and keep them conscientious.

It's wise to get to know the liquor inspector in your area. As with every other inspector, show that you want to learn the laws and to cooperate

with them. You can learn about the liquor laws in your area by visiting the National Conference of State Liquor Administrators' Web site at **www. ncsla.org/states.htm**.

Internal Revenue Registration

When you get a liquor license, Internal Revenue Service tax stamps. Call your local IRS office to obtain Application Form #11. Supply information about your pizza shop to the IRS, and they will assess your fee. This notifies the IRS that you sell liquor.

Federal Identification Number (Employee Identification Number)

All employers, partnerships, and corporations must have a Federal Identification Number. Many sole proprietors use their Social Security number, but they can also acquire a Federal Identification number. The number is used to identify your business on all tax forms and licenses. File Form #55-4 to obtain your number. You can download critical publications at **www.irs.gov** or request the IRS send them to you.

1.   Publication #15, circular E "Employer's Tax Guide."

2.   Several copies of Form W-4, "Employer Withholding Allowance Certificate." Each new employee must fill out one of these forms.

3.   Publication #334, "Tax Guide for Small Businesses."

4.   Request a copy of "All About OSHA" and the "OSHA Handbook for Small Businesses" from the Occupational Safety and Health Administration. The number of employees you have will dictate

which laws apply to you. OSHA can be contacted at:

OSHA, U.S. Department of Labor, 200 Constitutional Avenue NW, Washington, D.C. 20210 (**www.osha.gov**).

5. Get a copy of "Handy Reference Guide to the Fair Labor Standards Act" from the Department of Labor (**www.dol.gov**). The Department of Labor can be reached at:

Department of Labor, Frances Perkins Building, 200 Constitutional Avenue NW, Washington, D.C. 20210.

State Tax Assistance

Your state offers assistance to small business owners through the Department of Revenue. Your local office can be found at: **www.aicpa.org/yellow/ yptsgus.htm**.

There are many rules, regulations, inspections, and laws to learn. These are in place to monitor businesses and to ensure public safety. As I mentioned several times in this chapter, let the authorities know that you want to learn the requirements and to cooperate with the local authorities.

6

Internal Bookkeeping

You have all the permits you need. All the state and federal paperwork is done, and now we need to focus on how to keep track of the money. You must keep track of the money that comes in and the expenses that are paid. If you don't keep up with the money, you can have big problems, and they can happen fast. We're going to discuss how to find the right accounting software for you, how to handle cash, payroll, and tips.

Budgeting

Your internal bookkeeping includes any financial transactions for the business. These need to be tallied, reviewed, and balance your accounts. Even if you choose to hire an accountant for some of your accounting needs, it is important that you are personally involved in the internal financial details. This helps you identify potential problems early.

Set aside a couple of hours each day for accounting. A part-time bookkeeper can be a good idea, but be sure he/she is qualified and trustworthy. Purchase a good accounting program and have your bookkeeper enter all of the sales, invoices, and checks on a regular basis. These programs allow you to print a wide variety of reports to help you track income and expenses.

Something that I found helpful was to review the end of the week and one of the month reports. This is especially helpful when you compare it to previous weeks and months. Once you are familiar with the computer program, play with the report possibilities. A good tracking program can offer invaluable information about your pizza shop.

One of my biggest concerns with anyone who handles the money in a business is that he understands the confidential nature of any accounting. No one else needs to know what you are making or what your employees are being paid and your bookkeeper needs to respect that confidentiality.

Your accountant can audit the records, prepare tax reports, and offer advice when you need it. Keep in mind that a qualified bookkeeper is much more reasonable than an accountant. Ask local businesspeople if they can recommend a bookkeeper, or you can locate a certified bookkeeper with the American Institute of Professional Bookkeepers at **http://aipb.org**. If you cannot get a satisfactory recommendation for an accountant, you can find a Certified Public Accountant at **www.findaccountingsoftware.com**.

Accounting Software

QuickBooks® is a popular accounting package for the small business (**www. quickbooks.com**). There are payroll and inventory features that are very helpful. If you are a sole proprietor, you may also be able to use TurboTax to file your taxes. I've used QuickBooks in a variety of businesses over the last eight years and have learned how to customize many reports to get the information I need. It never hurts to experiment with the reports menus. See what possibilities are available in the program.

Another popular accounting program is Peachtree (**www.peachtree.com**). This program also offers various features. It is good to check the different versions, and buy the one that has the features you need. You can locate QuickBooks and Peachtree certified accountants and bookkeepers to help you with the programs. I've found the programs simple to use, and the help features have always answered my questions. You may not need help, but it's available if you do.

To evaluate the software available, go to **www.2020software.com/default. asp** to compare the top 20 software programs. The site offers comparisons, free demos and selection assistance.

Payroll

Your bookkeeper can handle paying employees, making withholding deposits on time and filing the necessary paperwork. QuickBooks and Peachtree offer payroll features which make this less complicated. But, you might prefer to have your accountant or a payroll service handle this for you. Either way, your bookkeeper will compute daily payroll amounts. If you use a payroll service, fax or call in the information within the time frame they provide.

You can divide the hours worked into different categories. This will help you monitor what you are spending for various activities. Payroll can get out of hand quickly in a pizza shop if you aren't conscientious. In the store I managed, we had a software program that tracked our sales and the payroll being spent. It was very valuable to keep an eye on payroll costs and to help me identify when to cut employees. You still have to rely on your experience and knowledge of your store trends, but it can prompt you to take action when it is warranted.

It is better to keep manager and owner salaries separate. They are budgeted differently and don't affect your staff payroll. When you look at your payroll

amounts, you can divide your month-to-date sales by your month-to-date payroll costs. Keep your payroll expenses to a certain percentage of your sales, in order to stay in line with your budget.

A DAILY CHECKLIST FOR YOUR BOOKKEEPER	
Duty	**Completed**
1. Gather time cards or reports.	
2. Verify employees clocked in on time and not early. If early, make sure they were needed and working.	
3. Compute the hours for each employee and include fractions.	
4. Enter hours on time cards or payroll form. Denote overtime in a different color or on another line. Notify the manager about any overtime or when employees are near overtime.	
5. Note hourly wage for each employee.	
6. Extend gross amount to be paid.	
7. Divide salaried employees' monthly salary by number of days in the month. Or, figure yearly salary, and divide by 52 for a weekly salary amount.	
8. List manager and owner salaries in a different part of the report.	
9. Total gross amount for each day at the bottom of the form. At the end of the week, total each employee's gross pay. Double check by totaling each employee and each day.	

A DAILY CHECKLIST FOR YOUR BOOKKEEPER	
Duty	**Completed**
10. Enter daily sales and labor amounts on Labor Analysis Form. (*A sample of this form is on the accompanying CD.*) Remember to keep employee pay separate from manager and owner salaries. The form has sections for daily and month-to-date payroll totals. Add each day's totals to figure your MTD totals.	

*Check the accompanying CD to print a copy of this list
and for a copy of the Labor Analysis Form.*

Keeping these numbers up-to-date will keep you aware of your budget. Know where your budget numbers stand for the month-to-date in order to maintain your monthly budgets. Maintaining your payroll costs is critical, and these methods will help you manage the costs and keep them in line.

Taxes

A study was conducted by the Providence District of the IRS, and it determined that "skimming" in "mom and pop" pizza shops is likely because they are usually a cash business. That means the IRS will keep an eye on independent pizza shops. Every business owner needs to keep accurate and thorough written records, but if you are in a business the IRS watches, it's even more critical.

Taxes can be a confusing maze for business owners, so I suggest that you spend some time on the Web site at **www.irs.gov**. We've included a tax calendar on the accompanying CD for your use. The calendar features these three federal taxes:

1.   Income tax withheld from employees' wages or non-payroll

amounts paid.

2. Social Security and Medicare taxes (FICA taxes) from employees' wages and the Social Security and Medicare taxes you pay as an employer.

3. Federal unemployment (FUTA) tax your business pays.

The calendar lists dates to file returns and make deposits for these taxes. The calendar should be used with IRS Publication 15, which outlines deposit rules.

Forms You May Need

These are descriptions of the employment tax forms you may need:

*   **Form 940** (or 940-EZ), Employer's Annual Federal Unemployment (FUTR) Tax Return. This form is due one month after the calendar year ends. Use it to report your FUTR tax. Most employers can use Form 940-EZ.

*   **Form 941**, Employer's Quarterly Federal Tax Return. File this one month after the calendar month or quarter ends. The amount of your payments will dictate how often to file. This form is used to report Social Security and Medicare taxes and federal income taxes withheld on your employees' wages.

General Tax Calendar

This tax calendar has the due dates for 2007 that most taxpayers will need. Employers, and persons who pay excise taxes, should also use the Employer's Tax Calendar and the Excise Tax Calendar.

Fiscal-year taxpayers – If you file your income tax return for a fiscal year rather than the calendar year, you must change some of the dates in this calendar. These changes are described under Fiscal-Year Taxpayers at the end of this calendar.

A complete calendar of tax deadlines for businesses is available on the accompanying CD. You can print it out for easy reference.

Tipped Employees

There are many opinions about how people should handle reporting their tips. Many people just don't report them. This is illegal. Owners of any food service business have to contend with this situation. Make it clear that the IRS requires the employees to report their tips. As with most things that involve the IRS, the rules are confusing. Since tax laws change all the time, verify the details with your accountant periodically.

The tipping information is included on the CD.
You can print these regulations for your employees.

Review the tipping information on the CD, so you will be familiar with the regulations that apply to employees who are tipped. You are responsible for educating your tipped employees on the tax laws that affect them.

Handling Cash

Cash Flow

The amount of cash your company earns and spends during a certain amount of time is called your "cash flow". There needs to be enough cash on hand to pay bills, suppliers, payroll, and other expenses.

Manage Your Cash Flow

When you pay your bills on time, you save money and can sometimes negotiate a better rate. Many suppliers offer a 10 percent discount if you pay by the tenth of the month. All of these things save you money; and when you stay on top of the bills, it's much easier to avoid penalties and problems.

Once you are established for a short time, many suppliers will give you an account which gives you 30 days to pay. This is very helpful because you have a chance to earn money off of these products before the account is due. If you do not pay these accounts when they are due, the supplier will add interest. Most of the accounts I've seen have high interest, so it's in your best interest to pay invoices on time.

CODs and Your Cash Flow

When you are new in business, the suppliers usually want you to pay for the order when it's delivered. A simple way to handle this is to ask for the total amount when the order is placed, and then have a check ready when the supplies arrive. You can pay for small deliveries from your till. But, this requires a person who is authorized, and you must have a receipt for the items. This is more random to track, but can work when limited people get into the till. At the end of the shift or the day, you will need to make a notation on your closing paperwork about why the money was spent. Otherwise, your accounts will be short. Make it clear that only certain people can accept COD orders. Once you pay for a purchase, it's much harder to resolve problems.

Being Paid

You can offer your customers a full range of options to pay. Evaluate any options that will cost you money, for example, credit and debit cards. There

are a plethora of credit card services, but you should search for the best service and price. Also, be careful because some services do not allow you to include a tip line, or they charge significantly more for that service.

Customers like to have the following options to pay:

- Cash
- Traveler's checks
- Business or Personal Checks
- Debit or Credit Cards

You can also add:

- Gift cards (giveaway for promotions or can be purchased for gifts)
- Store vouchers for returns or dissatisfied customers
- Discount coupons

Each of these options needs to be handled like cash/credit in order to balance your accounts at the end of the day.

Cash is a safe option as long as you know how to identify counterfeit bills. Checks can be risky, but you need a strict return check policy. These policies MUST be enforced, or it will get out of control. Debit and credit cards are slightly risky since they can be stolen, but you can minimize the risk by asking for a photo ID to verify the owner is using the card.

Cash Handling

Cash must be handled properly. Here are some tips to help you:

- Each cashier should have a separate drawer. Only the cashier and the manager should have access. Computer programs allow each user to code their transactions and to keep individual tallies.

- The owner or manager needs to have cash drawers prepared and assigned each day. The cashier needs to recount the drawer to verify the right amount and sign a receipt for the funds at the beginning of the shift.

- At the end of each shift, cashiers count and balance their drawers using the register report.

- If the drawer is over or short, it needs to be written up and signed off by the manager after double checking the amounts. The drawers then need to be stored in the safe, ready for the next shift.

- Checks and credit card receipts need to be tallied and stored in the safe until they are ready to be deposited.

- Credit card machines allow you to close out the machine for a shift. This saves time and processes your money quicker.

- When you get guest checks, have them numbered, so you can keep track of them. This is an easy way for an employee to steal. Employees need to turn in any void checks at the end of the day and explain why it was void. You can have a policy that the owner or manager must approve voids.

- For phone or Web orders, include the credit card's ID code.

- When a customer comes into the store, write his phone number on the check. This allows you to contact the customer if there is a problem. Most computerized systems use the customer's phone number for identification.

Counterfeit Bills

Meet with your bank's loss prevention department. They can teach you how

to identify counterfeit money and supply training manuals to help your employees learn to spot phony money. Counterfeit money detector pens are another option.

Travelers' Checks

Traveler's checks are usually handled like any other check. But, it is good to verify this with your bank before you accept any. Your employees need to be trained on how to accept traveler's checks. They need to be signed on the front, and ask for identification.

Checks

Each business needs to develop a check acceptance policy. Once the policy is in place, train all employees on how to accept checks. Most businesses never accept counter checks or starter checks. My policy has always been to only accept checks with the person's name printed on the front (not handwritten). It is also good practice to refuse a third-party check. Each state has "bad check" laws, and use these rules in your business.

There are more and more confirmation systems for checks. They confirm that the money is available and hold the funds for you until the check clears. This can be costly, but a mountain of bad checks will cost you more. Each business owner needs to evaluate whether he needs a check confirmation system, although some localities are requiring they be used. Check with your bank for the local rules. Valuable information is available from Check Fraud (**www.checkfraud.com**).

You don't need to be obnoxious about this. A simple sign that outlines your acceptance and return check policies is usually sufficient.

Debit and Credit Cards

Debit cards (or ATM cards) and credit cards are different ways to pay. Debit cards transfer funds from your bank account while credit cards issue money against a line of credit. The laws about how the money will be collected vary, and your amount of risk is different. This is another case where you can to talk with your banker and get full details.

Other Forms of Payment

A nice way to promote your business and to get new customers is through gift cards or gift certificates. These are very popular because they are a simple gift. It's like "one size fits all" buying. This allows the recipients to come to your pizza shop and purchase what they want.

When customers use gift cards, they have cash value. You subtract the amount on the card or certificate against their purchase. Store vouchers can be used for returns or dissatisfied customers. These can be an easy way for employees to steal from the company, unless you insist that only the owner or manager can issue them. These should also be printed with consecutive numbers in order to track them. If someone makes a mistake when filling one out, he needs to turn that ruined voucher in to you. Coupon amounts are subtracted from the current price. These aren't cash, but track them like cash to keep track of the activity. Your daily summary sheet should include a place to list all of these "alternative" forms of payment. All certificates, coupons, etc. need to be put in an envelope and included with your daily paperwork.

Many of these things may seem tedious, but they will help you keep track of the money and prevent potential theft by employees or customers. You must keep a tight rein on the money coming into and going out of your business. Keeping track of gift certificates and coupons helps you track your promotional efforts, but we'll discuss that later.

Managers need to keep track of many bits of information. I've included many forms for your use on the accompanying CD. If you need other log books, you can take a look at **www.commlog. com**. Some of these logs include: manager's, request shift, switch shift, kitchen, bar, guest relations, and much more. You can contact them at on their 24 hour toll-

free order line at 800-962-6564 (outside the U.S., contact them at 602-232-2956).

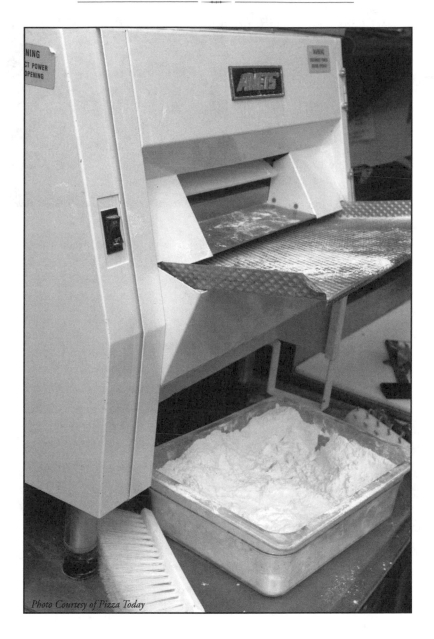

Photo Courtesy of Pizza Today

7

Budgeting and Operational Management

Successful businesspeople set realistic budgets and adhere to them. Setting a budget is admirable, but sticking to your budget is what will set you apart from your competitors. A simple principle I try to use is: If you don't have the money for something you want, you don't buy it at that time.

There are some exceptions in business, like times when you must have something critical. Those things are a necessity and are the exception. Before you borrow money or charge a purchase, evaluate whether you can use something else or if you can find something more reasonably priced. When you can't find another alternative, then you must spend the money.

A long range financial plan is needed for businesses. I like to do these for a year at a time. This gives you an overview of upcoming revenue and expenses. With your plan and budget, you will know how much money your pizza shop needs to generate to pay the bills. If you are in a college

town, you should see a noticeable difference in your store's revenue in different months.

It is good for you to make friends at local college campuses. Get a copy of the school calendar as soon as possible. This will give you all school breaks, dates when students will arrive, and special events. It is critical that you have this information in order to make accurate sales projections. My school calendar was prominently placed in my office. While you are making friends on campus, find a way to get into the fraternities and sororities. They have a lot of special events and will need a lot of pizza.

When you review your expenses and revenue, look at your actual numbers and your budgeted amounts. When you see problems, identify the cause, and fix them right away. If you create a yearly overview of your finances, break it down to monthly budgets to allow for fluctuations in revenue and expenses.

Monthly Budgeting

The time to evaluate your expenses is minimal once you have the original numbers established. For subsequent years, you can use your actual costs to develop future financial plans. The first one will be the most complicated, but it helps you become familiar with the full range of expenses you will face.

Once you start making decisions about your store, put a financial plan in place. There are one-time expenses which will include equipment, signage etc. You also have repetitive expenses which will recur each month or every two months. Your budget will help guide your business to your goals.

Your budget helps your manager, or other key employees, be aware of ways to control costs. These records are invaluable when you apply for a loan. It shows the lender how you use the revenue that is generated. Don't underestimate the value of a well developed budget. You can make consistent

financial decisions about your pizza shop and forecast future revenue. This work drives many business owners crazy because they don't have a financial plan in place. Expect your initial projections to be inaccurate. As time goes by, you'll project numbers that will be much more accurate.

Total Sales

Projecting sales is crucial and a difficult part of your budgeting. It's impossible to figure your sales from the very beginning. This makes this task complicated and confusing. Some costs are based on your sales. Obviously, food costs increase when you sell more pizzas and subs. In order to sell more pizza, you buy more food, more boxes, and so on. This shows why it is critical to start with a reasonable sales amount. That will impact everything.

In the beginning, your sales will be low because you are establishing your reputation and clientele. During this time, money will be tight. The cost of doing business will be high, but it will improve as you build sales. After a couple of months, you should notice a difference in your operating expenses and your sales. Realistically, in the beginning, there may be no profit.

It can take one to three months to work out the initial kinks, perfect your pizza and subs, and other items you sell. During this time, spend some additional money to get things right and to train your employees. The additional money should be included in your startup expenses. Doing these things right in the beginning will ensure you will be in business for years.

This is the time you want to try out the production, serving, and delivery of your products. When you find problem products, you can work out the problems or eliminate them from your menu. We've all seen the big name pizza shops offering various specialty items for a short time then they are gone. There's no reason you can't do that, too.

You want to offer the best quality product, and that takes experimenting

and perfecting. The beginning is the time to figure out these things. Keep this idea in front of your employees at all times. Create a great menu, serve a wonderful product, give excellent service, and build a solid reputation; then the budget will work for you.

Track Sales Growth

If you bought an established store, you can determine the sales based on the store's history. Sales usually drop when a new owner takes over. Review the records to see highs and lows. You should have similar trends. Use these trends to help you determine staff and purchasing needs. You may find ways to boost sales during the traditionally slow times.

Keep in mind that the number of weekends can make a difference in the numbers. Evaluate not only the sales numbers, but also what days the sales were done. I made notes about especially high or unusual sales. That helps you, in following years, account for unusual sales that may upset your trends. You will notice the trends and get to know the average sales for each day of the week, each weekend, and for special events. Be patient and it will all come together.

One of the first projects I had was to create a graph chart for the previous store sales. I wanted to track what the store did in the past. Each year was plotted in a different color and we added our sales each week. This gave the crew a visual aid to see how we were doing and helped them to see the sales as they increased. We had a goal for exam week and drew a mark on the target amount. We exceeded the number and it looked great on our chart.

Sales Categories

"**Actual Month-to-Date Sales**" is a tally of the daily sales.

"**Cash Over/Short**" accounts for errors on the register.

Every item and sale is accounted for and reconciled against other transactions. Keep the forms for at least five years in a fireproof storage file. It is convenient to keep your daily forms in a three-ring binder in the main office. If you use a computer, back up the system daily, and print your reports. Your backups should be stored outside the store. Again, special notes on the daily sheets are a big help when you look at sales numbers over the years.

Labor

- **Manager Salary.** The manager and owner salaries should be a fixed monthly cost. Use this formula to find the exact pay per month: Manager's Salary for Year divided by number of days in the year multiplied by the number of days in the month. When the salaries change during the year, your projections should be updated to reflect these changes.

- **Employee Salary.** The employee salary expenses will fluctuate based on your sales. Employee labor costs have a break-even point. This is the point where labor is within the profit from your sales. If you can maintain the same labor cost, but increase your sales, your profits increase. Don't do this to the point where service and quality suffers, but it keeps people working at their best. The cost of labor is determined by efficiency and the sales volume produced.

- **Overtime** should be nonexistent. If it's unavoidable, keep it at a minimum. Don't budget for overtime because you shouldn't need it. When you find a need for overtime, you may need to hire more employees. Your bookkeeper needs to alert you about employees who are near overtime hours. Keep an eye on the scheduled hours when the schedule is written. With practice, you can get employee hours close to the number you want. There will be times when employees need to exchange shifts. You can avoid

overtime by approving any shift changes. Check hours before you approve shift changes.

Controllable Operational Costs

When you work on your budget, the following categories and the actual amounts are generally tax deductible. Once your taxes are completed, you can determine how close your projections are to the actual costs. There are a wide variety of expenses to budget and to deduct. Many are listed here:

- **Large Purchases.** In the beginning, you may need to buy equipment, vehicles, computers, and software which can be depreciated over a set lifespan or may be deducted the year it's purchased. Once you are established, you can finance or lease these items and spread the payments over time. Search for the best possible deal before signing a finance or lease agreement.

- **Staple Supplies.** These include consumable goods that are replaced frequently. As you become better with inventory, you can keep these costs down.

- **Office Supplies.** These costs should be fairly consistent. Sometimes I stock up if prices are very good and then I don't need to make monthly purchases.

Services

Following are typical services that you will need to budget for:

- **Security** costs should be a consistent monthly charge.

- **Freight.** Most supplies that are delivered have delivery charges figured in, especially with the rising cost of fuel. You may evaluate

if there are some supplies you can pick up to save on delivery charges. I used to have my drivers pick up various store supplies that were close to their deliveries, and we saved on some freight and delivery charges.

- **Legal.** At times you must get legal advice. Hopefully, these visits will be sporadic as the costs can vary greatly. Many attorneys will give you an estimate for their services, but you can set aside a little each month for future legal fees.

- **Accounting.** In the beginning, there will be additional accounting fees. However, once you are operating, it should be a consistent monthly fee. Plan for tax time and the additional accounting charges.

- **Maintenance.** Make every effort to keep maintenance at a reasonable and consistent monthly amount. Problems do arise, but most things can be spaced out to work within your budget. These include: cleaning the parking lot, window and other cleaning.

Utilities

Following are typical utilities that you will need to budget for:

- **Telephone** charges should be relatively consistent. Any long-distance phone calls should be recorded in a notebook. Your bookkeeper should compare the list to the phone bill. If there are excesses or problems, identify who was working and address the problem.

- **Water** should be a consistent. In many locales, water is billed every two months.

- **Gas** may be a variable or semi-variable expense depending on what type of equipment you use. If you heat with gas, talk to the company about their budget payment plan. This will keep your bill consistent and alleviate excess bills in the winter.

- **Electricity** may be a variable or semi-variable expense depending on the type of equipment it operates. Electricity bills are normally higher during the summer months, as this is when the air-conditioning units are used.

- **Heat** includes the cost of any heating material used, but not listed above, such as coal, wood, oil, etc.

Fixed Operating Costs

- **Rent** or lease should be a monthly payment. You may have an agreement that includes a payment which is a percentage of your total sales or profit amount. Budget your actual payment, and base the percentage on your projected sales.

- **Insurance.** Divide your insurance cost by 12, which gives you the monthly amount. Types of insurance you must have include workers' compensation, fire, theft, liability, etc.

- **Property Taxes.** If you pay property taxes, divide the annual tax amount by 12.

General Operating Costs

- **Labor Taxes.** These include the amount you are required to contribute to the state and federal government. You should establish a separate account to hold withholding tax from each

payroll. These taxes include: matching social security, federal, and state unemployment tax.

- **Other Taxes.** There are miscellaneous taxes. Enter the total miscellaneous taxes you will need to pay each month. This is any tax the store pays for goods and services.

- **Equipment Repairs.** This includes scheduled and emergency repairs and maintenance for equipment. Budget a base amount for normal service, and adjust for major expenses.

- **Building Repairs.** These are minor scheduled or emergency repairs and maintenance to your building. Include a base amount for normal repairs and maintenance in your budget. You should budget for large remodeling or rebuilding projects.

- **Entertainment.** The only entertainment expenses you can deduct are those that are directly related to conducting your business.

- **Advertising.** This includes all advertising for your pizza shop (your Web site, television ads, radio spots, mailing circulars, newspapers, etc.).

- **Promotional Expense.** These are promotional items with your logo or sponsoring sporting events, etc.

- **Equipment Rental.** These are short-term or long-term rental of equipment or machinery.

- **Postage.** Include postage that is paid for business purposes.

- **Contributions.** Include all contributions paid to recognized charitable organizations.

- **Trade Dues, Business Associations.** Dues to professional

organizations, such as local and national retailer associations and business organizations like the Better Business Bureau, are included. Trade magazine subscriptions can be entered. Divide your annual fees by 12 to determine the monthly amount.

- **Licenses.** These are all business and government licenses: operating licenses, health permit, liquor licenses, etc. Divide by 12 to determine the monthly rates.

- **Credit card expenses** include monthly service charges and the percentage you are charged for your monthly credit card charges.

- **Travel** expenses for necessary business travel for yourself and your employees.

- **Bad Debt.** Businesses don't want bad debt, but improper handling of credit cards and checks can cause bad debts. The full amount of the debt is tax deductible. This amount is worthless and uncollectible.

Total Net Profit

To determine your net profit, subtract "Total Budgeted Expenditures" from "Total Sales." This will give you a net profit or loss.

Depreciation

Depreciation may be defined as the expense derived from the expiration of a capital assets quantity of usefulness over the life of the property. Capital assets are those assets that have utility or usefulness of more than one year. Since a capital asset will provide utility over several years, the deductible cost of the asset must be spread out over its useful life–over a specified recovery period. The IRS publishes guidelines for the number of years to be used for

computing an asset's useful life. Each year a portion of the asset's cost may be deducted as an expense. Your accountant can advise you on the rules and benefits of immediate deductibility of equipment and vehicles as compared to depreciating these.

Some examples of depreciable items commonly found in a store include: office equipment, kitchen and dining room equipment, the building (if owned), machinery, display cases, and any intangible property that has a useful life of more than one year. Thus, items such as light bulbs, china, stationery, and merchandise inventories may not be depreciated. The cost of franchise rights is usually a depreciable expense.

As you progress in your business, you might find other unusual expenses, and these need to be added to your budget. The details listed above will help you determine your expenses and the sales amounts needed to meet your expenses. It will also help you determine when you are making a profit. I used to mark a chart graph with the breakeven line and then plot weekly sales. It was great to post a sales number above the breakeven line.

Photo Courtesy of Pizza Today

8

What to Serve

Now let's get to the fun part. What do you want to serve at your pizzeria and sub shop? The easy answer is pizza and sandwiches, but what kind do you want to serve? Do you want to offer additional menu items or keep it simple? When making these decisions, keep in mind any special staff, equipment, and space needs. If you have a small kitchen, keep things simple, and stick with pizza. If you have a large kitchen and/or a skilled staff, branch out! Utilize these abilities, and give your staff freedom to use their skills, creativity, and every square inch available to make your pizza shop more profitable!

Pizza Marketing Quarterly Annual Report for 2005

The Industry as a Whole

There are three bits of good news when looking at the industry as a whole.

First, there are 1.7 percent more pizzerias in America. Second, sales rose 2 percent indicating more growth than the previous year. A third sign of positive change is that only 388 pizzerias went out of business according to statistics from *InfoUSA*, which is down from 1,139 that closed the previous year. The total number of pizzerias in the U.S. reached 69,844 as of July 2005 compared to 68,694 at the time of the 2004 Pizza Power report.

Average per unit sales for pizzerias in the U.S. for the period between July 2004 and July 2005 was $442,492 per location, which was up 0.3 percent from the previous year. The reason the per unit percentage change is lower than the overall growth rate is a result of the growth rate of total pizzerias being higher than the overall sales growth.

The National Restaurant Association's (NRA) Restaurant Industry Forecast for 2005 predicts a total of 900,000 restaurants and total sales of $475.8 billion by the end of 2005. This will average $528,667 per unit, leaving the pizza industry falling short of the national per unit average for all restaurants. The NRA's per unit sales prediction for 2004, was $501,253 per unit. The NRA's numbers show a change in average sales per unit for all restaurants between 2004 and 2005 of 5.5 percent. While the pizza industry is gaining sales and locations, it is still behind the national per unit averages for all restaurants in the U.S.

NPD Crest reports serving of pizza at restaurants were up 2 percent, which is a positive shift from being down 1 percent the previous year. According to NPD Crest, traffic in the QSR Pizza Category was flat and traffic in the Casual Dining Pizza Category was up 5 percent.

The Independents

For this report, independents are classified as all pizzerias not in the Top 25. Once again the independents gained market share of the total number of pizzerias in the U.S. and now comprise 64.3 percent of all the pizzerias

in the U.S., which is up from 64.2 percent the previous year, but lost market share of total sales. Between July 2004 and July 2005, independents earned 49.22 percent of the industry's total sales compared to earning 50.7 percent of the total industry sales the previous year. For 2004, independents earned an average of $338,745 per/unit compared to $341,534 per/unit the previous year. This marks a decrease of 0.8 percent. What does this mean? Independents are opening more locations than the Top 25, but the Top 25 are outpacing independents in sales. While this may be true, it does not necessarily mean the Top 25 are doing the best job of expanding our industry as a whole. We'll explain more as we go here.

The Top 25

The Top 25 chains are ranked based on sales. The big news of the Top 25 is that they are not expanding the number of locations so much, but are finding success in capturing sales in the pizza category. Let's look at the basics. The Top 25 increased their share of the total industry sales and now posses 50.78 percent of the $30.9 billion dollars in pizza sales. This means that of their 24,935 units (which represent 35.7 percent of all pizzerias in the U.S.; Source: Technomic), they are being more successful at increasing average per unit sales. Average per unit sales for the period between July 2004 and July 2005 was $629,334, which is up 3.6 percent from $607,364 per unit the previous year.

Here are some interesting notes about the Top 25. In the Top 25 category, there were three new companies that were not ranked as a Top 25 pizzeria last year. Those pizzerias were Greek's Pizzeria, Jet's Pizza, and Imo's Pizza. Of the Top 25, only three chains showed lower sales than the previous year and they were Donato's Pizza, Pizza Inn, and Mr. Gatti's. Ten of the Top 25 chains showed a decrease in the number of units from the previous year. They were (in no particular order) Pizza Hut, Papa John's, Little Caesars, Sbarro, Donato's, Pizza Inn, Mazzio's Pizza, Papa Gino's, Mr. Gatti's, and Pizzas of Eight.

Some of those Top 25 who appear to have performed better than others either in sales or overall growth were as follows. Pizza Hut's sales were up 4.5 percent while units were down 0.3 percent from the previous year. Chuck E. Cheese's sales were up 9.2 percent and units were up 6.3 percent from the previous year. CiCi's Pizza's sales were up 14.5 percent and units were up 11.2 percent. Papa Murphy's sales were up 13.2 percent and units were up 12.1 percent from the previous year. Peter Piper's sales were up 10 percent while units remained the same from previous year. Fox's Pizza Den showed a rise in sales of 28 percent while units were up 6.1 percent from the previous year. Greek's Pizza showed sales increases of 16.9 percent with number of units up 0.8 percent. Jet's Pizza's sales were up 31.9 percent while units increased 32.5 percent from the previous year.

What Should We Do?

As seen by comparing the pizza industry to the entire restaurant industry, pizza is failing to pull customers away from the hamburger, taco, sandwich, and chicken guys. It appears that rather than fighting to expand pizza's customer base, the deep discounting by the major chains is simply a war of attrition that is pulling pizza customers from one pizza place to another. Perhaps there needs to be a shift and an effort with marketing towards expanding your customer base, introducing new products or a healthy angle to keep this industry fresh and exciting. The Big Four's move in early 2004 to offer new items was a step in the right direction, but the "555 Deal," "$5 National Pizza Sale," and numerous low-priced pizza offers and coupons are simply going to make customers "bargain hunt" for the cheapest pizza they can find. Americans' love for pizza won't go away, but there needs to be a movement to educate customers on the quality, uniqueness, and value of pizza.

A $15 to $20 meal from a pizzeria can feed three to four people. Try feeding the same number of people chicken, burgers and fries, or sandwiches for around $5 each. It's hard to do and maybe this is a point pizza companies

need to push rather than short-term discounts. Pizzas are made to order and this ability to customize and feed multiple persons for around five dollars each is a unique selling point that few other restaurant categories can boast. Are you being suckered into the price wars? It's a no-win situation and it's hurting our industry.

Healthy Choices and "Buzz Words"

While the low-carb and no-carb trends have run their course, healthy alternatives and choices are something that have taken a root in the restaurant industry. According to a survey by the NRA, here are trends restaurant operators are reporting as in popular demand. As you will note, nearly all of these relate to healthy lifestyles. Percentages represent the percent of operators reporting an increase in popularity:

Entrée Salads	78 percent
Bottled Water	69 percent
Poultry	62 percent
Sandwiches w/o bun/bread	50 percent
Side Salads	48 percent

Also in the NRA report, a consumer research survey they conducted identified 10 keywords and phrases that "add a lot of interest" to the consumers' menu choice when deciding on what they will order. These words are: "Fresh, farm fresh," "homemade," "grilled, charcoal-grilled," "roasted," "charbroiled, broiled," "baked," "barbecued," "marinated," "sautéed" and "hearty." The report also cited a percentage of consumers who have never tried certain foods but said they would be interested in trying the following items; Ciabatta, empanadas, Tandoori, Falafel, goose, California rolls, lemon grass, and gnocci.

This report also found that there were words that at least one out of five

consumers gave low marks. These words are: "raw," "deep-fried, fried or flash-fried," "blackened," "infused," and "pureed."

Conclusion

The past year was positive for the pizza industry, but performance is still lagging behind the restaurant industry as a whole. While we are growing, so is every other restaurant...but at a faster pace than pizza. The Big Four took a step in the right direction with new product launches last year and saw increased sales by broadening their customer base, but once again resorted back to the price war in their fight to capture each others' customers rather than target other segments' customers like burgers, chicken, and sandwiches. With several chicken products being introduced by the Big Four and increased sales, a broader menu may be the answer to the pizza industry's below average gains compared to the rest of the restaurant industry. Deep discounted pizzas are an option for those needing a lot of food at a low price, but rather than being the primary marketing message, it should be further down on the list behind new menu offerings and customer loyalty.

The answer may be in enticing new customers in your doors and giving them multiple reasons to come back through rewards for loyalty and more choices. Customers who chose KFC, Taco Bell, Subway, and Quiznos are the ones we need to target. Let's learn from others, like Quiznos and Subway who are competing and building their brands on quality and taste rather than price. Subway promotes healthy and fresh while Quiznos promotes taste. (Source: **www.pmq.com/mag/2005september-october/pizzapower.php**)

Pizza Trends You Should Know

Delivery and Drive Thru

Your customers want pizza, and they want it to be ready fast. Domino's,

with their "30 minutes or less" delivery, set the standard for all delivery pizzerias. Pizza delivery is going strong. Papa John's has also been successful with delivery. Their sales increased by 23.4 percent in 1999 with delivery.

The pizza drive-thru is the latest convenience option. Tom Potter, the founder of Eagle Boys Pizza in Brisbane, Australia, played with the idea of a pizza drive-thru at his store. The drive-thru items are limited to four pizzas. The staff pre-bakes these pizzas and stores them in warming cabinets. The pizzas only last for 30 minutes then must be thrown away. Donato's and Flying Pizza, in Columbus, Ohio, has had success with drive-thrus. There are also some Taco Bell/Pizza Hut restaurants which offer some pizza items at the drive thru. Service was prompt, and the pizza and breadsticks were good and hot.

Take-and-Bake Pizza

Another possibility is take-and-bake pizza. Uno's successfully offered this for several years. Several varieties of their medium, thick crust pizzas are in a refrigerator near the hostess. This allows customers to stop by and pick up a pizza on their way home. This is more cost effective for the pizza shop since the pizzas don't need to be thrown away after 30 minutes.

Non-Traditional Locations

More and more convenience stores, hospitals, and grocery stores are offering pizzas to their regular customers.

Pizza Ingredients

To make pizza, you use three critical ingredients: sauce, cheese, and dough. There are many options, but these are the basics. Keep in mind there are also sauce options.

Dough

You must have dough to make a pizza, and the remainder of the pie will be built on top of the dough. Experiment with the dough to ensure it isn't gummy or uncooked.

The three types of dough include fresh, frozen, and par-baked. Fresh is the most labor intensive and gives you control over the quantity and quality of your dough. Pizza shop owners who make their own dough should promote that fact. This allows you to promote a "homemade product made from scratch."

If you use fresh dough, be sure to keep an eye on expiration dates. Pizza shops that order dough from a commissary have expiration dates on the trays. The closer you get to the expiration date, the worse the dough handles. You are more likely to get thin spots in the crust and the dough doesn't rise completely when it gets old.

This seems like too much work to many pizza shop owners, and that is why you have other options. You can use frozen or partially-baked crust. This should also guarantee a more consistent product for your customer.

You can make your own dough, but be sure you have a good recipe. It is also important to get some background information on how to make pizza dough. One large pizza business holds dough classes for their managers in order to help them understand how to get the best quality product.

First, understand that you need to follow recipes and formulas when you bake. These formulas are tried-and-true. In other words, stick to the recipe.

You can attend the Pizza Crust Boot Camp™ which has a technical and practical section. The technical portion deals with the dough formulation. The practical portion gives you a "how-to" perspective. You can find a Pizza

Expo™ near you at **www.pizzaexpo.com**.

When you make dough, start with yeast, water, salt, and flour. Some recipes call for oil, herbs, milk, or sugar, but they aren't necessary.

Most people believe that all flour is created equal, but there many kinds and not all are suitable for pizza dough. Some of the types include:

- White flour
- All-purpose flour
- High gluten flour
- Wheat flour
- Bread flour

The amount of protein in flour is critical for pizza dough. This affects how the dough will bake. For bread and pizza dough, use bread flour or all-purpose. Here is a list of the percentage of proteins in flours to help demonstrate:

Hard wheat flour	13-14%
Bread flour	12-13%
All-Purpose flour	10-12%
High gluten flour	13-14%
Whole wheat	13-15%
Pastry	8-9%
Cake	6-8%

In *Getting Your Slice of the Pie*, Tracy Powell says:

- Deep dish pizza needs all-purpose flour.
- An all-around choice is bread flour.
- Thin crust and hand-tossed should be made with high gluten flour.

The gluten content is also important. Gluten helps to trap air in the mixture when water is mixed with the flour. This enables the dough to rise and expand when it is baked. The gluten increases along with the amount of protein. So, a high gluten and protein content are needed for pizza dough.

Anyone who has baked bread knows how important yeast is in a dough recipe. It's a living, single-cell organism which grows and converts into alcohol and carbon dioxide. The dough rises in a healthy yeast environment. Rising can be enabled with a little salt to promote growth, and the right temperature. Add a little warm water to the yeast, and let it sit for a few minutes, while the yeast activates. This only works when the water is between 75 and 105 degrees. Use a thermometer to verify the temperature.

You can use instant dry, compressed, or active dry yeast. Some pizza shop owners prefer one over another, but any type is fine. Whether you have the compressed blocks or dry granules, they need to be stored in the refrigerator and should be used within two weeks.

Some recipes can be found on Pizza Marketing Quarterly's site at **www. pmq.com/cgi-bin/pizzacookbook/recipe.cgi?action=view_category&cate gory=Pizza+Dough**.

Domino's and Pizza Hut are just two of the pizza businesses that use frozen and par-baked dough. It would be good to find out what your food distributors offer.

Sauce

The most common pizza sauce is a red sauce, but we will discuss some other options. The consistency is important. Is it thick or thin? Are there chunks of tomato? You don't want the sauce to break down, so you should use a sauce with 16 to 20 percent solids, or spray a thin layer of oil on the dough before spreading the sauce.

All red sauces contain tomatoes, onion, garlic, and spices, but there are regional differences in the taste. Sauces in the south are sweeter, more acidic in New York, and thicker in the Midwest.

Decide if you will make your own sauce or buy canned sauce. This depends on your situation. Some pizza shops make their own sauce each day while many others buy prepared sauce. But, if you have a family recipe and can cook, it would be great to make your own. This sets you apart from the other pizza shops and provides a fresh product for your customers. You can also experiment with tomato paste, balsamic vinegar, a small bit of sugar, wine, olives, ricotta or parmesan cheese, crushed red pepper, olive oil, fresh herbs, fresh peppers, carrots, or even vodka. There are a million possible combinations, and you could create the next wonderful sauce.

Keep in mind that you will save labor dollars on pre-made sauce, but the sauce you buy will cost you more. A pre-made sauce can cost 0.20 cents per 16-inch pizza. Research all the possibilities before you make a decision. Pizza Today has links to sauce distributors who can help you get started (**www.pizzatoday.com**).

California Pizza Kitchen has several gourmet, hearth-baked pizzas, including barbecue, salsa, Caribbean, peanut-ginger sauce, white wine and garlic shallot butter sauce, and hosing sauce. Most pizza shops don't offer this wide variety.

The pizza toppings you choose will help you evaluate how many sauces you should offer.

- Mexican pizza – Offer salsa
- White sauce or Alfredo – Seafood toppings
- Barbecue sauce – Chicken

Here are some additional sauces you could try:

- Roasted red pepper
- Pesto
- Sun-dried tomato
- Teriyaki
- Spicy Chipotle
- Butter and garlic sauce

- Fire-roasted tomato
- Tzatziki Sauce
- Honey mustard dressing
- Country gravy
- Ranch dressing

Cheese

Some gourmet pizzas are made without cheese, but for most people, cheese is synonymous with pizza. A 2003 Market Facts study revealed that 75 percent of pizza eaters want at least two types of cheese on their pizza. Their favorites include: mozzarella, Monterey Jack, parmesan, provolone, and white or yellow cheddar.

- Whole-milk mozzarella and white cheddar blends are common in the East and South.

- A mozzarella-provolone blend is popular in Ohio.

- The west coast prefers mozzarella, cheddar and provolone, or mozzarella-Monterey Jack or mozzarella-Muenster blends.

You should have mozzarella and provolone, but you should see what blends are available, especially if you want to offer gourmet pizzas.

Pizza shop owners believe provolone is a better quality cheese which has a sharper flavor and higher fat content than mozzarella. The taste becomes sharper with age. Provolone is more expensive, so you can consider a provolone-mozzarella blend to have a good quality cheese and cut costs.

With cheese, you have the choice of buying grated cheese or grating it yourself. This has the same principles as sauce. You will save labor dollars if

you buy grated cheese, but it will cost you more. Keep in mind that freshly grated cheese will have a strong flavor and aroma.

You can also blend brie and gorgonzola cheese to create a flavorful four-cheese pizza, which will give you a different flavor and texture. They also melt well, but be careful not to overcook them. When it is overcooked, the cheese breaks down and becomes greasy.

Would you like all sorts of information about cheese? This includes recipes, what cheese to serve with specific wines, and how cheese is made. You can find these answers at **www. realcaliforniacheese.com**. Check into the "World

Photo Courtesy of Real California Cheese

of Cheese" for details about all types of cheese. This Web site is a good resource for restaurant owners who use various cheeses. The information can be helpful when you experiment with recipes. You can contact them at ed@successfoods.com.

Other Pizza Ingredients

We have the basic ingredients, and now you can be very creative. The possible combinations are unlimited. The Pizza Marketplace Web site offers a free download of "*Choosing the Right Toppings for Your Pizza.*" It explains how to choose the various toppings and discusses trends in toppings.

Some chapters in the book include:

- **Trends** – Are "gourmet" toppings cutting-edge?
- **Meats** – Sales show they're still the top toppings.

- **Vegetables and fruits** – Good tasting and good for you.

- **Seafood** – Tastes of the sea gain popularity.

- **Safe handling** – Temperature and sanitation are vital.

- **Cost and use** – A little math makes a difference in analysis.

- **Marketing** – How you sell is just as important as what you sell.

Visit **www.pizzamarketplace.com** for your free download.

Menu Add-Ons

Some popular add-ons include subs, appetizers, chicken, wings, pasta, soup, salads, and breadsticks or garlic bread.

Appetizers are a great way to increase your average ticket price. They also give some variety and make great impulse purchases. Customers can munch on them while they wait for their order or snack on them when they drive home. Children love breadsticks and cheese sticks.

Chicken wings, mozzarella sticks, chicken tenders, and garlic bread are offered by LaRosa's in Cincinnati. Uno's offers pizza skins, which are a deep-dish pizza crust with mozzarella, whipped and buttered red bliss potatoes, bacon, cheddar cheese, and a dollop of sour cream. Bertucci's in Baltimore offers several seafood appetizers, including Mussels Caruso and shrimp scampi.

You and your employees need to tell customers about your appetizers. Add them to your menu board, menus, and add promo pieces around the public areas to promote them. All order takers need to be trained to up sell and add appetizers to their orders. I used to hold employee contests each month. The employee who sold the most of our selected items won a gift certificate or something similar.

La Nova provides a variety of wing flavors to satisfy each customer's individual taste. These flavors include: Barbecue, Oven-roasted, Italian-style, and Hot-n-Spicy, there's one to please any palate. Customers love the taste, and you'll love the easy preparation of La Nova wings. According to Restaurants  and Institutions magazine, the best selling appetizers are chicken strips, followed by chicken wings. Strips and wings are popular with operators as well, because of their ease of storage, preparation, and serving. For full information, see their Web site: **www.lanova.com** or call 800-6LA-NOVA.

Subs are a good add-on to your menu. There are unlimited possibilities to what you can serve. You can offer subs that use the same toppings that are on your pizzas. These include: Italian subs, veggie subs, a meatball sandwich, and a steak hoagie. If subs do well, check with your suppliers and offer other varieties.

Desserts are a possibility, and dessert pizzas are popular. Donato's serves an apple and cherry dessert pizza. These are easy to make. You don't need different equipment, and most of the ingredients are in your shop.

Pizza shops with a dining area should consider a salad bar. Packaged salads are a good delivery item. You will also need to stock dressing packages. Pizza and salad are a good combination and will be a hit with your health conscious college students. Salads can help you target a new customer base.

Before you make a firm decision to add a salad bar, be sure that you have a good place for the bar. It needs to be convenient for customer flow in the dining room area. You also need enough refrigerated space for these ingredients. There is special equipment for the bar. Some are stainless steel, and others are lightweight plastic, which are portable. When you price the bars, be sure that you include an attached sneeze guard, lighting, rails, and plate chillers. The units are four to six feet long, and prices usually run from $3,000 to $8,000. You can also look for used supply stores.

You can also choose unique beverages. Some of these are offered by Jones Soda. The main categories are: soda, naturals, energy, and organics. Each category includes a wide variety of flavors. You can find complete details at **www.jonessoda.com**. You can contact them by phone: 800-656-6050.

The company has an interesting background which can be read at: **www. jonessoda.com/files_new/about.html**.

Specialty Items

Offering specialty items can set you apart from your competition. Finding ways to prepare menu items in a different way enables you to charge more for them. This can include a secret ingredient in your sauce or an unusual pizza combination. Make the most of these specialty items. They should be

promoted in your pizza shop and on your menu. Feature them on brochure menus and flyers.

Below are some gourmet pizzas being offered throughout the United States. These can help you with new creations. The list is from their menus.

The Gourmet Pizza Shoppe – Redlands, California

- **That's a Gouda** – BBQ sauce, chicken, cilantro, red onion, cashew, gouda, mozzarella

- **Mini Pearl** – Mashed potato, country gravy, fried chicken, mozzarella cheese, country gravy

- **No Kissing Tonight** – Ricotta, pesto sauce, tomato, bacon, red onion, garlic, mozzarella cheese

- **All American Burger** – Thousand Island dressing, ground beef, red onion, dill pickle chips, tomato, Jack cheese, cheddar cheese, and lettuce (after baking)

- **Wild Mayan** – Peanut butter, bacon, red onion, mozzarella cheese, Cholula sauce

Altieri's Pizza – Stow, Ohio

- **Mexican Pizza** – Refried beans and burrito meat topped with tortilla chips, provolone, cheddar, lettuce, black olives, and tomato

- **Ranch Pizza** – Ranch dressing, bacon, mushrooms, red onion, tomato, and provolone

- **Potato Pizza** – Sour cream, potato, pizza sauce, provolone, bacon, and red onion

- **Barkoukis Pizza** – Roasted garlic oil, spinach, gyro meat,

Kalamata olives, tomato, provolone, and feta

- **New Orleans Style Pizza** – Spicy white cheese sauce, provolone, chorizo sausage, chicken, roasted peppers, red onion, sour cream, and Tabasco sauce

Al's Gourmet Pizza – Washington DC

- **Chicken Kabob Pizza** – Marinated chicken, green peppers, onion, tomato, cherry hot peppers, mozzarella and feta cheese, and white garlic sauce

- **Surf and Turf Pizza** – Marinated sirloin, baby shrimp, mushroom, onion, mozzarella and American cheese, and white garlic sauce

- **Jerk Chicken Pizza** – Chicken marinated in jerk sauce and mozzarella cheese

Pomodori's – Cincinnati, Ohio

- **Figs and Prosciutto** – Turkish figs with prosciutto on a garlic and olive oil crust

- **Leeks, Pancetta and Goat Cheese** – Sautéed leeks, pancetta, and goat cheese on a garlic and olive oil crust

- **Gorgonzola and Walnut** – Gorgonzola, walnuts, tomatoes, and pesto sauce

- **Caramelized Onions** – Caramelized onions, gorgonzola, and fresh rosemary on a garlic and olive oil crust

- **Shrimp Asparagus** – Shrimp, asparagus, roasted red pepper with mozzarella and provolone on a fresh-pressed garlic and olive oil crust

California Pizza Kitchen

- **California Club** – Applewood smoked bacon, grilled chicken, mozzarella, Roma tomatoes, chilled lettuce tossed in mayonnaise, and fresh-sliced avocados

Photo Courtesy of Real California Cheese

- **Carna Asada** – Grilled steak, fire-roasted mild chilies, onions, cilantro pesto, Monterey Jack, mozzarella, salsa, and cilantro

- **Peking Duck** – Pan-roasted duck breast, mozzarella, soy-glazed shiitake mushrooms, crispy wontons, slivered green onions, and cilantro ginger Hoisin sauce

- **Thai Chicken** – Chicken breast marinated in a spicy peanut-ginger and sesame sauce, mozzarella, green onions, bean sprouts, julienne carrots, cilantro, and roasted peanuts

- **Wild Mushroom** – Cremini, shiitake, portabella and white mushrooms, Fontina and mozzarella cheeses, and wild mushroom pesto

Uno Chicago Grill

- **Spinoccoli®** – Spinach, broccoli, chunky tomato sauce, feta, cheddar, mozzarella, and grated Romano

- **Shrimp Sea Delico** – Shrimp, pesto, mushrooms, onions, mozzarella, and grated Romano.

- **Roasted Eggplant, Spinach and Feta** – Spinach, roasted eggplant,

sun-dried and plum tomatoes, caramelized onions, basil pesto, feta, and mozzarella

Healthy Options

In the United States, over 60 million people are classified as obese. This is one reason many restaurants are offering healthy sections on their menus. It's almost a public service to offer a healthy menu, but it's also a way to increase the profits for your pizza shop. You can even ask for suggestions about what new items should be added to your menu. This will show you care and can involve new people in your business.

The owner of Altieri's Pizza in Stow, Ohio, has a good friend who was allergic to gluten when he was a child. Altieri found one of his customer's was too, so he searched for a gluten-free crust. He now offers this choice and sells several each day.

LaRosa's, based in Cincinnati, has developed a "light pizza". Their Lite Topper has 60 percent less fat, than a comparable deluxe pizza, with fresh mushrooms and green peppers, red onions, pepperoni, capocolla, and diced Roma tomatoes.

If you decide to make these changes, you don't have to start from scratch. Try adjusting your blend of white flour and whole wheat flour, and add some honey or molasses to counter the bitter taste. Keep in mind you will need two percent more water because of the increased absorption rate. This will lower the gluten level. Wheat flour has a six month shelf life, but you can extend this by storing it in the cooler or freezer.

People are also interested in making other parts of the pizza healthier. This includes low fat cheese and healthier toppings. This can include a variety of vegetables.

Healthy eating is a trend, and it's worth your effort to offer healthy options. Reviewing the basics of nutrition will help you decide which items to include on your menu. The six basic nutrients include proteins, fats, carbohydrates, minerals, vitamins, and water. When you plan your menu, focus on carbohydrates and fats.

Carbohydrates include fiber, starches, and sugars. Carbohydrates provide an important source of energy for the body. Foods that contain carbohydrates include sugar, bread, potatoes, rice, pasta, and fruit. Vegetables contain lower levels of carbohydrates.

Fats provide concentrated energy and twice as many calories as carbohydrates and proteins. There are saturated and unsaturated fats which are differentiated by their chemical structure. Unsaturated fats are healthier. Sources of saturated fats include shortening and butter. Olive and canola oil contain unsaturated fats.

When you create a healthier menu, you can attract the portion of the population with heart disease or other chronic illnesses like diabetes. Ask customers to complete surveys for you, and find out what special needs they have. This will help you serve them better and make educated decisions about menu changes.

Customers with diabetes need to monitor their daily fat, carbohydrate, and protein intake. You can cater to their needs by offering low fat and low protein selections on your menu.

Some valuable resources to help you make these decisions include:

- American Institute of Cancer Research at **www.aicr.org**
- American Heart Association at **www.deliciousdescisions.org**
- American Diabetes Association at **www.diabetes.org**

Some good, healthy cookbooks include:

- *Vegetarian Cooking for Everyone* by Deborah Madison

- *The Joslin Diabetes Gourmet Cookbook* by Bonnie Sanders Polin, PhD, and Frances Towner Giedt

- *The French Culinary Institute's Salute to Healthy Cooking* by Alain Sailhac, Jacques Pepin, Andre Soltner, Jacques Torres, and the Faculty at the French Culinary Institute

- *Healthy Latin Cooking* by Steve Raichlen

- *Good Food Gourmet* by Jane Brody

- *Heart Healthy Cooking for All Seasons* by Marvin Moser, M.D., Larry Forgione, Jimmy Schmidt, and Julie Rubenstein

- *Moosewood Restaurant Low-Fat Favorites* by the Moosewood Collective

- *Canyon Ranch Cooking* by Jeanne Jones

It may be easier to make adjustments to your current recipes. These are some simple ways to tweak your existing menu to cater to additional customers:

- Offer a vegetarian pizza.
- Offer reduced-fat/reduced-calorie salad dressings.
- Use olive or canola oil instead of butter or shortening.
- Offer whole grain dough and breadstick choices.
- Offer low-fat mayonnaise for sandwiches.
- Offer sorbet for dessert.
- Include a simple fruit dessert that is low in sugar and fat.
- Offer smaller portion sizes for some dishes.

An unusual healthy option is available. If you decide to do something a little different, you can also offer smoothie's to your customers. This won't fit into all pizza and sub shops, but smoothies are a cool and refreshing treat for your patrons. The mission of Dr. Smoothie is to provide delicious, high quality beverage and food products that are good for your health, mind, and body. The explosive, full rich flavors of Dr. Smoothie will excite and tantalize your taste buds. Their special blends will amaze you taste

after taste and are available in Original or 100 percent Crushed Fruit varieties. Dr Smoothie offers the equipment and mixes you need to serve healthy and flavorful smoothies for your customers. Visit them on the web at **www.drsmoothie.com** or contact them at 888-466-9941.

Food Allergies

Food allergies can be serious and life-threatening. Common allergies and intolerances include nuts, peanuts, eggs, shellfish, and wheat. It is advisable to ensure ingredient information is available to your customers. You can list these ingredients specifically on your menu. If they are not listed on the menu, your server MUST communicate these details to the customers.

I have all sorts of food allergies and intolerances. This condition is much more prevalent than most people realize. Even a small amount of an offending food can cause the person to become nauseous, vomit, develop hives, have

trouble breathing, and anaphylaxis is even possible. It is critical that special order requests be taken seriously and that allergens are mentioned in person or on your menu.

You can obtain more information about food allergies from the International Food Information Council at 202-296-6540, or **www.ific.org**.

Alcohol

Alcohol Safety

Alcohol sales can be a profit maker if your pizza shop has a wine and beer or liquor license. This is not a completely positive possibility. More and more restaurants are being sued because customers drove drunk after leaving their establishment. If the customer hurts or kills someone, you could be liable. It is critical for everyone in your pizza shop to be aware of the laws and possible liabilities when you serve alcohol.

Blood Alcohol Concentration (BAC) indicates the amount of alcohol in the bloodstream. Alcohol is absorbed directly into the bloodstream from the stomach and intestines. Some factors that affect how alcohol is absorbed into the bloodstream include:

- How much alcohol was consumed
- How quickly it was consumed
- The person's weight
- The person's sex
- The amount of food he ate recently

How can you keep a guest from becoming intoxicated?

- Always check IDs – no exceptions
- Only serve one drink at a time
- Offer customers food while they are drinking
- Keep track of how much they consume
- Know the signs of intoxication

LEVEL 1:

- Talks louder
- Overly friendly

LEVEL 2:

- Difficulty walking or standing
- Slurred speech
- Argumentative
- Reduced muscle coordination – may have trouble picking up change, etc.

An alcohol sales policy – This policy needs to include the federal, state and local laws that govern your alcohol sales. It also needs to lay down rules for your servers. These would include: not selling to minors and not selling to customers who appear to be intoxicated. Set drink limits. For example, you can have a policy that a manager will be notified if a customer has four drinks. This allows the manager to monitor the situation and determine whether to cut off the customer. It's also good to set up a working relationship with a local cab company. This will help you when you suggest that a customer should call a cab.

Train your servers – Your servers MUST follow your alcohol sales policies. They need to track customers' intake, and there is a potential problem. They should offer a menu to customers who are only drinking. You can offer

intoxicated customers free food. They need some food in their stomachs, and this can save you potential problems. Your servers MUST check IDs. The employees who mix drinks need to measure the amount of alcohol they serve. You can hold role playing sessions with employees to allow them to practice these skills. They are critical to your pizza shop, and your employees need to understand this fact. Hold a group discussion after the exercise to find ways to improve.

Incidents will happen – Management needs to be involved right away and to document everything that occurs.

Atlantic Publishing offers a series of 10 full-color posters to help with alcohol awareness. This ten fundamental topics covered are: Right to Refuse Service, One Drink Equals, Spotting a Fake ID, Symptoms of Intoxication, We Check IDs, Drinking & Pregnancy, Blood Alcohol Content Chart—Female, Blood Alcohol Content Chart—Male, Don't Drink & Drive, and

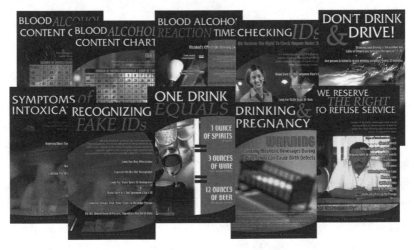

Alcohol Slows Reaction Times. Posters are in full color and laminated to reduce wear. They measure 11" x 17". To order call 800-814-1132 or online at **www.atlantic-pub.com**.

Resources

The National Restaurant Association Educational Foundation offers training materials for your pizza shop. You can find this information at:

- National Restaurant Association – **www.nraef.org**

- International Center for Alcohol Policies – **www.icap.org**

- Atlantic Publishing offers a book titled *The Responsible Service of Alcoholic Beverages: A Complete Staff Training Course for Bars, Restaurants and Caterers–With Companion CD-ROM* (**www. atlantic-pub.com,** Item # RSA-01). This book explains the legal and professional responsibilities of any food service business owner who chooses to search alcoholic beverages of any type. It also walks you through the process of training your employees to responsibly serve alcoholic beverages in your pizza shop.

Serving Alcohol

Beer and wine are popular at dine-in pizza and sub shops. You and your employees should be familiar with the associated terminology.

Wine

It's common for restaurants to serve red and white wine. But, wine is becoming more popular, and restaurants are expanding their wine lists. It's not necessary to stock all types of wine; you can focus on the wines that go with your menu items. Wine can improve the customers' experience and can make the meal more festive. This segment is meant to help you develop and promote a wine list that will work for your pizza shop. But, do not feel that you must serve wine or beer. This is only another suggestion for your menu.

Developing a comprehensive wine list can enhance your customers' experience and increase your profits. Once you develop the wine list, train your serving staff. Wine education can significantly impact the bottom line.

Wine is considered separately from liquor because there are nuances to wine service. Many people enjoy wine with their food, so the server needs a greater knowledge of wine than other alcoholic drinks. When guests order wine, they may pair it with the food they are ordering. This is a good reason to take a wine order after the meal is ordered.

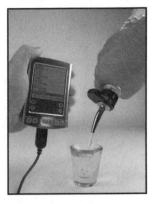

Portion control is critical with all food and beverage items. Nuvo Technologies offers a wireless free pour spout that mounts on the top of open liquor bottles. They are wireless and low profile. This product allows the bartender or server to go on with their responsibilities without being obvious or detracting from the ambiance. Their Web site is: **www.barvision.com/index.html** or you can contact them at 480-222-6000 or by fax at 480-222-6001.

A customer friendly bar needs to be kept clean. In order to keep the area neat and dry, the bartender needs bar towels and mops. Royal Industries offers a couple of choices in various sizes. The details are available at **www. royalindustriesinc.com/source/textiles.php** and they can be contacted at 800-782-1200 or by fax at 800-321-3295.

Serving Wine

These guidelines and tidbits of information will help you serve wine with flair:

- **Bottle sizes** – Most restaurants have 750-milliliter bottles for

sale. You can offer splits of wine or champagne, which are about half the size of a regular bottle. Most restaurants also stock larger bottles of house wines for individual glasses.

- **Wine language** – Your servers need to know the basics about wine, common grape varieties, and how people talk about wine. Your servers need to discuss color, smell ("nose"), and taste ("palate"). Some terms used to describe smell and taste include dry, sweet, earthy, and smoky. Servers should know which wines in your pizza shop are sweet and which are dry. These are the main categories on which guests base their wine decisions. For helpful advice about wine language, visit: **www.demystifying-wine.com**.

- **Reading wine labels** – Franklin Miami Publishing's guide *How to Read Wine Labels* summarizes how you can interpret wine labels. Go to **www.franklinmiamipublishing.com**.

- **Help customers choose wine** – Many customers want their server to offer wine suggestions. Your servers need to be comfortable in this role. For this to work, servers must be familiar with the pizza shop's wine list and how each wine tastes. Wine savvy customers should be helped by the manager or someone else with greater wine knowledge. Encourage your servers to let customers taste the wines you offer by the glass.

- **Serving wine** – Serve red wines at room temperature, and white wines should be chilled to about 50 degrees. Serve wine with the label facing the customer who ordered it. After the customer approves the wine, set the bottle on the corner of the table to open it. Cut the foil off the lower lip of the bottle top, and put the foil in your apron pocket. Remove the cork and pour an ounce or two for the person who ordered it to taste. You can set the cork beside this person so they can inspect it if they want.

After the customer has tasted and approved the wine, pour for all the guests partaking, starting with the women in the group. When you finish pouring a glass, give the bottle a half turn as you raise it to avoid making spills. Keep a napkin against the bottleneck to catch spills. Fill the wine glasses to one-half or two-thirds.

- **Pronunciation** – Your servers need to be familiar with the correct pronunciation of all the wines on your list.

- **Wine and food** – Instruct your servers about which wines compliment each entrée. Include wine suggestions on your menu. This can also increase sales. Your servers still need to be able to make suggestions for customers.

Wine Resources

There are many books and magazines on wine. They include:

- *Exploring Wine: The Culinary Institute of America's Complete Guide to Wines of the World*

- Robert Parker's *Wine Buying Guide*

- Oz Clarke's *Encyclopedia of Wine*

- Hugh Johnson's *Wine Atlas*

- Tom Steven's *New Sotheby's Wine Encyclopedia*

- *Hachette Wine Guide 2002* – "The Definitive Guide to French Wine" is recognized as "The French Wine Bible" and contains over 9,000 wines, chosen from 30,000, and described by 900 experts.

Online Resources

- Wine Spectator at **www.winespectator.com**

- Wine and Spirits – **www.wineandspiritsmagazine.com**

- Wine Enthusiast –**www.wineenthusiast.com**

- Tasting Wine – **www.tasting-wine.com/html/etiquette.html**

- Good Cooking's wine terminology: **www.goodcooking.com/ winedefs.asp**

- American Institute of Wine and Food has information on local chapters at **www.aiwf.org**

- Wines.com – **www.wines.com** offers expert answers, virtual wine tastings, and an online searchable database

Wine Training

A good way to train your staff about wine is to let them taste it! Hold regular wine tastings for your staff. You can use wine-tasting cards for them to fill out about the wine specifics. Wine vendors can help with the training. Hold sessions to taste menu items with wine to help the server understand how the wine and food items taste together. Train servers to pour wine from the bottle by using empty bottles with colored water.

Atlantic Publishing offers a series of five full-color posters to help train your staff on wine. This series covers all the basics—from service to pronunciation. Essential information for anyone serving, pouring, or selling wine, yet attractive enough to display in your dining room. Posters are laminated to reduce wear and tear and measure 11" x 17". The posters are $9.95 each and include: Wine Pronunciation Guide, Proper Wine Service, Red Wine, White Wine, and Sparkling Wine & Champagne. To order call 800-814-

1132 or visit **www.atlantic-pub.com**.

Beer

Beer may be packaged in bottles, can, or on tap. But, it is perishable and has a shelf life. It is best to adhere to some simple procedures to ensure a fresh and full flavor. Exposure to light and extreme temperatures are the enemies of beer. To counteract this problem you can store beer in a dark, cool place.

The hundreds of brands of beer fall into five categories. They include:

- **Lagers** – The most popular

- **Ales** – Contain more hops and are stronger in flavor

- **Porter, stout,** and **bock beer**s – Heavier, darker, richer, and sweeter

Of the hundreds of brands available, less than a dozen are primarily demanded by customers. However, "micro-brewed" beers have come on strong. It is common to have your most popular beer on draught—most customers prefer it that way and it is cheaper for you. Since beer is perishable, it is better to buy the less popular brands in bottles or cans to preserve their freshness. Most draft systems use three separate kegs. Use all three if you can.

Imported beers are gaining popularity. These are 50 to 100 percent more expensive than domestic beers, but customers still demand popular ones. You should stick to the three or four more popular imported beers.

Light beer has fewer calories than other beer and has been in greater demand in the past five years. A couple of light beers should be included on your list.

Draft Beer

If you plan to serve draft beer, know how much beer is in a keg.

A barrel = 31 gallons = 13.8 cases of 12 ounce bottles

Kegs of draft beer used at most on-premise establishments are actually half-barrels. Assuming a one-inch head, there are approximately two hundred 12-ounce servings per keg or about one hundred and fifty 16-ounce servings, depending on the glass used.

There is a specific way to pour a glass of beer. Draught beer should be poured in a way to produce a head that rises just above the top of the glass or pitcher. This settles to about three quarters of an inch in a few minutes. This head or foam has great economical and aesthetic value. You can control the size of the head by the angle of the glass or mug to the spout when you begin to pour. If the head is too small, you are pouring too much beer into each glass. This leads to lower than expected yield on each keg. If you pour

and make a bigger head than usual, it gives the impression that you are cutting corners on quality.

Beer must be served in cold, spotless glasses or mugs. A glass may seem clean, but may still have a buildup of soap or grease. Any trace of soap or grease breaks down the head, causes bubbles in the beer and will leave a stale-looking product. Rinse each glass in cold, fresh water before filling. Use a clean glass with each beer; never refill a glass.

Beer temperature is a crucial element. Proper flavor can be ensured when the beer is served at 40° F. When beer is served below 38° F, it loses its distinct taste and aroma. Beer served above 42° F may turn cloudy and loses its zest and flavor. Draught beer is not pasteurized, so it needs to be kept at a constant temperature. Set beer coolers at 38° F to maintain proper serving temperature. Always use chilled glasses and mugs (with thick glass and handles) to keep the beer at a cool, constant temperature.

It is important to flush your beer lines weekly. Beer quality is affected by the lines it flows through. Your professional tap and line cleaner are needed weekly. Ask your beer distributor to recommend a reputable company.

Other Types of Alcohol

Some pizza restaurants serve mixed drinks. You have the option of a full bar or select drinks. These can be divided into two basic categories: well items and call items.

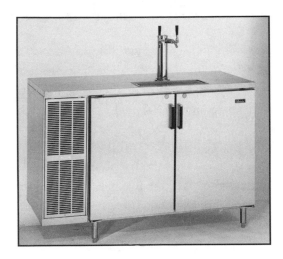

Select restaurants have a three-tier system which includes: well, call, and premium liquor. Premium liquor would have an additional surcharge.

Perlick's Bar and Beverage Equipment Division manufactures equipment used in the bar environment. This equipment includes refrigerated and non -refrigerated cabinets, stainless steel underbar equipment, glasswashers, and the revolutionary modular bar structure which completes the bar package. They have everything you need for beer and wine tapping. Check their Web site at **www.perlick.com** or you can contact them by phone at 414-353-7060 or by fax at 414-353-7069 or 800-558-5592.

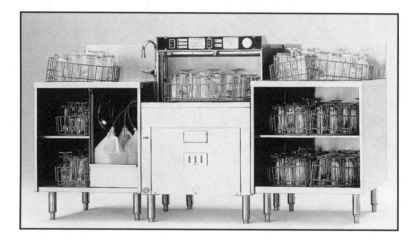

The items mentioned in this chapter are a wide variety of items you can serve. The choices are up to you and should fit your target customers. You can also adjust your food and beverage choices as you see how well the items sell.

If you do decide to sell alcohol, Atlantic Publishing offers an excellent series of alcohol service posters. Decorative and instructional, these full-color posters will be popular with both your employees and customers. Containing essential information, drink photos, recipes, and more, they will

help increase sales and grab attention. Posters are laminated to reduce wear and tear and measure 11" x 17". The topics include: 12 Classic Cocktails with Recipes, 12 Popular Cocktails with Recipes, Types of Beer, Categories of Liquor, 10 Types of Martinis, Drink Garnishes, and Common Bar Abbreviations. To order call 800-814-1132 or visit **www.atlantic-pub. com**.

GENERATIONS OF PIZZA

I come from a long line of pizza makers and pizza shop owners. Everyone sold hoagies too—they weren't subs—they were hoagies. Did I mention we're Italian? Both sides of the family. You learned a lot at family gatherings: what kind of ovens were the best, who had the best sauce, and where could you get pizza boxes for less. You also learned you were expected to work in the pizza shop. By the time I was middle school age, if I was not hanging out and doing small jobs for the family restaurant, I was putting together pizza boxes at my grandmother's pizza shop. I eventually graduated to checking the pizzas and taking orders.

What you decide to serve depends a lot on what you're good at. Sure, people's tastes change and they like different things, but the truth is if you make one thing really well, they'll keep coming back. New menu items entice them, but it's the old stand-bys that sell. My uncle's pizza is rated number one in the area where we live. He's been using the same recipe for 30 years. He's branched out and offers more variety than he used to, but his pizza is what sells. When Mexican food suddenly became popular (maybe 10 years ago in our area), he was one of the first to offer taco salads to go. He still offers them on the menu. Twenty-five years ago, my aunt struggled with the problem of drumming up more business and what could she make to lure the customers. Everyone already loved their pizza (like my uncle's, but the other side of the family!), so she decided to use the same pizza and fold it in half. With all of the "toppings" people requested in the center, it resembled a calzone in taste and appearance. But she didn't call it that. She called it Inside-Out Pizza. People bought it. By using the same ingredients as pizza and not having to stock anything more, it was a win-win situation for her and it did draw people.

It never hurts to add new items in a small way. You could have mushrooms for a topping, but when different types of mushrooms show up in the grocery store, they better show up on your pizzas, too. Portabella mushrooms are 'hot'. Offering baby portabella mushrooms on your pizza is not going to add much to the overhead, but it will give you bragging rights and bring people in to the store.

The best way to determine if you should add something to the menu is to shop around. Know your own market. If people are going down the street to buy a fish sandwich, and just pick up a pizza while there, you need to consider adding fish sandwiches so they'll think about picking it up at your place—where they would really have the pizza.

—*Tara Manderino,* **www.geocities.com/tjmanderino**

Recipe Development and Production

Your menu items and recipes can be an ongoing work-in-progress. People may request special topping combinations. Some of these combinations may appeal to other customers. You may want to add various appetizers and entrees to increase customer appeal. Never feel that your menu has to stay the same. You own the business and can alter items.

Ask your employees if they have suggestions. We used to make breakfast pizzas for the crew. This was a nice treat when we all came in early for a big event or to special order for the local colleges or schools. The possibilities are truly only limited by your imagination.

Experimentation

Experimenting enables you to find the best ingredients for a quality product that you can offer at a fair and profitable price. Perfection isn't always possible, so find a reasonable compromise for your customers, your employees, and your profits. You may find a product that is gorgeous and tastes incredible. But, if the price is unreasonable, rework it or forget it. Also consider the scenario that your customers love an item, but you have to hire an additional person or purchase costly ingredients, leaving you no profit.

- **Your ingredients** – Which dough will you use? Do you prefer canned mushrooms or fresh? Will you use one type of cheese or several blends?

- **Your formula** – Which ingredients should be used in which combinations and proportions?

- **What cooking temperature(s) and baking times?** – There are endless possibilities, and many depend on the type of oven you use. Do you have a computerized oven? Are they gas powered or conveyor ovens? You can use 450° for five minutes or 375° for 20 minutes. There is also the option to adjust your bake times depending on fan usage. One thing that made a difference for me was how busy I was and how quickly the pizzas needed to cook.

- **Your pan** – You can use a wide, shallow, or tall pan or maybe a screen.

- **Prep possibilities** – Will you purchase grated cheese or grate it yourself?

- **Tantalizing appearance** – Are your edges brown enough and did the dough rise enough?

- **Taste** – Does the pizza melt in your mouth? Will it make the customer want to come back?

Ask Employees for Help

When you hire your staff, remember people with experience can be invaluable. Others within the pizza business can offer suggestions. Qualified and helpful vendors and suppliers can be a wonderful resource for product testing and selection.

- **Equipment manufacturers** – Your sales representative can arrange for you to visit the company's kitchens. An alternative is to have your salesperson work with your employees. The oven manufacturers can help you learn to use their equipment for the best possible baking situation.

- **Utility company** – In some areas, the gas and electric companies have test kitchens with equipment. This will give you a chance to test the equipment before you make a decision.

- **Food distributors** – Have them bring you samples (enough to make one or two small batches) of various flour grinds/blends to test. Their representatives often have baking experience and other resources they can share.

- **Water company** – Your local water company can test your water and evaluate its condition. Water hardness and the pH factor can cause problems with your recipes.

We used to have fun experimenting with topping combinations. It might be chicken and barbecue sauce. Sometimes we played with breakfast pizza ideas. We even experimented with dessert pizza ideas. The possibilities are only limited by your imagination and the toppings you bring to the kitchen.

Test Your Ideas

When you are gathering ideas and suggestions about new products and menu items, consider whether these items will require different ingredients or equipment. You may also need to update menus and signage. This is a list of things to consider before you implement changes and additions to your menu:

- Offer the item as a daily special and let customers comment about the item. It might be good as an occasional special, but find out if enough people would want it on a regular basis.

- You can include a self-addressed, prepaid postcard with questions for carryout and delivery orders. Even though you don't see these customers in your pizza shop, you still need their thoughts.

- On a busy evening, you can pass out samples and ask customers for their comments. Do they like it? Would they buy it? Would it be good for lunch or dinner? Would they buy more than one?

Set Production Standards

First, decide which products you will offer. Second, be sure what needs to be done to produce each item. This includes what ingredients to use, what equipment is needed and how it will be produced. These are the beginning stages of developing your production standards:

- **Shift production volume** – Establish how much prep and what other duties need to be completed during each shift.

- **Quality standards** – Educate your staff on the quality standards for products and service. Let them know what is not acceptable.

- **Acceptable substitutions** – If there are w.
  adjustments, educate your staff about wha

Shift Production Volume

One technique is to set specific duties for each shift. In many pizza shops, the early or dayshift can do a lot of prep work with minimal staff. If you choose to buy foods and prep yourself, you will require an additional prep person. However, a shift manager and one delivery person can usually prep foods, boxes, etc. for the evening shift.

When the schedule writer knows it will be unusually busy, it is good to have an additional person to ensure your prep work is complete before the evening shift. These times can include special local events, sports' playoff games, local favorite sports teams playing during the shifts, special events at local colleges, etc. These events can make you much busier, and you need to be properly staffed to complete the prep work. If you get to a busy night shift without the proper prep, business can grind to a halt. This will cause all sorts of problems, and customer service and product quality will suffer.

Another thing that works well is to schedule an additional person for a "short" shift. While this employee will leave first, he is required to work until the minimal work is complete. Train your shift managers to know when to effectively let this person go home in order to save unnecessary labor dollars while ensuring the work is complete.

The nightshift needs to complete their work before they leave. This will include washing dishes, cleaning the makeline and prep area, ensuring minimal boxes are folded for the next day and enough food is prepped for dayshift, etc. When either shift fails to finish their assignments, the next shift will suffer. But, your customers will also suffer because the prep work was not completed.

 Standards

Determine what level of quality is and is not acceptable. When a product is substandard, it should be thrown away. Be careful that people don't make substandard products in order to get free food. You may be skeptical, but it does happen.

Your quality standards can include many things:

- Ingredients
- Appearance
- Temperature
- Taste
- Smell
- Texture

These are just some of the things to consider, but each is important in presenting a professional and quality product and service.

Acceptable Substitutions

When your pizza shop is swamped with business or someone under-ordered supplies, you need to have substitution requirements. There will be times when you sell more than you expect, and you must offer an alternative or tell the customer that the particular item is not available. Either solution can work if your employees and managers understand how to handle the situation.

We've all been to restaurants that ran out of the special or another item. If your policy is to tell the customer the item is unavailable, the server must handle it in a courteous way. Some people will be upset, and you can only prevent a certain number of problems. But, courteous behavior will cut down on the number of complaints you receive.

Do you want to plan substitutions when you run out of a prepared item or ingredients? This is acceptable as well, but decide what substitutions are

acceptable before there is a shortage.

Another possible solution is to offer a similar product at a slightly lesser cost. This needs to be done on a limited basis, but can be a solution when you run out of particular dishes. The practice can keep established customers happy when there's a problem.

You want to maintain a certain quality standard for your pizza and sub shop. All employees, and particularly your managers, need to know what is expected. When you find problems or substandard products and services, deal with the problems right away. Many people will let your standards slide if they feel you aren't committed to them. By enforcing the standards, you will confirm that you believe in them and expect your employees and managers to live by these standards.

RECIPE CREATION

The most important thing in developing recipes for a restaurant is to make sure all ingredients and procedures are accurately documented, because in the food service industry the turnover is very high, so you want to make sure that you do all you can to be sure the product will be the same at all times.

Also make sure that the ingredients placed on the pizza are specified in what order (do you want the cheese on top, should there be a splash of olive oil on the top of the cheese to help it melt, etc), and remember cooking times in the order the ingredients are placed on the pizza. The ingredients that need the least time to cook (such as pepperoni) should go underneath the ingredients such as fresh bell peppers, so the peppers have time to cook. Also, any ingredients that are flat should go underneath the thicker items. Note things such as: will you use pre-cooked sausage or shaved, partially frozen sausage; will you use shredded cheese or sliced, what kinds of cheese (pre-mixed, if more than one kind, or not, what portion of cheeses). Much of the prep can be done beforehand, such as slicing ingredients; just make sure not to have too much on hand, because if they sit for too long they will lose their freshness.

The two most important things to remember are: your product has to be consistent, so when people come back they get the same thing they had before; and you want to create food that makes people want to come there. There are a lot of places people can go to buy pizza, [and] you have to make sure your food and service is distinctive, so they will want to go to you.

—Chef Kevin Smith, door2door gourmet (catering, menu planning, and consulting), Orlando, FL, **kjoel_arts@yahoo.com**

10

Recipes to Sample and Inspire New Creations

I've included some recipes for you in this chapter. Some are for dough, sauce, pizzas, entrees, appetizers and desserts. There are an interesting variety of recipes to give you some ideas when you plan your menu items.

There is also a list of website addresses at the end for other Italian recipes. You can use the recipes as they are, or play with them, and make some adjustments.

Photo Courtesy of Real California Cheese

Pizza Dough Recipes

BASIC DOUGH RECIPE

For a chewy and thick crust, use this recipe for one 14" pizza.

6 oz. warm water (105 to 115 degrees)	½ tsp. salt
4 tsp. sugar	1 tsp. active dry yeast
1 tsp. regular olive oil	2¼ cups high gluten flour – sift and pack lightly

Be sure the water is between 105 and 115 degrees (warm to the touch on the back of your hand). Do NOT use hot water because the yeast will not work. Mix the sugar, olive oil, salt, yeast, and warm water, until the yeast dissolves. (If the yeast doesn't foam, it is bad.)

Place flour in a mixer bowl, and pour yeast mixture over top. Knead on low speed for about 15 minutes. While the dough is mixing, remove dough from the dough hook in order to mix all dough thoroughly.

Once dough is mixed, place it in a large bowl and mix with a sturdy spoon to be sure all liquid is absorbed into the dough. (If you are used to kneading bread dough, you will be surprised at the elastic consistency of pizza dough.) Place the dough on a sturdy table and knead vigorously – press, fold, and stretch dough for about 15 minutes. (Larger batches will take longer.) When the dough is kneaded properly, it will be smooth and soft.

Dough will be sticky when you're kneading it, but it shouldn't stick to your hands. If it's not sticky, add water to your hands while you knead the dough. But, do not add any water or flour until you knead it for at least 5 minutes.

The dough should be formed into a ball after kneading. Divide the dough into the number of pizzas you want to make, and shape into dough balls. (If you tripled the recipe, divide into three balls.) Place each dough ball into a large plastic bag, and place on the counter. The open end of the bag should be placed under the dough ball. Cover dough with a towel while it rises for about an hour to an hour-and-a-half. After this time, punch down the dough, and put in the refrigerator with the end of the bag tucked under the dough ball.

This is an acceptable process for a few pizzas, but if you plan to sell a lot of pizza, you should consider buying a mixing machine. (Get at least a 250 watt motor, or it probably won't mix dough.)

BASIC DOUGH RECIPE 11	
This recipe makes enough for two 12" pizzas.	
1½ cups warm water	1½ tsp. salt
2 Tbs. sugar	2 Tbs. olive oil
1¼ oz. dry yeast	3½ cups all-purpose flour (may need to add a little more)

Pour warm water in large bowl and add sugar and yeast. Stir until yeast and sugar dissolve. It will take about 10 minutes for the yeast to activate. It will get foamy as it reacts. If it doesn't become foamy, the yeast is old. Replace it and start over.

Stir in salt and oil and mix well. Add one cup of flour, and mix until combined. Add second and third cup of flour individually and combine. The mixture will become thicker with each cup of flour. Add ½ cup of flour with your hands. You may need to add ¼ to ½ cup of flour to make the right consistency. Take the dough from the bowl and place on floured tabletop to knead. Add more flour to tabletop, if needed. Fold the dough over in halves and quarters for about 8 to 10 minutes or 100 times. This is an important step and it's better to knead too much instead of too little. The dough should become a smooth consistency and stop sticking to your hands.

Rub the dough with a light coat of olive oil and place in a bowl which is also coated with small amount of oil. Cover bowl, and leave in a warm place or unlit oven. The dough should be left alone and will rise for 60 to 90 minutes. It will be at least double in size at this time. Remove dough from the bowl and cut in half with a knife to create two dough balls. Mold them into balls, press flat to remove any air, and reshape into a ball. Smooth the ball and tuck the dough inside itself from the bottom. You are now ready to store the dough.

THIN CRUST PIZZA
This 30 pound recipe is enough for 30 to 40 medium pizzas.

2-½ oz. of yeast	10 Tbs. salt
70 cups or 20 lbs. high gluten flour	20-22 cups or 10-11 lbs. water

Crumble yeast in the flour and add salt. Combine with water with mixer at medium speed for 12 to 14 minutes or until dough pulls away from the side of the bowl and is not sticky. Knead and shape into balls, as needed.

NEW YORK STYLE PIZZA DOUGH
One 12-14" pizza.

1 cup warm water	1 Tbs. corn meal
2 Tbs. milk	1 Tbs. olive oil
2 tsp. brown sugar	1 package yeast
1 tsp. salt	3 cups all-purpose flour
1 Tbs. shortening	

Mix water, milk, brown sugar, salt, and shortening on low speed for 1 minute. Add corn meal, olive oil, and yeast and mix for another minute. Let mix sit for 5 minutes. Add flour and combine with your hands till smooth. Place flour on tabletop, and knead for 8 to 10 minutes. Form into a ball, and place in a warm place to rise for 1 hour.

CORNMEAL PIZZA DOUGH
This creates enough dough for two 15" pizzas.

3 cups bread flour	1 Tbs. sugar
½ cup finely ground yellow cornmeal	½ tsp. kosher salt
	2 Tbs. olive oil
1½ tsp. yeast	1 cup water

Combine yeast, 1 Tbs. sugar, and ¼ cup warm water and set aside. Combine flour, cornmeal, salt, oil, and 1 Tbs. sugar in a mixing bowl. Yeast will become foamy, then add to the flour mixture and mix. Add the remaining water and mix well. Knead dough on a floured surface until smooth and elastic (about 5 minutes). Place in oiled bowl and cover to let it rise until doubled (1 hour). Punch down, and allow it to rise again. Once it rises again, it's ready to use.

GLUTEN-FREE AND WHEAT-FREE PIZZA DOUGH

You don't need to sacrifice taste with this pizza dough. Enough for 4 pizzas.

1 Tbs. gluten-free dry yeast	1 tsp. unflavored gelatin powder
⅔ cup brown rice or bean flour	1½ tsp. Italian seasoning
½ cup tapioca flour	⅔ cup warm water
2 Tbs. dry or non-dairy milk	½ tsp. honey
2 tsp. xanthum gum	1½ tsp. olive oil
½ tsp. salt	1 tsp. cider vinegar

Preheat oven to 425 degrees.

Combine dry ingredients in medium bowl at low speed. Add warm water and remaining ingredients on high speed for 3 minutes. Add additional water if necessary, one tablespoon at a time.

Spray pan with cooking spray, and place dough in a 12" pizza pan or on a baking sheet for a thin crispy crust. Sprinkle rice flour on dough then press into pan. Shape higher edges and keep bottom of dough consistent in thickness. Bake crust for 10 minutes. Remove from oven and top with sauce and toppings. Bake for 20 to 25 minutes or until browned.

WHOLE WHEAT PIZZA DOUGH
Healthy pizza dough with a gourmet taste.

1½ cups warm water	2 Tbs. olive oil
2 Tbs. sugar	3 cups bread flour
2½ oz. yeast	1 cup whole wheat flour
1½ tsp. salt	

Pour warm water in a large bowl, and add sugar and yeast. Stir until yeast and sugar dissolve. It will take about 10 minutes for the yeast to activate. It will get foamy as it reacts. If it doesn't become foamy, the yeast is old. Replace it and start over.

Stir in salt and oil and mix well. Add one cup of flour, and mix until combined. Add one cup of whole wheat flour and mix well. Add second and third cup of flour individually and combine. The mixture will become thicker with each cup of flour. Add ½ cup of flour with your hands. You may need to add ¼ to ½ cup of flour to make the right consistency. Take the dough from the bowl, and place on floured tabletop to knead. Add more flour to tabletop if needed. Fold the dough over in halves and quarters for about 8 to 10 minutes or 100 times. This is an important step, and it's better to knead too much instead of too little. The dough should become a smooth consistency and stop sticking to your hands.

Rub the dough with a light coat of olive oil, and place in bowl also coated with small amount of oil. Cover bowl and leave in a warm place or unlit oven. The dough should be left alone and will rise for 60 to 90 minutes. It will be at least double in size at this time. Remove dough from the bowl and cut in half with a knife to create two dough balls. Mold them into balls, press flat to remove any air, and reshape into a ball. Smooth the ball and tuck the dough inside itself from the bottom. You are now ready to store the dough.

TYPES OF CHEESE FOR PIZZAS*

Do not overuse sharp cheeses because they are salty. When you blend cheeses, use sharp cheese for half of the combination.

American	Muenster
Asiago	Parmesan
Feta	Provolone – domestic or imported
Fontino	
Goat	Ricotta
Mild cheddar	Sharp American
Monterey Jack	Sharp cheddar
Mozzarella	

CHEESE CHOICES FOR TOMATO PIZZA – MOZZARELLA AND PROVOLONE MIX

Mozzarella – ¾	
Provolone – ¼	

ALTERNATIVES TO PROVOLONE

Mild cheddar (white)	American
Muenster	Monterey Jack
Swiss	

CHEESE CHOICES FOR VEGETABLE, MEAT, AND SEAFOOD PIZZAS – BLEND

Provolone or Mozzarella – ½	Sharp American – ½

Pizza Sauces

BASIC PIZZA SAUCE
This recipe will produce enough sauce for one 14" pizza.

6 oz. tomato product	2 tsp. sugar (tone down the acidity of the tomato)
1 Tbs. tomato paste (no salt added)	¼ tsp. garlic powder (1 garlic clove)
1 Tbs. regular olive oil	¼ tsp. salt (only if no salt in any tomato products)
¾ tsp. fresh, chopped oregano, or basil (¼ tsp. ground oregano)	Dash of pepper

Don't overuse the oil because it will pool on top of the pizza when it cooks.

BACARDI BBQ PIZZA SAUCE
Yields 2 cups.

1 cup – butter or margarine	½ cup fresh lemon juice
1 ½ cups BACARDI Rum Gold Label	2 Tbs. chopped garlic
1 ¼ cups ketchup	1 tsp. salt
1 cup orange juice	½ tsp. black pepper
¾ cup honey	¼ tsp. cayenne pepper

In saucepan, over medium-high heat, melt butter. Stir in Bacardi rum, ketchup, orange juice, honey, lemon juice, garlic, and seasonings. Cook, stirring occasionally, for about 40 minutes or until thickened, leaving you plenty of time to find other things to do with the remaining contents of the bottle.

Chicken: Cut a 3-pound chicken into serving size pieces. Brush sauce on chicken during the last 10 minutes of grilling, turning, and brushing frequently.

Ribs: Grill three-pound pork or beef ribs and brush on sauce during the last 10 minutes of grilling, turning and brushing frequently.

CLASSIC TOMATO PIZZA SAUCE
Yield 2 quarts.

3 Tbs. butter or margarine	¼ tsp. black pepper
16 oz. tomato puree	2 large yellow onions, minced
3 Tbs. olive oil	1 tsp. whole oregano
1 tsp. salt	2 Qt. canned whole Italian tomatoes
3 cloves garlic, minced	
	1 tsp. whole basil

In a Dutch oven or large skillet, melt the butter with the olive oil, and slowly but completely sauté the garlic and onion. Add the tomatoes, salt, pepper, oregano, basil, and puree. Bring to a boil, then simmer covered for 2 hours. Stir occasionally, crushing the tomatoes with a potato masher. Continue to mash; stir, and simmer partially covered until the sauce reaches the consistency of a rich soup.

If you find you have too many, or too large, tomato seeds left in the sauce, you may run the sauce through a sieve (strainer). Set the sauce aside to cool or refrigerate before applying it to your pizza dough.

MAMA MIA PIZZA SAUCE
Yields 2¼ cups.

12 oz. tomato paste	¼ tsp. black pepper
1½ cup water	¼ tsp. sugar
1 tsp. ground oregano	⅛ tsp. garlic powder
½ tsp. basil	⅛ tsp. onion powder
¼ tsp. salt	

Combine dry ingredients into a small container and set aside. In a pan, combine tomato paste with water until it's a uniform consistency. When it bubbles, add spices and reduce heat to medium-low. Simmer, uncovered, 35 to 40 minutes until it reaches desired thickness. Stir occasionally. Cover and cool.

Refrigerate in an airtight container, until needed, or for 4 weeks maximum.

NEW YORK-STYLE PIZZA SAUCE

14 oz. Roma or Furmano's whole peeled tomatoes	¼ tsp. dried basil, crushed
	¼ tsp. dried marjoram, crushed
14 oz. Roma or Furmano's pizza sauce	
	½ tsp. Garlic salt
½ tsp. dried oregano, crushed	¼ tsp. Cayenne black pepper

Combine all ingredients in a large pot, bring to a boil, and then let simmer for 1 hour.

MARINARA SAUCE
Serves 6.

¼ cup olive oil	3 basil leaves – washed, dried, and chopped
4 cloves garlic minced	
35 oz. can of imported Italian tomatoes	1 tsp. of oregano
	Salt & pepper to taste

Sauté garlic in a sauce pan with olive oil. Lower heat to medium until garlic is soft and browned. Crush tomatoes and use their juices. Fill ¼ of an empty can with water and add to tomatoes. Mix basil, oregano, salt, and pepper. Bring mixture to a boil and lower heat to simmer until sauce is thickened, in about 20 to 30 minutes.

RANCH & CREAM CHEESE SAUCE (CHILLED)

1 small package Philadelphia Cream Cheese	⅔ cup mayonnaise
	⅔ cup sour cream
1 envelope Hidden Valley Ranch Dressing Mix (Dry)	⅛ tsp. seasoning salt
	1 Tbs. parsley, fresh, minced

Prepare this sauce, whipping these ingredients to a smooth texture with the consistency of a cake batter. Chill for 1 hour, stiffening the sauce like topping. Spread over a pre-baked pizza crust, then add pre-cooked or cold toppings for a chilled appetizer pizza.

SMOKY BAR-B-Q SAUCE

15 oz. canned tomato sauce	¼ cup light molasses
¼ cup apple cider vinegar	1 tsp. dry mustard
2 Tbs. virgin olive oil	1 tsp. Concentrated Hickory
7 to 10 oz. Lipton Recipe Secrets Onion Soup Mix	Seasoning Liquid Smoke or equivalent

Combine all ingredients in a sauce pan and bring to a boil. Simmer for 10 minutes, stirring constantly. Let cool and store in the refrigerator, or use immediately on cooked ribs, chicken, or seafood. It's great for dipping, too.

WHITE SAUCE FOR PIZZA

This rich, creamy smooth white sauce recipe is a nice alternative to tomato pizza sauces. Use this buttery sauce with your shrimp, chicken, or vegetable pizza.

⅓ cup flour	¼ tsp. onion powder
1 tsp. salt	2 cups milk
⅛ tsp. black pepper	1 Tbs. sweet, lightly-salted butter
⅛ tsp. paprika	1 Tbs. fresh minced garlic (optional)

In a sauce pan, on low heat, melt the butter and slowly add the flour, combine and stir constantly with a whip for 3 minutes. Raise heat to medium. Add ½ cup of milk, whipping until the sauce begins to cream and add another ½ cup milk, then repeat. Add the last ½ cup of milk, stirring until the sauce is bubbly (low boil), and creamy, about 3 minutes.

Add the remaining seasonings and cook a final 2 minutes, or until the sauce reaches a rich, heavy, gravy-like consistency.

Don't walk away from the stove...keep stirring! Remove from heat. Let the sauce cool to room temperature before saucing your pizza with it.

NOTE: Optional Preparation: Add Extra Garlic Zing. Try adding the garlic, along with the rest of the seasonings, to this sauce for extra flavor.

Pizza Sauce Toppings

BASIL PESTO PIZZA SAUCE TOPPING

Sprinkle this on top of your pizza or place on tables for your customers to try.

14 walnuts, shelled	4 Tbs. sweet, unsalted butter
3 Tbs. pine nuts, shelled	3 cups fresh, whole basil leaves
1 tsp. sea salt or kosher salt	8 oz. grated parmesan cheese or 4 oz. grated Romano cheese and 4 oz. parmesan cheese
4 black peppercorns	
3 garlic cloves	1 ½ cups extra virgin olive oil

Place all ingredients, except olive oil, in a food processor to grind until fine.

Add 1 cup of olive oil and combine well. Add remaining olive oil, and blend until sauce is very smooth. Use immediately, or refrigerate in an air-tight, glass container. Use at room temperature.

Appetizers and Miscellaneous

FETTUNTA

Toasted bread with olive oil

Loaf of bread	Garlic clove
Extra virgin olive oil	Salt & pepper

Cut the bread about 1-inch thick. Toast or grill on both sides and rub with garlic clove. Place bread on serving platter and drizzle oil over it. Add a dash of salt and pepper to taste. Serve while hot. The bread can be topped with chopped tomatoes or tomato sauce. Or, you can dip in warm pizza or marinara sauce.

ITALIAN SAUSAGE PIZZA ROLL BREAD

DOUGH:	FILLING:
4 cups flour	1½ lb. sweet Italian sausage
1 tsp. salt	12 oz. tomato paste
2½ oz. dry yeast	3 Tbs. minced onion
1¼ cup warm water	3 tsp. minced garlic
2 Tbs. olive oil	3 tsp. oregano
1 Tbs. sugar	⅔ cups shredded Romano cheese
	1½ cups shredded mozzarella cheese
	2 Tbs. olive oil

Dough: Mix flour and salt in a large bowl. Create a well in center and add yeast, water, oil, and sugar. Let stand for 5 minutes until yeast becomes foamy. Beat ingredients with a spoon to make soft dough. Knead on a floured surface until smooth and elastic. Add more flour, if needed. Place in a greased bowl cover and let double.

Filling: Crumble sausage and cook over medium-high heat. Drain fat and stir in paste, onion, and seasonings. Remove from heat and let cool. Punch down dough, and divide in half. Roll each part into a 14 x 9 inch rectangle. Spread ½ of filling within ½ inch of the edge. Top with ½ of cheeses. Drizzle with oil. Roll like a jelly roll—roll on one long side. Pinch edges and tuck under to seal. Place on large baking sheet seam side down, 2 inches apart.

Bend each roll into a crescent shape. Bake in a 400°F oven for 45 minutes, or until golden. Cool 30 minutes before cutting. Serve warm or at room temperature. You can dip in warm pizza or marinara sauce for a variation.

PIZZA BREAD

Served warm or cooled. You can dip in pizza or marinara sauce.

2½ oz. dry yeast	16 oz. canned chopped tomatoes
¾ cup warm water	5 large fresh basil leaves
3 cups all-purpose, unbleached flour	2 cloves garlic, minced
1 tsp. salt	⅛ tsp. salt
6 Tbs. olive oil	

Dissolve the yeast in ½ cup of warm water and let sit until it becomes foamy. Combine flour, salt, yeast mixture, and remaining water. Mix thoroughly with a wooden spoon then with your hands. Place on a floured work surface and knead for a few minutes until smooth. Place in a well oiled bowl, cover with plastic wrap, and let rise until doubled, about 1½ hours.

Punch down and place on an oiled 9-inch cake pan. Drain the chopped tomatoes and spread across the surface of the focaccia, then sprinkle with garlic and shredded basil leaves. Dimple the top surface with your fingertips, and drizzle with oil, sprinkle with coarse salt. Preheat the oven to 425°. Bake about 20 minutes or until golden. Serve warm or at room temperature.

PANE DORATO

Golden fried bread

6 slices of bread – cut pieces 1-inch thick	Extra virgin olive oil
8 oz. or 1 cup milk	Salt to taste
2 eggs – beaten	4 oz. gruyere cheese – optional

Fill half of a heavy iron frying pan with oil. Soak pieces of bread in milk for a few minutes then dip bread in beaten eggs. Heat oil and place bread in the pan individually, to fry each side for 10 minutes or until golden brown. Remove from oil and drain on a paper towel. Sprinkle with salt and serve hot. Sandwich bread is best for this recipe. An alternative is to place thin slices of Gruyer cheese on top of hot fried pieces of bread. This bread is good with soups or dipped in pizza or marinara sauce.

POSSIBLE PIZZA TOPPINGS: MEATS

Bacon	Pepperoni (Higher grease content, especially when the pepperoni is doubled)
Canadian bacon	
Chicken (Better if pre-cooked)	
Ground beef (Fresh ground beef may contain a lot of fat.)	Pork
	Pork sausage
Ground pork (Low-fat content)	Prosciutto (Italian ham – should be used sparingly)
Ground turkey (Low-fat content)	Salami
	Turkey (Pre-cooked)
Ham	Turkey sausage
Lamb	Veal
	Veal sausage

POSSIBLE PIZZA TOPPINGS: VEGETABLES, ETC.

Artichoke hearts	Kidney beans
Asparagus	Mushrooms
Bamboo shoots	Peas
Banana peppers	Pineapples
Black olives	Red onions
Broccoli	Red kidney beans
Carrots	Red peppers
Cauliflower	Red potatoes
Celery	Spinach
Corn	Sweet potatoes
Cucumbers	Tomatoes
Eggplant	Water chestnuts
Garbanzo beans	White kidney beans
Green beans	White onions
Green olives	White potatoes
Green peppers	Yellow onions

POSSIBLE PIZZA TOPPINGS: SEAFOOD

Anchovies	Mussels
Clams	Oysters
Crab	Scallops
Imitation crab	Shrimp
Imitation lobster	Smoked salmon
Lobster	Squid

Pizza Recipes

BACON & EGGS QUICHE DIANE

Vegetables, bacon, and eggs with Gruyere and Swiss cheese, in a pizza pie dough shell.

I cup quartered mushrooms, raw or sautéed	4 oz. Gruyere cheese slices, cut into strips
¾ cup chopped scallions or green onions	4 oz. Swiss cheese slices, cut into strips
5-6 strips cooked bacon, cut bite size	4 medium eggs
¾ cup broccoli flowerettes	⅔ cup heavy whipping cream
¾ cup spinach, cooked, drained, chopped	Salt & pepper
	Cayenne pepper
	15" round pie dough shell

Prepare and form pizza dough or pie shell in a 9" to 12" pie pan, then lightly coat the dough surface with olive oil. Layer mushrooms, onion, bacon, broccoli, and cheeses. Beat eggs and heavy cream; add dash of salt, pepper, and cayenne until the mixture thickens slightly. Pour egg mix over the contents in the pan.

Bake at 350°F for about 25 to 30 minutes, or until mixture is cooked thoroughly, and the top and crust have browned.

BBQ CHICKEN PIZZA "SOUTHWESTERN"

A tangy pizza with grilled chicken and Monterey Jack cheese. 6 to 8 servings.

3 Tbs. olive oil	1 green pepper, medium diced
2 chicken breast, skinned, cut into strips	8 oz. bar-b-que sauce
1 tsp. chili powder	8 oz. sharp cheddar cheese, shredded
1 tsp. garlic powder	Guacamole
1 yellow onion, medium diced	Sour cream
	Pico de Gallo

Prepare a 15 oz. ball of pizza dough, using any dough recipe.

Skin and remove chicken breasts from bone, or use boneless chicken and season with salt and black pepper. Heat oil in large skillet over medium heat until hot.

Sauté chicken, stirring 5 minutes or until lightly browned. Stir in chili powder and garlic powder then add onions and bell pepper. Cook and stir an additional 1 minute or until vegetables are tender.

Preheat oven to 425°F. Lightly oil 12" pizza pan. Roll the dough ball with a rolling pin into a 13" to 14" circle, center in the baking pan, and trim or crimp edges of the crust. Par-bake the dough at 425°F for 6 to 8 minutes, or until light golden brown.

Arrange chicken topping over the partially-baked crust. Drizzle bar-b-que sauce over chicken then sprinkle with the cheese. Place pizza in the oven, and bake 14 to 18 minutes, or until crust is golden brown. Serve with sides of guacamole, sour cream, or Pico de Gallo.

BREAKFAST PAN PIZZA

CRUST:	TOPPING:
2½ oz. active dry yeast	1½ cups grated mozzarella cheese
½ tsp. sugar	8 Tbs. freshly grated parmesan cheese
⅔ cup warm water	3 Tbs. minced fresh basil
1¾ cups bread flour or all-purpose flour	1 large clove garlic, pressed or minced
½ cup stone-ground cornmeal	1 tsp. crushed red pepper flakes
1½ tsp. sea or kosher salt	¾ tsp. dried oregano
	2 small plum tomatoes, thinly sliced
2 Tbs. extra-virgin olive oil	8 oz. bulk sausage (maple or sage flavored), cooked
	4 large eggs

Grease heavy skillet, preferably cast iron. Mix yeast, sugar, and water in small bowl until it becomes foamy. Use heavy mixer with dough hook or mix by hand with heavy wooden spoon. Mix yeast into flour and other dough ingredients. Mix dough until smooth and elastic.

Place dough on floured surface and knead for 2 minutes, adding an additional 1 to 2 Tbs. of flour until dough is no longer sticky. (Don't add too much flour, or the dough will be dry.) Form a ball and place in oiled bowl. Turn to coat and cover. Put in warm spot for about an hour, and let it rise to double its size.

Punch dough down and let rest for 10 minutes. Roll out dough to 11" to 12" in diameter. Transfer to ovenproof skillet and pull edges to form a ½ inch high edge. You can cover the dough and refrigerate overnight to use for breakfast. Let dough warm for 30 minutes before cooking.

Heat oven to 400°F. Combine topping ingredients in medium bowl. Arrange tomatoes and sausage on dough, and sprinkle cheese mixture on top. Bake pizza 18 to 20 minutes, until bubbly, and crust is crisp and light brown. While pizza bakes, scramble or fry eggs sunny side up. When the pizza is done, top it with the eggs. Slice into wedges and serve immediately.

Alternative – Pour beaten eggs into crust, then arrange tomato and sausage, cheese and toppings. Test consistency of egg mix to ensure cooked thoroughly.

CALZONE
Use basic dough recipe.

STUFFING:	4 oz. ham – thin sliced or chunks will work (pre-cooked and cut or sliced)
8 oz. ricotta (whole milk and part skim will hold shape – skim will be very juicy) 8 oz. provolone – shredded	

If cooking in a pan, punch fork holes in ½ of the crust, but not along the edges. Keep all filling away from the edges. Mix ricotta with provolone. Shape dough as you would for a pizza. Cover dough with cheese mixture and layer ham, then fold in half and seal edges. Poke holes in top portion of dough.

HAWAIIAN PIZZA
Use basic dough recipe and tomato sauce.

TOPPINGS:	3 oz. domestic provolone (shredded)
I cup pineapple – diced 4 oz. ham – cut into strips	6 oz. mozzarella cheese (shredded)

Spread sauce on the dough, apply a layer of ham, and cover with cheese.

RICOTTA PIZZA
Use basic dough recipe and tomato sauce (optional).

TOPPINGS:	4 oz. ham (cut into strips of thin slices-optional)
8 oz. whole milk ricotta cheese (skim or part skim will be thinner consistency)	3 oz. domestic provolone cheese (shredded)
6 oz. pitted black olives (optional)	6 oz. mozzarella cheese (shredded)

Mix ricotta with olives. Add a layer of tomato sauce (if desired) and ham and ricotta. Mix with olives and place on top or under shredded cheese mixture. (Toppings can be added in any combination—with or without sauce.)

CHICAGO MEAT-LOVER'S DEEP-DISH PIZZA
Prep the sauce and dough:

2½ to 3 cups marinara, pizza, or spaghetti sauce

28 oz. pizza dough ball

8-10 medium Italian, onion, or herbed meatballs, browned

1 lb. sweet Italian sausage, cut into 8 links, browned

8 slices Genoa Salami

8 slices Prosciutto or Capacola

8 slices bacon, cooked

8 slices pepperoni, large

1 medium red or yellow onion, sliced into ⅛ inch rings, raw

1 to 1½ cups white mushrooms, sliced or quartered, butter sauté optional

½ cup colossal black olives; pitted, whole, or halved

1½ to 2 Tbs. fresh garlic, minced

1 Tbs. Italian seasonings*

½ cup parmesan cheese, fine freshly grated

2 cups mozzarella cheese, grated

Roll out a 28 oz. ball of pizza dough into an 18" round and ⅜" thick circle. Place in a deep-dish pizza pan, and let edge hang over the top edge of the baking pan. Do not trim dough until you add ingredients.

Pour half of the sauce onto the dough and spread evenly over the bottom.

Arrange the meats around the bottom of the pan. Place vegetables over the meats. Sprinkle with garlic and seasonings. Place mozzarella cheese over the filling. Drizzle remaining sauce over cheese and sprinkle with parmesan.

Trim excess dough from the edge of the pan, leaving enough dough to "flute" with thumbs or a fork.

Bake in a preheated oven at 300°F to 325°F on the middle rack until bubbly and crust is medium brown, (45 to 55 minutes). Let cool before serving.

SEAFOOD PIZZA
Use basic dough recipe.

TOPPINGS:	Use any of the following:
9 oz. seafood	Clams
	Crab – real or imitation
5 oz. domestic provolone cheese (shredded)	Lobster – real or imitation
	Mussels
	Oysters
	Scallops
5 oz. sharp American cheese (shredded)	Shrimp
	Frozen seafood – Thaw and fry in a pan for a several minutes with 2 Tbs. of butter.
4 oz. mushrooms	Fresh seafood – Steam the seafood.
	Imitation and canned seafood – Use seafood as is.

Add a layer of cooled seafood. Cover with cheese and top with mushrooms.

WHITE PIZZA
Use basic dough. No tomato sauce on this pizza although a warm cup of sauce for dipping is nice with tomato or Alfredo sauce.

DOUGH DRESSING:	¾ tsp. fresh rosemary
2 Tbs. regular olive oil	Or – Mix melted butter or margarine with garlic powder to taste on dough.
1 clove of fresh garlic – pressed	
1 tsp. sugar	Or – Alfredo sauce spread on dough.

Spread dressing and sprinkle with combination of mozzarella and provolone cheese. You can add any toppings, but many people prefer fresh green peppers, onions, etc.

SICILIAN PIZZA

Basic dough recipe – 1 ½ times the original recipe for Sicilian crust.
Basic Sauce Recipe

TOPPINGS:	8 oz. mozzarella cheese (shredded)
4 oz. domestic provolone cheese (shredded)	Any toppings can be used.

This pizza is made in a deep, square pan. Grease the pan with 3 Tbs. of peanut oil and a dash of salt.

WARNING – Do not pile on too many toppings or the center of the dough may not cook thoroughly. A tip that will help is to move toppings away from the center.

WHITE PIZZA AUTHENTIC ITALIAN CRUST

4½ cups white flour	2 Tbs. olive oil
1¾ cups warm water	Olive oil
2½ tsp. dry yeast	Kosher salt
1 tsp. salt	Dried rosemary

Dissolve yeast in the warm water, and let sit until it becomes foamy. Add yeast mix to 3 cups of the flour. Add salt and olive oil a little at a time while you mix the flour and yeast. After it is thoroughly mixed add a little flour at a time, until the dough feels smooth and elastic.

Turn dough onto a floured board and knead; add flour or water in small amounts, as needed, to keep the dough from sticking to your hands. Place the dough in an oiled bowl and coat dough with oil. Let rise until about double the size (approximately 2 hours).

Remove the dough, punch down, and roll out on the floured tabletop from ⅜ - to ½- inch thick. Place dough in a pan or cookie sheet. With a pastry brush, paint with additional olive oil. Use thumb and two fingers to make dimples on the entire surface. Sprinkle sea salt and rosemary on the dough. Let rise a little more. Bake at 375° F for about 25 minutes then paint with more olive oil.

SHRIMP AND CRABMEAT SEAFOOD PIZZA RUSTICA

1½ cups peeled shrimp, bite size	½ cup grated parmesan or Romano cheese
1 cup crabmeat, bite size	1 Tbs. minced garlic
1½ cups shredded mozzarella cheese	½ cup diced mushrooms
2 eggs slightly beaten	1½ cup diced onion
1 cup shredded, extra sharp cheddar cheese	2 tsp. lemon juice
5 oz. chopped spinach, drained	1 tsp. minced parsley
½ cup ricotta cheese	¼ tsp. ground nutmeg
	Salt & pepper to taste

Combine all ingredients (less ¼ cup of mozzarella, shrimp, and crab) in a large bowl. Form a dough ball in a 10" to 12" pie pan. Spread the mixture evenly into the dough shell. Top with the reserved mozzarella, shrimp, and crabmeat pieces and a little more nutmeg or paprika. Drizzle olive oil over the toppings. Bake at 325°F for about 55 minutes, mid-oven, until filling is cooked, and the crust is browned. Remove from oven and cool for 10 minutes.

Miscellaneous Entrée Recipes

CHICKEN PICCATA

4 chicken breasts pounded thin	½ cup of white wine
¼ cup flour	Juice of 2 lemons
2 Tbs. olive oil	Salt and pepper to taste
3 Tbs. of butter	1 cup chicken broth

Coat chicken breasts with flour, shake off excess. Heat oil in sauté pan on medium heat. Place chicken in pan and brown on each side. Drain the oil and add butter, wine, lemon, salt, and pepper. Cook for 1 minute. Add broth and cook until liquid is reduced to half—about 5 to 6 minutes. Thicken with a little flour to when it starts to boil. Place chicken on plates and top with sauce.

CHICKEN MARSALA
Serves 2.

2 chicken breasts, pounded thin	⅔ cup Marsala wine
¼ cup flour	3 Tbs. of butter
¼ cup olive oil	⅔ cup chicken stock
½ lb. of mushrooms	Salt and pepper to taste

Heat olive oil in sauté pan on medium heat. Coat prepared chicken breasts in flour, shake off excess, and place in hot oil. Sauté chicken and turn once to lightly brown both sides. Place chicken on a warm plate.

Remove all but a little oil and add mushrooms. Sauté until they begin to lose their juices. Add wing and use wooden spoon to remove all browning residue in the pan. Add butter, broth, salt, and pepper. Cook until liquid is reduced by half—about 5 minutes. Place chicken in pan, and cook until heated. Place chicken on warm plates and pour sauce over them.

FETTUCCINE ALFREDO
Serves 2.

3 Tbs. butter	2 egg yolks
1½ cups heavy cream	1¼ cup freshly grated Parmigiano-Reggiano cheese
1 Tbs. salt	½ tsp. black pepper
½ lb. fettuccine	

Add butter and cream in large sauté pan, turn heat on medium and cook until cream and butter are melted together. Turn off the heat. Bring large pot of water to a boil, add 1 Tbs. of salt and fettuccine. Cook for 1 minute.

Strain pasta and add to butter and cream in the pan. Turn heat on medium. Add egg yolks, cheese, and pepper. Stir and mix well, coating pasta with the sauce. Serve from the pan, and sprinkle with Parmigiano-Reggiano cheese on top.

ITALIAN BAKED LASAGNA

1 lb. lasagna noodles, cooked	2 cloves garlic, chopped or minced
2 – 16 oz. jars meatless sauce	
16 oz. ricotta cheese	2 tsp. salt
¾ cup grated parmesan cheese	3 small or medium eggs, beaten
16 oz. mozzarella cheese, sliced thin	
	2 lbs. ground beef
¾ cup chopped onion	1 tsp. Italian seasoning

Cook lasagna noodles according to package directions until tender but still firm. Drain and keep warm. Sauté the ground beef, garlic, and onion in a skillet. Add sauce, salt, and Italian seasoning and combine. Simmer on low for 12 to 15 minutes. In a small pan, combine eggs and ricotta cheese. Grease a 9" x 12" or larger, deep-sided baking pan. Place some sauce and ground beef mixture on the bottom of the pan, then place the first layer of noodles, so the ends hang over the sides. Add thin layer of ricotta/egg mixture, mozzarella cheese, and cover with sauce. Add a second layer of pasta (lengthwise in the pan), the meat sauce, and cheese mixture. Repeat until pan is almost full, then fold over the ends of the first layer of noodles and top with more sauce. Bake at 350 degrees for 40 to 45 minutes or until cheese is bubbly. Allow to set for 5 to 10 minutes before cutting.

LINGUINI WHITE CLAM SAUCE
Serves 4.

¾ cup of olive oil	1 lb. linguini
4 cloves of garlic chopped	2 Tbs. chopped parsley
18 clams shelled and chopped with juices reserved	

Heat olive oil in sauté pan over medium heat. Add garlic and cook until browned. Add the clams with juices, bring to a boil, simmer for 5 minutes. Bring a large pot of water to a boil. Add 1 Tbs. of salt and pasta. Cook on high heat until softened, but still firm. Drain pasta, return to the pan, and add sauce. Dish pasta onto plates and top with remaining sauce.

CHICKEN CACCIATORE
Serves 4.

3 lbs. chicken cut into pieces	2 cups marinara sauce
1 large onion chopped	⅓ cup olive oil
1 lb. mushrooms sliced	Salt and pepper to taste
1 ¼ cup dry sherry wine	1 Tbs. chopped fresh parsley
1 ¼ cup chicken broth	

Heat oil in large pan over medium heat and brown chicken in the pan. Add onions and mushrooms, and cook for 2 to 3 minutes or until onions are translucent. Drain oil and add salt, pepper, and wine. Cook for 1 minute, stirring and scraping pan to mix thoroughly. Add marinara sauce and chicken broth. Bring contents to a boil and simmer for 25 to 30 minutes on low heat. Place chicken on serving dish and pour sauce over chicken to serve.

MANICOTTI

1 box manicotti shells (store bought is fine)	2 medium eggs
FILLING:	6 oz. grated Romano cheese
32 oz. ricotta cheese	1 jar of sauce
9 oz. shredded mozzarella	Salt & pepper to taste
2 tsp. parsley	

Cook manicotti shells according to instructions on the box. Filling: Preheat oven to 350 degrees. Combine ricotta, mozzarella, parsley, egg, and half of the Romano cheese. Add salt and pepper to taste. Coat a thin layer of sauce in a baking dish. Spoon filling into the shell carefully to avoid tearing. Continue until all the shells are finished. Cover with the remaining sauce and sprinkle the remaining Romano cheese on top. Bake for 30 to 45 minutes.

MIXED HERB SPAGHETTI AND SAUCE
Serves 6.

2 to 3 large tomatoes – chopped	¼ tsp. pepper ⅓ cup chopped fresh parsley
I cup tomato juice	2 Tbs. chopped fresh or
½ cup dry white wine or tomato juice	2 tsp. dried basil leaves
3 Tbs. lemon juice	20 oz. whole baby clams, drained
I tsp. olive or vegetable oil	6 cups hot cooked spaghetti
¼ tsp. salt	

Bring tomatoes, tomato juice, wine, lemon juice, oil, salt, and pepper to a boil in a Dutch oven; reduce heat. Simmer for 5 minutes or until slightly thickened. Stir in parsley, basil, and clams. Serve over spaghetti.

PASTA PRIMAVERA
Serves 2.

I cup nonfat dry milk	½ tsp. salt Dash of pepper
⅓ cup sliced mushrooms	⅓ cup frozen peas
½ tsp. basil	⅓ cup grated parmesan
I clove garlic	I oz. fat-free ham, Julienned
¼ cup. chopped onions	½ cup diced zucchini
½ tsp. salt	I Tbs. sliced pimentos
Dash of pepper	½ cup broccoli flowerettes
⅓ cup frozen peas	I cup uncooked pasta twists
¼ cup. chopped onions	

In saucepan, boil milk, basil, salt, and pepper. Mix cornstarch and water in a small bowl or cup. Add to milk and boil, stirring constantly. Add parmesan and cover. Cook pasta according to directions. Sauté garlic, zucchini, broccoli, mushrooms, onions, and ham in oil until tender. Add peas, pimentos, and pasta. Pour sauce over, toss, and serve immediately.

PASTA WITH SUN-DRIED TOMATOES, PINE NUTS, AND CHICKEN
Serves 4-6.

6 Tbs. olive oil	28 oz. can of Italian-style peeled tomatoes, chopped (reserve juices separately)
½ white onion chopped	
5 garlic cloves, sliced thick	¼ cup fresh chopped basil
⅔ cup of finely chopped sun-dried tomatoes packed in olive oil	½ tsp. salt
	½ tsp. pepper
⅔ cup of pine nuts	1 cup of chicken stock
1 cup chicken breast – boneless, skinless, broiled, and finely diced	⅓ cup whipping cream
	1 lb. of pasta (penne rigate, penne, or tortiglioni)
⅓ cup of brandy	⅔ cup grated parmesan cheese

Add olive oil to sauté pan along with onion, garlic, sun-dried tomatoes, pine nuts, and the diced chicken breast. Cook for 4 minutes over medium-high heat until garlic browns. Add brandy and mix well for 2 minutes. Add tomatoes and basil. Cook 2 minutes and stir well. Add chicken stock, reserved juice from tomatoes, and cream. Bring to a boil and simmer for 15 to 20 minutes.

Add pasta to boiling water 10 minutes before the sauce is ready. Cook according to instructions on the box. Drain the pasta and return to the pot. Pour the sauce on top of the pasta. Over medium-low heat, stir well to combine the pasta and the sauce for 3 to 4 minutes. Turn off the heat, add the cheese, stir well, and serve.

PROSCIUTTO LASAGNA

8 oz. lasagna pasta noodles, cooked	1 medium onion, chopped
8 oz. Italian Prosciutto, chopped	1 lb. lean ground beef
	4 Tbs. fresh basil, chopped
16 oz. canned whole peeled tomatoes, chopped	4 cloves garlic, chopped or minced
1 cup large curd cottage cheese or 1 cup ricotta cheese	½ tsp. oregano
	Ground black pepper
1 cup grated parmesan cheese	⅔ cup dry white wine *(optional)
1 lb. mozzarella cheese, sliced thin	2 Tbs. olive oil

Cook lasagna noodles according to package directions. Drain and keep warm.

In large pan over medium heat, sauté garlic, onion, and prosciutto in the olive oil for 4 minutes. Add the lean beef, oregano, a dash of black pepper and sauté for 10 minutes. Add the wine and cook until the wine is almost evaporated. Add tomatoes and basil. Reduce heat and simmer 35 to 40 minutes, or until most of the liquid has evaporated.

Grease a 9" x 12" baking pan with deep sides. Pour minimal sauce in the bottom of the pan. Place layer of lasagna noodles, a layer of the beef and prosciutto tomato sauce, cottage cheese, parmesan and mozzarella cheese. Add a second alternating layer of noodles, sauce, and other ingredients. Repeat until pan is full and pour remaining sauce on top. Sprinkle with parmesan cheese, and bake in a pre-heated oven at 400 degrees for 30 minutes.

SPAGHETTI WITH MEATBALLS
Serves 4.

MEATBALLS:	PASTA:
½ lb. ground beef	⅓ cup olive oil
½ lb. ground pork	3 cloves of garlic, halved
½ lb. ground veal	½ medium onion, chopped
¾ cup of breadcrumbs	2 – 28 oz. cans plum tomatoes with puree, crushed
½ medium onion, finely chopped	2 basil leaves
3 Tbs. parsley, finely minced	½ tsp. oregano
1 tsp. garlic powder	Salt and pepper to taste
½ cup grated Pecorino-Romano cheese	¼ cup of water
2 eggs	1 lb. spaghetti
Vegetable oil	

Combine all meatball ingredients, except oil, in a bowl. Knead the mixture without squeezing the ingredients. When well-blended, shape into 1½ to 2 inch meatballs. Place meatballs in a skillet that will hold all meatballs. Heat oil to cover ¼ of an inch of the meatballs, and brown on all sides.

Heat olive oil in heavy pot on medium heat. Add garlic, onion, and cook until onion is translucent. Add tomatoes, basil, oregano, salt, pepper, and water. Bring to a boil, and simmer for 45 minutes. Add meatballs, and simmer for 30 minutes.

Bring a large pot of water to a boil, and add 1 Tbs. of salt and spaghetti. Cook over high heat until softened, but still firm. Drain pasta, return to pan, and pour some sauce on top. Mix well. Dish pasta and top with sauce and meatballs.

RAVIOLI WITH MEAT

RAVIOLI:	FILLING:
2½ cups of flour	Meat – chicken, turkey, or veal – chopped fine
2 eggs	1 Tbs. grated parmesan
3 Tbs. of cold water	1 egg
½ tsp. of salt	⅛ tsp. nutmeg
	¼ tsp. lemon peel
	1 Tbs. chilled butter

Place flour on the counter or a bread-board. Make a hole in the middle and break the eggs into it. Add the water and salt, and mix with a fork until you have a paste. Use a rolling-pin and roll it out very thin, the thickness of a 10-cent piece, and let it dry. Cut into strips about 2½ inches wide.

Use cooked chicken, turkey, or veal. Chop the meat fine; add 1 Tbs. of grated parmesan cheese, one egg, a dash of nutmeg, a dash of grated lemon peel, and 1 Tbs. of butter, cold. Mix these ingredients in a bowl. Place a teaspoon of the mixture and on the extended paste, about two inches from the edge. Place another spoon about 2 inches from the first spoonful. Repeat this until you have a row of teaspoonfuls across the paste. Fold over the edge of the paste; cover the spoonfuls and cut across the paste at the bottom of them. Cut the paste into squares with the meat in the middle of each square; press down at the edges to seal. Repeat until meat and paste are used. Place the squares of paste and meat into boiling salted water a few at a time, and boil for 10 minutes. Serve with tomato sauce, or butter and grated parmesan cheese.

SWORDFISH SICILIAN STYLE
Serves 2.

4 swordfish steaks	Juice of 3 lemons
I large garlic clove finely chopped	⅔ cup white wine
4 Tbs. chopped fresh parsley	Salt and pepper to taste
½ cup olive oil	

Combine oil, garlic, parsley, salt, pepper, lemon juice, and wine in a small bowl. Place swordfish in oil baking pan, and cook under broiler for 10 minutes, or until done. Pour marinade over the fish and cook for 1 to 2 minutes. Place on plates and spoon marinade on top when you serve.

TORTELLINI WITH PEAS AND PROSCIUTTO
Serves 4.

15 oz. cheese tortellini	I cup peas, frozen
I ¼ cup whipping cream	4 oz. Prosciutto, fat trimmed cut
I tsp. nutmeg, freshly grated	I tsp. salt and ground pepper
6 Tbs. parmesan, freshly grated	

Boil tortellini in large pot until barely tender, stirring occasionally, and drain. Bring cream to a boil in heavy saucepan. Reduce heat; add nutmeg and simmer until slightly thickened, about 8 minutes. Return tortellini to pot. Add warm cream, parmesan, peas, and prosciutto. Simmer over low heat until tortellini are tender and sauce thickens; stir occasionally, about 4 minutes. Season with salt and pepper. Serve warm.

ZITI WITH RICOTTA CHEESE
Serves 8.

15 oz. ricotta cheese, part skim milk or 15 oz. cottage cheese	3 Tbs. fresh parsley, minced
2 eggs beaten	16 oz. pasta cooked and drained
⅔ cup grated parmesan cheese	30 oz. tomato sauce, seasoned
½ tsp. black pepper	1¼ cup mozzarella cheese, shredded

Preheat oven to 350 degrees. Combine ricotta cheese, eggs, parmesan cheese, and seasonings. In another bowl mix cooked pasta and sauce. Place half the pasta mixture in a 13" x 9" baking dish. Place half of the cheese, top with remaining pasta and remaining cheese. Bake 35 to 40 minutes, or until bubbly.

Sub Recipes

DELUXE SUBMARINE

½ lb. thin sliced Italian salami – cut into ¼" wide strips	½ cup mayonnaise
½ lb. mozzarella cheese – cut into ⅓" cubes	¼ cup roasted red peppers – chopped
½ cup chopped celery	18-inch French bread baguette
¼ cup black olives – pitted	2 cups radicchio – sliced thin

Combine salami, cheese, celery, and olives in large bowl. Mix mayonnaise and roasted peppers in small bowl to blend; season with salt and pepper.

Cut bread crosswise into four equal pieces, then cut in half. Scoop out some of the center from each bread piece, leaving ½ inch thick shell. Spread dressing in center of each piece of bread. Divide salad mixture among bottom bread pieces. Top salad with radicchio. Can be prepared 4 hours ahead. Wrap in foil and chill..

SALAMI CLUB SUB

2 – 16 oz. loaves of frozen or fresh Italian bread	8 oz. thinly sliced provolone cheese
½ cup mayonnaise	8 oz. thinly sliced salami
3 Tbs. mustard	8 oz. thinly sliced turkey
2 tsp. horseradish (optional)	8 oz. thinly sliced ham
8 oz. thinly sliced cheddar cheese	Leaf lettuce
	Sliced onions
8 oz. thinly sliced Fontina cheese	Sliced tomatoes

Thaw frozen bread in refrigerator overnight, at room temperature, or use fresh bread. Cover and let rest 1½ to 2 hours, or until doubled. Preheat oven to 350. Bake 25 to 30 minutes or until browned. Cool 5 minutes; remove from pan and cool completely.

Split loaf and spread with mayonnaise and mustard. Place cheese and meat in overlapping slices on bottom of bread. Add lettuce, tomatoes, onions, and top half of bread; press lightly and wrap in plastic wrap or foil. You can refrigerate for up to 6 hours before serving. Cut into 1 to 1½ inch slices.

ITALIAN SUB

⅓ cup Italian dressing	8 oz. smoked ham
¼ cup Dijon mustard	6 slices hard salami
2 tsp. dried oregano leaves	7 oz. roasted red peppers, drained, cut into strips
1 – 18" loaf Italian bread, split lengthwise	¼ lb. provolone cheese slices
2 cups shredded lettuce, divided	1 small red onion, thinly sliced

Mix dressing, mustard, and oregano until well-blended. Cut bread horizontally, and spread the mix on bread. Lay half of lettuce on bottom portion of bread, then ham, salami, peppers, cheese, onions, and remaining lettuce. Place top of bread on sandwich and cut into six pieces.

GREEK SANDWICH HEROES

½ cup fresh mushrooms – thinly sliced	3 Roma tomatoes – thinly sliced
⅓ cup cucumber – thinly sliced	I clove garlic – minced
2 Tbs. ripe olives	2 sub rolls (2½ oz.)
3 Tbs. crumbled feta cheese	2 to 4 leaves of lettuce
2 tsp. white balsamic vinegar	6 slices cooked ham
⅛ tsp. oregano	6 slices smoked turkey
	(Use personal preferences on type of ham and turkey.)

Combine first eight ingredients in a small bowl and toss gently. Let sit for 30 minutes and toss occasionally. Cut a 2-inch wide, V-shape wedge the length of each roll. Sit the wedges off to the side. Drain vegetable mixture. Line each roll with one or two lettuce leaves, and place ham and turkey over lettuce. Spoon vegetable mixture evenly over meat and cover sandwiches with wedges.

REUBEN

I – 8 oz. loaf French bread – cut lengthwise	½ lb. corned beef, chicken, or other deli meats, thin slices and in bite-size strips
¼ cup mayonnaise or salad dressing	8 oz. sauerkraut, rinsed and well drained
I Tbs. prepared mustard	
8 oz. Swiss cheese slices – cut diagonally	

Preheat oven to 425°F. Stir together mayonnaise and mustard. Spread on bread.

Top with cheese triangles. Place bread in a 15 x 10 x 1 inch baking pan. Mix meat and sauerkraut in small bowl. Divide meat between bread halves in pan.

Bake, uncovered, in the oven at 425°F for 5 to 10 minutes or until cheese begins to melt. Serve the sandwiches open face.

MEATBALL SUBS

3 lbs. ground beef	¼ cup breadcrumbs (plain, Italian, or parmesan)
8 oz. can of tomato paste	1 egg
¼ tsp. parsley	12 to 15 oz. tomato or pizza sauce
¼ tsp. basil	
¼ tsp. rosemary	4 oz. mozzarella cheese – shredded
¼ tsp. oregano	
¼ tsp. garlic	Italian sub rolls
Salt and pepper to taste	

Combine all ingredients, except sauce and cheese, in a large bowl and mix with your hands. Add more seasoning and breadcrumbs as needed for your taste. Form into bite size meatballs and place in a large skillet. Cook slowly and brown on all sides. Pour sauce into a pan and add spices if using tomato sauce. Be sure to use enough to cover the meatballs and heat the sauce. After meatballs are cooked and browned, add to the sauce. Heat sauce and serve on rolls with shredded mozzarella.

PHILLY STEAK SUB

6 oz. eye round roast – sliced so thin you can almost see through it ¼ cup thinly sliced onion	1 Tbs. olive oil
	1 French baguette, thin and sourdough
2 oz. mushroom sliced	2 thick slices provolone cheese

Heat oil in skillet. Sauté onions and mushrooms. When they start to look translucent, add the meat on top of onions and mushrooms. Mix thoroughly and cook until meat browns. Place on bun and add cheese.

SAUSAGE AND PEPPER SANDWICHES

I lb. fresh Italian sausage links (mild or hot)	I large onion – sliced in thin strips
½ cup water	½ tsp. dried oregano
I Tbs. olive or vegetable oil	½ Tbs. fresh basil or ½ tsp. dried basil
I medium green bell pepper – cut into thin strips	
I medium red bell pepper – cut into thin strips	4 French rolls or hoagie rolls – split and toast

Brown sausages in a skillet over medium heat, about 5 minutes. Add water and bring to a boil. Cover and simmer until almost totally cooked, about 10 minutes. Drain sausages on paper towels. Add I Tbs. of oil, if there's no liquid in skillet. Increase heat to medium-high and add peppers, onion, oregano, and basil. Stir frequently while it cooks, until vegetables are crisp-tender, about 5 minutes. Place sausage to skillet and heat through. Hollow out bottoms of rolls and place one sausage link in each depression. Top each with equal amount of the vegetable mixture and serve.

Desserts

FRIED DOUGH DIPPED IN HONEY BUTTER
Use a basic pizza dough recipe.

TOPPING:

3 Tbs. margarine or butter – softened

I Tbs. honey

Form dough into 4-inch round patties. Deep fry in peanut oil on medium heat until it is golden brown on both sides. Dough should sizzle and puff when placed in the oil. Dry each patty on paper towel. Whip softened butter and mix with honey. Spread honey mixture on fried dough.

ALMOND ITALIAN BISCOTTI
Yield: 3 dozen

4 eggs beaten	1 tsp. vanilla
1 ¼ cup sugar	4 cups sifted flour
½ cup margarine	4 tsp. baking powder
¼ cup milk	½ tsp. salt
1 bottle anise	1 ¼ cup toasted almonds

Combine margarine and sugar. Add eggs, milk, anise, and vanilla. Combine thoroughly and add flour, powder, and salt. Dough will be moist but not sticky. Add nuts. Roll into 2-inch and 4-inch strips. Bake at 350 for 15 minutes. Cool and cut.

CINNAMON ROLLS
Use a basic pizza dough recipe.

FILLING:	TOPPING:
1 Tbs. margarine (do not use butter)	1-½ tsp. margarine (do not use butter)
	4 oz. cream cheese (can alternate small amount of milk or water)
¼ cup sugar	¼ cup sugar (or use ¼ cup powered sugar and water or milk to moisten)
3 tsp. cinnamon	
	¼ tsp. vanilla

Roll the dough with a rolling pin to ¼ inch thick, and form into a rectangle. Combine the filling with a mixer and spread a thin layer over the top of the dough. Lift one edge of the dough and roll (jellyroll style). Cut the roll in 1-inch pieces. Place rolls closely on a small, deep, greased pan. Bake at 350°F for 25 to 30 minutes or until light brown. Combine topping ingredients and spread over cooked rolls fresh from the oven.

CANNOLI

SHELLS:	FILLING:
1¾ cups flour	15 oz. container of ricotta cheese
1 Tbs. sugar	½ cup of sugar
¼ tsp. of salt	2 tsp. of vanilla
2 Tbs. butter, melted	½ cup of mini chocolate chips
¾ cup Marsala wine	Confectioners sugar for dusting
Egg white	
2 quarts vegetable oil	

Combine flour, sugar, and salt. Add melted butter and Marsala wine. Place on a floured surface and knead until combined. Wrap dough in plastic and refrigerate for 2 to 3 hours.

Roll dough until very thin. Use a cookie cutter or glass rim to cut dough into 4-inch circles and roll again until very thin. Roll each piece around a cannoli tube and seal with egg whites.

Heat vegetable oil in deep pot to 350 degrees. Place dough rolls in hot oil, and fry 2 to 3 minutes until golden brown. Remove and place on paper towels to drain. Cool and gently twist tube to remove shell from the forms.

Whip sugar, vanilla, and ricotta until smooth then add chocolate chips. Spoon filling into a pastry bag with a large round tip. Pipe the ricotta cream into the pastry shells; dust with confectioner's sugar, and serve immediately.

LEMON ITALIAN ICE
Serves 1.

3 cups of water	1¼ cup sugar
1 tsp. grated lemon peel	¾ cup lemon juice

Combine water, sugar, and lemon peel in medium saucepan. Bring to a boil on medium heat, stirring constantly. Remove from heat and cool. Pour mixture into ice cream maker. Stir in lemon juice. Follow manufacturer's directions.

ITALIAN CREAM CAKE

1 cup butter	1 cup chopped nuts
5 egg yolks	1 cup coconut
1 tsp. baking soda	8 oz. package cream cheese
2 cups all-purpose flour	½ cup butter
5 egg whites	3¼ cups confectioners' sugar, packed
2 cups white sugar	
1¼ cups buttermilk	1 tsp. vanilla extract
	Chopped nuts for topping

Cream 1 cup of butter or margarine, egg yolks, and white sugar. Alternately, mix flour and buttermilk. Add baking soda, nuts, and coconut. Beat egg whites, and fold into batter. Pour batter into three greased and floured 9-inch round cake pans. Bake 20 to 25 minutes in a preheated 350°F (175°C) oven. Combine cream cheese, ½ cup of butter or margarine, confectioners' sugar, and vanilla extract. Spread onto cooled cake. Top iced cake with chopped nuts.

ORANGE SORBETTO
Serves 4.

2 oranges	1 tsp. grated orange zest
2 cups spring water	1 egg white
⅔ cup sugar	

Cut oranges in half and remove the pulp with a spoon. Don't puncture the skin. Place the pulp in a blender or food processor and add the water, sugar, and orange zest. Blend until the sugar is dissolved. Strain the pulp mixture through a fine-meshed sieve, pressing out as much liquid as possible with the back of a large spoon. Discard the pulp. Refrigerate the mixture for at least 2 hours, or until thoroughly chilled. Transfer to an ice cream maker and freeze according to the manufacturer's instructions, or until partially frozen. Add egg white and continue to freeze until firm. Scoop the sorbetto into the orange shells and freeze until ready to serve.

STRAWBERRY GELATO
Serves 20.

3½ cup cut-up strawberries 6 cup milk 1¼ cup sugar	12 egg yolks beaten Several drops red food coloring

Process berries in a blender or food processor, cover and blend until nearly smooth.

In large saucepan, combine 3 cups of milk, sugar, and egg yolks. Cook and stir over medium heat until mixture coats a spoon. (To test, dip a spoon into the custard and drag your finger through the mix. It's done when the edges along the line keep their shape). Remove from heat. Combine the remaining milk, the berries, and food coloring, if desired.

Cover surface of gelato mixture with plastic wrap. Refrigerate several hours or overnight until chilled. (Or, place the pan in a sink of ice water to chill quickly.) Freeze in a 4 or 5 quart ice cream freezer according to manufacturers directions. Ripen for 4 hours.

Additional Recipe Resources

www.cookingwithpatty.com

www.elook.org/recipes/european/italian1.html

www.ilovepasta.org/recipes/low_fat.html

www.italianchef.com

www.italiancookingandliving.com/recipes/index.php

www.italianfoodforever.com

www.italiansrus.com/recipes/recipes.htm

www.italylink.com/food.html

www.pizzaware.com

www.rumela.com/recipe/continental_recipes_italian.htm

www.virtualitalia.com/recipes

www.yourwaytoflorence.com/recipes

I hope you can use some of these recipes or use them to inspire you to create some of your own. There are many possibilities with appetizers, entrees, pizza sauce and topping combinations. Be creative and have fun with the possibilities.

11

Control Your Costs

In most businesses, expenses are on the rise and income is down. The pizza business is no different. To stay in business, you must make a profit. Watching the bottom line and controlling your costs are huge steps in showing a profit. It may seem boring, but studying your business costs will help you find ways to control your costs better.

Some things to watch include:

- Labor costs
- Food costs
- Inventory costs
- Marketing costs
- Adding new menu items
- Being competitive

It is critical to begin cost control measures from the beginning. You will find

businesspeople who learn to cut costs after they suffer losses. Why suffer a loss before you learn the lesson? You can control costs, in order to get the most value for the least cost, in every facet of your business.

Too many business owners spend all their time "putting out fires," but you need to prevent "fires" or problems. This enables you to maximize your profits. Controlling costs is another way to plan ahead for your business.

The statistics for the first couple of months will not be precise, but record the initial figures. When you buy an existing business, you can refer to the previous sale numbers. If you bought a franchise, you can acquire numbers from similar territories.

Profits Don't Guarantee Success

Don't assume that profits mean you are doing things the right way. There are instances when a business is making a profit, but you could increase that profit by controlling your costs. If you don't control costs, it will become obvious when your sales drop.

Controlling Costs Works

Control costs at all times. This allows you to get the most from every dollar. Controlling costs allows you to make a profit, while still serving a quality product and saving your customers money. This enables you to compete in the local marketplace.

To control your costs, evaluate where you are spending your money. It's hard to spot many of the ways you are wasting money in the pizza business. This is the reason to review your expenses and payroll costs. Learn to compile the records and analyze the reports. Pizza shop owners who are involved in the day-to-day operations are better qualified to monitor ways to save money.

When we talk about cost control, it's different from bookkeeping. To help you understand this better, we need to explain what you want to accomplish.

- Provide information to make day-to-day decisions.

- Determine the efficiency of each area of your pizza shop.

- Determine if your expenses are within budget for your sales.

- Prevent fraud and theft from employees and customers.

- Establish goals for the business.

- Prevent – don't correct.

- Maximize your profits instead of minimizing your losses.

It's important that you and your employees understand that controlling costs doesn't mean you don't trust your staff. Theft prevention or detection is a result of controlling costs. Do this to determine where the business is headed.

Atlantic Publishing offers a couple of books to help you find ways to cut costs and to save money in the operation of your business. *2,001 Innovative Ways to Save Your Company Thousands by Reducing Cost: A Complete Guide to Creative Cost Cutting and Boosting Profits* is perfect for any business owner who understands that every dollar counts. It offers practical advice on how to save money without sacrificing service and quality. These tips came from businesspeople who tried these techniques and know they work. (**www. atlantic-pub.com,** Item # IWS-02)

Another wonderful resource from Atlantic Publishing is *The Food Service Manager's Guide to Creative Cost Cutting and Cost Control: Over 2,001 Innovative and Simple Ways to Save Your Food Service Operation Thousands by Reducing Expenses.* This book shares experiences from successful business operators who found many practical ways to cut costs and save money. You can utilize this information in the day-to-day operation of your business

to cut costs which will increase the bottom line for your business. (**www. atlantic-pub.com**, Item # CCC-01)

Interpret the Numbers

Having the numbers isn't enough; you need to interpret them. Your first task is to understand the difference between controlling and reducing costs.

- Control requires compilation and interpretation of the data about your income and expenses.

- Reduction is making the effort to bring costs into budget standards.

Everyone in the business must cut costs. This includes management and staff. However, beware that you don't sacrifice quality or service in your efforts to cut costs and control expenses.

These are eight primary areas where you can control your costs in a pizza shop:

1. **Purchasing** – An effective inventory system is critical to purchasing. All orders need to be reviewed and placed carefully. When you place the order, you will be charged, and that ties up your working capital. With practice you will learn how much is needed for unexpected rushes and sales. Sending employees to the store for cheese and pepperoni is not cost effective. Your order amounts will depend on projected sales and the frequency that you receive deliveries.

   - Allow a cushion between deliveries but keep it to a minimum.

   - Analyze costs for non-perishables and usage to see if buying in volume is wise.

- Establish an order system and adjust for sales projections.

- Keep a list of suppliers, units ordered, product details, and prices.

- Try to renegotiate your prices with vendors every 6 months. Use your records to find the quantities you order and ask about volume discounts.

2. **Receiving** – Double-check your orders when they arrive.

   - Verify brand, grade, types, weight, amount, and prices.

   - Note any problems with your order and get credit or return items.

3. **Storage** – Foods must be stored with the proper temperature and ventilation to keep them from possible contamination.

   - Place expensive items in a safe place to prevent theft.

   - Organizing your storage makes it easier to manage your inventory.

4. **Usage** – Remove items from inventory when they are used.

   - Managers will take items from storage and put in the appropriate place.

   - Keep an accurate record of your beginning inventory, how much was sold, and the ending inventory.

5. **Portioning** – Set standards for the amount of each topping and other ingredients to be used. This is especially critical with cheese and other expensive ingredients. It is very easy to overuse cheese.

6. **Order taking** – Each item that is sold must be entered in the

computer or cash register.

- Everything needs to be entered, even drinks and snacks. Start this on the first day, and enforce it. You aren't accusing staff of theft, you but need to track your usage and profits.

  — Authorize "giveaways" for customer service, but only certain people should authorize and give their reasons.

  — You can provide employee meals, snacks, and beverages, but track these. (Details in IRS Publication 15-B.)

- There should be no verbal orders from anybody.

7. **Cash receipts** – You must monitor sales-to-cost controls. Discrepancies must be investigated daily. Your sales information is used to compile your financial record. This will help you make future projections.

8. **Bank deposits/accounts payable** – Verify deposit amounts. Each staff member needs to be involved in controlling costs. This is the reason to make the procedures easy to follow. Some employees will insist on knowing why it needs to be done. No matter how thorough your plan, review and improve it as needed. These are the five key elements to an effective cost-control strategy:

1. Plan ahead.

2. Make the procedures clear.

3. Monitor the program and make improvements, as needed.

4. Employees must comply.

5. Managers must enforce the program.

Ask yourself these questions:

- Are you gathering the information you need?

- Do you get the information in a timely manner?

- Do you have a system to assemble, organize, and interpret details?

- Are you gaining more than you are spending to control costs?

Look at that last question. If maintaining your cost control measures costs you more than you will save, you need to re-evaluate.

Set Standards

Standards are mandatory in order to implement your cost control program. Find the points you will use to compare and measure your results. Your resources can, and probably will, change. All managers can monitor variations in the established standards and what actually works. Use these steps to evaluate your standards:

1. Establish standards for each employee and department.

2. Staff members must be responsible to prevent waste.

3. You must monitor your staff's adherence to your standards.

4. Compare reality to your established standards and adjust as needed.

One thing that we used was a scale on the pizza makeline. We also had a small scale on the sub line. New inside help was trained to use the scale and it required effort from everyone. It was especially critical during busy times, because we would be in a hurry and weighing portions was the first thing to suffer. This is especially critical with cheese portions. Your food costs can be ruined during one big rush. It only takes a couple of seconds to reset the scale and to verify the weight is correct. You will be glad that you took the time.

Make sure the standards are used. Do your employees use measuring cups, spoons, and ladles? Do they weigh portions and count how much they use? These are simple ways to implement your standards to cut costs.

Inventory and Product Management

Buy quality inventory then turn it around to sell for the maximum profit. This starts with ordering the best quality ingredients and storing them properly. It's also critical to adjust your procedures as you find problems.

An important principle in inventory management is the "first in, first out" policy. This helps you to rotate your stock. These principles help you manage your inventory and avoid expired food issues. I can tell you from personal experience that I really appreciate a computer program that tracks food usage and assists you in inventory and ordering responsibilities. It can help you track usage, gives you control over inventory, and helps you compile orders.

The point is to maintain consistent quality in your product, and this helps you get the expected quantity from your supplies. This also helps you keep costs at a minimum. Be aware that employee turnover is high and setting standards will help you maintain consistency even with new employees.

The Uniform System of Accounts for Restaurants (USAR), published by the National Restaurant Association (**www.restaurant.org**), is an essential guide for food service accounting. This enables you to compare your results to other people in the food industry. These things will help you evaluate your controls and see if adjustments need to be made.

Beginning Inventory

At the beginning, you document the items in storage for your new store.

You will figure the supplies you will need for each month. This is necessary in order to place accurate food and supply orders. The supplies needed to replenish your stock are part of your operational costs.

Purchasing and Ordering

Determine which suppliers to use: what brands, grades, and varieties to order. Part of this process is to decide how the supplies will be delivered, paid for and returned as needed. Negotiate with your distributors and keep track of price increases on a regular basis. Once these procedures are established, you simply contact your suppliers to let them know what you need.

A quality and effective purchasing program includes:

- Standard purchasing specifics.
- Base these on your standardized recipes.
- This gives you predictable results and quantities.
- This gives you accurate costs based on portions that are served.

You can buy things face-to-face or over the phone. This requires verbal skills to convey your needs. You can also submit a written order form. Keep in mind that part of the package with your suppliers is their level of customer service. These people need to send you written statements with prices and details for your orders. Search for a good sale's representative. He can make your life easier.

The franchise I worked for had commissaries throughout the United States and they delivered most of our supplies. It was easier for us to purchase ground beef and tomatoes locally, but just about everything else came on the commissary truck.

I placed food orders twice a week from a commissary. We called their toll free number, read off the list of supplies we needed, and they repeated the

order back to us. The truck arrived the following evening.

Control Food and Beverage Costs

These four things will help you control food and beverage costs:

1. Forecast what you need and what you will sell.

2. Place orders based on your forecasts.

3. Portion your food, according to your standards.

4. Ensure everyone controls waste.

Food Cost Percentage

The simplest way to describe your food cost ratio is – take the cost of food and divide it by food sales. Determine the food you sold in comparison to the amount of food you actually used. This number can be radically different. This is where you find food over-usage. To have accurate numbers, you need to do a complete inventory at the end of each month. Your inventory is always changing, so do an accurate count to figure your actual usage.

> **Food Sold** = Food that was paid for by employees or customers at full price.

> **Food Used** = Food sold and food that was wasted, stolen, or given away.

Maximum allowable food cost (MFC) This is the maximum amount the food can cost and still allow you to make a profit. In turn, if your food cost exceeds this amount, you will not meet your profit projections.

> Labor Costs + Overhead Expenses – Food Costs =
> **Total monthly costs**

You can add the dollar amount or percentage of your profit goal.

Don't use your highest or lowest sales figures for calculating your operating expenses. It is more effective to use averages.

Subtract the total of the other expenses from 100 percent, and the remainder is your maximum allowable food-cost percentage (MFC).

Actual food cost (AFC) is how much you actually spent on food. If you deduct employee meals from your income statement, you will calculate the cost of food sold. If there aren't any deductions for employee meals, the food cost is food that was consumed. This amount is always higher than the food sold.

Potential food cost (PFC) is your theoretical food cost. This would be the lowest amount food can cost because it is based on the food usage amounts you set. These numbers do not allow for any waste. You can find this number by multiplying each item's ideal usage by the quantity of that item sold.

Prime food cost includes the labor dollars spent to prepare the food. You only need to figure this on labor-heavy items. This would be factored in if you do your prep work on site. Prime cost includes the total cost for food and beverages sold, payroll, and employee benefits.

Check Average

You can figure your check average by dividing the total sales and dividing the number of tickets. This will give you an idea of whether to increase your individual ticket prices. I used to have weekly contests for my staff to see who had the highest average ticket price and who improved the most each week. It was fun for the employees and helped the profit margin for the store. Another variation was to have them push a specific item that had a higher profit margin or something I had over-ordered.

You can figure your projected daily sales and the average number of customers. Then figure what your ticket price must be to reach your goals. It is easier to sell a little more to each table than to fill more tables.

Sales Analysis

Sales mix is the number of each menu item sold. This is important because each menu item impacts your food cost in a different way.

Breakeven point (BEP) means that sales equal expenses. Businesses can operate at the breakeven point, but they will not make any additional money.

Profit Analysis

Closing point means that the cost of being open was more than you brought in. If it cost you $1,500 to be open and you only earned $1,100, your closing point is $400.

Controlling Food Costs

To control food costs effectively, you need to:

1. Project what you will sell and how many of each item.

2. Purchase food and supplies for these projections.

3. Use the proper portions for each menu item served.

4. Control waste and theft.

The standards we discussed earlier in this chapter make this possible. But, your staff must adhere to these standards. The following standards will help you:

Standardize your recipes – The standardized recipe helps you determine the cost of each item. They also ensure consistent quality and cost. These recipes give you the ingredients, preparation method, yield, equipment needed, and how to present the item.

Standardized purchasing – This would include detailed descriptions of the ingredients needed in your standardized recipes. You already established the quality and brand when you negotiated with the distributor. These things make your quality and cost consistent.

Some of the advantages to using standardized recipes are:

- Product Consistency
- Control cost by controlling portion sizes
- Shows item cost used to determine the menu pricing
- Promotes smooth running and an efficient kitchen
- Easier to create inventory and order lists
- Assist with training employees

These are some key things to keep in mind when you develop recipes:

- Test each recipe in your kitchen. Verify and adjust times and temperatures for your equipment.
- List ingredients in the order they are used.
- Verify the amounts on the recipe are correct.
- Be sure the sequence is right and makes sense.
- Double check that you have the equipment you need to make the recipes. Using the wrong equipment will make consistency impossible.
- Dry ingredients need to be listed by weight and liquid by volume. Do you have a scale to measure the weight amounts?

- Have a designated person to make any changes to recipes.

- Make sure your staff uses the standardized recipes.

You can store your recipes on index cards or in a three-ring binder. A nice touch is to buy plastic sheet protectors for your binder or plastic envelopes to protect your recipes. The recipes need to be organized, so people can find the recipe they need. Group all categories together. This would keep all appetizers together, pizza recipes together, and so on.

NAME: SPINACH PIZZA	RECIPE NO. 126	
Portion size: 1 pizza		
Yields: 1 portion		
Cost per Portion: $4.44		
INGREDIENTS	**WEIGHT OR MEASURE**	**COST**
9 inch pizza dough	9 inch	.90
Olive oil	1 tsp	.03
Spinach, fresh	1/2 cup	.08
Red Peppers, roasted	3 oz	.80
Red Onions, chopped	3 oz	.03
Fontina Cheese	2 oz	.65
Parmesan Cheese	2 oz	.40
Feta Cheese	2 oz	.65
Hearts of Palm	1 oz	.70
Sour Cream	1/2 oz	.20
Total Cost for Recipe		4.44

Directions: *Brush olive oil on dough then top with the ingredients in the following order: spinach, red pepper, red onion, the three cheeses, and hearts of palm. The hearts of palm should be sliced into four pieces and placed to look like spokes on a wheel. Be sure that all ingredients are placed all the way to the edge of the dough (do not leave a border).*

Service: *Cut into six slices and serve with a dollop of sour cream in the center.*

As in the previous sample, each recipe needs the following information:

- **Name of item**.

- **Recipe number/identification** within file system.

- **Yield** – How many servings with the recipe prepare?

- **Portion size** – Use the cooked weight or number of pieces. Include the utensil you use to serve the item.

- **Garnish** – This needs to be specific in order to make every plate look the same. You can include a diagram or photograph to show the presentation.

- **Ingredients** – List these in the order they are used, and use the accepted abbreviations for quantity standards. Designate how the ingredient should be prepared, such as chopped, whole, sifted, etc.

- **Preparation instructions** – Include preheating details and use the correct terminology to describe all preparation that is required. Be sure to list any special warning instruction for each recipe. It should include pan sizes, cooking temperature, cooking time, how to test for readiness, and instructions for portioning.

- **Finishing** – This will include any special instructions on how to finish preparing the dish. It can include brushing with oil or drizzling chocolate on top. Include information at about what temperature the item should be kept. Can it sit at room temperature, or does it need to be refrigerated?

- **Cost** – You can include the cost on the recipe. To figure this, look at your invoices; add the cost of all ingredients then divide by the number of servings to determine the individual serving cost.

Sales Mix

The design and personality of your pizza and sub shop will come through in your menu choices. We discussed what to serve in Chapter 8, and we discussed how to pick the right location earlier. Your location affects your menu decisions.

When you decide what to serve, you can determine which equipment and supplies are needed. These things can impact the kitchen size and how it will be arranged. Keep in mind that large equipment changes can be very costly, so think through the equipment purchases and placements.

Your kitchen organization will also be affected by whether you will deliver, your preparation plans, decorations, packaging, and clean up. All of these things make a difference in your kitchen layout.

The equipment needs to be the best equipment for your needs and not based on price. Plan your menu, kitchen layout, and which pieces of equipment are needed then find the best price on that equipment. The same ideas are true for everything in your kitchen, even pots, pans, and utensils.

Once you have your food usage under control, you should analyze each item to make it as profitable as possible. See what sells and what doesn't, and determine what changes should be made. This may also reveal some items should be promoted more, and you can delete other items. It is good to determine which items are popular and profitable then you can promote those items more.

Study your profits for your whole menu. Some items will have a lower profit margin, but need to be on the menu. Is there a way to offer a special by combining these items with another item with a higher profit margin? This could be a way to offer a popular item and increase your potential profit. This is also a way to increase your per ticket price, which we discussed earlier. Remember that you can't offer only low-cost or high-cost items.

Choose a good mix of each.

Ask yourself these questions when you analyze your menu sales mix:

- How much of each item are you selling?
- What is your cost for each item?
- Is the item profitable?

Many restaurants have cash registers that track what was sold. This will give you a nightly, weekly, or monthly report. You can also figure these numbers manually, for a week or a month, by compiling the numbers from guest checks. Your cashier or hostess could compile this information for you on a tracking sheet. Emphasis of accuracy is critical in these figures.

Many consultants will tell you to focus only on the profitability of a menu item, but keep in mind that you need a mix of products. This can mean keeping some lower profit items.

Each item on your menu can be classified for these decisions. List all items in a particular category, and that gives you related items to help you make decisions.

- **Prime items** – Popular items that are low cost and high profit. Make these stand out on your menu and advertising.

- **Standard items** – These have higher food costs and high profit margins. One idea is to raise these prices, and make them your signature dishes. You can have these in all categories: appetizer, salad, soup, pizza, entrees, and desserts.

- **Sleeper items** – These include low cost items with low profit margins that rarely sell. You can increase the visibility of these items through specials and promotions.

- **Problems items** – The items in this group have high food cost

and are low in profits. It would be good to raise these prices, and tuck them onto your menu. If they don't start selling, delete them.

Pricing

Pricing is important on several levels. Over-inflated prices will keep customers away, and low prices can put you out of business. Pricing involves more than just adding a markup percentage.

You can determine the price by the market or the demand. The market is a determining factor in your pricing, but you also need to consider the demand for the items. You must also consider what your competition is charging and what your customers are willing to spend. Market driven prices must be responsive to the prices your competition charges.

If you and the other pizza shop in your neighborhood serve the same products, you have to price them competitive. Consider this when you add a new product to your menu, and there is no existing demand for it. The other instance is items that your customers demand and you can charge more. Once your competitors begin to serve it, you will have to re-evaluate your prices.

Your location will impact the prices you can charge. Another consideration is the atmosphere in your pizza shop. Remember, the price isn't the issue; it depends on whether your customers feel they are getting their money's worth. Your prices must be in line with how your customers view your pizza shop. A hot dog stand can't charge the same prices as a five-star restaurant. Each would lose their customers. Your image and prices need to fit with the image of your pizza shop.

There are a couple of processes you can use to determine the prices to charge: (1) Charge as much as possible or (2) Charge as little as possible.

There are negative and positive aspects to each approach. If you charge the most, your profit is higher, but you will have fewer customers and less business. The customers you have will demand a product that is worth the higher price. When you charge the lowest price, your customers are very satisfied with the value for their money, but your profit margin has shrunk.

These are four pricing strategies:

1. **Competitive pricing** – You must meet or beat your competitors' prices. This will have minimal effect because it depends on customers making a decision based on price alone, with no regard to quality, service, and ambience.

2. **Intuitive pricing** – You would base your prices on what you think customers will pay, with no regard to what others are charging. There is a slim chance this will work.

3. **Psychological pricing** – The price will have more impact on lower income customers. Some people will assume the items are good if they are high-priced. Another issue is how you place your prices on your menu. We'll discuss this more in Chapter 11. You can create a feeling that an item is a bargain by lowering the price.

4. **Trial-and-error pricing** – You can base your prices on the reactions of your customers. This could work on some items, but it is not a good way to price your entire menu.

In order to charge top dollar for your products, your customers need to believe you serve a special product that is worth the additional price. Do you have the best gourmet pizza shop in the area? Do you pique their interest with unique and different specials that tempt their taste buds? These things help to elevate you in their opinion.

You also need to insist your staff gives superior service to each customer, every time they deal with you. Some pizza shops make customers order at the counter then clear their own tables. The more you make the customer do, the less you can charge. Never underestimate the value of providing customer service. A very simple example is the difference in my drivers' tips when they delivered pizza with napkins. It's a very small thing, but when drivers included napkins with a delivery, their tips were higher. Often, tips were substantially higher. The tip was even larger when they offered coupons.

Financial Analysis

We've all eaten at pizza shops that have great food, service, and atmosphere and then we see them go out of business. Do you ever wonder how this is possible? Many times it's because they didn't manage the business finances. This doesn't mean they stole from the company, just that they didn't know how to manage the business income.

Managerial accounting includes managing the day-to-day operations of your pizza shop. The information reveals all aspects of the shop, including customer counts, sales mix and labor hours and costs. You can break down expenses by department, day, or meal, and can point out problem areas. But, to glean this information from the reports, learn how to compile and analyze the reports.

Theft

A 2002 National Retail Security Survey indicates that employee theft accounts for 48.5 percent of business losses, of which 31.3 percent is shoplifting, 15.1 percent is administrative errors, and 5.1 percent is vendor fraud. This is another reason to use strict policies and to ensure they are enforced.

When policies are in place, managers handle cash. Hourly employees may steal other things because they have access to them. Watch employees when they exit, especially when they leave with deliveries. They can try to take items out in the delivery bag, but this is usually obvious if someone watches. It might be necessary to have a camera on the doors to check for suspicious activity. Keep any food away from your doors, especially the back door.

In order to track sales and usage, all transactions must be entered into your system. This is true whether you use a computer or a manual system. I used to give my on call driver a free pizza as a bonus for being available if I needed him. Someone was on call every Friday and Saturday night, and this was a treat for being available in case I needed to call him in. When the employee got his pizza, I entered a zero amount in the computer to account for the food usage. It would hurt my average ticket price slightly, but it ensured my food count was correct.

The following cost-control concepts are crucial to make your system work:

- Documentation of all tasks, activities, and transactions.

- Managers must supervise employees to ensure standards are met.

- Different people should be involved in the tracking systems.

- Tasks need to be done in a timely manner. This helps you eliminate problems early.

- Evaluate if you spend more money to track these costs than you save.

Control Labor Costs

Many restaurant people feel the solution to labor cost overages is to fire people and to cut hours. This is very shortsighted and isn't the answer. The results are reduced productivity, decreased quality and service, and high turnover. You cannot keep valuable employees if they are concerned you will

terminate people each time there are problems. You can effectively control labor costs in your pizzeria by being involved in the daily management activities. Be involved each day, not just at the end of the month. Some suggestions to help you maintain labor costs are described below.

Scheduling

Effective scheduling is a wonderful tool to maintain and control labor costs. A bad schedule can cost you money. A qualified manager can overcome a bad schedule, but it can also create hard feelings with staff. Serious thought needs to go into creating a schedule. It is also good to review past sales records for the business, if you have them. If you don't, make thorough notes on your daily reports, so they will be useful in following years.

When you create a schedule, your goal is to operate effectively and provide quality products and service to customers. It's better to over-schedule than to under-schedule and be caught shorthanded. A technique I used was to schedule one or two short shifts. They could be 10 minutes or 2 hours, depending on how busy we were. There were a group of employees who liked the short shifts and when I needed them to work, they would stay. However, they were usually happy when I offered to let them go home. No matter how well you learn your customers, there can always be strange situations and its best to be prepared for these times.

It will take a couple of months to work out a scheduling system that works for you. In the beginning, it's important to have extra staffing until business gets established and settles into a routine. Keep in mind that your customers are paying full price and dealing with the snags in your system.

Effective Scheduling

The answer to controlling labor costs is proper scheduling, not low wages.

It's best to schedule your best people during the busiest times. Know the strengths and weaknesses of each staff member to make this work. Some employees are not good during a rush, but can be trained to do prep work. You can schedule people to start at different times and have overlapping shifts. This gives you the flexibility to send people home when business is slower.

- **Determine labor cost for a shift** – Write the schedule then multiply the employee hours by their hourly wage to determine the labor cost for the shifts. Take your projected sales figures, and divide that into your labor dollars to determine the labor percentage. If the percentage is too high, you need to get labor costs down or to increase sales.

- **Let team leaders write schedules** – Team leaders should help with writing schedules. It is a learning experience and can help them to be in touch with maintaining costs. You have to be able to count on team leaders to maintain costs, or they should be replaced.

- **Helpful hints** – Whoever writes the schedule should remember to:

  – **Give each employee one or two days off per week.**

  – **Avoid employee burnout from over-scheduling.**

  – **Schedule alternates in case of emergencies.**

  – **Schedule one team leader for each shift.**

On-call schedule – This is something I implemented on Friday and Saturday nights. It was difficult with all college students for employees, but we managed. One or two employees would be "on call," and I would only call if I was slammed. (Slammed = incredibly busy and we couldn't process the majority of the orders without help.) We had special college events and local events which packed the hotels, and it was impossible to plan for all of those things. Along with getting to know scheduling people at the college, it

is also good to know people at the local hotels and Chamber of Commerce. Their events will impact your business. Having someone on call gave me more peace of mind and allowed me to send a driver home when it slowed down, without being concerned we would get hit later. I only had to call people in a few times.

While I was an assistant manager, we had a huge motorcycle rally at a local hotel. We didn't know about this event when the schedule was written or the food order was placed and we were flooded with orders. It was so busy that we had to run to a local grocery store to get cheese. Sales were great for the weekend, but service suffered. If we had known about the event, we could have maximized the opportunity with coupons at the hotel and would have ordered enough food to handle the rush. Bottom line: get to know your community.

- **Cross Training** – In any business, you must hire people who can be cross trained. This makes them worth more to you and gives you more flexibility with their schedule. Your delivery personnel need to be trained to prep, and my drivers all knew how to make pizzas, subs, and tend ovens. This training was invaluable when we were really busy.

Computer Software To Improve Scheduling

Computer software is a wonderful tool for scheduling and tracking labor costs. You can find programs that track time, attendance, and payroll. These things will save you money and improve employee satisfaction and retention. The software ranges from a few hundred to several thousand dollars. One good scheduling system, with the option of an employee time clock, is available from Atlantic Publishing and costs less than $300 (**www.atlantic-pub.com** or 800-814-1132). Following are some other options:

- Visit Asgard Systems at **www.asgardsystems.com**.

- Staff Trak at **http://staftrak.com**.

- Madrigal Soft Tools at **www.madrigalsoft.com**.

- **www.restaurantresults.com** for a listing of other software.

Prepared Beverages and Foods

As discussed earlier, you will pay more for prepped food, but it will save labor costs. If you plan to buy prepared foods, be sure to test them before signing a contract. Can they supply the quality level you want? If not, talk to your sales representative and see if there are any quality options.

Work Area Layout and Equipment Design

The layout of your store and kitchen can have a big impact on your labor costs. Is your kitchen and store laid out to make it easier to work? If not, you should rearrange what you can. When you have to struggle to get to the sub makeline, you waste time on every sub that is ordered. If your drink cooler is in a back corner, you waste time on every order and each delivery. Placing the drink cooler beside the drivers' door is much more effective. Take a little time to watch your employees working in your pizza shop, and see if there are ways you can rearrange things to make it easier to work. This will save you money.

Every year new pieces of equipment are introduced to the market. Subscribe to trade magazines which will keep you informed about these new arrivals. But, be sure the cost is justified before you buy new equipment.

If the added expense can be justified, you can probably finance the cost over several years through the manufacturer or distributor. Verify the terms, and check about any penalties to paying this off early. The purchase is tax deductible, and your accountant can help you do this in the most advantageous way.

Here are some ways to help you with the store layout. When your pizza shop is laid out properly, it can increase efficiency, speed activity, and help your staff excel in their customer service.

- **Have self-contained workstations** where tools, equipment, supplies and storage are within easy reach for each task.

- **Keep cleaning supplies in a carryall** where they are needed.

- **Provide plenty of waste receptacles** – Divide waste if you implement a recycling program. Get the details from your waste management company.

- **Create work triangles** – Triangle or diamond layouts provide easy access to supplies and equipment while reducing steps.

- **Draw out traffic maps** to minimize unnecessary steps and crisscrossing paths for various workers.

- **Allow for ample open space** – People need room to work and move without bumping into other things and other people.

- **Listen to your staff** – Talk with your staff members, who have experience, to give you some suggestions about how to lay out the store and kitchen. They will appreciate being involved.

Creating Productivity

We've discussed many things that can impact your costs. Setting standards and ensuring people follow them will help maintain food costs. Monitor the financial management of the store. Ask your accountant for tips about how to manage your income. Learn to schedule your staff to your best advantage. These things may seem small, but together they can make a huge difference in the profitability and success of your pizza and sub shop.

12

Profitable Menu Planning

This chapter will help you determine your menu style, how to format your menu, projecting menu prices, developing menu items, portion control, and the importance of truth and accuracy in menus.

Menu Style

Menu styles can be described in terms of how simple or how many item varieties you offer. This decision can be dictated by your space, additional labor involved and, more importantly, what your customer base requires. Remember, more choices will keep your regular customers coming back and will attract new people.

On the other hand, a limited menu allows you to focus on certain items and will save on inventory, supplies, and labor costs. You've probably been to Chinese and Mexican restaurants that offer a lot of different things, but they use many of the same ingredients to create all of these items.

There are ways for you to offer many items and utilize some staple ingredients. What about spaghetti, lasagna, stuffed shells, manicotti, and similar dishes? These use many of the same ingredients and you can buy a variety of pasta to make the different entrees. You can make pizza, calzone, and stromboli from the same ingredients.

When you chose a limited menu, your ordering, storage, preparation, and service are simplified. You can charge lower prices when your costs are lower. In most situations it is better to keep things simple in the beginning and then diversify if it is warranted over time.

Decide how many items to offer. Your customers want variety, but sometimes too much variety causes confusion. Interestingly, research has proven that 60 to 67 percent of the menu items sold are the same 8 to 12 items. However, it's recommended that you offer 18 to 24 items.

Many pizza shop menus offer an A La Carte menu, which simply means that everything is priced separately, including salads.

Formatting Your Menu

Once your goals and menu style are defined, decide how to format your menu. Here are some questions that will help you get started:

- What menu categories will you offer? These include: appetizers, entrees, pizzas, salad, soup, dessert, beverages, etc.

- Will you offer specialties within these categories? This could include: healthy options, vegetarian, allergy conscious, etc. It would be good to include food lists with these items.

- How many items do you want in each category?

- Will certain items be served more than one way? One example is

chicken, which can be fried, broiled, baked etc.

• What recipes will you use? This helps you determine what ingredients, supplies, equipment, staff, and training you need.

These questions will help you develop the foundation for your menu. What you serve is important. It builds the character and personality of your shop.

Daily Specials

There are many ways to offer daily specials. In an earlier chapter, I mentioned using daily specials as a way to test new items. You don't have to offer it every day, but you can get feedback from your customers. If the feedback is good, you can consider adding it to your menu.

You can include a daily special card in your menu. Some restaurants offer the same daily specials week after week. Others list the specials on a special board. In some restaurants, the server lists the specials for customers.

A good thing about adding different specials is that it allows you to use up leftovers or items you over ordered. If you have cut up vegetables left over you can offer soup. It's better to make less than to throw away spoiled food.

Specials also offer some diversity for your regular customers without having to have so many items on your menu. You can allow employees or customers to offer suggestions for specials, but you need to have the final approval after evaluating the costs involved.

Developing the Menu Selections

You should have your menu planned before you choose your equipment,

hire your staff, and layout your kitchen. There will be changes while you are in business, but major decisions should be made before you move forward. For the people who buy an existing pizza shop, you may have to work around the kitchen and equipment that you have.

In the last chapter, we talked about how a disorganized kitchen can impact your production and labor costs. So, be sure your kitchen and staff compliment your menu. Here are some specifics to consider:

- Can inexperienced employees help with food preparation?

- Can your items be prepared ahead of time?

- Do you need employees with special abilities and if so, how often and for how long?

- Can everyone work in the kitchen at once without tripping over one another?

- Who will supervise the kitchen?

One way to produce consistent and less expensive food is to have some people work on preparation while others cook. I'll use these principals and insert personal experiences that may be helpful. Earlier I mentioned that your delivery drivers can help with a lot of your prep work. This is only true if you have drivers, and they must be trained to wash their hands thoroughly before doing any prep.

Points to Consider

- Items must be of superior quality.

- Be creative. Can you offer different things from other area pizza shops?

- Can you find quality ingredients year round? Are the prices reasonably stable all year?

- Is it easy to weigh and measure the items you plan to use? We had a scale on our pizza makeline which was handy and was used to measure many ingredients.

- Are your items affordable and in demand?

- Can your staff create the items on your menu?

- Can you duplicate the quality in all your menu items?

- How long is the shelf life of the foods you are considering? This isn't an issue with pizza since they are usually made fresh.

- Are the cooking times of most items similar? If not, it will be difficult to serve everyone at a table at the same time.

- Is the turnaround time for your items reasonable? If something will take a long time, your customers need to be told.

- Do you have a place to store the raw ingredients for your items?

Limiting the Menu

There may lots of great food ideas, but you are opening a pizza and sub shop which should include items to fit that atmosphere. In the beginning, you might be tempted to add "popular" items and extras to round out your menu. It's better to keep it simple and offer things you do better than your competitors.

A simpler menu makes things easier for your servers, hostess, phone staff, kitchen help, delivery drivers and for you. Everyone's job is easier when there

are fewer things to keep straight. When you focus on less things, you will need larger quantities of specific items. This should enable you to negotiate better prices which is helpful in controlling costs.

You and your staff need to be familiar with every item. Can they describe each item? Have you shown them ways to subtly upsell the customer? Can they explain what ingredients are included for customers with special dietary needs? Have your employees tasted each item on your menu? Offer samples to your employees because many customers will ask about an item before they order. The more positive things your staff can say about your menu items, the better they can help your customers.

Portion Control = Savings

We discussed this in some detail in the last chapter. Set standards about portion sizes. They should offer as much as possible for a value price. Anyone in the kitchen who prepares food for the customers, must understand the portion sizes and abide by these standards. You cannot overemphasize the importance of portion control.

Portion control is also a great way to maintain consistency. I've been to restaurants where the portion sizes changed on different days. Some days it was larger while other days it was less. Your customers need to know they will receive the same amount each time they order an item.

There will be small variations, but these shouldn't be noticeable for your customers. For example, you may allow five ounces of pepperoni, and there is actually 5.25 ounces. That won't make a big difference. But, what if the pizza has 3.5 or 7? Many restaurants enforce an eighth-of-an-ounce variation.

Since you will enforce the portioning standards, you must supply good scales and measuring items. I had a new employee who had a horrible time getting the right amount of cheese on a pizza, and on his second day our

scale broke. He made it very clear that he couldn't portion properly without a way to measure the items. I couldn't argue, and we had a new scale before his shift was over.

Take a look at the areas where food will be prepared to decide how many scales to buy. One scale on the pizza makeline is invaluable, and another in the kitchen where entrees are prepared, may be all you need. If you discover overages in certain items, take a look at where they are made, and see if a scale or better measuring utensils would help.

It's also good to verify the weights and amounts of your orders. This is especially true with a new supplier. Record discrepancies and address the problems. If one or two people handle this each time you receive a delivery, they should be able to spot problems quickly.

You could have someone pre-measure sliced meats for your subs. The items for each sub could be separated with deli paper or put in plastic bags. This is especially handy for a rush and enables the sub maker to be more consistent. Salad dressing can be dipped with a specific ladle to keep the portions even. The size of your sauce ladle will also make a difference. Become familiar with how full the ladle should be, and it will speed up your pizza making while remaining consistent.

Keep the portion lists at all appropriate places in the kitchen and on the makelines. This keeps the amounts in front of your employees at all times. On the occasions when you revise the amounts, make an announcement to all employees and replace all existing portioning charts. You must be responsible to make sure these standards are used.

Your Recipe File

In the last chapter, we discussed how to create a recipe file and what to include on each "recipe card." These files need to be in the kitchen for the

cooks to use each time they prepare an item. We also discussed keeping these cards or files in plastic, so they can be cleaned easily.

Menu items should not be prepared from your memory. Following the recipe each time will ensure consistency in taste, presentation, and food costs. For most pizzas and subs, you can have a list of the ingredients along with the portions for each ingredient.

Ordering Manual

This contains a list of all the products to be ordered. If you do not have a computer system, create a form that lists all items and your ideal amount to keep on hand. This will simplify your ordering, and you can simply place a mark beside anything you know needs to be ordered. However, do not forget to check sales history, local events, and special events to determine whether to order more than usual. You can simplify your list by keeping similar products listed and stored close and in a logical order for inventory.

Figure Menu Prices

To maintain a profit, keep your food cost at 35 to 45 percent. This is also dependent on controlling your other costs, but it gives you a starting point. This amount is the total food cost divided by the total food sales for the same period.

Figuring what to charge is reasonably simple. You should have already figured the portion costs for your recipe files. Take the total food cost and divide by proposed menu price to find the percentage. It should be 35 to 45 percent. There will be some exceptions to that rule. But, that percentage is a good rule of thumb. Some products will have higher percentages while others are lower. One item I used to love to push were breadsticks. We made

them by hand, and the cost was almost nonexistent. When you can charge two dollars, and your cost with sauce is about 40 cents, you should promote that product at a 20 percent food cost.

$$\text{Portion Costs} \div \text{Menu Price} \times 100 = 35\%\text{-}45\%$$

You can insert various menu prices and estimated costs to figure all percentages.

When you use this for each menu item, you will get some strange results. To maintain a 35 to 45 percent cost on each item would make some items far too high. But, they are balanced by others which have lower percentages. Create a good mix of both type of items.

It's also good to research what similar pizza shops are charging in your area. This will help you determine what local customers are willing to spend. Your side orders, beverages and appetizers have very low cost percentages which will help to lower your overall cost percentages. This was one of the reasons I set up contests for my staff to promote certain items. They should "hard sell" your customers, but can suggestive sell items that help your bottom line.

You must maintain a reasonable food cost percentage to maintain your overall costs. One item we always overused was cheese. It is costly and very easy to overportion. Check your reports. Determine which items you overuse and make everyone aware of the problem. Each person who helps prepare food needs to maintain food costs.

Preparing Your Menu

There are many options to produce your menu. It can be laminated, a one-page or two-page flyer, posted on your Web site, on in store sign, or it can be listed with a delivery service. However your choose to display the menu, consider some principals about the menu design.

Menu Design

Your menu needs to highlight the positives of your business. Focus on "fresh," "handmade," and brand names. How you word your descriptions and present your food items will have an impact on what your customers buy. You can draw their attention to specific items while drawing them away from others.

You can print a single page, two-panel, three-panel, or multi-page menu.

Menu Size and Cover

You've heard the adage that you can't judge a book by its cover. But, we all know people who do that. Your menu is the same. Your promotion starts with the cover of your menu. This is especially true if you print menus to circulate for promotion. Include something on the cover that distinguishes your pizza shop from others. It might include a picture of your building or logo. It can be nice to add some family information inside the front page or on the back to help customers know you better.

When you design your menu, you can use 8.5" x 11" paper because most menu covers are 9" x 12". You can play with those dimensions, but keep it a size that customers can look at comfortably. They also need to have room to read it at their table with drinks on the table.

Make your cover durable, or laminate the menus. There are many choices on the market. The personality of your pizza shop will give you an indication of the sort of cover to use. You also need to choose your cover color with care. It needs to tie into your pizza shop theme. Colors also affect people in different ways. We'll discuss colors in Chapter 19 about decorating your pizza shop.

Your cover should include your hours of operation, address, phone number,

a list of the credit cards you accept, and any special services you offer. These services could include eat-in, carryout, catering etc. Keep in mind that you want to attract new customers with your menu and they can learn more about your pizza shop.

Menu Content

Menu content can help customers make their decision. It needs to clearly state the details about what you offer. This content can reflect the personality of your pizza shop. Be careful not to make any false claims. These claims will cause bad feelings with your customers, and they could decide to stop dealing with you.

Ways to write your menu content:

- Use short descriptions.
- Use descriptive terms which reveal details ("roasted," not "cooked").
- Don't use unnecessary adjectives.
- Don't over-describe because this can confuse your customers.

Which description would persuade you?

Veal Parmigana – Tender veal lightly breaded and fried to perfection, then smothered with thick marinara sauce and topped with layers of melted provolone cheese, served with a mound of linguini.

Veal Parmigana – Lightly breaded and fried veal topped with marinara sauce and provolone cheese. Served with a side of linguini.

Either description will work, but the first gives too much information. Do your words make the customer feel full?

There are three general categories of menu copy:

1. **Name of the item**

2. **Descriptive content**

3. **General content**

The name of the item is self explanatory: pizza, veggie sub, lasagna, manicotti, stuffed shells, breadsticks, and so on. You can use theme names which may not reveal as much: Nora's house salad, Chris' pizza, University Spaghetti, and so on.

Descriptive content will include ingredients, how the item is prepped and any side dishes or condiments that are included. This would include marinara or Alfredo sauce with breadsticks. There is no need to list common items, but lesser known items should be explained.

General content includes hours of operation, location, and ownership.

Descriptions are the most important part of your menu and the most complicated. When you prepare to write your descriptions, think about how much description your items need. Longer descriptions aren't usually needed unless you are offering something really complicated. If you offer detailed special pizzas, you should describe the ingredients.

You might be tempted to used Italian phrases on your menu. Remember that most customers won't understand these, and it could cause confusion.

Key elements to include in your descriptions:

- Method of preparation (grilled, sautéed, fried, etc.)
- Main ingredients
- How it is served and any accompanying items
- Grades and/or freshness claims
- Geographic origin (Italian Ice, Sicilian Spaghetti, etc.)

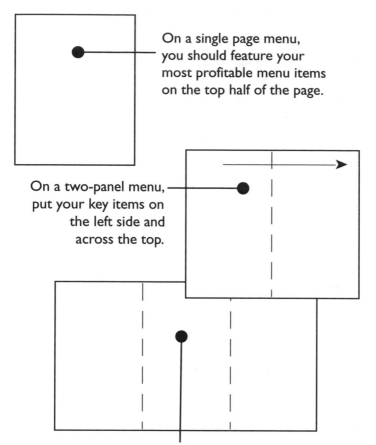

On a single page menu, you should feature your most profitable menu items on the top half of the page.

On a two-panel menu, put your key items on the left side and across the top.

The three-panel menu should feature your key items in the center.

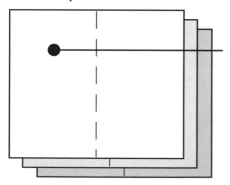

It is hard to find the focal point on a multi-page menu. Treat each opening like a single page or two-panel menu.

Price Placement

Customers need to read the description before the price. Some restaurants place the price directly across from the name. Instead, list the name and place the price under the description. This shifts their focus away from the prices.

Example 1

Steak and Cheese Deep Dish Pizza 13.95
Spaghetti and Meatballs 8.95
Pepper Steak Hoagie 6.95

This is a much more effective menu layout:

Example 2

Steak and Cheese Deep Dish Pizza
16-inch deep dish crust, filled with tomato
chucks, green peppers, slices of marinated steak,
and topped with provolone cheese. 13.95

Spaghetti and Meatballs
Spaghetti with garlic tomato sauce, meatballs,
and Parmesan cheese. 8.95

Pepper Steak Hoagie
Onion, peppercorn beef, melted Swiss cheese, and
roasted red pepper 6.95

Arrangement of Text

Menus are usually organized in the order food is served: appetizers, soups, and salads come before entrees, and desserts are the final menu item. This is one way of helping customers find the items they want.

It's been proven that people remember the first and last thing they read or hear. So, it would be good to place the items you want to feature at the beginning and at the end of your menu. This increases your chances of selling the items you want. By the same principal, you can draw attention away from things that are in the middle of the list.

Menu Psychology

A well-designed menu will influence what customers buy. Their decisions can be affected by the font, the colors, and how you place the words you choose. Menus are another way to promote your business.

We read from left to right and from top to bottom. You can attract the customers' attention by using different font sizes. Using boxes or graphics will draw the readers' eye to that spot. Place items you want to sell in these spots.

Have a clear picture of what you want to convey to your customers. What do you want them to know about your pizza shop? This message needs to be conveyed on your menu.

Menu Layout

Your menu needs to have sufficient white space around the context. Promotional material needs to convey a clear message and should be uncluttered. Use each section to promote something. If there's an empty area, promote your delivery service or daily specials.

Your printer can offer suggestions about the type styles and font sizes. The type needs to reflect the style of your pizza shop. No matter what you chose, be sure it is readable. Don't make potential customers struggle to figure out the name of your pizza shop or your phone number.

Serif looks traditional or old-fashioned. Sans serif type is simpler with a blocky shape and looks more modern. Script should have slanted letters which creates eye strain for the reader.

Tips for creating your menu's physical appearance:

- Use upper case letters for each category and lowercase for descriptions.

- Mix bold or italic type to provide some variety. Menu groups can be bold, item names can be italic, and use regular type for descriptions.

- Be careful not to use more than three type styles on your menu. It's confusing and looks amateurish.

- You shouldn't use type smaller than 12 points, but be sure the size you use fits the space. You don't want to overwhelm customers.

This can give you an idea of some available font sizes:

This is 8 point type

This is 9 point type

This is 10 point type

This is 12 point type

This is 14 point type

This is 20 point type

This is 24 point type

- You can adjust the space between letters. This is called kerning, and it can make your text more readable.

- You can also adjust the space between lines of text which is called leading. There should be at least three points between lines for maximum readability.

Graphic Elements

Graphics are another element you can add to your menu. Here are some things to consider:

- Your printer can include a photograph for you.

- Several online sources for free clipart include: **www.clip-art.com**, **www.barrysclipart.com**, and **www.clipartconnection.com**.

- Check with local colleges or high schools if you would like an original illustration at a reasonable price.

Printing Your Menu Production

When you talk with a printer, decide on paper style, color and weight, and ink colors. Keep in mind that additional colors get expensive. The quality of paper depends on how permanent the menus will be. In the beginning, you will probably make changes. Also, if you plan to use plastic menu holders, you don't have to spend a lot on heavy paper. Once you feel confident about the menu plan, you can laminate your menus to help them last longer. This also keeps them clean. You don't want to offer a customer a stained menu.

Decide what color paper to use and the colors should blend with your décor, personality, and logo, etc. The printer can help you with this.

Many office supply stores offer laser printer papers you can use for your menu, and menu covers come in a wide variety of styles. You can also order papers online at **www.ideaart.com/cgi-bin/sgdynamo.exe?HTNAME=_ index.html**.

Menu Design Dos and Don'ts

To review some of the specific things you should and shouldn't do:

- Don't list your prices down the right-hand side of the page.

- Leave "white space." Too many words be overwhelmings.

- Make the type large enough to read. This is especially important if you will have dim lighting or candlelight. Print a sample of your menu and read it in similar lighting before you place your final order. Don't use a type size lower than 12-point.

Carefully consider how much text to use. There is no need to describe common items unless you plan to give them a new twist.

It's better for you to work on the layout of your menu. The printer can give it a more pleasing appearance, but figure out the placement. You and someone else should proofread your menu before sending it to the printer. It is very unprofessional to have typos on your menu.

Truth and Accuracy in the Menu

When you proofread your menu be careful that everything you say is accurate. Most business owners don't want to deceive their customers since that would hurt them. There might be an unintentional mistake that could cause problems. You want to make your customers' mouths water, but you must describe your products accurately. Here are some examples:

- Are there three eggs in your three-egg omelet?

- Are you sure your organic produce is certified organic?

- Be clear about your promotional offers.

- Do you charge customers to share plates or make substitutions?

- Do you clearly identify ingredients that are common allergens?

- Is there a special notation on items that are prepared different?

- Instead of calling it "homemade," do you describe it as "homestyle," "homemade style," "made on the premises," or "our own"?

- If you use any of the following terms, are you sure you can substantiate them?

  —Fresh daily   —Fresh-roasted

  —Flown in daily   —Kosher meat

  —Our special sauce   —Low calorie

- Do you misrepresent fresh orange juice as frozen?

- Do you use commonly accepted ways to preserve, such as canned, chilled, bottled, frozen, and dehydrated appropriately?

- Do you use the right terminology to describe the food preparation techniques you utilize?

- Do pictures on your menus, wall placard, or advertising materials contain pictures that accurately represent your menu items?

- Could you put the public's health at risk by misrepresenting the content of your food?

- Is your food really "salt-free" or "sugar-free"?

Disclaimers

Many restaurants include a disclaimer on their menus. This simply says that what you have printed is accurate to the best of your knowledge, but the pizzeria cannot be held responsible for any actions beyond its immediate control. Here's an example:

> *We serve only the finest food available. However, at certain times during the year we may not be able to obtain the exact product desired; therefore, we may substitute a similar product that will be equal or superior to the original item. Should this be the case, our staff will inform you of the substitution.*

Set the menu aside then look at it with fresh eyes to be sure there are no misrepresentations. Restaurant owners need to self-regulate to maintain the high standards and reputation they enjoy.

Nutritional Claims

If you want to include menu items that are marketed as healthy (i.e., heart-healthy, low-fat, reduced-fat, cholesterol-free, etc.), make sure you have the nutritional information for these items readily accessible. Items described as "fresh" are included in this category.

The FDA regulations say if you make health/nutritional claims on your menu, you must demonstrate your basis for making them. There is some flexibility in how restaurants may support the claim, but they must be able to show their claims are consistent with the claims established under the Nutrition Labeling and Education Act.

Some restaurants list ingredients and Nutritional Facts labels on their menus. The label gives the item's calories, total fat, cholesterol, sodium, carbohydrates, protein, etc. Some states require take-out foods be labeled in this manner.

You don't have to include the nutritional information on the menu but it needs to be available. Many chains post this information on a poster in a public area. Decide if you have room on your menu or if a poster or separate brochure would work better.

Menu Design Help

It is best to have a professional print your menu or to use professional menu design software. You can use an unusual and readable style to dress up your menu. Discuss ideas and possibilities with your printer or graphic artist.

Artwork should be used if possible. You can use your logo. Your printer may have an artist on staff or there could may be freelancers who can help you.

- Microsoft Office offers templates and more templates and graphic art (including menu-specific) are available at **www. office.microsoft.com.**

- Restaurant MenuPro software is available – **www.foodsoftware.com.**

- Soft Café offers menu design software – **www.softcafe.com.**

- Custom menu covers can set you apart. Check out Impact Enterprises – **www.impactmenus.com.**

- Atlantic Publishing has several books dedicated to menu design. You'll find books with sample menus for inspiration at **www. atlantic-pub.com.**

Your menu will represent your store and needs to reflect it's personality. Menus can be used for wide spread promotion. Get your menus in as many hands as possible. Keep these promotional possibilities in mind when you design the menu. Keep it simple and useful for your customers.

MENU PLANNING

The most important aspect of menu planning is consistency, your design and image presented for the menu has to fit the type of setting you will be having in your restaurant. Also make sure it is easy to read, and make sure the different categories are well-defined and easy for people to find what they are looking for. Be sure to specify some of the ingredients, as well as any different procedures, used in making the pizza. Let people reading the menu know what you do that is distinctive, that makes your pizza not like everywhere else's...so they should want to go to you all the time. If you use fresh mozzarella and fresh herbs, let them know that.

Anything that is fresh or distinctive should be stated on the menu clearly. If you only use fresh herbs, for example, state that at the top of the menu, so they can see it soon as they look at it. Do you make your own pizza dough? If so, tell them you make it fresh daily. Diet and healthy eating is of increasing popularity, so make sure to state any menu items that are health conscious, vegetarian friendly, heart friendly, diabetic friendly, etc., perhaps with small symbols next to the menu items with a key at the bottom of the page. Also keep in mind you want them to remember your name and slogan, (future free advertising; if they like it, they will tell their friends, and there is no better advertising than a satisfied customer) so make sure it is prominent (but not overbearing) on the menu, and visible on every page if there is more than one page to the menu. Perhaps having your logo watermarked under each page of the inside menu.

—Chef Kevin Smith, door2door gourmet (catering, menu planning, and consulting). Orlando, FL, **kjoel_arts@yahoo.com**

Your Staff

Your pizza shop will be different from others. In small shops, your staff will handle many different tasks. This was mentioned in Chapter 11 about cross-training your employees. Decide what you will serve and how many people you can afford to hire. This will make a difference in the skills to look for in prospective employees. It is usually easier to start with less people and add more as the business gets busier. But, don't understaff and let customer service or quality suffer.

Cook

Your menu will dictate how many cooks and the experience level needed. You and your manager can usually do a good amount of the cooking. This will depend on your menu. So, let's plan for one multi-talented cook, and the manager can help when needed. I also recommend that other employees be trained to help with simple cooking tasks and health concerns.

The cook will be responsible for all cooking duties; setting up for the next shift and ensuring sufficient prep is done before the next shift or before closing and cleaning the work.

Prep Cook

Once your pizza shop gets bigger, you might need a prep cook, but other employees can be trained to help with preparing simple entrees, pizzas, subs, etc.

These duties also include prepping food for the next shift. The responsibilities will depend on how much food needs to be prepped, including lettuce, sauce, cheese, and so on. Take a close look at your menu and determine how many hours you actually need a prep person.

Manager

In larger operations you will have a manager. Until you get to that size you can train an employee who excels to be a shift runner. This will give you some flexibility as the owner and will still ensure the work will be done. Always pick your managers or shift runners carefully. A manager may be responsible for:

- Hiring, training, supervising, and scheduling employees.
- Monitoring quality control.
- Control waste and food cost.
- Ordering, receiving, storing, and issuing food.
- Health and safety oversight.
- Setting safety standards and training employees.
- Inform owner of possible problems.

- Encourage employee communication and morale.

Dishwasher

There may not be a lot of dishes, but you will have pans, sauce buckets, cutters, knives, and bowls to be cleaned, even if you don't have eat-in service. For pizza shops that also offer a dine-in option, you will obviously have more dishes.

It is possible that your prep employee can also wash dishes. This is a good position for someone who wants to learn a lot from the ground up. They can also learn a lot from the cook and the manager.

Some duties can include: tracking cleaning supplies, tracking dishware and cookware breakage, coordinating recycling, cleaning waste areas, along with the things mentioned above.

Delivery Personnel

You will need to hire delivery drivers if you decide to offer delivery service. Their main duty is to deliver orders, but they can also be cross-trained to help with prep, cooking, cleaning, and so on. My drivers helped with all aspects of the business and did a great job.

Front Counter

Your front counter person can set the mood for your pizza shop. Any business is judged by the people who interact with your customers. The front counter person needs to help with many duties, but his primary duty is to handle customers in a professional and courteous manner. The counter person's duties include making change, taking orders, answering the phone, keeping areas in the public view clean, food prep, and possibly helping in

the pizza and sub preparation.

Job Descriptions

Numerous books have been written about developing job descriptions. You can also write your own job descriptions to fit your pizza shop. These descriptions include:

- Job title.

- Title of supervisor.

- Job summary – Description and responsibilities of the position.

- Essential functions or primary responsibilities – Outline the job tasks. Always include: "all other duties as assigned" which allows you the flexibility to change responsibilities as needed.

- Qualifications and special skills.

- Working Conditions – This includes noise level, extreme temperatures, lifting, etc.

You can use this template for your job descriptions.

JOB DESCRIPTION TEMPLATE

Job Title: _____

Inside or Delivery: _____

Reports to: _____

Salary or Pay Rate: _____

Last Revision Date: _____

SUMMARY

PRIMARY RESPONSIBILITIES

KNOWLEDGE AND SKILL REQUIREMENTS

WORKING CONDITIONS

Check the accompanying CD to print this template. The following job descriptions are also included for your reference.

Job Title	**ASSISTANT MANAGER**
Reports to	General Manager or Owner

SUMMARY
- Oversee kitchen and dining room staffs.
- Responsible for operations in the absence of the General Manager.
- Promote staff/customer relations.

PRIMARY RESPONSIBILITIES
1. Manages and oversees business operations.
2. Writes schedules.
3. Performs and analyzes daily and monthly reports.
4. Monitors food and labor costs and takes corrective measures.
5. Provides and coordinates training for all staff.
6. Monitors performance and assists with annual performance reviews.
7. Receives, reviews, and acts on guest complaints.
8. Monitors safety and sanitation guidelines.

KNOWLEDGE AND SKILL REQUIREMENTS
1. College degree in applicable field.
2. Three to five years of restaurant management experience and proven skills in cost and labor controls.
3. Requires bending, climbing, reaching, standing, walking, sitting, lifting, carrying, repetitive motions, visual acuity, and hearing.

WORKING CONDITIONS
High noise levels, hot, must be able to lift 50-plus pounds.

Job Title: **BUS PERSON**

Reports to: Manager/Owner

SUMMARY

Assists food servers to maintain service efficiency, and ensures guest satisfaction by maintaining cleanliness of the front-of-the-house area.

PRIMARY RESPONSIBILITIES

1. Greets guests appropriately when they are seated.
2. Communicates with host/hostess and wait staff to maintain service efficiency and ensures guest satisfaction.
3. Maintains cleanliness and sanitation of the front-of-the-house, including all tables, chairs, floors, windows, and restrooms.
4. Serves water, bread, and butter to guests and provides refills as needed.
5. Restocks dining room with china, silverware, glassware, utensils, condiments, and linen and maintains adequate supplies in the work stations when dining room is opened.
6. Prepares beverages required for service, including coffee, iced tea, and hot water.
7. Removes dirty dishes and utensils from tables between courses and clears tables after guests leave.
8. Replaces dishes and utensils for next course, and cleans and resets vacated tables.
9. Returns dirty dishes, silverware, glassware, and utensils to dish-washing area.
10. May assist wait staff in serving tables with hot beverages, such as coffee or tea.
11. Performs all other duties as assigned

KNOWLEDGE AND SKILL REQUIREMENTS

1. Some high school.
2. No previous foodservice experience required.
3. Must be able to stand and exert fast-paced mobility for periods of up to four (4) hours in length and to lift, bend, and

stoop. Must have the ability to frequently lift and carry bus tubs, trays, and other objects weighing 25 pounds or more.

WORKING CONDITIONS

High noise levels, hot, must be able to lift 50-plus pounds.

Job Title: **CASHIER**

Reports to: Manager/Owner

SUMMARY

Collects payments of guest checks from servers and/or guests. Ensures accurate accounting of all transactions, collections, and disbursements.

PRIMARY RESPONSIBILITIES

1. Receives cash drawer at beginning of work shift, and counts money in drawer at beginning and ending of shift to verify its accuracy.

2. Itemizes and totals food and beverage orders, or rings food and beverage checks into register. Collects cash, check, or credit payment from guest; makes change for cash transactions; checks identification for personal checks; and prepares voucher for credit card purchases.

3. May reconcile checks, cash receipts, and charge sales with total sales to verify accuracy of transactions at the end of work shift.

4. Responsibilities may include greeting guests, taking food and beverage orders and giving them to kitchen staff.

5. Performs all other duties as assigned.

KNOWLEDGE AND SKILL REQUIREMENTS

1. High school graduate or equivalent.

2. Must possess basic math skills and have the ability to handle money accurately.

3. Basic knowledge of the functions of cash registers.

4. Must have the ability to remain stationary for periods of up to four hours in length, be able to bend and stoop on occasion, and be able to escort guests to other parts of the facility as circumstances dictate.

WORKING CONDITIONS

High noise levels, hot, must be able to lift 50-plus pounds.

Job Title: **COOK**

Reports to: Manager/Owner

SUMMARY

Responsible to cook the prepared food items in the standardized method. Ensure food products are prepared correctly before cooking.

PRIMARY RESPONSIBILITIES

1. Arrive on time for work.
2. Ensure proper preparation procedures are completed.
3. Prepare work areas for the shift.
4. Maintain the highest food quality.
5. Communicate with all co-workers.
6. Be aware of what happens in the dining room.
7. Account for every food item used.
8. Maintain a clean and safe kitchen.
9. Follow health and safety regulations prescribed.
10. Follow restaurant regulations prescribed.
11. Control and limit waste.
12. Communicate problems and ideas to management.
13. Attend all meetings.
14. Fill out all forms required.
15. Maintain all kitchen equipment and utensils.
16. Keep every area of the kitchen clean and organized.
17. Follow the proper food rotation procedures.
18. Label and date all products used.
19. Follow management's instructions and suggestions.
20. Performs all other duties as assigned.

KNOWLEDGE AND SKILL REQUIREMENTS

1. One year of cooking experience and/or degree in culinary

arts field
2.   Knife skills
3.   Knowledge of HACCP
4.   Basic cooking knowledge

WORKING CONDITIONS

High noise levels, hot, must be able to lift 50-plus pounds.

Job Title: **COUNTER PERSON**

Reports to: Manager/Owner

SUMMARY

Greeting and serving customers, cold food preparation, stocking counters, and steam table.

PRIMARY RESPONSIBILITIES

1. Maintains sanitary standards.
2. Interacts with customers in a friendly and efficient manner.
3. Stocks display refrigerators and salad bar accurately, and efficiently.
4. Maintains hot or cold temperature conditions as per standards.
5. Maintains appropriate portion control.
6. Cleans tables and chairs by the start of each meal period. Arrange per diagram. Check for salt, pepper, and napkins and stocks accordingly.
7. Cleans equipment, as assigned, thoroughly and in a timely fashion.
8. Keeps floor in public, work, or service area clean and free of debris.
9. Completes shift work timely and thoroughly in accordance with standards.
10. Performs other duties as assigned.

KNOWLEDGE AND SKILL REQUIREMENTS

1. High school diploma or equivalent.
2. Demonstrated ability to understand and implement written and verbal instructions.
3. Must be able to lift 25 pounds and stand for periods of up to four hours.

WORKING CONDITIONS

High noise levels, hot, must be able to lift 25-plus pounds.

Job Title: **DISHWASHER**

Reports to: Manager/Owner

SUMMARY

Responsible to supply spotless, sanitized dishes to the dining room and clean kitchen utensils to the cooks.

PRIMARY RESPONSIBILITIES

1. Correctly operate dishwasher.
2. Bus, sort, and rack dishes.
3. Place clean dishes in appropriate storage areas.
4. Keep dish area, back kitchen, and restrooms clean throughout shift.
5. Empty trash in kitchen area.
6. Performs all other duties as assigned.

KNOWLEDGE AND SKILL REQUIREMENTS

1. High school diploma.
2. Must speak, read, write, and understand others in the business.
3. Must be able to lift up to 50 pounds.

WORKING CONDITIONS

High noise levels, hot, must be able to lift 50-plus pounds.

Job Title: **HOST/HOSTESS**

Reports to: Manager/Owner

SUMMARY

Primary responsibilities are to greet and seat guest upon arrival, or to take orders for carryout customers if you offer that service.

PRIMARY RESPONSIBILITIES

1. Assign service stations to servers and bus persons.
2. Inform staff of menu changes and daily specials.
3. Coordinate the dining room.
4. Balance customers among the various service stations.
5. Graciously greet and seat guests promptly.
6. Provide menus to guests.
7. Manage special seating requests for guests.
8. Relays appropriate messages to servers and bus persons.
9. Assist servers and bus persons as needed.
10. Check table settings for completeness, and check service tray stations for adequate supplies for refill or replacement.
11. Perform all duties as assigned.

KNOWLEDGE AND SKILL REQUIREMENTS

1. High school graduate or equivalent.
2. At least one year experience in foodservice.
3. Stand and walk for up to four (4) hours in length.
4. Lift up to 40 pounds.
5. Speak clearly, and listen to guests and other employees.

WORKING CONDITIONS

High noise levels, hot, must be able to lift 40-plus pounds.

Job Title: **PREP COOK**

Reports to: Cook/Manager/Owner

PRIMARY RESPONSIBILITIES

1.   Prepare food products according to the prescribed methods.
2.   Maintain highest quality of food.
3.   Receive and store all products as prescribed.
4.   Maintain a clean and safe kitchen.
5.   Follow all health and safety regulations.
6.   Follow all restaurant regulations.
7.   Control waste.
8.   Communicate problems and ideas for improvement to management.
9.   Communicate and work together with co-workers as a team.
10. Arrive on time and ready to work.
11. Attend all meetings.
12. Fill out all forms as prescribed.
13. Maintain all equipment and utensils.
14. Organize all areas of the kitchen.
15. Follow proper rotation procedures.
16. Label and date all products prepared.
17. Follow management's instructions and suggestions.
18. Perform all other duties as assigned.

KNOWLEDGE AND SKILL REQUIREMENTS

High school diploma

WORKING CONDITIONS

High noise levels, hot, must be able to lift 50-plus pounds.

These are examples of some of the jobs that need to be filled in your pizza shop. You can adjust these to suit your business. Copies of these job descriptions are included on the CD.

14

Successful Employee Relations and Labor Cost Control

There will be many things to invest your time and money in, but none are as important as your employees. You must have employees to make the business work, and great people can make your pizza shop great. In order to have great employees, you must be a great employer.

The Value (and Cost) of Employees

Your employees are directly responsible for the quality of your food and the presentation to your customers. To maintain quality, train your employees and keep them motivated and satisfied. One great way to do this is by helping them feel like part of the team and making their job rewarding.

A few simple ways to show you how to make working conditions better are: employee lockers, separate restrooms, break room, air conditioning,

sufficient lighting, and the right tools and equipment for the job. These things aren't usually difficult and make a big difference in the employees' attitude and performance.

In an ideal situation, you should provide the following for your employees:

- Higher salaries
- Thorough training
- Insurance programs – if possible
- Flexible scheduling
- Shorter work weeks
- Tools to increase productivity, reduce stress, and maximize safety
- Safe, clean working conditions
- Effective employee evaluations
- Benefit packages – if possible
- Opportunity for advancement
- Pleasant and structured work environment

When you review the things valuable employees want, you must consider the cost of replacing employees. Keep in mind that most of these things are not provided by other foodservice businesses.

First, you have the indirect cost when you have unmotivated and unhappy employees preparing food. They won't usually do their best if they are unhappy. So, your customers aren't getting a quality product and aren't getting outstanding customer service. We all know positive word-of-mouth advertising can be great, but you can also get negative word-of-mouth. This can happen if the food was wonderful, but the server or cashier was rude.

Second, unhappy employees aren't concerned with what is best for your business. This can mean breaking things, losing things, being rude to others,

not showing for a shift, and so on. It's hard to get employees to care about the store's profits when they feel they are underpaid.

Now, consider the cost of replacing that employee:

- Advertising the position.

- Interviewer's pay and time taken from other duties.

- Administrative cost for paperwork and payroll, etc.

- Time to train the new employee and added work for others.

- Loss of sales and the cost of supplies because of training mistakes.

- Labor expenses while employee is less productive.

- Expense involved in terminating an employee: paperwork, exit interviewing and, possibly, unemployment compensation.

The American Management Association says the cost to replace an employee is, conservatively, 30 percent of his annual salary. If the employee was more skilled, the cost can be one-and-a-half times his annual salary. Needless to say, retaining good, quality workers will have an impact on the profitability and effectiveness of your pizza shop.

All good employees want to work for an employer who appreciates their skills and who will give them adequate compensation. It is good to check the Department of Labor in Washington, DC. You can also check with your state Employment Commission. The office in your state capital will have more detailed breakdowns for the current pay rates for various jobs. This will help you ensure your pay scale is within local parameters.

Atlantic Publishing offers a book titled *365 Ways to Motivate and Reward Employees Every Day – With Little or No Money* (**www.atlantic-pub.com**, Item # 365-01). Rewarding and motivating employees is necessary to keep them happy. When you find quality employees, find ways to keep them with your company. Many people will tell you the only way to keep employees is

to give them more money, but other things work just as well and can work better.

Hiring Pizzeria Employees

First, hire quality people to work in your pizza shop. To determine the best candidates for the positions requires effective interviewing skills. Even before that, the quality of your help wanted ad can make a difference in the people you attract. Be honest in your ad: You want hardworking and skilled applicants with previous experience and with the drive to do a superior job. You can rework that, but that will attract a different person than an ad that says, "Busy Pizza Shop in desperate need of anyone with a driver's license." Do you see an immediate difference in how you respond to the ad? The quality individuals are not usually attracted to a desperate business. Once applications come in, what should you do next?

Atlantic Publishing offers a book titled *501+ Great Interview Questions for Employers and the Best Answers for Prospective Employees* (**www.atlantic-pub. com,** Item # 501-02). This book contains 501 carefully worded questions which will help interviewers get the answers they need from a potential employee. There are techniques to help you ask your questions in ways that will help you get the answers needed in order to screen applicants for the position to be filled.

Screening Potential Employees

Pre-screening applicants allows you to eliminate candidates who simply are not qualified for the position before conducting a lengthy interview. This saves the pizza shop, and the applicants', time and money. This should be done by someone who knows what qualities and experience are needed for the job. Interviews with job candidates may be scheduled with the manager. All applicants should leave feeling they have been treated fairly and had

an equal opportunity to get the job. This is an important part of public relations.

Base your preliminary screening on the following criteria:

- **Experience** – Is the applicant qualified to do the job? Examine past job experience. Check all references.

- **Appearance** – Is the applicant clean and neatly dressed? The applicant will deal with the public, and people usually dress better for an interview than they will on the job.

- **Personality** – Does the applicant's personality complement your other employees', and will it impress customers? Is he outgoing, but not overbearing?

- **Legality** – Does the applicant meet the legal requirements?

- **Availability** – Is the person available for the hours you need to fill? Does he have a ride to work?

- **Health and physical ability** – Can your applicant do the physical work required? Some businesses require potential employees to have a complete physical examination by a mutually approved doctor.

- **Make certain the application is signed and dated.**

At this point you can divide all applicants into one of three categories:

1. **Refer for interview** – Refer to manager for interview.

2. **Reject** – Describe reasons for rejecting applicant and list on application.

3. **Prospective file** – Any applicant who could be considered for

other areas of the business should be placed in a prospective applicant file.

Key Points for Conducting Employment Interviews

- **Show a genuine interest** in all applicants, even if it's unlikely you would hire them. Consider that each applicant could be a potential customer.

- **Be on time and be ready to talk with the applicant.** Being late or changing the appointment time gives the impression you are unorganized. This will discourage quality applicants, and they may not reschedule.

- **Know all details about the job you are offering.** It's impossible to find the right person for a job when you don't understand what the job requires.

- **Conduct all interviews in private.** The best place for the interview is in your office. Be sure your staff knows to keep interruptions to a minimum.

- **Make the applicant feel at ease.** This can include a comfortable place to sit and possibly a cold drink. Be conversational and be interested in what applicants say.

- **Applicants will have questions** about the job, its duties, the salary, etc. Allow time for their questions. The questions they ask will also reveal their needs and desires. Listen carefully.

- **Let the applicants speak.** Again, give them a chance to talk and then listen. They will tell you a lot about themselves, past jobs, past supervisors, and school experiences. Watch for

contradictions, excuses, and defensive and negative reactions. If they avoid certain questions, this is an indicator of possible problems.

- **Don't show any disapproval** of something an applicant does or says; appear open-minded. But, don't condone obvious mistakes.

- **Ask a few questions they don't expect and aren't prepared for:** What do they do to relax? What are their hobbies? What is the last book they read? These questions will reveal things about their attitudes, personalities, and energy levels.

A very useful thing you can ask prospective employees is: What did they like most about their last job and their last supervisor? Do these things fit into the job you need to fill? Another thing I like to ask is what they didn't like about their last job and supervisor. There have been times when this told me right away that they wouldn't be happy. Most people who apply for foodservice positions are people who "like dealing with people" while the others "like dealing with food." Is the applicant the person needed for the job?

Ask at least one behavior-based question; this helps you see how the applicant responds in real-life work situations and how well he or she can handle them. For example: "How would you help a customer who complained his 'soup just doesn't taste right'?" Or, "What would you do if a seemingly happy patron did not leave a tip?" This last question is especially important for delivery personnel. You won't see the applicant's reaction when a customer doesn't tip, and he needs to understand that not all people tip.

Unlawful Pre-Employment Questions

This section will offer suggestions about equal and fair employment practices, but it does not replace talking to your attorney or state and federal

labor offices, who can give you complete information. You should have your attorney review any specific information or forms before you use them for your pizza shop.

The Federal Civil Rights Act of 1964, and other state and federal laws, ensure that a job applicant will be treated fairly and on an equal basis, regardless of race, color, religious creed, age, sex, or national origin. To support these regulations, there are certain questions you cannot ask. It is good to use common sense about these things, along with the suggestions provided.

Age/date of birth is important for pizza shops that serve any alcohol. Age is a sensitive pre-employment question, because the Age Discrimination in Employment Act. (**www.eeoc.gov/policy/adea.html,** protects employees 40 years and older.) You can ask applicants if they are under 18.

Drugs, smoking. You can ask if the applicant uses drugs or smokes. The application gives you a chance to have the applicant agree to be bound by the employer's drug and smoking policies and to submit to drug testing.

Other problem areas:

- Questions about credit rating or credit references are discriminatory against minorities and women.

- Asking if an applicant owns a home is discriminatory against minority members, since a greater number of minority members do not own their own homes.

- You can ask if the person was in the military, but not about his discharge.

- The Americans with Disabilities Act prohibits general inquiries about disabilities, health problems, and medical conditions.

These are some questions which are prohibited:

- How tall are you?

- What color are your eyes?

- Do you work out at the gym regularly?

- Do you, or does anyone you know, have the HIV virus?

- Did you get workers' comp from your last employer?

- How old are you?

- Have you been in prison?

- Are you really a man?

- Do you rent or own your home?

- Have you ever declared bankruptcy?

- What part of the world are your parents from?

- Are you a minority?

- Is English your first language?

- I can't tell if you're Japanese or Chinese. Which is it?

- Which church do you go to?

- Who will take care of the kids if you get this job?

- Is this your second marriage, then?

- Are you gay?

- Are you in a committed relationship right now?

- How does your boyfriend feel about you working here?

Check the accompanying CD to print a copy of this list for your use.

Things to Look for in Potential Employees

- **Stability** – You want to hire someone who will stay around. Look

at past employment records. Stability includes the applicant's emotional makeup.

- **Leadership qualities** – You want employees who want to achieve and do, not individuals who have to be led around by the hand. Review their past employment records for growth.

- **Motivation** – Why is the applicant applying to your pizzeria? Is he interested in the pizza industry in general? Is he looking for a career or a temporary job? Is he domineering or appear to be motivated by someone else?

- **Independence** – Is the applicant on his own? Does he appear to be financially secure? When did he leave his parent's home and why?

- **Maturity** – Are the applicants mentally and emotionally mature enough to handle a stressful environment? Can they communicate with employees and customers who may be older or younger?

- **Determination** – Does the applicant finish what he starts? Does he look for, or retreat from, challenges?

- **Work habits** – Does the applicant understand the physical work involved in a pizza shop? Has he done similar work? Is he neat and organized? Is the application filled out properly? Look at the applicant's job history for pay increases and promotions.

Maturity is an interesting quality to find in pizza shop employees. My store in the college town was staffed with a large number of college students. I was selective in hiring because I knew the qualities we needed and the personalities and characteristics to avoid. By choosing students who needed to work and who held jobs in the past, I avoided many potential issues. A good friend who managed another local store liked to hire college students who liked to party and their job would provide extra spending money.

The quality of the work between some of his employees and most of mine was very different. During homecoming, his staff members didn't want to work, while mine knew they were needed. Don't get me wrong, my staff liked to party and have fun, but they also understood their responsibilities and what was expected of them. Make this line clear in the beginning and you will save yourself a lot of hassles later.

The Final Selection and Decision

Deciding who to hire can be very difficult. Sometimes there are too many qualified applicants and other times you can't find any. When you are making the final decision, look at the applicant as a "total package." At times, I've created a pros and cons list to help me.

Did others in the pizza shop meet the person or talk to him or her? Ask about their impressions. Their input can and will help them realize you value their input.

It's also important to feel good about the person, feel he or she will enjoy the job and have a feeling he or she will be successful in the job.

When you offer the applicant the job, you have one more time to ensure he or she fully understands what the job entails:

- **Salary** – Starting pay, pay range, potential and realistic growth rate, payday, company benefits, vacations, insurance, etc.

- **Job description** – Explain job duties, hours, your expectations, etc.

- **Time and date** of, and to whom he should report, on the first day of work.

At this point, ask the applicant if he is interested and would like to accept

the job. Some people say no, but by this time in the process, they usually say yes.

Rejecting Applicants

Rejecting applicants is a hard task, but the majority of the applicants will be rejected. There might be some people who want to know why they were rejected. Be honest and tactful. It doesn't need to be a confrontation, and it might help them to target jobs they are more qualified to do. It could be enough to say that there was a more experienced or better qualified applicant.

Employee Handbook/Personnel Policy

The federal government mandates that all employers need to have written policies. Employee handbooks are a great way to ensure consistency with employee training and understanding. This gives you a written record of the policies and what you expect from your employees which will help when there are problems. A written employee manual can also help you overcome some common communication problems in business. Require employees to read the manual then sign a statement for their personnel file. This is good for you when problems arise.

Writing a comprehensive employee manual is time-consuming. Atlantic Publishing has a standard employee handbook for the foodservice industry. You simply edit the information to make sure it matches your policies. It is written in Microsoft Word, making it easy for you to customize. The title is *Design Your Own Effective Employee Handbook* (**www.atlantic-pub.com** Item # GEH-02).

Topics to Be Covered in Employee Handbook

STANDARDS OF CONDUCT	EMPLOYEE CONDUCT	BONUS PLAN
Absenteeism and Punctuality	Work Performance	Performance Reviews
Neatness of Work Area	Availability for Work	Benefits Program
Personal Telephone Calls	Personal Mail	Benefits Eligibility
Mandatory Meetings	Communications	Insurance
Employee Relations	Problem Resolution	Insurance Continuation
Use of Company Vehicles	Disciplinary Guidelines	Personal Appearance
Confidentiality of Company Information	Employment Classification	Conflicts of Interest
Violence and Weapons Policy	Workplace Monitoring	Holidays
Severe Weather	Suggestions	Vacation
Orientation	Equal Employment Opportunity	Bereavement Leave
Harassment	Criminal Convictions	Social Security
Personnel Files	Employment References	Pre-Tax Deductions

STANDARDS OF CONDUCT	EMPLOYEE CONDUCT	BONUS PLAN
Employment of Relatives	Outside Employment	Military Leave
Rehiring Former Employees	Searches	Medical Leave of Absence
Substance Abuse	Solicitations and Contributions	Family Leave of Absence
Company Property	Office Equipment	Employee Discounts
Tools and Equipment	Safety	Workers' Compensation
Hours of Work	Break Policy	Jury Duty
Recording Time	Overtime	Unemployment Compensation
Salary and Wage Increases	Payroll	Educational Assistance
Travel Expenses	Reimbursable Expenses	Job Abandonment
Voluntary Resignation	Performance-Based Release	Acts of Misconduct
Termination Procedures	Other Forms of Separation	Affidavit of Receipt

Check the accompanying CD to print a copy of this list for your use.

Personnel File

When the applicant is hired, create a personnel file for him or her. Over time, the file will include the following information:

- Completed Application.

- Form W-4 and Social Security number.

- Name, address, and phone number. (Update as needed.)

- Emergency phone number.

- Employment date.

- Job title and beginning pay rate.

- Performance evaluations.

- Signed form to confirm he read and understands the Employee Handbook/Personnel Policy Manual.

- Notes regarding any problems or positive events during his employment.

- Termination date, if applicable, and a detailed account of the reasons for termination.

Check the accompanying CD to print a copy of this list for your use.

Training

Employees cannot be expected to do the job right without proper training. This training needs to explain what to do, how to do it properly and the reasoning for the procedures. Training is more than just providing information, and managers and owners soon understand the importance of effective training.

Get the trainee involved in what is being done. It won't help to just let him or her watch. Be sure he or she can do the job tasks. You should have a list of the job description and physically check off each thing on the list. When you train someone, learn about his or her interests, goals, and desires. These will help you determine what will motivate him or her to do a good job.

I've mentioned cross-training several times. When the new employee is trained, he or she needs to understand the job and how it fits with other responsibilities in the pizza shop. This also helps the employee to see how his or her job fits into the big picture. You can use this to show how important he or she is to the business.

Orientation and Instruction

Do a simple orientation for your new employees. This should only take about 30 minutes and is a great way to get them started. Here are some basic orientation practices:

- Introduce employee to the company.
- Introduce employee to the other employees.
- Introduce employee to trainer and supervisor.
- Explain the company policies. Present the employee manual.
- Outline the objectives and goals of the training program:

    —Describe the training, where and how it will take place.

    —Describe the information to be learned.

    —Describe the skills and attitudes to be developed.

- Set up a schedule for the employee which includes:

    —The date, day, and time to begin training.

    —Who will train him and who is the supervisor.

—What should be learned and accomplished each day.

—The date to complete training.

After reviewing the training program, introduce the employee to the trainer. Choose your trainer carefully because he must be a model employee with the ability to train. Remember that not everyone can teach. A qualified trainer needs to communicate well and be patient and understanding.

It's important to know how fast the trainer is learning. The trainer should give you daily updates in writing, and these can be filed in the employee's personnel file. New material needs to be added as the new employee learns. It's also effective to show the employee how tasks build on each other.

The trainer should submit a report to you when the training is complete. It should include details on how the trainee has done. What are the trainee's strengths and weaknesses, quality of work, and understanding of all aspects of the job?

Congratulate the trainee on successfully completing the training. It's helpful to ask the employee about his training, what was helpful, anything that would be helpful for future trainers and so on. After a couple of weeks, ask if the training prepared him for the actual job.

Outside Help in Training

You can bring in outside help for some facets of your training. Find people who are experts in their fields. Many times all you need to do is ask, and be sure to reward them for their help with a complimentary gift certificate.

There are great resources for outside-training information to assist you in training programs: videos, posters, books, software, etc. One great source for all these products is Atlantic Publishing (**www.atlantic-pub.com**).

Outside Help: Speakers and Subjects

- **State liquor agent** – Liquor laws, compliance, etc.

- **Health Department** – Health and sanitation practices/ requirements.

- **Wine distributors** – Wine tasting, promotion, etc.

- **Red Cross instructor** – First Aid, Heimlich Maneuver and CPR procedures.

Scheduling

We discussed scheduling in the chapter about controlling costs. Your goal is to schedule the most efficient employees in the job or shift where they can give you maximum productivity for the minimum expense. Many managers and owners tend to rush through writing a schedule.

It can take an hour or more to create an effective schedule. But, you can reduce the time frame as you become more familiar with schedule writing. These are some of the factors to consider when writing a schedule:

- Proper staffing for peak periods (specific hours or days of the week).

- When will you need the maximum production?

- Plan for special events that require additional staff or that require staff to work outside the pizza shop.

- The skill and productivity of each employee.

- Each employee's desired schedule: days off, hours, etc.

It takes time to assess the labor that is needed. In the beginning, it's better to have some additional help to maintain customer service. Schedule employees throughout the day, and be sure your best people are there at the most critical times. Is this when you open, dinner rush, or late night? Whenever your critical time is, be sure that you have sufficient staff to handle the work load.

Cross-train your full-time employees to perform at least two different jobs. This allows you to fill your schedule even during vacations and illness. This will make every week schedules and emergency situations more workable. The variety can also prevent employees from being bored with your duties. Employees who are involved, interested, and concerned about the pizzeria are better performers than people who remain uninvolved.

Each team member that I hired was told in the beginning that they were being hired for a specific job, but would be expected to help wherever they were needed. If that was a problem, they could be passed over for the job. Flexibility is key in a business and especially in the beginning. The more flexible your staff members are the better service you can offer your customers. Be specific in the initial interview and new team members will know what is expected.

In times when you have too many employees, you can assign tasks in the pizza shop. This can include food prep, folding pizza boxes, or any other tasks. Depending on the time of day, you can start closing work or prepare for the next shift. On some occasions, I sent employees to distribute coupons to local apartment complexes or to door hang coupons in target neighborhoods. A word of warning, however: Check local laws and apartment regulations before you do this. Many places allow this, but some localities have strict policies. There is always the option that you can send people home. It might be best to ask for volunteers. I never had a shift where someone wasn't willing to leave early.

There are a variety of software programs which are very helpful in scheduling

employees. They can help you track labor as the shift progresses and alerts you about good times to cut staff. You still need to factor in your knowledge, but the software is very helpful.

Evaluating Performance

Employee evaluations are a great way to help your employees understand how they are doing and what needs to be improved. You also need to acknowledge the positive things about each employee. Evaluations can be quarterly or annual or on a schedule that works for you. These sessions give you a chance to discuss thoughts, ideas, and problems with the employee.

Check the accompanying CD to print a copy of an
Employee Evaluation Form for your use as well as a list of tips such as the
following to keep in mind when performing an exit interview.

Consider these things when you complete evaluation forms:

- **Know the employee's job description thoroughly** – You must understand the job duties in order to evaluate how an employee performs the job.

- **Conduct the evaluation in private.** Schedule enough time to discuss everything in one session.

- **Don't let one incident—positive or negative—dominate the evaluation.** Consider the whole picture of the employee's work since the last evaluation.

- **Evaluations should balance positive and negative attributes.** A totally negative evaluation doesn't motivate a poor employee. Focus on his positive contributions, and describe the changes he needs to make. A totally negative evaluation can scare an employee. If the employee deserves a totally negative evaluation,

he should be terminated.

- **Review past evaluations, but don't dwell on them.** Look for areas where improvement or a decline in performance has taken place.

- **Support your appraisals with specific examples.** Allow enough time for the employee's comments because your conclusions could be wrong.

- **Don't cover too much material or expect drastic change overnight.** An evaluation is only one of the steps to direct the employee.

- **Begin with the employee's positive points** and then discuss the areas that need improvement.

- **Some traits and deficiencies may not change.** Don't overemphasize them, but explain how they affect the employee's performance and the performance of others.

- **Finish the evaluation on a positive note.** The employee should leave with a good feeling about his positive contributions to the business and direction on how to improve on his weaknesses.

- **After the evaluation, follow up** on the thoughts, recommendations and ideas that were discussed during the evaluation. Without a follow-up, the evaluation is of little value.

- **Evaluations are confidential.** File them in the employee's personnel file if no one else has access to them there.

Check the accompanying CD to print a copy of this list for your use.

If you decide to create your own customized Employee Evaluations, you should check out a book from Atlantic Publishing. The book is titled *199*

Pre-Written Employee Performance Appraisals: The Complete Guide to Successful Employee Evaluations and Documents (**www.atlantic-pub.com,** Item # EPP-02). We've discussed how important effective evaluations are for you and your employees. This book will help you understand what to include, how to ask, responding to employee concerns and more. There is also an accompanying CD which will help you create your own employee evaluations.

The Decision to Terminate an Employee

When an employee is not performing to your expectations, you have to take further action. Give the employee a chance to correct the problems. If this doesn't help, the employee needs to be terminated. Terminating employees can be difficult, but it is necessary. It is much worse to keep unsatisfactory employees. They can impact the morale of your entire staff.

Weigh the pros and cons of whether to retrain the employee or to terminate him. Ask for input from any managers or shift runners to get a complete picture of their performance. Review their past reviews, training, and performance. Once you decide to terminate the employee, you should schedule a meeting with the employee.

If the employee has a direct supervisor other than you, that supervisor should be present at the meeting to offer support and witness the meeting. Conduct the exit interview in private with no interruptions. If the employee disagrees with you, give him or her a chance to discuss it. Have facts to support your comments. No matter how the employee reacts, stay seated and calm. Be sure not to touch the employee, unless you shake hands.

Fill out a report about the exit interview and file it in the employee's personnel file. This will be important if the employee decides to challenge the termination. Begin to advertise for a replacement right away. It can take several months for a new employee to be brought up to full productivity, and he may not work out at all.

Be honest with the employee about his performance and the reason for the termination. Document the chances you gave the employee to improve prior to your decision to terminate him. Keep all your records in case the employee challenges the termination. The notes don't have to be very detailed, but should include the pertinent facts, the date and any recommendation you made to the employee.

Other employees can perceive the termination of an employee as a threat to their security. On the other hand, it's likely they will be relieved the problem is resolved. It also helps employees understand that substandard work will not be tolerated. If necessary, give your other employees a simple explanation. Remember to document everything.

Photo Courtesy of Pizza Today

15

Equipping Your Pizza and Sub Shop

The equipment and tools you purchase are an investment in your pizza shop. You cannot have an efficient business that turns out a quality product without the right tools. All equipment should pay for itself over time. For your profit margin, you want to find equipment that will be paid for quickly. There are several ways to figure the return on investment:

- Increased sales with fewer employees.

- Faster production which turns out products faster.

- Improved and consistent quality gives you happier customers.

- Reduced risk of injuries and stress.

- Can sometimes give you exclusive products, enhanced service, and more choices for your customers.

Create an Equipment Budget

The first big question is "How much should I spend?" Equipment quality and pricing levels vary a lot. One common sense idea is not to spend more than is necessary, although that distinction can be difficult. Be sure you know what items you want to include on your menu before you shop for equipment. That will determine the types of equipment you need.

A couple of options are to buy light-duty equipment. Light duty or heavy duty really depends on the volume of business you plan to do. There are less expensive and very serviceable brands on the market.

How do I keep within my budget?

- Develop an equipment/fixture/tool wish list.

- Divide your list into three priority categories:
  1. Must Have
  2. Would Make Life Easier
  3. Dreaming

- Your budget needs to focus on the Must Have category. These items will make money for you.

- Do the items in the second category have the potential to save time and money? If so, they could become must have items.

- The third category contains things you don't need at this time. If you find an incredible deal, it might be worth considering.

- Analyze your second and third category items.

  —How long will it take to pay for itself?

  —Will it honestly make you money?

- What would your CPA think of each scenario? A slick salesman can convince most people to buy anything. Be sure the money is in your budget and that you really need the item.

- Work with a food service consultant, or do your own research. Ask for comparison charts to be sure which items will fit your needs. Also, evaluate maintenance specifics and costs.

- Negotiate for a better price. Start with 50 percent of the list price. There is almost always some negotiating room.

- Check major restaurant supply stores since factory discounts could give you negotiating room that isn't available with smaller suppliers.

- They may offer specials on last years' models. They could have overstock items that would fit your needs.

- Search the Internet for "pizza equipment" and "restaurant equipment." Do everything you can to verify the legitimacy of the company. Try to have the equipment shipped COD, so you can pay for it after you receive it and can check it over.

Pizza Equipment Supply, Inc. offers a variety of pizza specific equipment. Their Web site is located at **www.pesi.us/index_files/Equipment.htm**. They sell new and refurbished equipment. I like that they include the brand name and model number to enable easy price and product comparison. They can be contacted at 704-629-0000 or e-mail sales@pesi.us.

Used Equipment

This is the same as buying a used car. Equipment depreciates after a year or two, and you can usually find a restaurant that is going out of business and

needs to liquidate. Some of this equipment can be "almost new."

- Shop for new items first. Never shop for a used item without knowing the price for a new item. Focus on top manufacturers with a reputation for quality.

- Review the repair history of the make/model. Your dealer should have personal experience with the equipment.

- Understand "reconditioned" and "rebuilt."

  —**Reconditioned equipment**. Cleaned, worn/broken parts replaced, short dealer warranty. Typically priced 40 to 50 percent of new price.

  —**Rebuilt equipment.** Totally dismantled and rebuilt, longer dealer warranty. Should perform to the manufacturer's specs. Typically priced 50 to 70 percent of new price.

- Verify age and history. Use manufacturer serial numbers and service records to check age and care. Don't rely on a story from the owner or a salesman.

- Is there a trade-in policy? Some suppliers offer above-average trade-in values when you want to trade up for a new version.

- Used equipment online (auction and direct purchase) at bankruptcy auctions, from new equipment dealers and food equipment groups.

- Do they have demo models available? Trade show, showroom, and test kitchen models can be discounted, and they could have reduced prices for "scratch 'n dent" items.

- Save time by buying used. Delays for new equipment may be an issue.

- Don't buy:

    —Equipment or fixtures with cosmetic problems customers will see.

    —Any items with rust, except for restorable cast iron.

    —"Married" equipment (where pieces have been interchanged between different models).

    —Foreign-made equipment that wasn't made for the United States.

Leasing Your Equipment

Leasing might be an alternative for you which will provide 100 percent financing. It is good to talk with your accountant about tax benefits with leasing. Here are some ideas to help you make a decision about whether to lease equipment.

- Leasing isn't easy money. The actual cost can be much greater than the purchase price. Interest is included in your lease.

- Avoid personal guarantees. This makes you personally responsible even if the restaurant closes or the equipment doesn't last.

- Research leasing details before searching for a leasing company. Leasing companies pull credit reports, and repeated inquiries negatively affect your credit reputation.

- Who is responsible for service and maintenance? Verify details about the manufacturer's warranty for a lease. But, usually you are 100 percent responsible for maintaining the equipment in good working order and resalable condition.

- Compare total annual lease costs to your annual depreciation

benefits. Food service equipment has a 7-year depreciation rate while the typical lease is 36 to 60 months.

- Don't lease items with a short life or items that are fully deductible that purchase year, such as flatware, glassware, or dinnerware.

- Some leases have low buy-out provisions. The IRS classifies it as a purchase agreement subject to depreciation instead of a 100 percent expense.

- Verify your insurance covers leased equipment for fire, theft, or losses.

- Get the fair market value information in writing. Equipment can have excessive buyouts. Check the used market to compare values.

- Read the lease before signing. Lease agreements are legal contracts! It could be good to have your lawyer review the document.

- Estimate your monthly payments. You can learn more about leasing from GE Leasing Solutions – **www.geleasingsolutions. com**.

- Leasing used equipment – This can be a cost-effective way to obtain expensive equipment.

Make Wise Purchases

Always get the best value for your money. These suggestions can help you get the quality, service, and performance you need.

- Seek out recommendations. Ask other restaurant owners, used equipment dealers, and equipment specialists for advice and

suggestions. This can help you determine the features you choose, how long the equipment should last and the brands to consider or to avoid.

- Contact your local gas and/or electric utility company. Ask if the utility companies have a test kitchen, rebates, or promotional programs.

- Don't overlook custom-built equipment. The best option for you might be custom built equipment. Research what is available and see if custom equipment is needed.

- Comparison shop. Ask for first, second, and third choices by your consultant or equipment dealer and compare features, costs, and life expectancies.

- Substitution is an option. Sometimes the equipment you want isn't available in a reasonable time due to discontinued products or price changes. Is another option suitable for your needs?

- Commercial-grade materials and superior construction:

  —High-grade stainless with welded joints.

  —Verify the gauge used is steel (small number is thicker steel).

- Don't receive until you're ready to install. This helps prevent the risk of dents and dings, and dust can damage fragile equipment.

Sitram has manufactured high quality cookware in Europe for over 40 years. For the past 20 years SITRAM's products have been available in the United States. SITRAM supplies products to both food service professionals and discriminating home users. They have 8 fine product lines to fit the needs of each type of cookware user. The details can be found at **www. sitramcookware.com/products_foodsrv.htm**. To obtain the most up-to-date information regarding pricing, availability, dealer locations, or to order

directly, contact Frieling USA at 800-827-2582.

Genpak is a one-stop shop for bakery display packaging, oven ready baking trays and oven ready meal trays. The display packaging is made from crystal clear APET which helps extend shelf life while displaying your product at its best. Display packaging won't crack and may be opened and closed multiple times. Genpak oven ready baking trays are more economical than bulky permanent trays. Fill, freeze, bake, and display in the same package. The attractive design and clear lids will help you market items at the counter.

Genpak oven-ready meal trays work with all automated equipment. They are available with clear lids, or may be film sealed equally as well. See the full line of products at **www.genpak.com** or contact them at **www.genpak.com/cfm/inforequest.cfm**. Genpak also offers a selection of disposable dinnerware and carry out containers.

What Quality Level?

Should I buy the top brand or purchase a practical low-end model? Each person wants the newest and best equipment, but is it a wise investment for you? Evaluate your emotional, creative, and business needs to assess whether that specific equipment, tool or fixture serves your immediate and future needs. Consider these questions:

- Does it fit into my budget?

- Will smaller, more efficient equipment save precious space?

- Will this equipment improve my food or service quality?

- What is the return on investment?

- Can I sell enough to pay for specialty equipment?

- Will it save energy costs or reduce overhead?

- Will it help make employees more productive?

- What routine maintenance does it require?

- Can I get local and affordable service?

- Is it difficult or expensive to operate?

- Is an economical service or maintenance contract available?

- Is it the most productive and energy-efficient equipment available?

- Will it last beyond the lease terms?

- Can I trade-in or trade-up?

- What's the resale value if I need to sell or trade-up?

- Does it meet sanitation, plumbing or building code requirements?

Regal Ware Food Service, a division of Regal Ware Worldwide™, provides top quality beverage and food preparation products for the food service industry. The craftsmanship dates to 1945. Regal Ware Food Service offers various

products which were designed with your needs in mind. Visit their Web site for the full range of products which are available at **www. regalwarefoodservice.com.** Contact them by phone at 262-626-2121, by fax at 262-626-8532, or via e-mail: rfsinfo@regalwarefoodservice. com.

Service Contracts

Many gas/electric companies and equipment manufacturers have service contracts you can purchase. It's recommended that you purchase them. Regular maintenance will help your equipment last longer and more effectively. Be sure that calibrating of the baking ovens is included. All ovens need to register their temperatures accurately for consistent cooking results. Heavy-use ovens should be calibrated every month.

Equipment Records

Set aside a loose-leaf binder for your equipment information and maintenance schedules. Include warranties, brochures, equipment schematics, operating instructions, maintenance schedules, part lists, order forms, past service records, manufacturers' phone numbers, a chart showing which circuit breaker operates each piece of equipment, etc. Keep this manual from the beginning. Train your employees on the proper use of your equipment and it will serve the business well for years.

Pizzeria-Specific Equipment, Tools, and Supplies

Ovens

There are a plethora of choices when you chose ovens. These include gas, electric, or wood. Some are regulated by high-tech computerized systems or by hand. Your space limitations, product requirements, and budget will all be deciding factors on purchasing an oven. The two most important considerations are capacity (rack sizes, adjustability, pan sizes) and temperature control (accuracy and stability).

Many manufacturers offer test kitchens for you to test your dough samples. Contact the local restaurant equipment supply house and favorite manufacturers to locate a facility near you.

- **Revolving tray ovens** – Sheet pans and trays revolve for even baking.

- **Convection ovens** – Hot air is circulated through the oven to speed baking and keep temperatures consistent in the oven.

- **Deck ovens** – Flat steel or stone surface oven with single or multiple decks with various heights.

- **Rack ovens** – Multiple sliding racks for volume baking with same temp/time requirements. The best use of your floor space.

- There are also **tunnel, conveyor, and traveling tray ovens** that move the product through the oven. They need significant floor space and require professional installation.

- **Marsal 12 PIE COMBO** – This oven combines the power of the MB Series brick-lined oven with the efficiency of the SD

Series deck oven. The Combo Oven eliminates the issue of which type of oven will best fit your needs. You can have the choice to cook different kinds of pizza in the oven that will give it the best bake and taste. The Combo Oven has the same main features as the MB and SD Series deck ovens. All Combo Ovens are manufactured with a stainless steel finish all the way around. Contact the sales department at 877-FOR-OVEN (367-6836) or **www.marsalsons.com/combo.html.**

- **Amana's Commercial division** offers an oven that cooks 12 times as fast as a conventional oven. You can view all the details at **www.amanacommercial.com.** This page has a complete list of the benefits to using the Amana Veloci as compared to a conventional oven. The infrared radiant element works with the direct air flow which enhances browning, toasting and crisping. You can contact Amana for more information at 866-426-2621 or fax 319-622-8589.

DECK OVENS

Single or double deck gas pizza ovens are for baking, roasting, and pizza. Brick or deck ovens bake pizzas with exceptional taste, but they are more work than a conveyor oven. The pizzas taste different from pizzas cooked in conveyors because the pizza is cooked directly on the cooking surface, and this bakes the crust differently.

Deck ovens require some training and skill. The large "deck" is made from ceramic tiles, large bricks, or sections of stone. You place the pizza in the oven, usually with a pizza paddle.

These ovens work well because pizza is best when cooked from the bottom up. The crust becomes crispy on the stone which holds heat better than metal. Stone absorbs oils and moisture from pizzas, which makes the pizzas drier.

Tiles absorb oils and moisture, but they aren't as thick as stone. They are cheaper, but they don't maintain surface temperature as well as stone.

Your staff will need training and practice to use deck ovens. They can develop a sense of when it's time to pull the pizzas out. This is the type of oven I used, and it takes practice. Heat comes from various parts of the ovens, so your cooks need to rotate the pizzas so they will cook evenly.

Deck ovens have advantages over conveyor ovens. They are easier to clean, and the prices are more reasonable. Deck ovens can be cleaned by closing the doors, turning up the heat, and then scraping and sweeping any residue inside.

Each time you open the oven doors, you lose some heat. This adds to your cook time during peak times. The door must be opened to load, turn, check, and remove pizzas. The cooking is more inconsistent than conveyors, and your oven tender needs to be more intuitive. Deck ovens also require longer preheating and cooling times and have less capacity than conveyor ovens. One very busy evening, my staff proved you can serve and deliver pizza during a power outage when you have gas deck ovens.

My favorite type of oven are deck ovens. They do require more training and work, but I personally like the finished product better. A qualified oven tender can turn out a "perfect" pizza almost every time with deck ovens. I can testify with certainty that you will get burned

Bakers Pride VH-1828G Series Gas Countertop Impingement Oven

while you're learning. I had burn marks on my right hand and wrist for years, but I learned how to cook a gorgeous pizza in a deck oven.

Bakers Pride Deck Ovens – Bakers Pride offer a full line of deck ovens

for various production amounts and for several space requirements. The Y Series are the greatest selling Deck Ovens in the world. These are designed for high volume, quality pizza baking, with ceramic decks, 120,000 BTUH per deck and may be stacked two high. Some are ideal for kitchens with narrow aisles and traditional kitchen cook lines. The

Bakers Pride Bakers Pride Deck Ovens

space saving Stubby models are 33" deep, but still deliver high volume and the quality. Ovens are stackable three high and feature ceramic hearth decks. Stainless steel exteriors are standard. Visit the Web site and check the ovens at **www.bakerspride.com** or call toll free 800-431-2745 (U.S. & Canada) or e-mail sales@bakerspride.com.

In 1848, gold was discovered in California and Gardner S. Blodgett built his first oven. This was a turning point for California and the foodservice industry. Today, the Blodgett Oven Company is the leading manufacturer of commercial ovens in the world. Many businesses rely on the Blodgett name. Blodgett ovens have been in demand overseas since the late 1800s—many years

Blodgett Deck Oven Model 951/966

before international trade became a focus for our modern world. Blodgett offers a variety of deck ovens for your use. They come in a variety of sizes and configurations. Your choice depends on the volume of business you do. For the choices that are available, check the Web site at **www.blodgett. com/deck_roasting.htm** or you can call toll free at 800-331-5842 or 802-860-3700.

CONVEYOR OVEN

Your oven is critical for a pizza shop, so choose carefully. Some considerations when you choose an oven are: space, fuel requirements, and capacity. For example, old-style deck ovens make a high volume operation more difficult.

Consider your menu items and the atmosphere you want to create for your pizza shop. Will your patrons be able to see your oven? A conveyor oven doesn't have the same appeal as a deck oven.

Conveyor ovens are the most common ovens in the pizza industry today. Speed and airflow on these ovens is fixed, so consistency is assured. Most pizzerias do the majority of their business in two three-hour spans during lunch and dinner, and a conveyor produces pizzas fast enough to fill orders. Multiple conveyor belts or split belts increase your capacity and allow for varied cook times, if you offer pan pizza and thin crust pizza.

If you plan to have a high-volume operation, purchase a longer conveyor oven. With a conveyor with a chamber that is 18-inches wide and 30-inches long, you can cook two pizzas at once. However, a chamber that's 18-inches wide by 60-inches long can cook four pizzas at once.

These ovens are simple because you make a pizza, place it on the conveyor, and pick it up at the other end. The oven lets you have an assembly line of pizzas. You still need to have cooks with good timing. The pizza won't burn, but could land on the floor in a pile of steaming cheese and sauce.

Conveyor ovens only need 15-20 minutes to preheat, hold their temperature and then cool down quickly when turned off.

Consider the disadvantages to conveyor ovens. If there is a malfunction, the oven won't move the product through the oven and it has to be shut down, taken, and repaired. The oven fans are also noisy, and the cleaning and repair can be time-consuming. Another issue is that conveyors are usually more expensive than other types of pizza ovens.

Global Cooking Systems™ offers stainless steel conveyor ovens which are reliable and give you the maximum cooking potential with minimal effort and investment. These ovens are built to give you easy cleaning access. The heat is constant and even offering thorough baking and a consistent product time after time. This gives you a product that is moist and flavorful on the inside while offering a crisp crust. You can contact their customer service department at 316-721-1355 or their Web site at **www. globalcookingsystems.com/products.php**.

Blodgett Conveyor Ovens

WOOD FIRE OVENS

A decent number of pizza shops and restaurants have incorporated wood fire ovens into their operation. Pizzas cooked in wood-fired ovens look and taste different. Part of this is because they absorb the smoke, and the bottom crusts tend to be crispier because of the intense heat of the cooking stone.

Use the proper wood for cooking in these ovens. The most popular choices are oak, almond, and walnut, but cherry and apple are good, as well. Never use pine, or your pizzas will taste like lumber. Some disadvantages include:

- These ovens take longer to heat.
- It's usually necessary to keep them fired, even at night.
- Have a separate vent for this type of oven.
- You may need to preheat the oven one to two hours before starting to cook.

This can be a good oven for a skilled cook. It produces pizzas which have a distinct taste. An experienced cook can produce around 100 pizzas per hour, and you can fit about 12 to 13 12-inch pizzas in the oven at one time.

Earthstone Wood Fire ovens are one option for wood fire pizza baking. Their modular ovens may be the solution for an existing pizza shop which has limited space. Wood fire ovens can achieve a tasty combination of roasting, baking and smoking which give your patrons a healthy and delicious option that creates flavorful foods. Visit their Web site at **www.earthstoneovens. com/about.html** or you can contact them by phone at 800-840-4915 or via e-mail at earthstone@earthlink.net.

Pizza Pans

The type of pizza pans you use will make a difference in your oven. Choose

a pan that is made for the type of pizza you want to make, whether deep dish, hand tossed, or thin crust. Using the wrong pan will make you lose cooking time during a busy shift because the heat doesn't convey to the pizza properly. Extremely long cooking times during a rush can hurt customer service and cost controls.

Cheap pans aren't durable, and you will have to buy new pans soon. Take time to research the pans to get the ones that are best for the products you plan to offer. The difference could be the different metal finishes, or you can use discs instead of pans with baffles to increase or decrease heat penetration.

Most pizza pans are aluminum, but today many of these pans have a hard-anodized coating which increases the heat transfer. The coating can reduce your baking time by 6 to 12 percent. It also improves consistency and reduces waste since your pizzas won't stick.

Once you buy good quality pans, read the cleaning instructions. They may be pre-seasoned, or you may need to "oil-and-bake" the new pans. The pans are easy to clean, but don't toss them into a sink of water because it can damage the finish.

Other food items, including subs, can be cooked in pans on a conveyor oven. You will have to practice to determine the time that is needed to cook other items.

A great pizza starts with a great pizza pan. A deep dish pizza that is chewy on the inside and crispy on the outside needs a quality pan. Royal Industries offers basic aluminum pans and trays in various widths and depths. The choices are available at **www.royalindustriesinc.com/source/pizza.php** and they can be contacted by phone at 800-782-1200 and through fax at 800-321-3295. Here are some other pizza pan suppliers:

- Lloyd Pans – **www.lloydpans.com**

- American MetalCraft – **www.amnow.com**
- Allied Metal Spinning – **www.alliedmetalusa.com**

Brown Halco offers a wide selection of pizza trays and screens in a wide choice of sizes. These products heat evenly and can cook your pizzas to perfection. Brown Halco also offers pizza peels, cutters, pizza pan grippers and more items for your pizza shop needs. Some of the items can be used to warm various subs. Check their Web site at **www.halco.com** or you can call 888-289-1005.

Brown Halco offers a wide selection of pizza products

Polar Ware also offers many types of utensils for your pizza and sub shop. Polar Ware's products range from steam table pans and covers, chafers, stock pots, mixing bowls, kitchen utensils, and sinks. Their products are used

by various food service professionals. The majority of their stainless steel products are NSF listed or certified with other professional organizations. You can visit their Web site at **www.polarware.com** or contact them at 800-237-3655 or 920-458-3561.

Refrigerated Food Prep Tables – Pizza and Sub Prep

For pizza or sub preparation, you can use a refrigerated food prep table. These come in many shapes and sizes. Some offer refrigerated areas below the prep table. This is very handy during rush periods. You stock each topping in the individual containers on the prep table and can store additional supplies under the prep table. This saves you time when you are in the middle of a lunch, dinner, or late night rush. For additional information about the prep tables that are available, please visit Instaware Restaurant Supply's Web site at **www.instawares.com**. Enter "food prep tables" in the search block for a wide selection of products that can fit your needs. You can also call them at 800-892-3622.

Sub Supplies

We never needed a lot of supplies to make subs, but these are some items I would recommend. A refrigerated makeline on casters is helpful. This allows you to store the sub ingredients in one place, and I would recommend clear plastic covers for the individual compartments on the makeline. These will keep the items fresh and free from contamination by other items. I also found it was good to keep hot peppers on the far right end, so you don't accidentally drip hot pepper juice on other ingredients. Many of these makelines also have refrigerated space below the work area, where you can store additional supplies to refill the buckets on the top.

Clear plastic condiment bottles are great to hold mustard, mayonnaise, catsup, oil and vinegar, etc., to top the subs. The clear containers are great

for easy reference to ensure you use the right condiment and to keep you aware of the amount on hand. It's best to be sure these containers are filled and ready for your busy times.

A good quality, large, sharp knife is invaluable for a sub maker. A hearty sub will be difficult to cut without a good knife, and you can mangle the bread and toppings with a dull or small knife. Be sure to store the knife somewhere safe when not in use. A good knife will speed up your sandwich preparation time.

All subs need to be wrapped in thin deli paper and placed in a sub bag when offered for carryout or delivery. These long narrow bags are perfect for a long sub or half sub and will help contain the toppings during transport. You don't want your customers to lose the lettuce, tomatoes, and other toppings when they carry their subs to their car.

Purchase good containers to store all sub meats, cheeses, and toppings between shifts. I prefer clear containers for easy identification and inventory purposes. When you talk with your sub meat and cheese vendor, negotiate good prices, but keep in mind that you need to keep these items fresh until they are consumed. Their shipping packages or quantities could make this difficult.

Some of your subs will be heated, and these can be heated on pizza screens or in pizza pans, whichever is easier for you. The only real concern I had was with a new sub maker placing the cheese haphazardly, causing it to melt onto the screens. But, a little extra care can eliminate much of this problem.

Scales

Most commercial dough recipes use weight to measure raw ingredients. It's more accurate and much easier when you increase or decrease the recipe

size. This also ensures consistency in your bake times. Different scales can be used in your pizza shop:

- Use a floor scale at the door to weigh delivered items.

- Scales that measure ounces and pounds should be in all prep areas.

- For sub prep, use a small scale to control the costly ingredients like meats and cheeses.

Digital scales are faster to read and more accurate, and some show the weight after you remove the bag or bowl. Scales need to be calibrated periodically to ensure accuracy. When shopping for scales, ask about maintenance and calibration service.

Quality and accurate scales are critical to help you control food costs. This is not an equipment purchase where you should scrimp. Instaware Restaurant Supply offers many items for your pizza and sub shop. One of these is a variety of scales. Their Web site is **www.instawares.com**. Enter "scales" in the search block and you will find various scales for your pizza shop. Some of those choices include: dough scales, digital scales, and platform scales. The digital scales can be used to measure individual portions and platform scales are used to measure the accuracy of your delivery orders. Some scales are made to fit onto your refrigerated pizza prep table. You can contact them at 800-892-3622.

Fryer Equipment

General-purpose commercial fryers can be used for appetizers, fried chicken, eggplant parmesan, and French fries. Fries can be a great add on with subs. The type and size of your fryer depends on what you plan to make with it. Check these distributors:

- Anetsberger Brothers – **www.anetsberger.com**

- Cecilware Corporation – **www.cecilware.com/home.aspx**

- Henny Penny Corporations – **www.hennypenny.com**
- Autofry – **www.autofry.com**
- Keating of Chicago – **www.keatingofchicago.com**

Fryers are also available from major manufacturers such as:

- Vulcan Hart – **www.vulcanhart.com**
- Blodgett – **www.blodgett.com**

Henny Penny open fryer

Frontline International offers a system to pump waste from your fryer into a containment tank. There are a variety of systems so that you can find one to fit your needs. For more information, you can visit their Web site at **www. frontlineii.com**. You can contact them at 330-861-1100 or e-mail sales@ frontlineii.com.

Mixers

Commercial mixers are needed to mix dough. The industry leader is Hobart (**www.hobartcorp.com**). Their Web site has calculators to help you determine the capacity needed, shows you potential savings when using auto-scrapers, and offers advice. Hobart offers counter and floor model mixers. Your local restaurant supply house can also help you find the right mixer. If you plan to make your own dough, purchase a heavy-use mixer.

Precision dough mixers offer various size mixers depending on the amount of business you do. Precision North America's headquarters is located in Albany, New York. There is a complete stock of mixers, crated, and ready to ship today. Precision North America has distributors throughout the US who can help you find the mixer you need at a price you can afford, and get you mixing. You can contact them toll free at 877-7-MIXERS (877-764-9377) or on the Web at **www.precisionmixers.com**.

Packages

The packages will depend on what you offer and whether you have carryout and delivery. Look over your menu, and look through a supply catalog to decide what items are needed. If you are selling items other than pizza, you'll also need to investigate other types of packaging. There is a variety of materials to choose from: paper, plastic, and Styrofoam, for example. Some of the things you'll want to think about while investigating these options include cost, how environmentally friendly each is, and sturdiness. Check out **www.yourbaglady.com** for some packaging options.

Pizza Boxes

Your beautiful pizza needs to arrive at the customers' home or office in great condition. It shouldn't run out of the corners or soak through the box.

Good boxes are critical to making a good impression and to delivering a quality product. It might cost a little more, but it's worth it to develop loyal customers.

Corrugated board is preferred because it's sturdy. When you choose your boxes, consider the height and size of the items you will deliver. You can have different heights, but be sure they will be high enough for your pizzas and other items. There is also a choice of white or brown paper. The brown is more reasonably priced.

Many pizza boxes are square, but Domino's uses octagon because the pizza doesn't slip around as much. Papa John's also has corners that fold in to keep the pizza from slipping and to hold sauce and peppers.

Clamshell boxes are an alternative, and they don't take up much room and are easy to fold. These are more inexpensive and sturdier.

Wash Up Afterwards

After you cook and bake, wash the dishes and pans. Purchase a washing system that protects your customers while being efficient and cost-effective. Should you use a multi-sink configuration or a conveyor system? Your dishwashing decision will directly affect your bottom line. Should you have a more expensive dishwashing system, or can your staff wash the pans in a sink? Consider the price of a sink or a dishwasher and the labor hours for both options.

Sanitation is when water, chemicals, and heat are properly combined. When you wash dishes, the goals are: waste removal, washing, sanitizing, rinsing, and drying. Familiarize yourself with local health department codes.

- **Make certain your water pressure is ample** for your dishwasher. Poor water pressure can slow cycles, inhibit automatic settings,

and may not meet sanitation standards.

- **Review your hot water capacity and recovery times.** Use temperatures of 150°F and above, depending on the machine's capabilities.

- **Invest in a hot water booster.** Check with your local utility company for rebates on select equipment.

- **Calculate your water hardness.** Rinse aids may not be effective without a water softener.

- **What and when to wash.** Do you need a separate washer for glasses? Will you need a lot of storage area for dishes that must wait until after a rush? Will a lot of pans need to be soaked? Each of these things makes a difference in what you need.

- **Install a low-flow (1.6 gpm) pre-rinse nozzle** at your dishwashing station in order to save up to $100 a month in energy, water, and sewer costs.

- **Research equipment rental/chemical purchase programs.** The supplier owns and maintains the equipment. You pay a rental fee and purchase their chemicals. Auto-Chlor System, a well-known national supplier, may be in your local Yellow Pages.

- **Create ample, convenient, and secure storage for chemical dishwashing agents.** Rental/supply programs with monthly service require less chemical inventory.

Washing by Hand

A multi-sink configuration that complies with local regulations is a good option to clean oversized pots and equipment components. Be certain to:

- **Add ample counters and racks.** Local codes dictate the size.

- **Keep dirty and clean dishware separate** in order to avoid contamination.

- **Install a detergent dispenser.**

- **Maintain a consistent and hot water temperature** by placing sinks near a dedicated water heater.

Refrigerators and Freezers

To research efficient freezers and refrigerators, read the U.S. Department of Energy's pamphlet at **www.eere.energy.gov/femp/technologies/eeproducts. cfm** and the Consortium for Energy Efficiency at **www.cee1.org**.

Your menu and ingredient items require refrigeration. Walk-in units provide a place to hold your products, and you can wheel food in the door. There are many things you will need to store, and the way you decide to handle your dough will make a difference. Parbaked dough and trays of prepared dough take up a lot of space.

U.S. Cooler manufactures premium walk-in coolers, freezers, and combination units at competitive prices. These are used for all types of cold storage. These can be constructed to suit your needs and will arrive at your pizza shop pre-assembled to ensure a quality product. Check the Web site for the various configurations that are available. Each accessory that you need can be purchased from U.S. Cooler to accentuate your walk in cooler. These can include: outside ramp, rain roofs, strip curtains, shelving, glass doors, and many others. U.S. Cooler utilizes the latest technology to manufacture walk-in coolers and freezers which can be purchased from a dealer or an online discount dealer. For more information, visit **www.uscooler.com** or call 800-521-2665.

Henny Penny – Blasters and Chillers – Proper chilling is also necessary to reduce the risk of contamination and these blasters and chillers are just the item to safely store prepared food for use during peak times. See **www.hennypenny.com/pd/pd2.phtml?formTarget=bchillers** or call 800-417-8417.

Computers — How to Use Them and Profit From Them

The right computer system can be invaluable to a small business owner. It can give you capabilities that were once only available to major corporations. Even small businesses can benefit from owning a personal computer. This can be a desktop or a laptop that can run a word processor, spreadsheet, database, accounting package you choose, and other software packages that help you organize your business. Computers are integrated into every facet of the food service industry. Computers can:

- Track sales and purchases.
- Monitor inventory.
- Increase purchasing power.
- Maintain accounting and payroll records.
- Develop menus and minimize food waste.

Industry- and task-specific computer systems may not look like a typical computer. There may not be a monitor, and the keyboard may look like a cash register. These systems focus on functions such as ringing up sales. Computerized systems, with alarm and fire-suppression systems, can save lives.

Computers are valuable tools for the small business owner; however, they can also create headaches. You must have thorough training for a computer to become valuable and useful for your business. Local community colleges, computer stores, and private learning centers offer computer classes for

many popular programs.

When you research custom software or hardware, be certain the company offers sufficient training, easy-to-understand manuals, and ongoing support. Industry- and task-specific computerization is a long-term investment. New employees and new businesses need long-term support, so research the company before purchasing.

Business Computers

Your PC (personal computer) can be used for accounting, inventory control, personnel support, advertising, and business correspondence. Apple's Macintosh is popular, but there are more Windows-based programs available. Laptops are convenient, but your confidential data is at greater risk of being stolen.

Many major manufacturers and retailers offer small-business leasing. An extended warranty and/or service agreement (preferably an onsite agreement) can be an excellent investment, as your business will depend on your computer working full time. My business computers are leased through Dell, and I have a warranty that guarantees replacement by the following morning if I call before 5 p.m. They also send a repairperson the following day, when needed.

You can find computer reviews and recommendations at **www.zdnet.com** and **www.cnet.com**. A low- to mid-range small business system should satisfy your needs.

The World Wide Web

The Internet provides a wealth of information and resources for small business owners. You can research equipment, place your food and supply

orders, compare prices for paper goods, and advertise your restaurant.

Most computer systems include a 56K modem for dial-up service. Be sure to add a modem, even if you plan to use high-speed Internet. This is an inexpensive backup plan.

If you maintain a Web site or share files with a franchisor, spend the money for a significantly faster broadband service. Contact your local cable and telephone companies to determine service availability and prices. Many national companies also offer high-speed access.

More and more companies offer online ordering, order tracking, and technical support. If your typical order is stored online, it only takes a few minutes to schedule next week's delivery.

Most banks offer Web access to your accounts, including transferring funds from one account to another and paying loans and credit cards. Some banks offer free online banking if you get your statements online. Check Web-based bill paying services through your bank or third-party services such as MyCheckFree (**www.mycheckfree.com**) and PayTrust (**www.paytrust. com**). Most credit card companies and utility companies offer online bill paying.

Verify how long it takes for the payment to clear. Most have a delay of several days, which must be taken into consideration when paying your bills. This is a cheaper, easier, and quicker way to pay your bills once you set up the accounts.

Computer Networks

Small pizzerias probably won't need to network their computers. Networking allows multiple computers to "talk" to each other, share data, printers, and Internet access. Networks can be created via existing telephone wiring, data-only wiring, or a wireless setup. A local computer company can offer advice

about the best solution for your building. A network can be helpful if your budget allows for the additional units.

Industry-Specific Computer Systems

POINT OF SALE (POS) SYSTEMS

Touch screen POS (point of sale) systems are widely used in the food service industry. The POS system, an upgrade from the electronic cash register, was introduced in the mid-1980s and has penetrated 85 percent of food service establishments nationwide. Freestanding and integrated (networked with your accounting system) systems are available in a variety of price ranges, although all are more expensive than a cash register. The touch screen requires minimal training and provides extensive sales data.

Learning to decipher the number in the POS system enables you to have more control over your inventory, provides time-specific data (what sells during what hours or days) and provides detailed sales reports. This helps you schedule employees, minimize overtime, monitor shrinkage (waste, theft), and identify productive and non-productive areas. This allows you to clearly understand the bottom line and it will eliminate the guesswork.

InTouchPOS is a system that was developed by restaurant operators. That means that it is customized to fit your needs in the restaurant business. It includes performance, flexibility, security, and reliability.

The system can be set up to include your employee information, payroll details, all your discounts, promos, and special offers. It can include various meals and your ingredients and portions which are

programmed before it arrives at your location. This is a "turn key" system that might be just what your pizza and sub shop needs to control food and labor costs. For more information, you can visit **www.intouchpos.com/ product.htm** or call 800-777-8202.

Pizza shops that offer takeout, dine-in, carryout, and delivery can send orders to your office computer at the end of the shift or the end of the day to compile your reports. POS benefits include:

- Increase sales and accounting information.
- Offer custom tracking and reporting.
- Report product sales breakdown for forecasting.
- Show peak and slow periods for staffing projections.
- Report individual product performance.
- Monitor inventory usage.
- Process credit cards immediately.
- Eliminate math errors and minimizes over/under-rings.
- Control discounting.
- End errors caused by poor handwriting.
- Highlight possible theft.
- Record employee timekeeping.
- Tally employee sales and performance.

GENERAL RETAIL POS SYSTEMS

There are literally hundreds of POS systems. Don't ask a computer consultant for a recommendation. Your accountant should be able to provide you with recommendations. Your local restaurant supply distributor will also offer POS systems or can provide local references.

In selecting a POS system and other accounting software, look for convenient

training and support and fast, local repair service. Research the software company for history of performance and long-term stability. You will need the company long after the sale.

VITAL LINK POS SYSTEM

Vital Link POS helps you to track orders, modify any items, verify the productivity of your servers and drivers. You can evaluate individual menu items. It is able to manage your orders by a variety of variables including: customer, table, or server. You can oversee your inventory and scheduling for 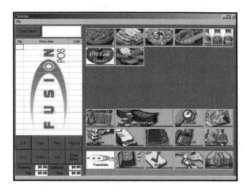 better cost control. The customer history which is stored in the system will give you the opportunity to target your marketing efforts to your customer base. For more information, visit **www.vitallinkpos.com/products.htm** or e-mail loconnor@vitallinkpos.com.

CHOOSE YOUR SOFTWARE FIRST

Find software with the features and reports best suited for your pizza shop. Then find the hardware (cash register, computer, printers, etc.) to operate it. A versatile choice is Window's-based. But, you may find excellent programs that are Unix or Linux operating systems, which need the right hardware/operating system to access. Custom-programmed software, which only works with their hardware, ties you to that company, even if you're unhappy with their product or service.

Below are just a few general-purpose POS systems for retailers:

- **QuickBooks Point of Sale Software** (**www.intuit.com**) integrates

your QuickBooks for Retailers accounting software and offers various merchant services, including credit card processing.

- **Microsoft Business Solutions (www.microsoft.com/ BusinessSolutions)** offers various POS and credit card systems and accounting.

- **The Retail Solution** offers general retail and restaurant-specific POS systems (**www.nwns.com**).

- **IBM Retail Store Solutions (www.pc.ibm.com/store/products/ pos/sureone)** offers a system for budget-conscious retailers.

PIZZERIA-SPECIFIC SYSTEMS

Pizzeria-specific computer systems are available for POS activities. These may be stand-alone POS systems or customized systems that include production, inventory, and accounting capabilities. There are various manufacturers and resources for food service or computer systems.

- **Point of Success** – POS software for restaurants and pizzerias – **www.pointofsuccess.com**

- **Point of Success** – Pizza delivery software – **www.pointofsuccess.com**

- MicroWorks – POS systems for pizzerias – **http://microworks.com**

- PlanMagic – Pizzeria business plan software – **http://planmagic. com/business_plan/restaurant/pizza_delivery_business_plan.html**

Food Service Software

The following food service software packages are "stand alone," and are not

part of a POS system. These are not pizzeria-specific, but your business may benefit from one of these.

SpeedLine's comprehensive point of sale, restaurant back office, and enterprise solutions give you all the tools you need to manage the business of pizza. It is the #1 most recommended POS of the top 100 pizza companies. With SpeedLine you can:

- Make the right decisions, based on real numbers
- Control food costs and manage labor
- Evaluate your sales performance by the minute
- Track your best-selling menu items
- Bring customers back with stellar service and low-cost promotions

SpeedLine is the POS of choice for better service, bigger profits, and instant access to the information you need to grow your business. With a 15-year reputation for excellence and an impressive roster of satisfied customers, SpeedLine delivers the complete restaurant management solution that your business needs.

For more info, visit their Web site at **www.speedlinesolutions.com** or phone toll-free at 888-400-9185.

CHEFTEC

ChefTec is an integrated software program with recipe and menu costing, inventory control, and nutritional analysis.

Nutritional Analysis: The nutritional analysis module gives you a quick and accurate analysis of nutritional values for up to 5,000 of the most commonly used ingredients.

- Add your specialty items.

- Calculate nutritional values for your recipes.

- Verify which menu items are low fat, low-calorie, etc.

- Print a "Nutrition Facts" label.

Inventory Control: Preloaded inventory list for 1,900 commonly used ingredients and capacity for adding additional ingredients.

- Import purchases from online vendors' ordering systems.

- Track fluctuating food costs.

- Compare vendor pricing.

- Evaluate price increase impact on recipes.

- Automate ordering with par values.

- Use handheld devices for inventory.

- Generate custom reports.

- Compare vendor pricing at the touch of a button, from purchases or bids.

- Enter invoices quickly using the "Auto-Populate" feature.

- Generate customized reports on purchases, price variances, bids and credits. Speeds up physical inventory, ordering and maintenance of par levels. Lists ingredients in different languages (Spanish, French, German, and others).

There is also a ChefTech PDA (personal digital assistant) version available. ChefTech is available from Atlantic Publishing Company (**www.atlantic-pub.com** or 800-814-1132).

NUTRACOSTER

NutraCoster calculates the product cost (including labor, packaging, and overhead) and nutritional content for any size serving. Ingredient database

contains nutritional information for approximately 6,000 ingredients (USDA Handbook 8). It also includes unlimited ingredients and process statistics. You can print camera-ready "Nutrition Facts" labels that comply with the requirements of the Nutrition Labeling and Education Act (NLEA).

The "Overhead Calculator" allows you to factor overhead costs into your cost. No more fudging or guessing. Nutritional analysis accounts for nutrient changes during processing, such as water lost during baking, water gained during boiling, fat lost during broiling, fat gained during frying, or other changes in nutritional value. Print multiple "Nutrition Facts" labels per page. It includes ingredient listings with Nutrition Facts. It can be used by unlimited simultaneous users.

NutraCoster offers libraries with nutritional information for specific brand name ingredients. An accompanying StockCoster Inventory Module handles inventory control, production, and vendor data and quotes. NutraCoster is available from Atlantic Publishing Company (**www.atlantic-pub.com** or 800-814-1132).

MENUPRO

MenuPro allows you to create professional menus at a lower rate than print shop menus. You can create "Daily Specials" or take-out menus with MenuPro. MenuPro is available from Atlantic Publishing Company (**www. atlantic-pub.com** or 800-814-1132).

EMPLOYEE SCHEDULE PARTNER

Employee Schedule Partner is a complete software package for employee scheduling.

- Point-and-click: make a schedule without touching the keyboard.
- Click a button, and fill your schedule with employees automatically.

- Click a button to replace absent employees and a list of available employees, with their phone numbers, will appear.

- The online coach offers helpful hints to new users.

- It accommodates an unlimited number of employees and positions.

- You can manually override selections and track employees' availability restrictions.

- You can schedule employees to work multiple shifts per day.

- Track payroll and hourly schedule totals for easy budget management.

- Use any day of the week to start your schedule.

- Specify maximum hours per day, days per week, and shifts per day for each employee.

- Lock employees into a scheduled shift, and the program will not move them when juggling the schedule.

- Save old schedules for reference when needed.

The software is password-protected to prevent unauthorized use. Employee Schedule Partner is available from Atlantic Publishing Company (**www.atlantic-pub.com** or 800-814-1132).

EMPLOYEE TIME CLOCK PARTNER

Employee Time Clock is a favorite software. It's powerful and easy to use.

- Employees can clock in or out using their employee number.

- Employees can view their time cards to verify information.

- It's password-protected, so management can edit the information.

- It calculates daily and weekly overtime.

- Management can assign Employee ID number or PIN (personal identification number).

Employee Time Clock Partner is available from Atlantic Publishing Company (**www.atlantic-pub.com** or 800-814-1132).

Accounting Software

Computer programs, such as QuickBooks® (**www.quickbooks.com**) and Peachtree® (**www.peachtree.com**), are a solid choice for in-house bookkeeping. These programs are inexpensive, easy to use and save time, money and countless errors. See Chapter 6 for discussion about accounting software.

Other Computer Uses

Small businesses use computers in a variety of ways to make their businesses run smoother. Some of these ways include:

- Improve communi line ordering has become increasingly popular with pizzerias.

Many items and ideas were discussed in this chapter. Not all will be appropriate for you, but you should have enough information and additional resources to make informed decisions about the equipment you need.

Photo Courtesy of Pizza Today

16

Successful
Kitchen Management

To effectively manage anything, you must be organized. You also need to develop the ability to analyze the things that are needed and the ability to supervise and motivate.

Purchasing

Purchasing is the activity that supplies your pizza shop with the best items at the lowest prices. In order to be effective and get the best prices, you should maintain a good working relationship with your suppliers. Take time to meet them face-to-face, if possible, and develop a good relationship with them.

The purchasing person needs to be familiar with the needs of your pizza shop. If you have a kitchen manager, he or she would be an ideal choice. However, you can do this, and delegate someone qualified to work with

you. It's better not to have a lot of people doing the purchasing. This can cause inconsistencies and potential problems.

Inventory Levels

Determine the minimum and maximum inventory levels for your store. When your supplies reach the minimum, you must reorder before you run out. It is easier to handle the purchasing in an effective manner when you understand the daily, weekly, and monthly usage and the delivery schedule. Your maximum inventory signals you are over-ordering and tying up too much money for items that will sit on the shelf. The key is to have enough stock without overstocking!

You must take a physical inventory on a regular basis and always before you place a food order. If you have a computerized system, you can rely on those numbers, but I always double checked the inventory numbers before placing an order, especially for costly and unusual items. We inventoried daily, but some pizza shops inventory weekly or monthly. Remember, the less often you do any actual inventory the less control you have over food costs.

To figure your "Desired Inventory," you need to know when the deliveries are made and how much you use between deliveries. For a normal week, add 25 percent for unexpected usage. There are some special situations that will affect these figures.

I've mentioned checking for special events in the area or at local colleges. Special events can drastically affect the supplies you order. If students are a big part of your business, their events and vacation will impact your usage. When they are on break, usage goes down and when they have Homecoming or exams, usage can soar. I used to get student events calendars and checked the sales from previous years to determine the amount of food to order.

Your order will be the difference between "Desired Inventory" and the amount "On Hand." Placing food orders gets easier with practice. Also, the

more familiar you are with your customers and your sales figures, the easier it becomes.

Establish a buying schedule and stick to it. In a franchise you could be assigned a delivery schedule. Your calendar can show the following:

- Which day to place orders.

- Which day the delivery will arrive.

- What items will arrive from each company.

- Contact information for each vendor.

- Your negotiated prices for items.

Post the schedule on the office wall. When a delivery doesn't arrive on time, call the company immediately.

A Want Sheet can be posted on a clipboard in the kitchen. Employees can list items they need to do their jobs more efficiently. Consult the sheet on a regular basis. These can be inexpensive items that need to be replaced, but they can also be bigger items. Buy what you can, and place the rest on a list for future review.

Cooperative Purchasing

A group of small restaurants can work together and form purchasing groups to increase their buying power. When the various stores place large orders, you can get substantial price reductions. If it works out very well, you could have your own warehouse, trucks, and personnel. In the pizza franchise I worked for, we ordered everything through their commissary, and it saved negotiating prices and placing a lot of different orders. I called one number to order and had two deliveries per week.

Receiving and Storing Supplies

Most deliveries arrive during the day. Set specific hours for your deliveries—typically after the lunch rush and before dinner. Most of my deliveries were made after dinner and late night. The manager or owner should be responsible for receiving and storing all items. If someone else placed the order, he should ensure that each item is what he ordered. Receiving and storing is critical, and the people who are involved need to be trained to handle it right. Mistakes can cost you a lot of money. How to process all products:

1. Check delivery against order sheet.

2. Verify the amount ordered (weight, size, and quantity).

3. Check items against the invoice.

4. Verify price, totals, date, company name, and receiver's signature.

5. Weigh any items to verify delivery amount.

6. Date, rotate, and put products in the assigned storage area immediately.

7. Note discrepancies on bills of lading, invoices, and related paperwork. Contact the vendor immediately about overages and shortages. Revise COD amounts to reflect the correct price when an error occurs. Have the delivery person acknowledge and sign the corrections.

Keep a box in the kitchen to store invoices and packing slips from the day. At the end of the day, the invoices must be brought to the manager's office and placed in a designated spot. Handle all invoices with care because missing invoices will complicate the bookkeeping, financial records, and statements.

Rotation Procedures

Use the "first in, first out" (FIFO) rotation method. Date each package, and

place the incoming items behind existing stock. When people pull supplies, they pull the first package to ensure they use the oldest items first.

1. New items go behind or on the bottom.

2. Older items move to the front and to the left.

3. Always use the oldest item first.

4. Date and label all items.

    —You can use an office self-inking date stamp or a big marker.

    —If multiple people handle this, have them initial items they mark.

    —Dissolve-a-Way labels are useful. Visit **www.dissolveaway.com**, or call DayMark Food Safety Systems at 800-847-0101.

Issuing

Issuing ("checking out") raw ingredients is an important part of inventory control. All raw materials must be issued on a daily basis. When bulk items are removed from a freezer or storage area, they must be signed out. Create a Sign-out Sheet for all items. The Sign-out Sheet should be placed on a clipboard near the storage area.

When items are removed, the weight or quantity removed must be recorded. The weight must be placed in the "Amount Used or Defrosted" column on the Daily Preparation Form. This will show the items were used in the store. From this information, you can compute a daily yield on each item prepared. This yield shows the portions were weighed accurately and shows the bulk product that was used to prepare menu items. The signing-out procedure eliminates pilferage and helps you create waste reduction procedures.

Restroom or cleaning supplies can be issued that way. If any items are stolen, the cost shows up in the cost analysis at the end of the month.

Kitchen Controls

Combine kitchen controls with your established procedures and policies to help you have an airtight food cost control system. The key to food control is reconciliation. Each step is checked and reconciled with another person. First you must set up the systems, and then its management's responsibility to enforce and monitor them daily. When all employees follow these steps, you know where each dollar and ounce of food was used. You and your managers must help to train and supervise all employees. Daily involvement and communication is needed to succeed.

When employees don't follow the pizza shop policies, correct them. No matter how good your control systems are, they must be enforced and followed. You should be able to oversee these controls in less than an hour a day. Consider it an investment in reducing waste, maintaining quality and productivity, and mentoring your employees.

Identifying Inventory Theft

Check the invoices every day against the items that were delivered. Be sure the items signed off are in the storage areas. When you find discrepancies, check with the employee who signed for the delivery. When you take your original inventory, add any deliveries and subtract usage, and that is the amount you should have on your shelf. If there is a difference, there could be a problem.

Be sure items aren't stocked in the wrong place before accusing anyone of theft. Well-meaning employees may put away deliveries on the wrong shelf.

There were also times when items appeared to be missing, but they were left in the pizza makeline at the end of the night. Check thoroughly for items before hurling accusations at employees. You can discourage a good employee by jumping to wrong conclusions.

Public Areas

What will your customers think when they drive by your pizza shop? Will they notice trash in the parking lot, or will their attention go to the bushes and flowers that line the sidewalk leading to your door? Once they get inside, they will scan the waiting area, counters, and dining room. These areas must be:

- **Attractive** – Is the appearance of your shop appealing?

- **Clean** – The majority of your customers will never see inside your kitchen, so they draw conclusions from what they can see.

- **Efficient** – Your staff must be well-trained to offer good customer service.

- **Organized** – An organized staff and work space allow you to offer quicker service while you maintain a high level of quality and service.

- **Inviting** – A pizza shop has a welcoming combination of sights, smells, and personality which can draw people to your shop and encourage them to return.

Some of the large pizza chains are working to offer an upscale design. When food is served in an upscale environment, the pizza shop can place a higher value on their food. This is just another way to set yourself apart from your competition.

Outdoor Areas

The exterior of your pizza shop is usually the first thing people will see. What do they see? Is it appealing enough to make them venture inside? One very critical issue for a restaurant is to be clean. If the outside is dirty, it would seem obvious that the kitchen is dirty as well.

These are some consideration when you think about the exterior of your pizza shop:

- Review zoning regulations for possible restrictions to your present plans and future expansion.

- Place all plants, trees, and decorations in a way that hide unattractive views, shelter customers from the wind, and soften noise levels. This is especially critical if you offer outdoor seating.

- Provide ample lighting to prevent accidents.

- You can add gas heaters, fireplaces, and fire pits for chilly nights.

- Attractive umbrellas can fill several needs. They can protect customers from the sun or unexpected rain. Awnings or patio covers might be a more conducive possibility for your pizza shop.

- Use tables and seating that are easy to clean and safe. They also need to endure the weather in your area.

Parking

Can your shop be seen from the street? When customers park, ensure there is sufficient signage to help them find the door. This is especially critical when there are doors you don't use. Make it obvious how to get inside.

Ensure that customers have easy access to your entrance. Check local laws and ADA requirements for accessibility by disabled customers.

Pizza shops are a favorite hangout for young people. Do you offer a bike rack that is easy to find, but out of the way of most foot traffic? If your pizza shop is in an area that charges for parking, you can offer validation for your customers. It is inexpensive and is a thoughtful touch.

First Impressions

You want a front door that welcomes customers into your pizza shop. The same is true for the exterior of your shop. Does it grab their attention and draw them to your door? It should. One important thing is sufficient lighting. Consider these possibilities when you walk to your front door:

- What is the first thing that catches your attention?
- Does it look clean and well-maintained?
- Is the appearance comfortable and inviting?
- Do you see trash and debris or overflowing, ugly trash cans?
- Can approaching customers smell fresh pizza baking?
- Can the counterperson be heard over the "cooking noises"?

Does the appearance send a consistent message of quality and concern for your customers? If not, make some changes to give that feeling. Ensure that people are assigned to keep all public areas clean throughout the day.

Window Displays

There are many ways to dress your windows. A word of caution; don't overdo the window dressing. Make it inviting, but not overwhelming. You can do amazing things with some fabric, a few tools, and your creativity. It's also good to change the windows from time to time. Simple changes can be effective. You can use bright colors that work with your décor, nice props, and signage.

Window ledges can be spruced up, and you can use fabric in many appealing ways. Secure items on your shelves or ledges, or create a small rail or barrier that doesn't hide your decorations. Be sure to work with the theme you picked for your pizza shop.

Another concern that I kept in mind with window displays was the safety of the store and the team. We had a series of thefts in the area and my store was on a dark side street. Everyone's safety was a concern, so we left areas of the windows open to ensure a clear view of the parking area and the street. There's no sense in placing so many signs on your windows that you give a potential robber the upper hand. Place signs and ads, but be sure you can still keep an eye on the exterior of the shop.

Use Some Greenery

Plants can be used in a variety of ways both inside and outside. They add life to your pizza shop. Interior plants filter the air and provide oxygen. Outdoor plants add an attractive and welcome environment and can be used to hide unattractive elements. You can also use them to lead the customer to your

door through effective use of plants and landscaping.

Talk to a landscape professional to ensure you have the right light, moisture, and drainage for your plan. Here are some tips to help you get started:

- Find a landscape firm to maintain your area. Keeping your plants alive and looking good is time-consuming good. These professionals can keep out the weeds, pluck dead leaves and flowers and mulch, and maintain your landscaping. You also need to assign someone to rotate your indoor plants on a regular basis. It's possible that you will need to replace indoor plants from time to time.

- Go faux! Sometimes silk plants are a better choice. Only use high quality artificial plants, and work within your existing color scheme, using colors that are natural. Unusual colors will stand out and look phony.

- Portable gardens can be created with pots, planters, hanging baskets, barrels, or antique or unusual kitchen items. These can be filled with plants and moved around the pizza shop.

- Unfriendly plants shouldn't be used in your shop. These include foul smelling, prickly, and plants with stickers. Some plants have poisonous leaves or berries, and you shouldn't use these in your pizza shop.

- Right plants in the right place. Remember light and watering needs. Consider the full grown size of the plants. Vines should be directed away from seating and customer service areas.

Your Restrooms

Your restrooms are a small part of your business, but they are important.

They need to be sufficient for your shop capacity and must be clean. This is an easy way to show your consideration for your customers.

This is another area where you must verify plumbing and health department requirements. The ADA requires handicapped accessible restrooms. Insufficient restrooms can delay your opening and cause issues with the health department. Consider these factors when you design your restrooms:

- Remember your customers' physical needs. You can offer sinks, hand towels, or dryers at levels for adults, children, and handicapped customers. The ADA can offer advice at 800-514-0301.

- Choose lasting materials that won't show dirt and tolerate strong cleaners. Ceramic tile is great, but the grout may become discolored.

- Avoid public unisex rooms. You may have no choice, but if feasible you should provide separate women's and men's restrooms. Some individuals may feel uncomfortable in a unisex restroom, and it could keep them from your pizza shop. This is most critical in a dine-in restaurant.

- Provide separate staff restrooms.

Countertop Displays

Generate interest in your specialties or temporary specials with countertop displays. These are also great for impulse purchases like appetizers and desserts. It's important to keep it simple. Too many signs and displays are too busy and won't influence the customer in a positive way.

Use a variety of signs or cardboard displays to promote various items. If there are ones you use often, you might upgrade them with glass units, bowls, or

special stands. These can help you sell more add-on items when the orders are being processed. They are a great way to increase your ticket prices.

Front Work Areas

There are setups which make it impossible to do all prep work in a closed kitchen. I ate at a Carabbas in North Carolina, and they had cooks lining two walls of a dining room. Many chain pizza shops also have the pizza makeline and ovens within view of their carryout customers. Here are some additional things that are needed in your front work areas:

- Display prepared food
- Packaged food for travel
- Order taking areas
- Ring up on cash register or enter sales in computer
- Areas to prepare food and drink items
- Finish and pack food items
- Storage items, forks, knives, spoons, and cash in the till

Suggestions for the layout of your front work areas:

- Find an attractive and functional layout.
- Maintain a clean and orderly work environment visible to customers.
- Have rollers on all carts and trash cans.
- Be sure to offer adequate lighting and avoid glare on customers.
- Use non-slip flooring and mats.
- Install drains in the floor, and use vinyl baseboards to eliminate scuffs. Equipment on casters is easier to rearrange.
- Work areas should be laid out to avoid stooping, reaching, and lifting.

- Handle "wet" and "dry" tasks in different areas to avoid damage, electrical problems, and food contamination.

- Have hand sinks handy for workers. Mine was behind the ovens and about 10 feet from the pizza makeline. This made it easier for drivers to help between deliveries.

- Plan to have sufficient counter space to store deliveries, to pass food items to servers, and to talk with servers.

Shelving

Your staff needs adequate storage areas to work efficiently. There are tools, equipment, and food items that need to be handy. Makelines can be a huge help. These store the food in a refrigerated setting, and there is room to store additional food and supplies underneath. There are many sizes and varieties, depending on what you offer. Keep these areas clean, and they can be within customer view. Many customers enjoy watching their pizzas and subs being made.

You can keep cleaning supplies and cash registers out of view, but handy for your employees. Remember, the work area needs to look good, but must be functional.

Dedicated Work Areas

There are work areas in your pizza shop other than the kitchen and the public area. How will you handle the space and supplies needed for delivery? Your food and supply storage area can take up considerable space in your pizza shop.

Delivery Areas

It is best to have a back door for all deliveries. This gives you a separate point of access for the supplies to be delivered, especially during peak hours. You need information from any perspective vendors. Some specific questions may be:

- What method do they use to package heavy bulk items?
- Do they leave racked goods?
- Do they drop items inside the door?
- Will they move heavy bags of flour to storage areas?

Set up an effective delivery and storage area. Here are some tips:

- Provide gloves and heavy-lifting belts for your employees.

- Check-in can be handled quicker with a computer in the delivery area. Compare packing slips with orders, then accept, and sign off on the delivery. But, you can also do this with a clipboard and copies of orders.

- Have an established procedure to accept deliveries and train all staff members. There will be written damaged goods and return policies, which should be stored in the binder to support employee training.

These procedures will help employees catch ordering and shipping errors:

- Note all visibly damaged merchandise on packing slips or bills of lading, or refuse the item. Your action depends on the vendor's recommendations.

- Note any hidden damage on the packing slip; advise management immediately, and file a claim.

- Inspect all items for damage, signs of pests, excess debris, or mishandling.

- Note overages or shortages on the packing slips or bills of lading.

- Sanitize hands and remove soiled aprons to avoid potential contamination.

- Take complaints to vendor's customer service department or your sales representative.

Storage

You will need various storage locations. These include raw ingredients, finished products, refrigerated areas and dry storage, along with equipment and supply storage. Sometimes you should have short-term storage. I did this on unusually high volume weeks, when I ordered substantially more supplies and assigned someone to move supplies to the usual storage area as we used items. Take a close look at your menu and the necessary supplies in order to determine how to arrange your storage areas.

These ideas will help you work more effectively by creating three types of storage areas:

1. **Active** – Storage that you will access regularly. Keep these things close to the work area.

2. **Backup** – When you use your active items, you will pull from the backup area to refill. Use this area for items you use occasionally. This area should be farther away from the main work areas.

3. **Long-term** – Store your non-perishable, special-use, and seasonal items in an out-of-reach area in the back of the building and less accessible areas.

Dry Storage

Establish your dry storage are near your delivery door. Be sure there is enough access to move items in and out without difficulty. Any shelving needs to be at least 6 inches off the floor to avoid posts. Keep the following tips in mind when you create storage areas:

- Any public storage cabinets need to be attractive, blend with the décor, and be easy to clean.

- Store your chemical cleaners or hazardous materials in a separate place. Check any local regulations on how to store hazardous materials.

- Evaluate your storage plans with cross contamination in mind. This will include what you store, how you store it, and how things are handled.

- Movable storage shelves, etc., are a great way to add flexibility to your plan.

- For safety, place items at waist level and below. On the rare times you must store things higher, supply sturdy stepstools and ladders.

Waste & Recycling

The way you dispose of your waste products is important. Here are some tips to help you to manage your waste and lower disposal costs.

- A waste disposal unit. Stainless steel systems with automatic reversal controls are best. Buy a unit with enough horsepower and rotor size to handle your food waste. Review expected lifespan when comparing units.

- Build a recycling center. Include recycling equipment in your rear storage area layout.

- Arrange for grease/meat waste rendering companies for pickup.

- Use sorting bins and convenient waste receptacles. Install color-coded recycling containers on wheels for easy use.

- Plan for large quantities of paper, cardboard, plastics, glass, metal cans, and food waste.

- Cardboard balers can pay for themselves through reduced hauling costs.

- A commercial-grade trash compactor. You will have some trash even if you have an aggressive recycling program. A compactor can pay for itself by saving you bin use and hauling fees.

- Discussions with local recycling companies and government waste management agencies. Recycling companies can handle grease/oil waste and pick up glass and cardboard. Some companies specialize in food service waste. Your city or county can help you develop waste-reduction programs.

Last But Not Least — Your Office

You should have an office at the pizza shop, even if you do bookkeeping at home. It doesn't need to be big and showy, but it needs to be centrally located and organized. Be sure you have sufficient lighting, file cabinets, shelves, a desk, and a chair. It's also good to have another chair for meetings. When you arrange your office, consider these things:

- Be organized, so others can find files and paperwork in your absence.

- Store confidential and personnel documents in locked file cabinets.

- Have copies of Policy and Procedural Manuals available for employees.

As a business owner, you'll be spending a good deal of time in your office, so be sure to make it comfortable—physically and emotionally. Your office is like every other area of the store. Organization is a key to making your pizza shop run smoothly and profitably.

Photo Courtesy of Pizza Today

18

Marketing Your Business

Many business owners think they must have a big budget to promote their businesses. I'm glad to tell you that isn't true. I'm sure you would like to run an ad for your pizza shop during the Super Bowl, but that won't be possible.

Marketing can be described as any activity to create an image and recognition for yourself and your business that relays a message to potential customers.

Hiring Marketing Experts

One tactic is to hire an advertising or public relations (PR) agency. This can be an excellent investment. They will work for an hourly rate, set a fee or a percent of your advertising purchases. These are some services they can offer:

- **Develop your image** – Logo, mascot, or tagline.

- **Construct an advertising message** – A slogan to represent your business. It reminds potential customers about what you offer.

- **Develop advertising campaigns** – Suggest the media campaign to reach your ideal customer.

- **Design and produce print, TV, radio, and Web ads.**

- **Create positive buzz** – A way to get people talking about your business.

- **Make media buys** – Negotiate and purchase ad time or space.

Your budget may not allow you to hire a full-service advertising agency. There are alternatives such as hiring independent marketing consultants and freelance business communication writers.

What to look for in marketing experts:

- Experience with restaurants.
- Working with the experienced marketer, not underlings.
- Well-developed and thorough proposals.
- Willing to work with your set budget.

Spending money with marketing professionals can pay for itself. They should keep you from costly mistakes, and they will create a consistent and an effective message.

You Can Do It Yourself

Millions of entrepreneurs successfully advertise and promote their businesses. They make wise buying decisions, track their ads, and grow their businesses. Alternately, there are those business owners who spend too much and fail to increase sales, so they are unable to create an image for their businesses.

Before you start to spend money on promotion, be sure you know what you're doing. This chapter will provide ideas on how to promote your pizza shop, and I will share some tips from my time as a manager and marketing director in a pizza franchise. Ask yourself these questions:

- Do you want to learn about marketing?

- Should you use your time to promote?

- Are you objective?

- Do you have the personality to handle aggressive ad salespeople?

- Are you creative?

I'll help you learn to promote your business even if you don't have any marketing experience. These are some resources to set your plan in motion:

- E-mail Marketing can be a great way to reach people. Constant Contact, at **www.constantcontact.com**, provides user-friendly services. E-mail Factory (**www.emailfactory.com**) and Got Marketing (**www.gotmarketing.com**) are cost-effective e-mail services.

- Learn about specific marketing techniques at Market It Right, **www.marketitright.com**.

- Explore creative marketing ideas at Idea Site for Businesses, **www. ideasiteforbusiness.com**.

Guerilla Marketing

Guerilla Marketing is one of my favorite types of marketing. Marketing guru Jay Conrad Levinson is the father of Guerilla Marketing. This is a principle that gives small businesses owners the ability to be active and effective marketers without spending a lot of money. His marketing and PR

books, business tools, and his Web site (**www.gmarketing.com**) are filled with hands-on, practical advice. You can purchase his books at his Web site or from your favorite bookseller. His Web site contains dozens of free marketing articles, which will give you an idea of what Guerilla Marketing includes. Jay has free newsletters, radio programs, seminars, and individual coaching.

These are some Guerilla Marketing books, CDs, and DVDs you will find helpful:

- Guerrilla Publicity
- Guerrilla Marketing Attack
- Guerilla Advertising
- Guerilla Marketing Excellence
- Guerilla Marketing for Franchises – CD's
- Guerilla Marketing 101
- Guerrilla Marketing in 30 Days
- Guerrilla Marketing: Secrets for Making Big Profits from Your Small Business
- Guerrilla Publicity: Hundreds of Sure-Fire Tactics to Get Maximum Sales for Minimum Dollars
- Guerrilla Marketing Weapons: 100 Affordable Marketing Methods for Maximizing Profits from Your Small Business
- The Guerrilla Marketing Handbook
- Guerrilla Marketing Excellence: The 50 Golden Rules for Small Business Success

Something that I really like about "guerilla marketing" is that it requires more effort, creativity, and imagination. Most "guerilla marketing" ideas are low cost marketing solutions for your business. Some of these ideas are things you are probably already doing, but you can learn ways to do it

better. One example is your business card. You can learn techniques to make better use of the limited space on your cards and tips to use the cards more effectively. There are many other ideas in the books and pages of the **www. gmarketing.com** Web site.

Advertising

Advertising is purchasing time or space for your ads in any type of media. Take time to figure your return on investment for advertising. First, figure the number of customers you have and how much it cost to reach these customers. You will have better results when you use advertising that targets your ideal customer. To do this, you must determine your ideal customer. Have this clearly in mind when you talk to an advertising sales representative. Some sales reps will push to sell you unnecessary things, so be sure about what you need before your meet with them.

Here are tips to gather information about your ideal customer:

- **Interview potential customers** – These may be friends or customers.

- **Know Your Competition** – Try your competition; dine-in, carryout, and order delivery. How do they market and how do they serve their customers?

- **Talk to others** – Talk to restaurant owners who are not your competition. They can be a wonderful source of information.

- **Trade magazines** – You can learn a lot from *Restaurant Hospitality, Pizza Today,* and *Restaurant and Institutions.*

- **National Restaurant Association** – The National Restaurant Association can provide some customer research.

- **Corporations and franchises** – The franchise company or a corporation will have a wealth of information to help you.

Effective Advertising

In order to ensure your advertising is effective, determine whether your advertising attracted new customers. How did they find you? Did they see your yellow page or newspaper ad? There are ways to incorporate these checks into your advertising. Tracking your advertising will help you eliminate advertising that isn't working. These tips will help you determine if your ads are working:

- Ask your customers how they heard about you.

    —Provide a form on your Web site for customers to submit.

    —Have employees ask customers how they heard about you.

    —Include a postage-paid reply card in carryout or delivery packages.

    —You can increase submissions from Web site forms and postage-paid cards if you offer a free or discount offer.

- Set up automatic data gathering systems.

    —Unique e-mail addresses for specific promotions.

    —Unique phone numbers for specific promotions.

    —Something I have used is to assign a coupon code on each offer. If you distribute the same offer in different places, use different codes. Then log the code for each offer that is ordered.

This will help you determine the promotions to continue and those to stop. The information is invaluable when making marketing decisions. This eliminates the guesswork and provides statistics.

Is Your Ad Effective?

A good ad must:

- **Attract customers.**

- **Reactivate customers.**

- **Lead to increased sales per customer.**

If your ad doesn't increase sales, you're wasting money.

Patience is Crucial

Some ads draw people in; others generate future business. Some customers need you on an ongoing basis while others only need you occasionally. You can generate business from the ongoing customers by adding an expiration date to your coupons and offers. The special event customers will be motivated to buy only if your coupon is there when they need you.

To add a sense of urgency to your advertising:

- **Expiration dates** – Include expiration dates on any offers. Consider the "life" of the advertising medium, and pick an appropriate expiration date. Be aware of their release date to make the date effective. Never include a coupon that expires before it reaches the customers.

- **Motivate the consumer** – Encourage the customer to use your offer right away.

I'll share an interesting story about expiration dates. We had about 20,000 coupon books that would expire in a week, but they didn't expire until the following Monday. It was a calculated risk, but the books had done well, so we decided to send the remaining coupons to targeted neighborhoods. I ordered some additional food in the hope that I would need it for the

coupons. We were swamped with calls from Thursday through Monday from those coupon books and had a very busy weekend. We took a chance, and it paid off with people trying to utilize their coupons at the last minute.

Repetition for Emphasis

Running an ad once won't get decent results. Repeat the ad to be effective. So you may need to place a smaller ad in order to increase the frequency. Many advertising experts say it takes three to seven exposures to your offer before people make the decision to buy. You can make some small changes, but be sure there is consistency in your message. Your customers are busy, so you must keep your name before them. Advertising can also regenerate customers who haven't dealt with you for some time.

An interesting way to get people's attention is by giving them useful items. One of these items is a durable and attractive plastic cup, or a set of cups. Berry Plastics has a great selection of cups in various sizes. They can also customize these with your logo, slogan, address, phone number, etc. Check their selection at **www.berryplastics.com/souvenir.html** and **www. berryplastics.com/specialty.html**. You can contact them at 812-424-2904 or e-mail them at **www.berryplastics.com/contact.html#phone**.

These are wonderful items to give to carryout or delivery customers. Send your dine in customers home with a drink refill, and you can also stuff these cups with coupons, magnets, menus, or anything else and then put a lid on them. Students, families, and most anyone will appreciate these at special events. Use the stuffed cups to promote your pizza and sub shop with local colleges, fraternities, schools, businesses, and any other place you want to attract customers. I used these very successfully in various situations.

What Benefits Do You Offer?

To draw customers in, tell them "what you can do for them."

- Are you open late? Tell students and second and third shift workers.

- Do you offer multi pizza discounts? Promote to businesses and schools.

- Are you near the park? Promote to mothers with children on sports teams.

- Do you deliver to the local college campus? Promote to the students.

- Do you cater special events? Promote to skating rinks and other facilities.

- Partner with other companies with compatible products or services. For example, you could pair with a local marina and offer a lunch and sightseeing cruise. Look into other types of opportunities. For example, **LunchandEarn.com** brings the pharmaceutical industry's online lunch orders to you! All you need is a fax line. They market your restaurant online at no cost. There are no set-up fees, no monthly dues, and no fees to join **LunchandEarn.com**. Sign up at **www.LunchandEarn.com** or call 888-70-LUNCH.

Improving Your Skills

As your skills improve, evaluate your marketing message and where you promote. Here are some tips:

- Repeat your ad on radio spots and end with call to action.

- Provide easy direction and a map to your pizza shop.

- Use normal terminology in your ads and never talk down to customers.

- Include ways to track response (coupon codes etc.).

- Make the appearance and content of your ads consistent. Create a tagline and logo for your business to then use in all advertising efforts.

- Promote your food and how it benefits your customers.

- Don't focus on public relations activities, like sponsoring teams, until you are established. Use your money for advertising to bring people in.

- If an ad campaign isn't working, change it!

Utilize Your Computer in Another Way

There are endless reasons for you to have a computer for your pizza shop. One of those reasons is to save time and money in your advertising. These are a few ways to use your computer to save time and money in your advertising:

- Print customer newsletters, table tents, coupons, flyers or postcards, menus, business cards, gift certificates, and advertising posters.

- Microsoft Publisher® is an easy program that includes templates you can use. Microsoft's Web site contains free enhancements for Publisher.

- One way I save money is to supply digital, press-ready flyers, cards, etc., to my printer. You can design these on your computer and e-mail to the printer.

- You can hire a graphic designer for complicated work, your logo, or menu design. It might be more cost effective to have someone else do this work, so you can focus on things you must handle.

These are the most popular desktop publishing software programs. Click to learn more about these programs at **http://desktoppub.about.com/cs/win/index.htm**:

- Adobe InDesign
- Adobe Pagemaker
- Greenstreet Publisher
- Microsoft Publisher
- QuarkXpress
- Ragtime Solo

Use E-Mail Effectively

E-mail is very convenient to contact customers, suppliers, and others. You can establish an e-mail address with your Internet Service Provider or use a free online account. Free accounts are nice because you don't need to change your address if you change providers. E-mail marketing is inexpensive, and the cost is basically only the employee's hourly wage to compile and send the messages.

Choosing E-mail Over the Post Office or Telephone

There are two reasons:

1. **Convenience** – E-mail can be sent or received at any time of the day or night.

2. **Cost** – E-mails are sent at no charge. You can also attach files, instead of paying to fax them, and the quality is much better.

There are some important differences between e-mail and postal mail:

- E-mail is faster.

- E-mail is free.

- E-mail is simple.

- E-mail requires a password and is safe to use.

- E-mail is fast, but you cannot retrieve it. Be sure before you send.

- E-mail can be sent to many people at once.

- E-mail often contains typos and misspellings, so spell check.

- You must have an e-mail account to receive and send messages.

Do you like the idea of contacting potential and existing customers through their e-mail? It's fast, inexpensive, and I know that I check my e-mail more consistently than my mail box. Surely, other people do the same thing. If this is a promotional avenue that appeals to you, call 800-309-7228 or check **www.loyalrewards. com/merchant.asp** for more information about a program to promote your business through e-mail. They offer an interesting program and ways to build your mailing list.

E-mail Etiquette

- **Avoid flaming**. A flame is a personal attack for something that was written, said, or done.

- **Delete irrelevant info**. When you respond to an e-mail, only include the relevant parts of the message. Use a descriptive subject for your message. If responding to an e-mail, the subject line should be the same as the original and preceded by "RE:."

- **Be clear and careful**. Be sure you understand the message before you respond.

- **Avoid CAPS**. Do not use all caps—it is perceived as yelling.

COMMON E-MAIL MISTAKES:

- Typing the message in the subject line instead of in the body of the message.

- Forgetting what you write can be misinterpreted by the recipient.

- Not signing off before leaving the computer (this allows others to use your e-mail address).

- Not checking e-mail and missing something important.

- Forgetting your password.

- Sending messages to the wrong e-mail address.

Promote with Your Logo

Your logo should include your pizza shop's name and an appropriate image. Consider the font, or typeface, and colors. The logo will be used on all your

promotional pieces, so don't scrimp on it. You can hire a professional to design it for you.

T-shirts are a wonderful way to promote your business whether you give them to customers or have your staff members wear them. You could hold a drawing each week and award a t-shirt to one customer. This can be a great way to get business cards from customers, or e-mail addresses for other promotional pieces. One business that offers custom t-shirts which would include your logo or other information is **www.campuscollection. net/custom.php3** or call 800-BUY-T-SHIRTS (800-289-8744).

Business Cards and Brochures

It's almost never too early to design and produce business cards and brochures. These are an inexpensive and convenient way to market your new pizza shop. There are design programs and many online sites that allow you to layout your cards. Consider having a professional design them for you. Local colleges could be a good source, too. College students can help you and add to their portfolios at the same time.

Many artists do freelance work. You can contact the American Institute of Graphic Arts (AIGA) for a directory of freelancers. They can be contacted at: AIGA, 164 Fifth Avenue, New York, NY 10010, or by phone at 212-807-1990. Their Web site is **www.aiga.org**. Also look at **www.sologig.com** for freelancers. You can also post a project on online freelancing sites to get additional bids for your project. Some of these include **www.elance.com** and **www.guru.com**.

Keep these principles in mind when you design your card:

- Alignment
- Contrast
- Repetition
- Proximity

When you layout your business card or brochure, think of the paper as a grid, and place each element on the grid. This will help you balance items and create a pleasing design. Place some elements outside of it for visual interest.

Contrast should be obvious, or it can look accidental. A good contrast is to make all headings bold, and keep remaining text a regular font. Bullets are another useful element.

When you design a brochure, repeat certain elements to tie the content together. Use the same text for all headers. You can place your logo on a couple of different pages. This is another place where you don't have to fill every inch. Leave sufficient white space.

Proximity can provide a relationship between your business card and your brochure. When you design a brochure, hold the page at arm's length. If everything looks gray, work on your proximity.

Practice using these elements in your design. Consider colors, but remember two- and four-color copies are more expensive to print. There are many times when a clean black-and-white design might be better.

Simple brochures can be a tri-fold or letter fold, or six-panel like below:

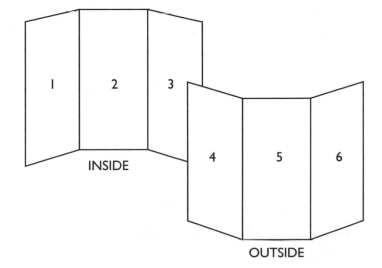

Place your logo or picture on the front cover (panel #4). Include copy about your pizza shop and menu items on panels #1, 2, and 3. Inside you can also include information about your specialties. Make your contact information obvious and in several places. You can design the back page (panel #5), so it can be used as a mail piece.

Business cards can be difficult to design because they offer such a small area. So, be careful not to include too much information. Design it to grab attention, or it will be tossed into a drawer and forgotten. These are things to include on your card:

- Logo
- Name of your business
- Address
- Phone and fax numbers
- Web site address
- E-mail address

- Business tagline, if you have one

This doesn't leave much room for anything else. An interesting way to make people keep your cards is to print a special offer on the back.

Poynter Online has several helpful design pages you might want to investigate. Articles include:

- Understanding Color – **www.poynter.org/column.
  asp?id=47&aid=38564**

- Elements of Typography –
  http://poynteronline.org/column.asp?id=47&aid=50927

- The Grid: The Structure of Design –
  http://poynteronline.org/column.asp?id=47&aid=37529

Keep in mind that there are many things you can do with business cards, and they are a very inexpensive way to advertise. I recently purchased 1,000 heavy card stock, color cards for three cents each from **www.vistaprint.com**. It's hard to get your business name and contact information into someone's hand for three cents. Give your cards away freely. Many businesses will let you leave a stack of your cards in their offices/buildings or on their message boards. When you go to networking events, be sure to take a pile of your cards, and hand them out freely.

Paper Types and Colors

In Chapter 19, we discuss the effect that different colors evoke in people. So, it's important to pick your colors carefully. Many pizzerias use green, white, and red (colors of the Italian flag) or red and white like checkerboard tablecloths. Or, you can so something totally different.

Paper comes in many different colors and weights. Colored and heavy paper

costs more, so don't use heavier paper than necessary or colored paper, if it isn't needed. Brochures are good in a slightly heavier weight. Business cards should be a card stock. I've gone to the printer and touched many types of paper to be sure about what I want to use. Heavier paper and colored ink is more expensive. Be sure about your choices, and don't skimp on primary promotional items.

Any time you plan to buy something, you should compare prices. Check with your local printers, office supply stores, and online printers. Be sure you get estimates for comparable items. It's also good to get references from other businesses. These things help you make an educated decision. Sometimes printers have excess paper and might give you a discount to take it off of their hands.

How to Use Your Brochures and Business Cards

What should you do with your brochures and business cards? Don't be afraid to be creative. Here are some ways to use your brochures:

- Local attractions, museums, and theme parks

- Local hotels – This can be a great way to get business, especially on weekends, holidays, and special events. Talk to the manager of budget hotels that cater to families and do not have a restaurant.

- Local colleges – Do everything possible to get your cards, brochures, and anything else in the hands of the students.

- Chamber of Commerce – Put brochures in their office for travelers.

- Event planners and music venues – You could work out a contract to sell pizza during events.

Be creative, and don't be afraid to ask. The worst they can do is say no, and they may say yes.

An unusual promotion we did at a local college was to take trucks onto campus the day underclassmen were moving in. The temperature was miserably hot, and we filled big tubs in the truck bed with ice and cans of Coca Cola. We gave them away with coupons and menus. The students appreciated the cold drinks. That evening, there was a bad storm that knocked out the electricity. The other pizza shops in town had electric conveyor ovens, but my gas stoves stayed on. We had to pick up our phones randomly since the electricity was out, but we stayed busy for hours that night while our competition was stranded in their dark stores with no pizza cooking.

Should You Have a Web Site?

Every day there are millions of people using the Internet for work, play, shopping, and research. Even if you only want to serve the best pizza in your town or neighborhood, a Web site can be invaluable for you. Anyone can see your Web site, including new people moving or traveling to the area.

Your Web site is a wonderful way to tell people:

- About your pizza shop
- Who you are
- What you make
- Who you serve
- Where you are located
- When you are open
- Why to buy from you
- How to place special orders

Your site can also:

- Be changed quickly. You don't have to throw out items to make changes. You can also share mouth-watering pictures of your menu items.

- Be a menu.

- Allow people to place orders.

- Be any size you want and need.

- Be interactive. Give people a chance to respond to your information.

- Build community spirit and promote community and charity events.

- Sell your specialties to people around the globe through e-commerce.

Some businesses have password-protected sections to share information with their employees, to explain benefits, and to post work schedules.

You can reach local customers through online city guides and other community-oriented sites where you can place an advertisement, free directory listing, or link to your Web site. Chambers of Commerce, virtual travel guides, and guide sites, including About.com at **www.about.com**, offer chances to promote your business. This is also very effective in attracting college students.

These are potential benefits for your business:

- Gather marketing information.

- Evaluate marketing information.

- Generate additional sales.

- Establish meaningful communication with customers and employees.

- Supplement employee training through updates and bulletins.

- Broadcast press releases.

- Submit invoices and expenses more quickly.

- Identify prospective employees.

- Provide immediate access to your menu.

- Permit customers to place orders online.

According to Nielsen ratings, 67.8 percent of the U.S. population uses the Internet. Many people go online to find information about your location and hours, so get listed in the online yellow pages, and place ads on sites your customers would visit. Include an obvious link to your menu online. You can offer coupons on your Web site or specials that can only be found on your Web site.

What to Put on Your Web site

Are you curious about what information you should put on your Web site? A Web site should reflect the personality and atmosphere of your pizza shop. Use fonts, color, and graphics that are consistent with your store. Here are some suggestions for things to include on your site:

- **Show what you have to offer.**

  —What do your pizza and other food items look like?

  —What do customers see when they walk in your pizza shop?

  —How does the building look?

  —Show the atmosphere in your shop.

  —Show a picture of your friendly and cheerful staff.

  —Show how you make your dough or sauce, etc.

- **Share the news** – You can develop a web-based newsletter to share

information about your pizza shop, employee news, and specials.

- **Menus** – Your Web site gives you a chance to include full color pictures with your online menu.

- **Directions** – You can include a link to **MapQuest.com**, or I prefer **www.randmcnally.com**. Customers can enter their address and get directions to your door.

- **History** – Is there interesting local history or neighborhood history that Web site visitors would find interesting? Share the story. You can also have local individuals share some interesting stories.

- **Area attractions** – You can promote your store and help new residents and visitors by adding information about what the local area has to offer. You could include a local events page for tourists. All of these things make your site valuable.

- **Local sports teams** – A great addition would be information about local youth and sports teams. These groups have reasons to buy a lot of pizza and by dedicating a page to local sports news and updates, you will draw the participants and their families to your site.

You are only limited by your imagination. But, I really like to incorporate things in my sites that educate the visitors. This gives your site wider appeal. Give your visitors a reason to tell others about your site.

Develop An Effective Web Site

There are many easy-to-use Web site design programs, or you can have someone else design your site. I use Microsoft FrontPage® which offers templates for the beginner, or you can build your site from scratch. I personally design and

maintain my Web sites, but that's because I like immediate access to make changes and the satisfaction of seeing a new site develop.

Make the decision about the domain name for your Web site. You can use a free Web site service, but I wouldn't recommend that for a business site. Most domain names end with .com or .net. There are many Web sites you can use to check if the address you want is available. If your desired domain name is not available, you might have to use a name that ends with .biz or something similar. When you are choosing a domain name, remember that you don't want a really long name. The names are hard to remember, and they don't fit on business cards. Dashes and underscores are confusing and should also be avoided. When you are ready to register your name, be sure it is a reputable site that allows you to be the owner and administrator of the name. Before you create a site, be sure you "own" the name. Once you have a domain name, it must be "pointed" to a location on the web. This is done through a hosting company.

Some important things to remember:

- **Professional looking site** – An unprofessional or amateurish site can reflect badly on your pizza shop.

- **Does your site work** – Be sure visitors can navigate your site. Do all your links work? Are there links to all of your pages? Broken links give people a bad impression of you and your pizza shop.

- **Search engine friendly** – Seventy-five percent of all online activity comes from search engines. Design your site with keywords that will bring targeted traffic to your Web site.

- **Content that promotes sales** – You may need to hire someone to write the content for your Web sites. The person who writes your content needs to have flair and excellent spelling and grammar skills.

- **Where should you spend your time** – As the manager, evaluate whether you should spend your time designing the site or hire someone else to do it.

Hiring a Web Designer

A professional Web site can cost $3,500 to $15,000. This would include layout, design, copywriting, programming, and the first year of hosting. Keep these suggestions in mind if you decide to hire a web designer:

- You can find a web designer online.

    —Search for "web design [your city name]" or "restaurant web design" for people with experience designing food service sites.

- Look at pizzeria sites.

    —When you find a design you like, contact the Webmaster. The webmaster is usually listed at the bottom of the homepage.

    —Visit sites, and take notes about what you like and what you don't like.

- Review designers' portfolios and samples.

    —Do they grab your attention?

    —Do the links work, and do the graphics load quickly?

    —Are there annoying sounds and pictures?

    —Is it immediately obvious what the site is promoting?

PRECAUTIONS

- Pay attention to the details.
- Invest time and money wisely.

- Can your site grow with your pizza shop?
- Know all the "hidden" costs.
- Promote your site.

A quality Web site is an investment. Use this with your other advertising to maximize all of your marketing efforts.

Coupons

Don't ever underestimate the value of coupons in the pizza business. Consumers love coupons. There are all sorts of coupons you can use. These include:

- A dollar amount discount
- A percentage off
- Offer a free item with order
- Special price for multiple pizzas
- Additional toppings for free
- Additional pizzas for $5

These are just a few ideas. Be creative, and figure your food costs to be sure it's cost effective for you. To create effective coupons that will attract your customers, you must know what those customers like. Some computer programs will create a mailing list based on the customers' order history. This can be an invaluable feature once you are established.

How will you circulate your coupons? If your city allows it, you can have people place them on vehicles, on door knobs or in neighborhoods. Verify this with the city or police first. You can also mail coupon flyers or coupon books. If you plan to mail a lot, it could be worth your time to buy a bulk permit. But, be sure you have what is needed to get the bulk rate.

After you get used to your customers' preferences, you can customize

coupons to suit their tastes. Many computer programs allow you to track the sort of offers your customers order on a regular basis. Some programs let you track sales and orders based on specific days of the week and even the time of day. This is ideal for lunch or late night specials.

Vital Link Back Office – Vital Link POS contains customer history which allows you to target your marketing efforts to your customer base. For more information, visit **www.vitallinkpos.com/products.htm**.

Never underestimate the value of coupons. They come in all shapes, sizes, and colors, but the best ones offer a deal to drive your customers and potential customers to call or visit. A company who prints custom coupons is National Tickets. Their Web site is: **www.nationalticket.com/Ticket_Printing/coupon_books.asp** They offer coupons, coupon books and gift certificates for your pizza and sub shop. For more information call 800-829-0829 or e-mail ticket@nationalticket.com.

Direct Mail

Direct mail is useful for large franchises and local, independently owned pizza shops. The U.S. Department of Commerce says 80 percent of your business comes from a three-mile radius. This makes direct mail a great option for pizzerias that deliver. Focus on the addresses or zip codes within three miles for the best success.

Direct mail prices range from pennies to 25 cents or more per home. The cost fluctuates depending on the weight, size and volume. For more details, you can visit **www.usps.com/directmail/createdirectmailonline.htm**.

As a pizza shop owner, one important part of your promotional plan is to target people who are new to your neighborhood. These people will be looking for a pizza shop in their new area. You should be the first one to contact them. Moving Targets is a company who specializes in attracting

new neighbors. Their Web site is **www.
movingtargets.com/ourprograms.html**.
Check their Web site and contact their
customer service department at 800-926-
2451 for more information about how
they can help you.

Another promotional idea is to send
postcards to specific groups of people.
This could be certain neighborhoods,
business districts, students, or any other
sort of people. They can be utilized with existing customers and to reactivate inactive customers. Postcard Press also offers specialized mailers for
businesses (see examples below). Their Web site is **www.postcardpress.com**
and they offer a variety of sizes, shapes and patterns. Call 800-957-5787 for
more information.

Packaging

A very easy way to advertise is by putting your logo and pizza shop name
on top of your pizza box. This is especially effective at large gatherings
and colleges. These customized boxes usually cost 15 to 20 percent more.

Research has proven there is a mental connection between packaging and perceived quality. Put your packing to work.

Band Together

To save on your advertising, you can work with other complimentary businesses.

This works well to promote each of your businesses, while allowing you to share the advertising costs. You can do this in a neighborhood, shopping center, or small town. Keep in mind that this will cut down on your advertising costs, but someone needs to coordinate the ads, the proofs, printing, and distribution. A local printer might do this for a reasonable fee, especially if you provide a list of the interested businesses.

Here are some possibilities:

- Split a larger newspaper ad with other businesses.

- Create ways to cross promote each other.

- Create a punch card or frequent buyer program with another business.

- Have an open house or a special event and provide refreshments and display business cards.

- Have a special event with nearby businesses. You can each supply samples, coupons, seating, and possibly prizes.

The local chamber of commerce, business associations, and networking groups are a great way to connect with other businesspeople.

Market to Your Existing Customers

When you develop a marketing plan, don't overlook your existing customers. You got them in the door, and then you need to know how to keep them coming back. It is a common belief that if you take care of your guests, your sales will take care of themselves. We all like "customers for life." These are customers who won't be satisfied if they deal with your competitors. This proves that the product they are served, and how they are treated, is an important part of your promotion.

Talk to Your Customers

Your customers pay attention to how you treat them. This is especially important in small towns and neighborhood pizza shops. Make your guests feel important, and they will be loyal and will send their friends.

This is an interesting statistic: It costs five times as much to attract a new customer as it does to retain an existing one. This is another reason you want to encourage loyalty in your customers. Focus on repeat customers–your most profitable clients–and keep them coming back. Two ways to retain clients:

- Find out what they want and need and why they've chosen you.
- If they leave, you need to find out why.

Every Sunday night, a man and woman came into my store. They were a good-hearted country couple who seemed to live a simple life. You might not pick them out of a crowd, but they came in every Sunday night and bought pizza. You could count on them to come in. We even gave them an old hot bag to carry their pizza home, and I let them know we appreciated their business.

Have comment cards for your customers and encourage them to fill them out. This can be a great way to find out what they think of your pizza shop.

An incentive to complete the cards is a discount coupon for completed cards. A critical question to include is "Would you dine with us again?" Find out more and act on each "no".

There are an infinite number of ways to enhance your guests' experience and to show your appreciation. These can include frequent buyer cards. Your customers earn points they can use toward another purchase. Dennis Altieri, owner of Altieri's Pizza, gives a snack to their carryout customers. He jokes that it keeps them out of the pizza box on the way home. Whatever his reasoning, it's a great marketing tool and a great way to build customer loyalty. Here are a few ideas to get you thinking about possibilities:

- Create a mailing database for your customers.
- Track food and table preferences, entertainment, and special needs.
- Update information based on your customers' thoughts.
- Recognize customer birthdays, anniversaries, and special occasions.
- Show appreciation with various types of customer recognition.
- Thank customers for their business.
- Send individualized communications.
- Listen to and act on customer suggestions.
- Inform guests about new or improved services.
- Explain inconveniences like renovations, and stress the benefits.
- Answer all customer inquiries, including complaints.
- Accommodate reasonable requests for meal substitutions, etc.
- Train your employees to solve customer problems.
- Let customers and employees know you're listening to them.

Open communication between you, your customers, and employees is critical. Let them know their opinions are important to you. Never forget that your customers have many options of where to spend their money.

Make them want to come back to your pizza shop.

Delight Your Guests

Satisfying your customers isn't enough. You must exceed their expectations every time they deal with you. Many businesses have horrible customer service and that gives you a chance to surpass your customers' expectations. Remind your staff that you are in the hospitality business. Serve one person at a time, and make sure that service exceeds their expectations. Guests want a quality product, served by a friendly staff, at a reasonable price. It is a tall order, but it's possible to achieve.

Public Relations

Public relations (PR) is the message you send to the public about your business. Work to build positive opinions, among your customers, through your actions and communication. PR is any contact you have with other human beings. This doesn't guarantee they will form the right opinion, but it is formed from the things the public reads, sees, hears, and thinks about you. Effective PR can be described as becoming a positive member of your community (and getting credit for it). Basically, good PR sends a positive message to the public about your business.

PR should be included in your marketing plan. This can include:

- Advertising
- Communications
- Sales promotion
- Speeches
- Contests
- Promotions

- Personal appearances
- Publicity

Each of these things affects how people view you and whether that view is positive or negative.

What PR Can and Cannot Do

Effective PR can set you apart from your competitors. It gives customers a positive impression of you and gives them information about your pizza shop they can share with their friends. It can also help to get you through a crisis.

Good PR will help people want to spend their money and their time at your pizza shop. It enhances the positive aspects of your business and will create a lasting impression. But, PR cannot create a lasting value if there's no value to start with.

Remember that people are interacting with your staff and your shop. The building needs to be in good condition and reflect positively on your business. Keep the building repaired, clean, and aesthetically pleasing.

Have a clear idea of the image you want to project in order to have an effective PR campaign. Then determine how to create that image for the public.

Clearly define your goals, and create a plan to implement them. PR will not gloss over or hide problems. You must resolve problems.

Implement Your PR Plan

Determine your PR objectives then work them into your marketing plan. These questions can help you:

- What should you use to get the word out?

- Who should you contact?

- How strong are the personal relationships needed for the plan?

- Should you establish or reestablish these relationships?

- Have you developed a thorough plan?

- Did you consider all the risks?

- Is your media kit ready to be delivered to the media?

Your media kit needs to contain a description of your business, an explanation of what you are offering, a contact name, phone numbers, an e-mail address—all the information to direct the media to you. It's possible that the media won't use any of your information, but your details will help them get the specifics correct.

These are the practical factors to help you gain recognition:

- **Honesty** – The media is looking for credible, honest information and relationships. Include thorough and truthful details.

- **Respond** – Don't lie. If you don't have an answer, simply tell them you don't have that information, but you will provide it soon. Then provide it as soon as possible.

- **Follow up** – Provide a list of key facts and you lessen the chance of being misquoted. Once the information is sent, follow up with your contact. If the contact needs more information, supply it quickly.

- **Be precise** – Think carefully before you answer questions and give a precise answer without exaggerating or making up things.

- **Nurture** – It is valuable to build strong and lasting relationships with the press. Acting hostile or argumentative can ruin these relationships. Treat journalists with respect, courtesy, and

professionalism, no matter what you think about them.

What and how you communicate is crucial. Have a clear focus when you speak to the media. This list will help you find a purpose and communicate it effectively to the press:

- **Your purpose** – Why do you want public exposure? To what are you drawing attention? Be sure you know, and focus on it.

- **Your target** – Who is your target? Decide who you want to reach and then figure out who in the media can reach them effectively.

- **Your thinking** – Why do you think this would interest the media? Find a way to interest the media. Make them want to print your story. Is it a story that will sell papers or gain listeners? That will help you.

- **Your materials** – Define your purpose, your target, and the angle for the media. Then supply the story and the pictures to the media.

- **Send your materials** – Should you submit your story as a news story or a feature? News stories go to the city desk. Feature stories go to the appropriate editor: travel, lifestyle, etc.

- **Make it easy on them** – Learn the ground rules before you talk to the media. You can also build good relationships with them by doing some of their work for them. When the media contacts you with questions, answer right away. If a reporter calls and you don't answer or return the call, your story could end up in the trash.

Here are some tips to work effectively with the media:

- Deal with the facts.
- Never ask to review an article before publication.

- Never ask if an article will appear.

- Follow up by phone to be sure your fact sheet or press release arrived, to determine if the reporter is interested and if anything else is needed.

- Provide requested photos, plans, etc.—ASAP.

Charity for PR

Supporting charities is something everyone should do. Businesspeople can donate to charities and improve their images in the community. That's a win/win situation. Purchasing decisions are based on emotions, so associating a face with your business will create a positive image in your community.

First, find a worthwhile charity. Find one that is respected and supported in the community. Second, find a connection between your business and the charity. This allows you to raise money for the charity and showcase your products. It is fine to verify how your support will be recognized. Fundraisers understand the amount of work involved and won't act like you are buying advertising.

Charity events also offer an opportunity to do some good and have fun.

- Coach a Little League team you sponsor.

- Operate a fundraising booth.

Take the chance to get out and discover the benefits of helping others.

Special Events

Special events can generate publicity and community interest. This is useful when you open a new pizza shop, remodel, or have an anniversary. These are just a few of the chances to plan a special event.

Be clear about why you are holding the event. I'm going to guess it is not because you're bored. So, why are you doing it? Be clear about your motivation and goals. Finding a way to tie your event into something in the community will help the media see it as a way to help, instead of free promotion.

I can tell you from personal experience that special events require a lot of work. Every little detail needs to be organized and planned. That may not seem like a lot of work, but you will be amazed.

One thing that I've done successfully, with charity events, is to have people and businesses donate printing services, prizes, and so on. I developed a successful fundraising event which garnered television and radio exposure, positive word-of-mouth for several businesses, and donations for a local animal shelter. The cost for us was less than $100 because many items were donated by others. This is why it's critical to find a charity that others want to support. For details about this event, visit **www.nikkileigh.com/pets_n_portraits**.htm and **www.prestigecontracting.net/spa.htm**. This event was to promote other types of businesses, but it might give you ideas of ways you could garner reasonable and positive PR for your business while helping the community.

Find a day that doesn't conflict with local events or a holiday. Invite local officials, etc., who have a connection to your event. Guided tours are a wonderful part of a new store opening. Be sure to have cards, coupons, and menu brochures easily accessible during the event. Press kits, with relevant information, should be provided to the media. It is a lot of work, but make it fun for the community.

Create your own banners for special events and pricing. Banners Across America offers banner kits to create custom banners. The sizes and prices can be seen at: **www.bannersacrossamerica.com**. These kits include reversible letters, built in grommets, heavy duty vinyl, durable plastic pockets to

hold letters and numbers, and nylon rope to secure signage. Call 214-352-7015.

Maintain Employee Relations

When your employees are happy, they treat the customers better and are more productive. They will also say positive things outside of your pizza shop. Customers want to be treated right, and they judge the food and the service. Happy employees will keep your customers happy and eager to return.

Another way to keep your employees happy is by ensuring they are well-trained. They need to know how to do their jobs and understand that you expect a high level of service. Allow them the power to give the best possible service. This type of employee generates repeat business and helps your business grow.

These are some ways to communicate with your staff and keep them involved:

- How is the business doing?
- What are you planning?
- How is your competition doing?
- What do you plan to do about your competition?
- What do you plan to do to help the community?

- Communicate information about training and job openings.

- Discuss staff weddings, birthdays, accomplishments, and other happenings.

- Don't say they are important; show them.

These things help your employees feel you care and will create a unified work atmosphere. Show that you understand the difference they make in your business. This is all done through effective communication with your staff. They can be an invaluable source of information and suggestions on how to improve your business. Have meetings with your staff, create a newsletter, and offer orientations and training for employees. This shows you care and want to encourage them to make a difference.

The Other PR – Press Releases

An easy and inexpensive way to generate interest in your business is through the use of press releases. You can use press releases to promote many things within your business. The first priority is to find something newsworthy to include in the press release. This can be your business opening, expansion, new manager, special events, anniversary events, promotional projects, the launch of your Web site, and anything else the public might be interested in reading. Be careful not to overuse press releases, especially with your local media.

Write Effective Press Releases

- FOR IMMEDIATE RELEASE – In the top left corner of the page.

- Include contact name, phone number, and e-mail in the top right corner.

- Make the headline capital letters, bold print, and centered. Any

great headline must catch the reader's attention. It needs to draw the reader into the body of your release. A good way to grab the reader's attention is to tie the subject of your press release in with current events. Relate it to something people are concerned about. Give the reader a reason to read more.

- The most important information should be in the first paragraph. List the top five reasons someone would be interested in what you have to say. Keep the content focused and simple. Know your target market before you write your release. They are the people you can reach through your press release.

- The press release must be no more than one or two pages – no longer. One way to stay with the page count is to avoid the sales hype. Stick with the basic and relevant facts of your subject. You can make it look like an advertisement, but it might not get the response you want. Focus on how your product or service will benefit readers, and let them know why your product or service is the only thing they need.

- Use an easy to read and common font like Times Roman. Do not use fancy fonts on your press release. Do not mix fonts or use more than one. You can make a limited number of things bold, but don't go overboard with that either. It will only make your press release look unprofessional. That won't get good results.

- Anything about your product or service that would be of special interest in a particular area needs to be included in the first paragraph.

- Check and recheck your spelling and grammar. Then check one more time.

- Include your quotes and quotes from satisfied customers. Create interest, and establish yourself as an expert and the best person to

offer that particular product or service. Make the reader believe that no one else is qualified to offer the same product and service. This is a good time to work in a testimonial from a customer who thinks your product or service is invaluable.

- Never use exclamation points.

- Don't use words like best ever, or anything like them. It makes you look amateurish and also lowers your credibility when it isn't a bestseller.

- Use short sentences.

- Edit to eliminate any unnecessary words and any repetition. Any writer will tell you this is hard. Every word may seem like a treasure, but cut any excess wording. Make it lean and effective.

- The first time you list the name of your product or service, order information, your web site, and e-mail address be sure to use all capital letters.

- The first time you use a name, write the full name. All other references should use only the last name or a salutation and last name.

- At the bottom of the release, type "###" to denote the end.

Once you have written an effective press release, you must circulate it. This can be to your local daily and weekly newspapers, local radio and television stations, and magazines. If you are located in a tourist area, it wouldn't hurt to submit your press release to national sites. You can submit your press release quickly, and it is circulated for you. Here are some free submission sites:

- **www.clickpress.com**

- www.prfree.com
- www.press-world.com – BIG site
- www.prweb.com – BIG site
- www.pr.com/
- http://press.arrivenet.com/
- www.press-base.com/
- www.webnewswire.com/submit.html
- www.prleap.com
- www.przoom.com
- www.marketwire.com

All of these ideas help you generate positive PR and a great environment for your employees and customers. Give back to the community, and boost the image of your pizza shop. There's a lot of satisfaction in helping others.

PHARMACEUTICAL REP CATERING

Michael Attias operates a restaurant and helps restaurant owners expand their profits through his company, The Results Group. You can download his FREE report: "Tapping Into Your Hidden Catering Profit$" at **www. ezRestaurantMarketing.com**.

How would you like to add an extra $2,000 to $5,000 a month to your sales? I have quite a few clients in the pizza and sub business that I've helped do just that by increasing their weekday, drop-off catering business. Pharmaceutical reps are a perfect catering target market as they regularly bring lunch in for a doctor's entire office and have an expense account to use each month. Charlie, a sub shop owner in Pennsylvania, followed my plan for attracting pharmaceutical reps.

He mailed a series of letters to each pharmaceutical rep in his trade area promoting his menu, delivery service, and the fact he would provide a "hassle-free" experience for the pharmaceutical rep. He did not stop there. He initiated our Pharmaceutical Rep's Club and provided a rebate in gift certificates to his store as an incentive to continue utilizing his catering services. He also mailed each rep a monthly newsletter, Pharm Rep Monthly, to stay top of mind with his prospects and alert them to new menu offerings and promotions. Pharmaceutical reps are a lucrative catering niche for you to add to your marketing plan.

—Michael Attias, The Results Group, 615-831-1676 office, 615-831-1389 fax, "High Return, Low Cost Marketing Systems for Restaurants", **www.ezRestaurantMarketing.com** **www.ezRestaurantPromotions.com**

19

Carryout and Delivery

Will you offer carryout? Should you offer delivery? Carryout offers substantial profit and very little additional expense. There are some things that are specific to a store that offers carryout, which we will discuss. Delivery also offers benefits and some unique needs and expenses. Those will be discussed in this chapter.

Carryout

I won't say that creating a carryout business is easier than developing a dine-in business, but it does require different skills and focus. Dine-in customers usually want to take their time. On the other hand, carryout customers are in a hurry, and your pizza shop is just one of their stops. They want to run and be served quickly. Your counter staff needs to understand this and be efficient.

All business owners want to cut costs and I highly recommend cross training

your employees. Be careful not to cut your staff too short as that can cause customer service to suffer.

If you offer various services, distinguish which areas are for carryout, delivery, and dine-in. I've been in some restaurants where the decoration and flooring are different in the various areas. It's a simple way to set areas apart. Signage is another good way to direct customers in the right direction. It is best to have a separate entrance for your delivery drivers, so they don't push past your customers. Use some sort of menu in the carryout area.

Delivery

Delivery can be a wonderful addition to your pizza shop. Your operating expenses will be less if you only offer carryout and delivery. It eliminates the need for all dine-in extras, and your pizza shop will require less space, which could save money on your rent or lease. However, keep in mind there are additional expenses when you offer delivery service. These are some of those expenses:

- **Cars** – There are two options with delivery. You can supply company vehicles, or your drivers need to use their vehicles. These work in different ways. If you supply the delivery cars, you will have the added expense for vehicles, gas, insurance, and maintenance. You would probably need at least two or three vehicles over the weekend. Speaking of maintenance, figure more than your personal car. Delivery driving is hard on a vehicle. You can also put your sign on the vehicle. We've all seen car top signs on pizza delivery vehicles. These can be strapped to any vehicle, and they will promote your pizza shop all over town. Another more reasonable option is to buy metallic door signs for your drivers to use.

- **Auto insurance** – Any company vehicle needs sufficient

insurance. Talk honestly with your insurance agent to be sure you have enough coverage. If your drivers use their vehicles, you must have a proof of insurance, proof of a valid driver's license, and proof of a good driving record.

- **Drivers** – You need drivers to deliver. Your drivers will make a minimal wage then receive tips and commissions for each delivery. This is done differently in different pizza shops. You have the option of not hiring a dishwasher, and your drivers can help with prep work during slack times. *On the CD, there is information about reporting tips, which should be circulated to your drivers.*

Liability Insurance for Delivery

All businesses should carry liability insurance. Remember the saying, "Bad things happen to good people." That is true of your drivers. No matter how good their driving records, things happen when you are on the road. Talk to your insurance agent about delivery liability insurance.

These are some things to consider before deciding to offer delivery:

- **Know the risk.** You are responsible for the behavior of your drivers when they are delivering for you. Tell your drivers in writing that you will not tolerate bad behavior in the pizza shop or on the road. You need to see new copies of their driving records every six months.

- **How much risk?** Figure the dollar amount of the worst case scenario.

- **Minimize your risk.** You will either decide there is too much risk or that the risk is part of doing business. But, make that decision for your business.

- **Transfer your risk.** This is why we have insurance companies. Ask your agent about high limit liability insurance policies. This will cover expenses over your drivers' policies.

To Charge or Not to Charge

There was a time, not so long ago, when pizza shops offered free delivery. The current price of gas has made this difficult. You can still make the decision to offer free delivery. It is becoming common to charge for delivery. The companies I spoke with are charging $1 for delivery. If you consider it, you couldn't usually drive to their pizza shop to pick it up for $1. Pizza Hut, Domino's, and Papa John's are all charging a delivery fee at this time. Ironically, Papa John's has seen an increase in business. Even at $1 for delivery, it's still a deal.

What to Deliver?

You will deliver pizza, but will you offer more? Many items travel well, so review your menu to see what you can deliver. Also consider how you will pack the items to ensure they get to the customer.

Most sandwiches and salads travel well, especially if you deliver the salad dressing separately. Prepackaged salad dressing is a great option. You can offer soup, if you find 100 percent leak proof containers. Many pasta dishes can be delivered. There are wonderful pans secured with cardboard lids. These are a great option.

Here are some non-pizza items that travel well:

- Lasagna
- Ravioli
- Caesar salad
- Baked ziti
- Chicken or eggplant parmesan
- Meatball sandwich

Does this short list give you some ideas of additional menu items to deliver?

Delivery Containers

When you choose the menu items to deliver, you need to find containers to transport the food. WNA is a supplier of a very wide selection of quality plastic plates, cutlery, cups, serving ware, and you can choose custom packaging. View the products by category at **www.wna-inc.com/products/selectCategory.php**. To find the customer service information for your area, check **www.wna-inc.com/company/contactus**.

People have become more conscientious about the environment and they are looking for biodegradable products. That is where Biocorp excels. They offer environmentally friendly products for your pizza and sub shop. They provide quality products at reasonable prices. They also supply a line of cutlery that is heat resistant, doesn't have an after taste or allergy concerns. Their full product line can be viewed at **www.biocorpaavc.com/index.asp**. Contact BioCorp at 866-348-8348.

Wes Pak's food service carriers are an affordable alternative to transport food. They are one time use packages. The packages are quick and easy to use. Their lightweight design makes them an ideal choice. They can be used to cool drinks or store ice and hot foods. After the

food is delivered, the packages can be thrown away. The selection can be viewed at **www.wespakinc.com/section.asp?secID=5**. Call 800-493-7725.

Lollicup USA, Inc. provides their customers with a complete restaurant solution. They wholesale/ distribute beverage ingredients, restaurant equipment, and disposable Hot and Cold cups at competitive rates. The sealing feature for cups could be an asset if you plan to deliver fountain drinks or any other drinks which are not in cans or bottles. For more information, visit their Web site at **http://www.bobateadirect.com/Equipment-Machines-c-4.html**.

Delivery Equipment

There are a variety of ways that your delivery personnel can get your menu items to your customers. These are the more popular choices:

Hot Bags

At one point, pizza delivery drivers carried awkward metal boxes and we still use them for multi pie orders. But, for one or two pizza deliveries, a hot bag is easier. The bags are thermal and keep the heat from escaping the pizza box. The original bags, from the 1980s, have evolved into an extremely effective way to transport pizza while ensuring it remains hot.

The following information will help you understand the options and the benefits. Some important things to consider are:

- How far are your average deliveries?
- Do you live in a warm or a cold climate?

- Does delivery make up a major part of your business?

Some bags hold heat while others generate heat. Here are some options:

THERMAL BAGS

These bags are usually made out of nylon or vinyl and are more affordable. Be sure you are buying bags that will last. Vinyl is cheap, but they don't last and tend to trap moisture. This causes the pizza to become soggy. On the other hand, nylon bags are durable and can be washed. They also allow moisture to escape. To evaluate the strength of the bag, look at the "denier." A number of about 500 is desirable.

Your Bag Lady can supply you with insulated bags to deliver pizza, subs, and any other food items. Their selection of insulated bags is at **https://upowerit.com/yourbaglady.com/insulated_bags/index.php**.

They offer bags designed to carry pizzas at **https://upowerit.com/yourbaglady.com/pizza_bags/index.php**.

There is also variety of bags for carryout and for your patrons to carry their leftovers home. To contact Your Bag Lady call toll-free 888-569-9903, fax 718-788-4218, or e-mail marjorie@yourbaglady.com.

DISK-HEATED BAGS

These bags have preheated disks. They generate heat to keep the pizza warm. The bag is warm, instead of cold, when the pizza is put in the bag. Most disks hold their heat for an hour before they need to be recharged. Change them on a regular basis because they need about 30 minutes to heat. However, they can usually be recharged in about ten minutes. The disks fit in most bags and don't need cords to stay warm. Teach your drivers to be careful, so they don't drop the disks. You can sew a pocket in the bag to hold the disk.

INTERNALLY HEATED BAGS

You can also buy internally heated hot bags. Heat elements run through the bag and are plugged into a cigarette lighter to maintain a temperature or 170 degrees. They don't require preheating, but they cost more.

INDUCTION HEATED BAGS

Induction heated bags use pellets that are heated by magnetic waves. The pellets are stored in the heat resistant pouch at the bottom of the bag. These bags usually heat up in three minutes. The pellets can keep a pizza at 160° for about 45 minutes. They can be heated and recharged.

Do your customers complain about your delivery pizzas being soggy? Then you need to check **www.dripie.com**. Dri -Pie enables you to deliver a top quality pizza. Insert this into your delivery bags and get rid of the excess moisture and your delivery drivers can deliver a better quality pizza. Contact Dri-Pie at 203-723-1514.

Hot Delivery Tips

These are some tips to help you deliver steaming hot pizzas to your customers:

- If you use a conveyor oven, leave the pizza on the end of the conveyor until ready to deliver. When the pizza is boxed, it steams and loses heat and crispness.

- Have good support in the bag, so it won't tear.

- Keep the bags clean. The drivers carry the hot bag to the customer's door, and it represents your pizza shop.

Food Safety for Carryout and Delivery

Food safety is an important issue. This is important whether you wrap leftovers from the dining room or deliver food to a customer's house. In the pizza shop, the server will bring a box to the table for the customer to box the food. (Most health departments don't allow you to take a plate back into the kitchen – check with your local health department).

According to Pizza Today, 36 percent of people eat leftover pizza from the night before, even if it wasn't refrigerated. It would be good to provide reheating instructions on your box. This can give typical reheat times and whether the pizza should be reheated in the original packaging. Giving customers reheating and storing instructions is a good safety practice. Let your customer know they should store their salad dressing in the refrigerator.

The decision to offer carryout and/or delivery is your decision. Evaluate the business potential, and the risk or cost involved, in order to make an educated decision.

Safety and Delivery

We've all heard hair-raising stories about delivery drivers, and this is especially true about pizza delivery drivers. The U.S. Bureau of Labor Statistics says pizza delivery drivers are in the fifth most dangerous job in the country. Precautions in your pizza shop can create a safer work environment. One very good way to do this is to promote a policy that your drivers only carry a small amount of money. We had a $20 limit. To make this easier for them, have convenient and locked drop boxes for your drivers. They should drop any additional money after each run. This is a safer situation for them and saves time in the pizza shop between deliveries.

Cell phones are a safety device for your drivers. You can enact a policy where you call each delivery when the driver leaves the store. Furthermore, have a policy about delivering to abandoned houses or telephone booths. We used to have people outside the delivery area who wanted to meet drivers at the outer limits of our delivery zone. These things can be a setup to rob or hurt your drivers, and you need to make a judgment call about how to handle them.

Your drivers need to stay alert on deliveries. If they feel a situation isn't safe, they should come back or call the store. The manager can call to verify the delivery or have someone come outside. Train your drivers to know how to handle unusual situations. Most importantly, it is not worth fighting over money.

Delivery Driver Tips

The best advice is to simply take pride in your work. Although being a delivery driver may not be the most glamorous job, it is essential for the success of the company. Pay attention to the everyday details of the job. The knowledge you gain will serve you well in your career, whether or not you stay in the food service industry. Punctuality, professional appearance, great attitude, hustle, and keeping the customer's best interests in mind are traits that all employers value highly.

Delivery Driver Kit

- Map of delivery area
- Flashlight
- Pad and paper
- Radio

- Map of surrounding area
- Money bag
- Cell phone or calling card

Recommendations for a successful delivery experience:

- **Be on time to work.** In fact, arrive a few minutes early, so you can be ready to hit the road when your shift begins.

- **Hustle.** Delivering pizza is a time sensitive enterprise. Look for ways to improve your in-store and at the door performance to ensure that every customer gets your best effort.

- **Be diligent about information sharing with management.** Let your shift supervisor know you're out the door and delivery times when you return. Doing this allows management to make adjustments to staffing levels, ensuring that the restaurant stays within its budget targets.

- **Pay attention to your appearance.** You are the frontline customer service representative for your company. Use this opportunity to make a good impression.

- **Be a problem solver.** Make each customer's experience as pleasant as possible. Don't shirk responsibility when a problem presents itself. Managers appreciate someone who takes initiative and offers solutions to problems.

- **Keep careful records.** Knowing how much you make in tips will help at the end of your shift and could alleviate problems with your check out. It is also helpful to keep brief notes about customer service issues you may encounter during your shift. Make a note of the issue and how you resolved it. This will help management decide if more needs to be done and provides a record of your

good work.

- **Smile.** In person and on the phone. If you enjoy your work, you will put others at ease and ensure comfortable relationships both with your customers and your co-workers.

- **Be flexible.** Offer to do other tasks when deliveries are scarce.

- **Enjoy your work!** Who doesn't like to see the pizza guy?

BE SAFE

- **Be aware of your surroundings.** Don't deliver to locations that are inadequately lit. Call the homeowner and request that an outdoor light is turned on. Bring your flashlight. Always go with your gut feeling. Your safety should always come first.

- **Do not speed.** Quick delivery does not mean reckless delivery. Not only is speeding dangerous, but it also carries with it the risk of damaging the reputation of the company in your community.

- **Don't carry large amounts of cash.** Use your money bag and the lock box provided by the restaurant to hold your delivery proceeds and tips.

In conclusion, keep in mind these points

- Be prepared for every shift
- Be safe
- Treat the customer with respect
- Work harder and smarter
- Take pride in your work

Whether you are a CEO, a manager, a supervisor, or a delivery driver, do the best job that you can do. When you take pride in your performance, you will find job satisfaction and will be rewarded both by your employer and your customers.

—Jason Clarke, Delivery Driver for Eight Years

20

Dining In

Will you offer a dine-in menu? Many pizza shops do, and you can too. There are things to consider if you are going to have a dining room, and we will discuss those things in this chapter.

Create a Design Focal Point

Your design and layout should highlight and accentuate your products. These tips can help you choose and design your pizza shop's focal point. Your focal point should reflect your vision. Is your focus gourmet pizza? Incorporate your theme in your:

- Pizza shop name
- Logo or signs
- Uniforms
- Decorative accents

- Your design focal point may not have a point. You may just want to convey an elegant, cozy, warm, or safe feeling.

- Plan for expansion. Your décor should have a five to seven year lifespan. When you buy floors, lights, ceiling, and fixtures, try to purchase neutral items that wouldn't need to be changed when you change your décor.

- Spend money for quality basics – save on decorative touches. You can easily accessorize, to carry your theme throughout your pizza shop, without spending a lot.

- Don't over do it. Every wall and surface should not be covered. Leave some blank spaces.

Set the Mood

- Make your pizza shop stand out from the competition. We've all seen the single color and stark leased spaces. Can you add interior or exterior accessories to your pizza shop?

- Play music in your pizza shop. Does it fit your atmosphere and is the level appropriate for your customers and staff?

- Post menus and "daily special" signs. Don't underestimate the promotional potential of these signs.

- The smell of fresh baked pizza. You can add other pleasant scents, but don't underestimate the sales potential of fresh pizza.

Table, Chair, Booths, and Bar Stool Options

Art Marble Furniture is designed to bring a unique elegance to your pizza

and sub shop. These granite top tables are affordable, durable, and lightweight. They offer a beautiful choice for your dining room. Check the selection of chairs and stools which were designed to compliment granite top tables. The Web site is **www.artmarblefurniture.com**. Call toll-free 866-400-1688.

If you are looking for a variety of chair options, you might be interested in the Gasser Chair Company. They were the first to design a unique style of aluminum framed seating specifically for the hospitality industry. The second generation of the Gasser family is guided by the founders' principles and proudly continues the tradition of introducing new ideas and innovations. They work to resolve the requirements of resolving customers' seating needs with quality seating. Visit their Web site at **www.gasserchair.com**, call 330-759-2234, or e-mail sales@gasserchair.com.

Have you been to a restaurant, your meal was delivered, but the table wobbles? We all hate a table that wobbles. There is a solution and you can find it at **www.tableshox.com**. The site explains how and why it works.

Wobbly tables are number one customer complaint. Will you fix the problem? Call 800-457-6454.

Hilden America offers fine table linens for restaurants. The standard linens range from 100-percent Egyptian cotton products, 50/50 cotton and polyester and 100-percent spun polyester. Their most popular 100-percent cotton products include: Satin Band, Partridge Eye, Rose, and Ivy. The full catalog can be viewed at **www.hildenamerica.com/prod01.htm** or you can contact them at 800-431-2514 or by fax 434-572-4781.

Royal Industries offers a wide variety of table and chair options. They also offer highchairs, children's chairs, and booster seats. For the full line of products, please visit **www.royalindustriesinc.com/source/furniture.php**, call 800-782-1200, or fax 800-321-3295.

Cover Your Floors

You shouldn't expect people to rave about your floors, but you might receive some comments if you have ugly floors. The floor you choose will add to the

overall appearance of your pizza shop. Remember to plan for high traffic, and your floors will need to be long-lasting.

These are some things you want to consider when buying flooring:

- Commercial grade offers a longer lifespan.
- Verify manufacturers' warranties for commercial coverage.
- Characteristics for flooring in public areas:

    —Doesn't show scuff marks.

    —Holds up when chairs and equipment are pulled across the floor.

    —Not marred by high-heels.

    —Medium color to hide spots and dirt between cleanings.

- Hardwood vs. vinyl vs. acrylic-infused look-alikes.

    —Wood can be refinished easily, but look-alikes must be replaced.

    —More expensive strip vinyl flooring has a longer lifespan than cheaper vinyl. You can also replace small areas that are damaged.

- Concrete use in commercial buildings. There are new options and color choices that are attractive and durable.

- Say "No" to dark, high-gloss floors. These will show every bit of dirt and may look wavy and reveal any structural damage.

- Is your floor:

    —Easy to clean and maintain?

    —Able to handle chemical exposure?

    —Slip-resistant in all conditions?

    —Up to the sanitation code in food prep areas?

Dur-A-Flex flooring offers a variety of flooring options. You can visit their Web site at **www.dur-a-flex.com/ProductLine/productLine.html**. The attractive and functional flooring systems are ideal for your pizza shop. They are formed from heat resistant epoxy to withstand temperatures to 250 degrees F. This can be used to resurface your floors in the dining area or restrooms. It resists penetration of grease, stains etc. Here are some examples:

DURAFLEX FLOORING OPTIONS
Choose a category below to get flooring system, product listings, and information.
PRIMERS AND SEALERS The best flooring systems begin with a low-viscosity epoxy or acrylic primer coat that penetrates, seals, and reinforces concrete floors prior to resurfacing.
MEMBRANES AND CRACK FILLERS In areas where containment and stress relief head the list of priorities, an elastomeric waterproofing membrane is an ideal foundation layer.
RESURFACERS Clear or pigmented epoxy binders fuse with multi-colored or natural quartz. These fast curing Acrylic (MMA) Systems combine the benefits of an ultra fast cure with UV stability, which makes them perfect for exterior or cold interior environments.
PERFORMANCE TOPCOATS The perfect finish for epoxy or methyl methacrylate flooring systems, a performance topcoat makes your floors more chemical- and abrasion-resistant while imparting a high-gloss, low-glare satin, or flat finish, depending on your preference.
COATINGS— FLOOR AND WALL Quality resins are the key components in any flooring system. High-strength, abrasion-resistant, epoxy, or acrylic coatings can be further enhanced with Bio-Pruf® antimicrobial treatment, corrosion, and heat-resistant Novolac™ and other special formulations.

This link will show you the full line of restaurant flooring options: **www. dur-a-flex.com/ByIndustry/industries/restaurant.html** or contact Dur-A-Flex at 800-253-3539 or fax 860-528-2802.

Looking Up – Selecting Ceilings

Many restaurant owners may overlook their ceiling. Be aware that customers do notice the interior decorations and ugly, stained ceilings. A clean ceiling shows that you want a clean and pleasant environment. It's best to use soundproofing materials that are easy to clean.

Here are some things to consider when you shop for ceiling materials:

- Use moisture-proof, mildew-resistant materials that meet your local sanitary standards on ceilings in high-moisture areas (food prep, dishwashing, and restroom areas).

- Transform ceilings with wallpaper, wood paneling, fabric, or other suspended treatments. All materials need to be fire-resistant and meet, or exceed, local codes.

- Exposed beams, pipes, and vents can be used as great color accents and high-tech art pieces. The paint and other treatments must be fireproof and heat-resistant for heating and steam pipes, and waterproof for water pipes.

- Reflect more light and make the room feel larger with light-colored ceilings. On the other hand, light-colored ceilings also show dirt stains. The health department may require light ceilings in work areas for the benefit of their inspectors.

- You can eliminate ceiling stains by having properly maintained and vented HVAC. Not maintaining is unsightly and wastes electricity.

- Skylights, sky tubes, and well-placed windows can bring more natural light into your pizza shop. Plan to clean these quarterly or more often, if necessary.

- The ceiling is another surface to decorate. Some decorative options include: tin ceilings, faux painting, mirrors, posters, faux beams, fabric, and decorative molding.

Let a Little Light Shine

We know that effective lighting can enhance a mood, improve your décor, and make your pizza shop safer. It can also make your food look more appealing. There are some things you should know when you choose lighting for your pizza shop:

- Natural light will be affected by the seasonal changes.

- Various activities in the room-work areas, walkways, tables, and waiting areas all impact the light that is needed.

- Do you want to create a bright and simulating, or soft and romantic atmosphere?

- Your use of light and shadows can provide accents for attractive features or help you hide less attractive areas.

Candle Lamp Company has offered quality lighting options for over 25 years. These lamps enhance your atmosphere and the dining experience. The design team and staff are available to help you make the right purchase for your pizza and sub shop. Check their Web site at **www.candlelamp.com** or contact them at toll-free: 877-526-7748 or fax at 951-784-5801.

Another alternative is Dining by Candlelight. The company offers, candles,

holders and lamps to fit any décor. Below are a few examples and more can be seen at their website at **www.diningbycandlelight.com**. Restaurant customers in many areas like the ambiance created by candlelight. These candles and lamps offer various designs and options. Call 800-375-8023.

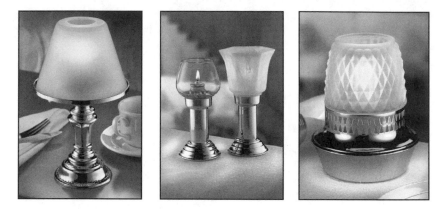

Some additional ways to change the lighting are with wall sconces, chandeliers, track lighting, table lamps, spotlights, and candles.

- **Indirect lighting**. Well-placed wall sconces add subtle lighting.

- **Enhance the food's appearance**. Incandescent lighting has a warmer, yellow-orange cast; fluorescent lighting has a blue-green cast. Halogen lights are closest to true white light. Use lighting and shades that flatter your food.

- Should you use **full-spectrum lighting** in your work areas? It's said that it makes people feel healthier.

- **Hire a lighting designer**. This person can help improve your existing lighting to improve appearance and save energy or develop a new look.

- **Visit GE Lighting online** for design, selection, and energy savings at **www.gelighting.com/na/business/restaurant_solutions.html**.

Colors That Complement

Colors affect people, and that's something to consider for your dining room. These are the feelings that specific colors promote:

- **Yellow** – Sunlight, cheery, vital. You can have a bit of yellow in each room.

- **Red** – Passion stimulates appetites. Use boldly or to accent.

- **Blue** – Cool, clean, and refreshing. Blue isn't complementary to your food.

- **Green** – Well-being, nature, fresh, and light. It can make food look off-color.

- **Gold** – Wealth and power. Warms other colors and brightens dark wood.

- **Neutrals** – Hues make food and people more attractive.

- **White** – Clean, fresh, and new, but white can look institutional, boring and ordinary.

- **Black** – Black can add elegance and style. Avoid black as a background color.

A Little Artwork

Picking the appropriate artwork isn't always an easy project. You may need to commission an artist to create the perfect piece. Hiring an artist isn't like hiring another professional. Reputations, egos, and biases can mean head-bumping and unhappy outcomes. Keep in mind that different people have various ideas about what "art" is. To guarantee you get the artwork you want, work closely with an artist during the conceptualization stage. If you are having an artist do a mural, you can have him prepare a sample board, which is a miniature version of your mural.

Amusement

Pizza and sub shops tend to attract young people and families. A vending machine could be a great addition to your pizza shop. Sports Blaster offers machines for your restaurant. There Web site is **www.sportsblaster.com** and you can reach them at 877-529-8169. They have eight different machines to add variety and entertainment for your patrons.

Serving

When your servers carry orders to the patrons' tables, they will need serving trays. America – American Corporation offers a variety of tray options. You can buy standard trays or have your logo or business name added to the trays. Their Web site is **www.america-americabirchtrays.com/products.html** or contact them at 800-621-5075 or via e-mail at info@american-americabirchtrays.com.

Self-Service Displays

Self-service displays and beverage dispensers save labor and move traffic through your pizza shop. These units should be placed away from the main traffic pattern to keep from disrupting other customers. You should limit your self-serve items to packaged goods. This can be slices of pizza, Italian bread, spaghetti, lasagna, and so on.

When you offer "self-serve" beverage dispensers, assign someone to keep the area clean and neat. Nozzles should be cleaned or changed regularly. Your beverage vendor will typically provide free or economical dispensers when you feature their products.

Self-serve displays are:

- Functional-traditional sliding or swinging glass doors.

- Elegant European-style wood racks.

- Temporary freestanding cardboard displays.

- Classic old-fashioned tubs with ice, holding bottles of water.

- Creative-combine boxes, shelves, stands, wagons, strollers, and décor for innovative displays.

These are many of the choices you have in your dining room area. Think about the atmosphere you want to create and what items and décor will allow you to do that. Some vendors will develop three dimensional layouts to show you what the finished rooms will look like. Over time you will want to make changes and updates to your décor. So, use neutral colors for your main walls and then rotate your accents. Well chosen artwork can also be a great addition to the dining room. Have fun with it, but be sure you have a firm budget before you start to shop. Like all other purchases, do sufficient research before you make final decisions.

Alto Shaam Display cases offer a wide selection of cases from full-service to self-serve. They are customizable to suit your individual needs. These cases keep food at peak quality and freshness throughout the day. The Halo Heat case eliminates the condensation and water that is common in  many heated cases. You will have less food waste and a consistent product for your customers. Check their Web site at **www.altoshaam.com** or call 800-558-8744 for more information.

There are many items that can be sold as an impulse buy as the customer pays their bill or when come in to pick up a carryout order. This is a great way to use display cases. For a variety of display cases, you can visit **www.calmil. com/products.asp?ID=9**. Or, you can contact them at 800-321-9069, or e-mail info@calmil.com.

Berry Plastics offers a wide selection of disposable plastic cups which are great if you have a self-serve beverage area. These cups offer high clarity, are crack resistant, decorative, and have a sleek design. The Web site is: **www. berryplastics.com**.

Photo Courtesy of Pizza Today

A Safe Work Environment

Safety should be a primary concern for you as a business owner. This concern extends to your employees and customers. This chapter discusses things you can and should do to ensure a safe environment for staff and customers.

Agencies

Below are some agencies that can come to your pizza shop and offer various types of safety training.

- **Red Cross** – The Red Cross offers training in first aid, abdominal thrust, and CPR. They can be contacted through their Web site: **www.redcross.org**.

- **Fire department** – Your local fire department offers training for your employees on how to use fire extinguishers. Fires are more common in restaurants than other businesses, so everyone

needs to understand how to operate fire extinguishers. Have fire extinguishers available throughout your pizza shop. Place one in any location where fires are likely, especially near ovens and fryers. Your priority is making them accessible in case of an emergency. In addition, train employees how to avoid fires as well as how to handle a fire in case of an emergency. This will include an evacuation plan for the staff and customers. All employees need to know your plan and how to help customers if there is a fire. REMEMBER...Always call the fire department before using a fire extinguisher!

- OSHA can also provide safety training information. The Occupational Safety and Health Agency (OSHA) is the federal agency that oversees safety in the workplace. Be sure that you are in compliance with their regulations. Details about their requirements for food service establishments and training materials are available at: **www.osha.gov**.

First Aid and Safety

A restaurant with poorly trained employees can lead to hazardous conditions. This is another good reason to thoroughly train your employees. They need to be trained on how to handle first aid safety emergencies.

Have a safety plan in place and train your employees to implement the elements of this plan. Train them, so they can respond in a calm and quick manner. Safety training materials can be found on The Training Network's Web site at **www.safetytrainingnetwork.com**.

Fire

Contact your local fire department for more information about their

regulations and recommendations. You need fire extinguishers, fire alarms, carbon monoxide alarms, and smoke detectors. Place a note on your calendar to replace the batteries in your fire alarms every six months.

When you consider fire extinguishers, there are several types, including:

- Dry chemical
- Halon
- Water and carbon dioxide

The type of fire extinguisher depends on the type of fire. This is the reason fire extinguishers are labeled:

- **Class A** – Ordinary combustibles
- **Class B** – Flammable liquids
- **Class C** – Electrical equipment

Many fire extinguishers are labeled with a graphic image that shows the type of fire. Once you have the fire extinguishers in your pizza shop, they must be serviced once a year.

Part of your Fire Safety Plan should include an emergency number by all phones, along with evacuation plans around the kitchen, near the doors and in the entryway and dining room area. There are interesting statistics and information on the NFPA Web site at **www.nfpa.org**.

Accidents and Security

Any person or business can have an accident, but you can reduce your risk. These are a few ways to do so:

- Ground your electrical outlets.

- Clean walkways and clear clutter.

- Shovel and salt walks and steps in the winter.

- Provide adequate outdoor lighting.

- Place rails along steps.

- Provide adequate interior lighting.

- Install solid doors.

- Put good locks on windows and doors.

- Have a quality security system installed.

These are only some of the possibilities. Assign someone to be your safety coordinator. The safety coordinator can plan and train employees about your evacuation plans, arrange training with local organizations, and be on the lookout for safety problems and concerns.

Kitchen Safety

The restaurant business has many potential safety hazards. Knives, hot ovens, fryers, slicers, grinders, glass, and wet or greasy floors are only some of the hazards your staff faces every day. Many accidents can be prevented with good training.

Heat and Burns

It's very easy for employees to get burns while they are working. A good amount of these can be avoided if they are careful. They can be burned on grills, stoves, ovens, hot food and drinks, splatters, slashes, and spills.

To prevent burns:

- Use thick, dry potholders and stir food with long-handled spoons.

- Use hot water carefully. Wear insulated rubber gloves for hot rinse water. Follow operating instructions, especially with steam equipment. Expel all steam before opening the doors.

- Lift lids and equipment away from yourself.

- Avoid splatters and splashes by not overfilling kettles. Don't let food boil over.

- Oil and water don't mix; ensure food is dry before frying.

- Point pan handles away from walkways, but within reach, to avoid knocking over other pans.

- Do not crowd hot pans. Remove cooked foods from cooking surfaces.

- Let oil cool and use caution when cleaning fryers.

- Wear insulated gloves or mitts when removing hot pans from the oven and be certain no one is in your way.

- Do not wear clothes that drape and could catch on fire.

Kitchen Grips offer a great way to grab hot items. They are safe for temperatures to 500 degrees F. They are heat resistant, safer grip, water repellent, and stain resistant. Visit the Web site for more information at **www.kitchengrips.com** or call 800-785-4449.

Cuts

Another hazard for your workers is cuts, but knives aren't the only potential problem. Some equipment has sharp edges and broken glass is a problem. Opening boxes can be a hazard, too. This includes nails, staples, and the edges of box tops.

Take these precautions:

- Use the proper tools to dispose of broken glass. Place broken glass in a separate garbage container.

- Cut rolls of kitchen wrap with the cutter.

- Watch the edges when opening cans. Don't use a knife to open cans or to pry items loose.

- Use a pusher to feed food into a grinder.

- Unplug slicers and grinders when removing food and cleaning.

- Utilize guards when operating grinders and slicers.

- Replace equipment blades when clean. Don't let them sit around.

- When you hire left-handed people, give them additional safety instruction about slicers and similar equipment. The safety features on this equipment are designed for right-handed people.

Some Additional Tips:

- Keep knives sharpened. Dull blades cause more cuts.
- Do not leave knives or blades in the bottom of a sink.
- Carry knives by the handle with the tip away from you.
- Never try to catch a falling knife.
- Cut away from yourself on a cutting board.
- Slice; do not hack.
- Use the proper knives for the project.
- Carefully store and clean knives and equipment.

- Store knives and sharp tools in separate areas.

- Wash glasses separately to prevent them from being broken in the sink.

- Don't stack glasses and cups inside of each other.

- Watch for nails, staples, and sharp edges while unpacking boxes.

Electrical Shock

Many pieces of restaurant equipment are electrical, so shock is a real concern. Some tips to prevent electrical shock are:

- Ground electrical equipment.

- Replace worn or frayed electrical cords.

- Ensure employees can reach switches without touching or leaning against metal tables or counters.

- Unplug equipment before cleaning.

- Use electrical equipment with dry hands.

- Know locations of electrical switches and breakers for quick shutdown in an emergency.

Strains

Your staff members can strain their arms, legs, or backs by carrying heavy food items or equipment. To prevent strains:

- Place heavy food items and equipment on low shelves.
- Use dollies or carts to move heavy objects.

- Use carts with rollers to move objects around the restaurant.

- Use a cart to carry excessive or heavy objects.

- Ask for help when lifting large or heavy objects.

- Bend from your knees, not with your back, when you lift heavy items.

Slipping and Falling

Anyone who slips and falls on a floor can be badly hurt. Implement practices and training to help avoid hazards that put workers at risk.

PREVENTION:

- Clean spills immediately.

- Use signs or cones to let people know when floors are wet.

- Wear shoes with no-slip soles.

- Don't stack boxes too high; they can fall and cause people to trip.

- Keep boxes, ladders, step stools, and carts away from walkways.

Matrix Engineering offers Grip Rock and Super G floor mats. These are ideal for preventing slip and fall accidents which are a leading cause of injury in workplaces. They are durable, lightweight and long lasting to make your wet, greasy and hazardous areas safe for your staff. To contact Matrix call 800-926-0528, fax 772-461-7185, or e-mail griprock@gate.net. You can find more information on their Web site at **www.griprock.com.**

These are some of the mat characteristics.

Grip Rock slip-resistant safety mat and Super G slip-resistant safety mat are:

- Slip-resistant in water, grease, and oil

- Extremely tough and durable

- Flexible even in freezing temperatures

- Lightweight and thin (⅛ inch thick, a 3' x 10' is only 25 pounds)

- No installation needed

- Easy to handle, clean, and maintain

Choking

Children are warned not to eat so fast or to talk when they are eating. Adults need to heed this advice, too. Restaurant safety means being aware of your customers. How to react:

- Hands on throat and unable to talk or cough equals choking.

- Do not pat a person's back if he can talk, cough, or breathe.

- Use the Heimlich Maneuver, and call for help right away if the person cannot talk, cough, or breathe.

- Every one of your employees needs to be trained in how to use the Heimlich Maneuver. Post posters with Heimlich Maneuver instructions in employee areas.

Exposure to Hazardous Chemicals

All cleaning chemicals, pesticides, and sanitizers can harm or poison people. Special precautions need to be taken to protect employees. The law requires that some of these steps be taken. OSHA requires a current inventory of all

hazardous materials.

Manufacturers must properly label all hazardous chemicals and must supply a Material Safety Data Sheet (MSDS) to be kept on file in your restaurant. The MSDS provides the chemical name, the physical hazards, health hazards, and emergency procedures in case of exposure. This notebook must be up-to-date and handy in the case of emergency. Train all employees to use the MSDS.

Prevent Improper Exposure to Hazardous Materials

- Only trained workers can handle hazardous chemicals.
- Use safety equipment when working with hazardous chemicals.
- Wear nonporous gloves and goggles for sanitizing and cleaning agents.

Even accidental mishandling of food products or neglecting safety can lead to health problems or injury. To be successful you must build and maintain a reputation for offering quality food in a safe environment. If there is a question in your customers' minds about the quality of your product, you can quickly lose your hard-earned reputation. The sanitation and safety procedures described here are simple to initiate, but they must be enforced.

Good Ergonomics

Ergonomics is "the study and engineering of human physical interaction with spaces and objects during activities." Any area that requires your workers to repeatedly stretch to reach the supplies they need is poor ergonomically.

Good ergonomics can positively affect your employee's wellbeing, safety, productivity, and comfort. This would include well-fitting tables and

comfortable chairs to enhance your customers' experience. Below are tips to help you reorganize your pizza shop to work well with people:

- Create mini-workstations with food, utensils, and prep space close.

- Rearrange your storage to minimize bending, lifting, and reaching.

- Provide stools or chairs that support the back and feet when sitting.

- Are your tools and equipment designed for men and women?

- Supply stable, heavy-duty ladders to access shelves and storage units.

- Purchase tools and utensils for left-handed employees.

- Consider how employees, customers, and vendors interact with your facility. Does the current layout make it easier or more difficult for employees to do their jobs or customers to enjoy dining?

- Choose fixtures and equipment that can be moved easily.

The Air We Breathe

Your pizza shop needs healthy air, inside and out. "Poor air" can contribute to employee absenteeism and unhappy customers. Many communities have rigid air and work environment regulations that pertain to proper ventilation, grease, smoke, and wood burning. Any unpleasant odors contribute to "poor" air quality.

Fresh Indoor Air

Wood burning ovens, charbroilers, and fryers can create unhealthy or unpleasant air conditions. Flour can also be a concern. Bring in enough outdoor air to supply sufficient indoor air quality, by properly filtering,

circulating, and redirecting airflow.

These are some ways to improve indoor air quality:

- Smoking and non-smoking areas – Direct airflow away from non-smoking tables. Ban employee smoking in the kitchen and dining room.

- Install an air cleaner/filtration system that reduces airborne particles and dust.

- Radon, mold, and biological dangers are possible when converting old or vacant buildings.

- Read EPA reports about air quality at **www.epa.gov/iaq/pubs/ insidest.html**.

- Unhealthy emissions from carpet, paint, and cleaning products. Sick Building Syndrome is explained at the National Safety Council site at **www.nsc.org/ehc/indoor/sbs.htm**.

- Hire an HVAC contractor or engineer with restaurant experience. Hire contractors to install new systems or to maintain existing systems.

Outdoor Air Quality

Ovens, fryers and other cooking equipment emit particulates, gases, grease, and odors that are regulated. Local and state standards vary greatly. The Federal Air Quality Standards may supersede these. You must pay close attention to the regulations, because the penalties can be severe. Here are suggestions to meet emission regulations:

- Hire an industrial air-cleaning firm to install emission-control

systems to handle grease, smoke, CO_2, and odors.

- Inspect and repair exterior vents, hoods, and intake ducts. Proper maintenance saves the air and your energy costs.

- Install a catalytic oxidizer that converts gases and smoke to water. Read the article at **www.pfonline.com/articles/010203.html**.

- Contact your natural gas and electric company and county or state environmental and health departments for air quality information, resources, and financial incentives.

- Hire an air quality consultant to help you comply with more complex emission issues and stringent regulations.

- The Environmental Protection Agency's Web site, **www.epa.gov**, provides information on restaurant-specific regulations.

A safe and healthy pizza shop is important to your customers and their families. Your employees appreciate and deserve a safe and healthy work environment. Some of these elements are simple and some are more complicated, but all are needed to provide the atmosphere to support your customers and employees.

Photo Courtesy of Pizza Today

The Essentials of
Food Safety, HACCP, and
Sanitation Practices

Preparing and serving quality food in a safe environment is each employee's responsibility. In order to guarantee the quality and safety of your food, you must understand the basics of controlling food contamination. The definition of food contamination is the spread of infectious diseases.

This is another issue that needs to be addressed in your employee training. Give them the know-how and necessary tools to allow them to establish and practice effective food-handling and sanitation procedures.

These are some things you must provide for your employees:

- Give your employees hands-on training, reminders, and training manuals.

- Provide hair nets, uniforms, gloves, hand and nail brushes, germicidal hand soaps, and first-aid kits.

- Provide hand sinks at each workstation, sanitary employee bathrooms and lockers, scrub brushes, gloves, and disposable towels.

- Equipment and storage supplies should have dated labels and standard rotation procedures. Give your employees color-coded utensils, test kits, and quality-control standards. These standards must be enforced.

Many types of bugs, animal pests and bacteria can reside within your pizza shop. These intruders search for food, water, and warmth. Since these unwanted things are plentiful in your shop, make conditions unfavorable for them.

HACCP Defined

Hazard Analysis of Critical Control Points (HACCP) is a system to monitor food preparation to reduce the risk of food-borne illness. HACCP focuses on how food is processed – beginning with purchasing to including how it is served. You and your staff need to understand the potential problems during each stage of preparation.

HACCP provides the necessary procedures to control food preparation in order to avoid the potential hazards. It helps you identify these critical control points (CCP). Each of these points can allow bacteria or harmful organisms to grow and contaminate food.

Atlantic Publishing offers a variety of HACCP products which can give you more in-depth information about HACCP regulations; a training kit, labels, and posters for employees, at **www.atlantic-pub.com/HACCP_ Main.htm**. You can order the items you need, or they offer a HACCP kit which contains many items that you can use with your staff. The special

sanitation package includes:

- *HACCP & Sanitation in Restaurants and Food Service Operations: A Practical Guide Based on the FDA Food Code: With Companion CD-ROM*

- A complete set of 20 Safety & Sanitation Labels (five each of four different labels)

- Sixteen sanitation and safety posters

- Ten workplace safety posters

Why Should You Use HACCP?

You are the owner of a pizza shop, and that means you are responsible to serve safe food to your customers. So, you must educate and motivate your employees to implement food safety procedures. These procedures must:

- Identify potential hazards.
- Implement safety procedures.
- Monitor how successful your safety system is on a consistent basis.

If the raw ingredients are safe and the process is safe, then the finished product is safe. Using HACCP allows you to identify potentially hazardous foods and stages in the food preparation process where bacterial contamination, survival, and growth can occur. This enables you to minimize the danger.

Implementing HACCP

These are the key steps to implementing HACCP:

Step 1: Assess the Hazards

- Have a system to track food from purchasing, receiving, preparation and serving, and reheating, if needed.

- Review your menu items. Identify the potentially hazardous foods and foods that could become contaminated.

- Risk can be reduced by removing very hazardous items from your menu.

- Review how you store, prep, cook, and serve items to identify any areas where contamination might occur.

- Rank the hazards based on whether they are severe or probable.

Step 2: "Critical Control Points"

Identify areas in your process that can be controlled or prevented. Develop a step-by-step list that details the preparation of potentially hazardous foods. Then, identify ways to prevent, reduce, and eliminate recontamination at each step you listed.

These are ways food service workers can reduce the risk of food-borne illness:

- Practice good personal hygiene.
- Avoid cross-contamination.
- Use proper storage, cooking, and cooling procedures.
- Reduce the steps involved in preparing and serving.

Remember to review how your vendors handle your food. This includes being sure the food is transported and handled properly during delivery.

Step 3: "Critical Limits"

Part of this process requires that you establish the critical limits. These are standards that can be seen and measured. Include time and temperature rules.

- What is required to meet each standard? Avoid vague descriptions like "cook until done," and use "cook to internal temperature of 170 degrees within two hours."

- Your thermometers need to be calibrated on a regular basis.

- Your recipes need to include the end cooking, reheating, and hot-holding temperatures; along with thawing, cooking, and cooling times.

- Have sufficient staff at peak hours to ensure food is prepared and served safely.

Step 4: Monitor "Critical Control Points"

Step-by-step charts will show you potentially hazardous steps. Review your process and compare with the requirements to avoid potential problems in your process. Identify any problems and make the needed changes.

Step 5: Make Needed Changes

Make changes as needed. Some reasons for change are:

- Food contaminated by hands or equipment must be rewashed or discarded.

- Food temperatures aren't sufficient after cooking. Continue cooking to the required temperature.

- If food temperatures exceed 55°F during prep or serving, discard it.

Step 6: Develop a Recordkeeping System

Develop a system to document the HACCP process to monitor your results. Your employees can log their compliance. This will also keep the procedures in their minds. These records can provide proof that food-borne illnesses did not originate at your pizza shop.

Step 7: Verify Your System is Effective

Verify that the HACCP process for your facility works. These are some ways you can do that:

- Note how often you need corrective actions. If frequent corrections are needed, evaluate the need to change, or fine-tune, your system. You may need to find time to retrain your employees.

- How can you test the strength of your sanitizing solution? Examine your records. Are employees entering actual valid data?

- Ensure your dishwashing and sanitizing equipment work properly. They need regular calibration and maintenance.

- The board of health can give you a non-biased assessment of whether or not your process is working.

HACCP Procedures

Purchasing

When you purchase the food for your pizza shop, you have several goals:

- To obtain safe and wholesome ingredients.

- Prepare food to meet your production and menu standards.

In order to accomplish this, carefully choose your vendors. They must meet the federal and state health standards. They should use the HACCP system in their operations and train their employees in sanitation. Delivery trucks need adequate refrigeration and freezer units. Foods should be packaged in protective, leak-proof, durable packaging.

Be clear with vendors, from the beginning, about what you expect from them. Include food-safety standards in your purchase agreements. Ask to see the most recent board of health sanitation reports, and tell them you will inspect their trucks quarterly, or more often if warranted.

Receiving

The goals of receiving are:

- To ensure food is fresh and safe when it enters your facility.

- To transfer food to proper storage as quickly as possible.

These are the two important parts of receiving:

1. Preparing to receive food.

2. Inspecting the food when it arrives.

Keep these guidelines in mind, and complete these tasks when you receive food:

- Stock sanitary carts in your receiving area to transport goods.

- Prepare sufficient refrigerator and freezer space before deliveries arrive, especially during special events of high volume time periods.

- Label all deliveries with the date they arrived and a "use by" date.

- The designated receiving area needs to be well lit and clean.

- All trash left after deliveries needs to be thrown into trash containers.

- Keep the floors free of food and debris.

How does the delivery truck look when it arrives at your store? Is it clean and are the refrigerator units working properly? Next inspect the food:

- Check expiration dates for all perishable items.

- Check that the shelf life dates have not expired.

- Check that frozen foods are airtight and moisture-proof.

- Check for any sign that food has been thawed and refrozen. If there are any signs of refreezing, reject the items. (Some signs include large crystals, solid areas of ice, or excessive ice in containers.)

- Check cans for swollen areas, flawed seals or seams, dents, or rust. Also, reject cans that contain foamy or bad-smelling items.

- Check temperature of refrigerated and frozen foods, especially items that spoil quickly.

- Check for signs of insect infestations.

- Check for dirt on flats or crates that are dirty. If you find any, reject them.

Storage Options and Requirements

There are four ways to store food:

1. Dry storage is ideal for holding items longer and for less perishable items.

2. Refrigeration is for short-term and perishable items.

3. Deep chilling units are good for short-term storage.

4. Freezing is recommended for long-term storage of perishable foods.

You and your staff need to be familiar with safety and sanitation requirements for each type of storage.

Dry Storage

When you plan your storage areas, keep in mind that many items can be stored in a sanitary storeroom. You can store canned goods, baking supplies, grain, items like flour, and any other dry items. Some vegetables like onions, potatoes, and tomatoes should be stored in dry areas. It's best to have proper ventilation in this space and a temperature that will discourage bacteria and mold. Remember this:

- Dry goods should be stored at 50 degrees, but 60 to 70 is adequate.

- Calibrate the wall thermometer to gauge the temperature in this area.

- Packages in this area should be in unopened cans or in tightly covered containers. These items need to be rotated using the "first in, first out" (FIFO). To ensure accuracy, date the packages when they arrive and place new items behind older ones.

- Clean all spills immediately and thoroughly to avoid pest infestation and cross-contamination. Don't store trash or garbage

cans in food areas.

- No items should be placed on the floor. The bottom shelf of your storage shelves must be 6 inches off of the ground. You can use pallets on the floor and store paper products on them.

- Never use or store cleaning agents or other chemicals where they could contaminate foods! Label all chemicals in a separate area, and label all containers. Always store chemicals in their original containers.

Refrigerated Storage

Fresh meat, poultry, seafood, dairy products, most fresh fruits and vegetables, and hot leftovers should be stored in the refrigerator at temperatures below 40°F. Keep in mind that food won't keep forever, even in a refrigerator. However, refrigeration does extend the shelf life and the cold keeps it safe from bacteria.

A refrigerator unit should have slotted shelves that allow air to circulate around the food. This is important, so you shouldn't line the shelves with foil or paper. Be careful not to overload the refrigerator or shelves. Empty space improves air circulation. Refrigerated food should also be dated and sealed.

Additional refrigerator tips:

- Use clean, nonabsorbent, covered containers for food storage.

- Dairy products are to be stored away from onions, cabbage, and seafood.

- Raw and uncooked food must be stored below prepared and ready-to-eat food to prevent cross contamination.

- Keep poultry, fish, and meat fluids away from other foods.

- The proper temperature for perishable items is critical to prevent food-borne illnesses. Check regularly to be sure the temperature stays below 40°F. Each time the door opens and closes affects the inside temperature.

Tucel Industries offers a color coordinated set of brushes. Each color is for a specific type of food. This is another way to prevent cross contamination. Additional details can be found at **www.tucel.com/html/haccp.htm** or you can contact them for more information by phone at 800-558-8235 or by fax at 802-247-6826. You can also e-mail them at info@tucel.com.

- **Red hygiene:** raw product preparation contact area.

- **Green hygiene:** cleaning produce and fruits.

- **White hygiene:** pasteurization and food contact areas.

- **Blue hygiene:** seafood preparation areas.

- **Yellow hygiene:** non-food contact surface areas.

- **Black hygiene:** drains and other non-food areas.

Have a backup thermometer for your refrigerator in addition to the built-in thermometers. Use several thermometers in different sections of the refrigerator. This is especially true in a walk-in unit. Be sure you have a consistent temperature throughout and ensure no area is too warm.

Deep Chilling

Deep or super-chilling foods, at a temperature between 26 and 32°F decreases the growth of bacteria. This extends the life of poultry, meat, and seafood without compromising their quality through freezing. This can be done in specially designed units or by lowering the refrigerator temperature.

Frozen Storage

Frozen meats, poultry, seafood, fruits and vegetables, and some dairy products should be stored in a freezer at 0°F to keep them fresh and safe for an extended period.

It's best to only freeze items that were shipped to you already frozen. When you freeze perishable foods, you can damage their quality. Storing food in the freezer for extended periods increases the chance of contamination and spoilage. Arrange your freezer to allow air to circulate through the shelves and around the food just like you do in your refrigerator.

Tips to maximize efficiency of your freezer:

- Store frozen foods in moisture-proof containers to minimize loss of flavor, discoloration, dehydration, and odor absorption.

- Monitor temperature using various thermometers to ensure consistent temperatures. Keep a written record of the temperatures of each freezer.

- Open freezer doors only when necessary, and take multiple items each time. A "cold curtain" can guard against heat gain.

- Maintain temperature by lowering the temperature of warm foods before storing.

- Use the first-in, first-out (FIFO) method to keep your inventory fresh.

- Date (with a freezer marker) "occasional-use" items. When anything has been in the freezer over the recommended time, it should be thrown out. The manufacturer or food vendor can give you their recommendations.

Preparing Food

Prepping

Most fruits and vegetables should be washed to remove dirt, sand, and insects. Soap and water should remove these and residual pesticides. You might use a food-safe disinfectant solution as a precaution for "high-risk" customers.

To prepare raw ingredients and to avoid contamination:

- Sanitize employees' hands and work surfaces before handling.

- Knives, choppers, and peelers should be sanitized between uses.

- Scrub produce before it's peeled or sliced to avoid transferring germs and chemicals.

When you prepare raw foods, it's necessary to do everything possible to avoid contamination. One way to do this is through the use of colored cutting boards. Each board is for a specific food item. An example can be seen and purchased at **www.halco.com**. These boards are available in the food preparation section on page 136. Many other preparation items are available on the surrounding pages. Contact Browne Halco at 888-289-1005 or fax 908-964-6677.

To prep many foods, you need the appropriate brushes. Some are used to clean the food items and others are used to clean your work area. Several types of brushes are shown at **www.tucel.com/cgi-bin/store/agora.cgi**, within the prep food area. You can contact Tucel by phone at 800-558-8235 or via fax at 802-247-6826.

Thawing and Marinating

Freezing keeps bacteria from multiplying, but it doesn't kill them. Any

bacteria, when food is removed from the freezer, will multiply rapidly when thawed at the wrong temperature. So, it's critical to thaw foods below the temperature danger zone. Never thaw foods on a counter or in a non-refrigerated area.

Two of the best methods to thaw food:

1. Place a pan on the lowest shelf in a refrigerator below 40 degrees.

2. Place under drinkable running water at 70 degrees or less for no more than two hours, or until the item is thawed.

Marinating Do's and Don'ts

- Always marinate meat, fish, and poultry in the refrigerator.
- Never marinate at room temperature.
- Never save and reuse marinade.
- With all methods, be careful not to cross-contaminate!

Cold Food Precautions

Preparing cold ingredients is a hazardous point in the process. These are the reasons:

- Cold food preparation is done at room temperature.
- Cold food is a common point of contamination and cross-contamination.

Be especially cautious of cold foods that will not be cooked. There is greater reason to properly clean and prepare these items. Chill the various ingredients, and combine them while chilled.

Important precautions to remember:

- Don't prepare food too far in advance.

- Prepare small batches, and place in the refrigerator immediately.

- Store prepared cold foods below 40°F.

- Wash all fresh fruits and vegetables with plain water to remove surface pesticide residues and other impurities.

- When you cut into thick-skinned produce, it can be contaminated.

- Scrub thick-skinned produce with a brush.

To avoid cross-contamination, you must:

- Sanitize hands before and after handling each item.

- Keep raw products away from prepared foods.

- Sanitize cutting boards, knives, and surfaces after each food item.

- Color-coded prep equipment can identify those used for produce, chicken, and other risky items.

- Discard leftover batter, breading, or marinade after it's used.

Cooking

Potentially hazardous foods can contain contaminates even when it's properly handled. Cooking to a proper internal temperature will kill bacteria. Keep in mind that conventional cooking procedures won't destroy bacteria.

Some "safe cooking" tips:

- Stir foods in deep pots frequently to mix and ensure thorough cooking.

- Consistent sizes make cooking time predictable and uniform.

- Don't interrupt the cooking process. Partially cooking poultry or

meat can create conditions that encourage bacterial growth.

- Verify the accuracy of heating equipment by using thermometers.

- Use a thermometer to ensure food reaches the proper temperature. Use a sanitized metal-stemmed, a numerically scaled, or a digital thermometer.

- Check food temperature in several areas, including the thickest parts, to ensure it's thoroughly cooked. Do not touch the pan or bone with the thermometer because this will alter the temperature.

- Always cook food to an internal temperature of 165°F.

We discussed pizza ovens in an earlier chapter. These ovens need to be cleaned. How you clean them depends on the type of oven you use. Deck ovens need to be scrubbed with a pizza oven brush like the one that is sold by **www.tucel.com/cgi-bin/store/agora.cgi**. The products are listed in the Equipment Cleaning Supplies. You will need many types of brushes to keep your pizza shop clean, many can be found in this section. You can contact Tucel at 800-558-8235 or by fax at 802-247-6826.

Serving and Holding

Food isn't guaranteed safe because it's been cooked. If your holding temperature is too low, the food can be contaminated. To avoid this type of problem:

- Keep hot foods in hot-holding equipment above 140°F.
- Keep cold foods in a refrigeration unit or below 40°F.

Safe Serving and Holding:

- Use steam tables and hot food carts during service but not to reheat.

- Stir foods consistently to ensure even heating.

- Use a food thermometer to check temperatures every 30 minutes.

- Sanitize thermometer before each use, or use a digital infrared thermometer that never touches the food.

- Cover hot-holding equipment to contain heat and prevent contamination.

- Monitor the temperature of hot-holding equipment.

- Discard food held in the "temperature danger zone" over four hours.

- Never add fresh food to a serving pan with food that has been served.

Important points:

- Wash hands with soap and warm water for at least 20 seconds before serving food.

- Use cleaned and sanitized long-handled ladles and spoons, so your bare hands don't touch food.

- Never touch parts of glasses, cups, plates, or tableware that come into contact with food.

- Never touch parts of dishes that come into contact with the customer's mouth.

- Wear gloves if serving food by hand.

- Cover cuts or infections with bandages or gloves.

- Discard gloves when they touch an unsanitary surface.

- Use tongs or wear gloves to distribute rolls and bread.

- Clean and sanitize equipment and utensils thoroughly after each use.

- Use lids and sneeze guards to protect food from contamination.

- Keep cash handling duties separate from food handling, when possible.

- Wash hands, utensils, and contact surfaces after contact with raw meat or poultry and before contact with cooked meat or poultry.

Sanitary Self-Service

Workers and customers can contaminate the food. Remember, your customers aren't trained in sanitation. Here are some things to watch for:

- Touch food and plastic ware with their hands.

- Touch edges of utensils and equipment.

- Sneeze or cough into food or self-serve displays.

- Touch salt and pepper shaker tops, sugar bowls, and condiment containers.

- Return food items to avoid waste.

It is critical that you remove any food that could be contaminated as soon as you see something questionable. If you are unsure, throw it out. Some ways to protect your customers include:

- Serve sealed packages of crackers, breadsticks, and condiments.

- Pre-wrap, date, and label sandwiches, if possible.

Rosseto – Salad Bar Dispensers are a good example of a way for your customers to serve themselves while you control the possibility of contamination. It's hard for them to resist your salad bar when you use Rosseto's patented dispensers for your salad bar toppings. Your salad bar toppings are beautifully displayed and you get measured portions that are neatly and hygienically dispensed. The unique design keeps all your toppings fresher, longer. And it's so easy to use and easy to clean! For more information visit the Web site

at **www.rosseto.com** or by phone at 847-491-9166.

Cooling

There will be times when you will prepare foods in advance and use leftovers. This can lead to problems. This can be the number one cause of food-borne illnesses. Two key precautions to prevent these problems at this point are rapid cooling and protection from contamination.

Chilling It Quickly

Leftovers should be chilled to an internal temperature of below 40°F. Quick chill any leftovers larger than a half a gallon or two pounds.

Simple Steps to Quick chill:

- **Reduce food mass** – Smaller amounts of food chill quicker than large amounts. Cut items into smaller pieces, or divide into several containers.

- **Shallow, pre-chilled pans** – (no more than 4 inches deep). Use stainless-steel containers because stainless steel transfers heat

better and cools faster than plastic.

- **Chill** – It's best to place food in an ice-water bath or quick-chill unit (26°-32°F) instead of a refrigerator. This is why these are your best options:

  —Water conducts better than air. Food cools quicker in an ice bath than in a refrigerator.

  —Refrigeration units keep cold foods cold, rather than chilling hot foods. It can take too long to cool foods to safe temperatures.

- Pre-chill foods in a freezer for about 30 minutes and then refrigerate.

- Separate items so air can flow around them. Don't stack shallow pans. Never cool at room temperature.

- Stir frequently – Stirring accelerates cooling and gets cold air to all parts of the food.

- Check temperature periodically – Food should reach 70°F within two hours and 40°F within four hours. This time must be reduced if food spent time in the "temperature danger zone" during preparation and serving.

- Tightly cover and label cooled foods. List preparation date and time.

- Store food on the upper shelves of the cooler and cover the container when they reach 45°F.

  —Uncovered foods cool faster, and they have an increased risk for cross-contamination.

  —Never store prepared foods beneath raw foods.

Reheating

Remember that leftovers are not safe. During reheating and serving leftovers, be careful not to allow contamination.

Tips to safely reheat and serve leftovers:

- Boil sauces, soups, and gravies, and heat other foods to a minimum of 165°F, within two hours of taking food out of the refrigerator.

- Never reheat food in hot-holding equipment.

- Never mix a leftover food with fresh food.

- Never reheat food more than once.

Heated holding cabinets – Keeping the product warm and free from contamination makes a difference in how much you sell and how much you throw out. Heated holding cabinets from Henny Penny can make this difference for you. They provide floor or counter top units. They are energy efficient and built to last. For more information, visit **www.hennypenny. com/pd/pd1.phtml**. Contact Henny Penny at 800-417-8417.

Clean Versus Sanitary

Heat or chemicals can reduce bacteria to acceptable levels. They can also combat other harmful microorganisms. Heat sanitizing requires exposing equipment to high heat for an adequate period of time. This can be done by placing equipment in 170° to 195°F water for at least 30 seconds, or in a dishwasher that washes at 150°F and rinses at 180°F. It's critical that you check water temperatures on a regular basis.

Equipment can be chemically sanitized by dipping in or wiping it with bleach or sanitizing solution. Use a half of an ounce, or one tablespoon, of

5-percent bleach per gallon of water. Commercial cleaning agents contain manufacturers' instructions. These chemicals are regulated by the EPA. Follow the instructions carefully. You can also use chemical test strips to test the strength of the sanitizing solution. Since exposure to air can dilute the strength of these agents test often.

The Quik-Wash Hand Wash Faucet Control – "Handwashing is the single most effective means of preventing the spread of disease." – Centers for Disease Control and Prevention. This faucet is an economical choice which can be better than the costly electronic faucets. The faucet offers automatic closing and hands-free positions. For additional information, visit **www.fmponline.com/featuredproduct.html**. You can contact FMP for more information by phone at 800-257-7737, by fax at 800-255-9866, or through e-mail at sales@fmponline.com.

Pre-rinse Basket – For use with a 20" x 20" (50.80cm x 50.80cm) dish rack, this also fits in a standard 21¾" x 21¾" (55.24cm x 55.24cm) pre-rinse sink.

Cleaning Products and MSDS – Henny Penny has a full line of quality cleaning products that are formulated to sanitize Henny Penny equipment. It is also useful for cleaning your food prep and serving areas. For more information, visit **www.hennypenny.com/pd/pd2.phtml?formTarget=cleaning**. Contact Henny Penny at 800-417-8417 or by fax at 800-417-8402.

Sanitize Portable Equipment:

- Proper cleaning and sanitizing portable equipment requires a sink with three separate compartments for cleaning, rinsing, and sanitizing.

- Have a separate area to scrape and rinse food and debris into the garbage or disposal before washing, and another drain board for clean and soiled items.

- This is the correct procedure to sanitize a piece of equipment:

  1. Clean and sanitize sinks and work surfaces.

  2. Scrape and rinse food into garbage or disposal. Presoak items like silverware.

  3. First Sink – Immerse the equipment in a clean detergent solution at about 120 degrees. Use a brush or cloth to loosen and remove any remaining visible soil.

  4. Second Sink – Use clear, clean water between 120°F and 140°F to remove all traces of food, debris, and detergent.

  5. Third Sink – Sanitize items in hot water at 170°F for 30 seconds or in a chemical sanitizing solution for one minute. Cover all surfaces of the equipment with hot water or sanitizing solution and keep them in it for the appropriate amount of time.

  6. If soapsuds disappear in the first compartment or remain in the second, if the water temperature cools, or if water in any compartment becomes dirty and cloudy, empty the compartment and refill it.

  7. Air dry. Drying with a towel can re-contaminate equipment and remove the sanitizing solution before it finishes working.

  8. Let equipment dry before putting it into storage; moisture can foster bacterial growth.

Sanitizing In-Place Equipment:

Larger and immobile equipment must be washed, rinsed, and sanitized. Use this procedure:

  1. Unplug electrically powered equipment.

2. Remove food particles and scraps.

3. Wash, rinse, and sanitize removable parts using the immersion method described in steps three through five of the previous section.

4. Wash the food-contact surfaces and rinse with clean water. Wipe with a chemical sanitizing solution, using the manufacturer's directions.

5. Wipe down non-food surfaces with a sanitized cloth and allow to air-dry before reassembling. Sanitize cloth before and during sanitizing by rinsing it in sanitizing solution.

6. Re-sanitize external food-contact surfaces that were handled when reassembled.

7. Scrub wooden surfaces, like cutting boards, with a detergent solution and a stiff-bristled nylon brush. Then rinse in clear, clean water and wipe down with a sanitizing solution after every use.

A First-Rate Facility

Safe and sanitary food service begins with a clean facility that is in good repair. The entire facility, especially work areas, should be laid out for easy cleaning.

Eliminate and reorganize any areas that are hard to clean. You should also replace overloaded refrigerators or other equipment. The easier it is to clean an area, the more likely it will be cleaned.

Work Areas

Choose nonporous materials in your work areas. These need to be able to withstand chemical and/or steam cleaning. You should also purchase tables and counters without seams or joints that are hard to clean. Worktables on

wheels can be moved to useful areas during busy times.

Floors, Walls, and Ceilings

- Keep dirt and moisture away from floors, walls, and ceilings.
- Clean walls by wiping down with a cleaning solution. Sweep floors, then clean with a spray method or by mopping.
- Swab ceilings to keep from soaking lights and ceiling fans.
- Don't ignore corners and other hard-to-reach areas.

With Sanifloor, the food goes in the floor, not on it. The potential for slip and fall accidents are dramatically reduced. It controls liquids, crumbs and other items which are dropped on the floor. This will limit the need to clean the floor during the work shift and allows you to offer better customer service. The ability to flush the floor eliminates unpleasant smells and situations that attract pests. Visit the Web site for more information at **http://sanifloor. com**. For information on pricing or installing Sani-Floor" units, call 760-345-7987 or e-mail info@sanifloor.com.

Various cleaning supplies are used to maintain a clean floor. You can find these items at **www.tucel.com/cgi-bin/store/agora.cgi** in the Floor and Wall Clean section. These items include: brooms, mops, and dust pans. They also offer mops to clean your walls. You can contact them at 800-558-8235, by fax at 802-247-6826, or by e-mailing info@tucel.com.

Ventilation

We discussed the importance of ventilation earlier. It is critical to a clean environment. Effective ventilation will remove smoke, steam, grease, and heat from your food-preparation area. This improves air quality and reduces the possibility of fire from accumulated grease. Ventilation eliminates condensation and other airborne contaminants. In addition, it:

- Reduces the accumulation of dirt.

- Reduces odors, gases, and fumes.

- Reduces mold growth by reducing humidity.

Ensure good ventilation by:

- Using exhaust fans to remove odors and smoke.

- Using hoods over cooking areas and dishwashing equipment.

- Checking exhaust fans and hoods to make sure they operate properly.

- Cleaning hood filters according to the manufacturer's instructions.

Restrooms

Provide public and private restrooms that are convenient, sanitary, and adequately stocked with the following:

- Toilet paper.

- Antiseptic liquid soap.

- Disposable paper towels and/or air blowers.

- Covered trash receptacles with a foot pedal for the lid.

- Someone needs to check public restrooms and clean throughout the day. Provide nail brushes and sanitizing solution in employee restrooms.

Cross-Contamination Concerns

Cross-contamination is a common cause of food-borne illness. This is

the transfer of bacteria and viruses from food to food, hand to food, or equipment to food.

- **Food to food** – Raw, contaminated ingredients can be added to foods, or fluids from raw foods may drip into foods that are not cooked. A common mistake is leaving meat on an upper refrigerator shelf where it can drip onto prepared foods stored below.

- **Hand to food** – Bacteria is located all over the body: in the hair, on the skin, in clothing, in the mouth, in the nose and throat, in the intestinal tract, and on scabs or scars from skin wounds. The bacteria can end up on hands where it can spread to food. People can transfer bacteria by touching raw food and transferring it to cooked or ready-to-eat food.

- **Equipment to food** – Bacteria can pass from equipment to food when the equipment touches contaminated food and is used to prepare other food without proper cleaning and sanitizing.

Plastic wrap can hold bacteria and transfer it to other containers and food. A can opener, boxes of wrap, or a food slicer can all create cross-contamination when they are not sanitized properly.

Contributing to Foodborne Illness

The Centers for Disease Control (CDC) reveals the most common reason foodborne illness occurs is because of food mishandling. According the Center for Disease Control's Surveillance for Foodborne Disease Outbreaks (1988-1992) these are the major factors:

CAUSES OF FOODBORNE ILLNESSES	
ACTION	**PERCENT CAUSED**
Use of leftovers	4%
Improper Cleaning	7%
Cross-Contamination	7%
Contaminated raw food	7%
Inadequate reheating	12%
Improper hot storage	16%
Inadequate cooking	16%
Infected people touching food	20%
Time between preparing and serving	21%
Improper cooling of foods	40%

Controlling Bacteria

Some good ways to control bacteria are:

- Good personal hygiene.

- Eliminating cross-contamination.

- Monitoring time and temperature.

- Employing a sanitation program.

Your first step is to limit access to the restaurant. All products need to be clean when they enter your pizza shop. Following all the suggestions that have been discussed in this chapter is a great start.

Time and Temperature Control

Controlling time and temperature can be a great way to avoid contamination. Most disease causing bacteria grows between 41 and 140 degrees. When food

is cooked, reheated, and stored in the correct temperatures, the potential problems are reduced.

Believe it or not, bacteria can double every 15 minutes, which will generate over 1,000,000 cells in just 5 hours. There can be enough bacteria within 4 hours in the temperature danger zone to cause food borne illnesses. But, you can prevent this by using correct storage practices.

There will be times when food has to be in risky temperatures. So, you must minimize those times. If you take a break, put the food back in the refrigerator briefly.

Bacteria

Bacteria can be found everywhere: in the air, in your restaurant, and all over your body. Not all bacteria are bad, and some are even beneficial. There are some types of bacteria that are added to foods. But, a small amount will cause food to spoil and can generate food poisoning when eaten.

Bacteria is in a vegetative state and reproduces like any other living organism. There are types of bacteria that form spores which enable the bacteria to live in less than ideal situations, including cooking, high-salt environments, and freezing. So, these activities won't kill those bacteria. These spores must have the "ideal" conditions to multiply and cause illness.

These are the things bacteria need to reproduce:

- Food
- Time
- Acid
- Oxygen
- Temperature
- Moisture

Food – high protein or carbohydrate foods like meats, poultry, seafood, cooked potatoes, and diary products.

Acid – Most bacteria flourish in a neutral environment, but they are capable

of growing in foods that have pH levels between 4.5 and 9.0. The "pH" is indicative of how acidic or alkaline a food is. pH ranges from 0.0 to 14.0, with 7.0 being neutral. High acid foods discourage the growth of bacteria. You can limit the hazard of lower pH foods by adding acidic ingredients to increase the pH level.

Temperature – Most disease-causing bacteria grow at between 41 to 140°F. Listeria monocytogenes is the bacteria that causes food borne illness related to processed luncheon meats, can grow below 41 degrees.

Time – Bacteria needs about 4 hours to reproduce enough cells to cause a food borne illness. This is the total time the food is in the temperature danger zone.

Oxygen – Aerobic and anaerobic bacteria have different oxygen requirements. Aerobic bacteria need oxygen to grow. Anaerobic bacteria do not. Anaerobic bacteria grow well in vacuum packed or canned items.

Moisture – The amount of water in a food to support bacterial growth is called water activity. It's measured on a scale of 0.0 and 1.0. The water activity must be greater than 0.85 to support bacterial growth.

The growth of bacteria is dependent on how favorable these conditions are. Bacteria prefer moisture-saturated foods. In turn, they won't grow in dry conditions.

DANGEROUS BACTERIA

There's an estimated 76 million cases of food borne disease in the United States each year. Most of these are mild and don't last long. The CDC estimates 325,000 hospitalizations and 5,000 deaths caused by food borne diseases each year. The elderly and the young are the most at risk.

The most commonly recognized foodborne infections are those caused

by the bacteria *Campylobacter, Salmonella,* and *E. coli* O157:H7, and by a group of viruses known as the Norwalk and Norwalk-like viruses.

Campylobacter causes fever, diarrhea, and abdominal cramps. Eating undercooked chicken, or food contaminated with juices dripping from raw chicken, is the most frequent source of this infection.

Salmonella causes fever, diarrhea and abdominal cramps. When this bacteria attacks a person with poor health, it can cause serious infections.

E. coli O157:H7 is usually caused by consuming water that's contaminated with microscopic amounts of cow feces. This causes severe and bloody diarrhea and painful abdominal cramps, without much fever. If the condition becomes more severe, it includes temporary anemia, profuse bleeding, and kidney failure.

Calicivirus, or Norwalk-like virus causes an acute gastrointestinal illness, which is characterized with more vomiting than diarrhea that only lasts about two days. It's usually spread from one infected person to another. Infected kitchen staff can contaminate cold foods when they are prepared.

More information can be found on the FDA's Web site at **www.cfsan.fda. gov/~mow/intro.html**.

Personal Hygiene

One of the best and easiest ways to stop bacteria is personal hygiene. Hands are a big source of contamination and need to be washed throughout the day. Any time you sneeze or scratch your head you expose your hands to bacteria and then pass those bacteria on to other things you touch. Some great things that help prevent the spread of bacteria are: nail brushes, disposable gloves, and anti-bacterial soaps. It is critical that you train your employees properly and follow up to be sure they are following these standards.

These are some basic ways to practice good basic hygiene:

- Short hair, and/or use a hairnet.

- Clean shaven face.

- Clean clothes/uniforms.

- Clean hands and short nails.

- No unnecessary and large jewelry.

- A daily shower or bath.

- No smoking in or near the kitchen.

- Hand washing prior to work, periodically, and after handling foreign objects such as any body parts, money, food, boxes, and trash.

Many hand cleaning supplies are available to maintain the hygiene of your employees. These can be found at **www.tucel.com/cgi-bin/store/agora.cgi** in the Infection Control Clean section. You can also contact them for more details call or e-mail info@tucel.com.

When employees are getting a cold or have a cut, they shouldn't be at work. This is a way to spread bacteria. Some businesses require employees to take a complete medical exam with blood and urine tests, but this is cost prohibitive for others.

Hand Washing

Hand washing is the most critical aspect of personal hygiene. Unless they are washing fruits and vegetables, employees should not touch ready-to-eat foods with their bare hands. Instead, they can use single use gloves, spatulas, tongs, or deli paper.

Always wash your hands after these activities:

- Smoking

- Eating

- Using the restroom

- Handling money

- Touching raw food

- Touching or combing your hair

- Coughing, sneezing, or blowing your nose

- Taking a break

- Handling anything dirty

Clothing

Dirty clothes can hold bacteria, whether these are your work clothes or personal clothing. It is common to touch your clothing while working, and this transfers bacteria to the food. Another problem is that customers get a bad message when they see employees in dirty clothes. There were days when we were so busy, I went through many aprons because of flour, sauce, and other ingredients getting all over my apron. Other days, the sleeves of my uniform shirt were several shades lighter from flour and spinning dough. These are signs of working hard, but change into a clean uniform or apron when needed.

Aprons, Etc provides a wide variety of apron options. There are washable and disposable choices. You have the opportunity to have your business name and logo printed on your aprons. Keep in mind that you will need a lot of aprons and will need to wash them. Some of the aprons available are displayed at **www.apronsetc.com/aprons.htm#1**.

Dickie's Chef Aprons and Hats are high quality products. These items are functional and have the durability that Dickie's is famous for. The aprons

provide oversized pockets and are constructed to be comfortable for your staff. They are available with a soil resistant finish. Dickie's has a wide selection of aprons, chef hats, shirts, pants, and vests. They can be seen at **www.dickieschef.com**. Call 866-262-6288 or fax 877-353-9044 for more information.

Royal Industries offers aprons, chef's coats, and chef's hats. These are all options for your cook staff. Royal Industries, Inc. is an innovative leader in the Foodservice Industry, serving a nationwide market of commercial products for the food service industry. Their Web site is **www.royalindustriesinc.com** and you can contact them by phone at 800-782-1200 or by fax at 800-321-3295.

Eating, Drinking, or Using Tobacco

Some employees feel it's acceptable to eat in the food preparation area since they work in a restaurant. But, this needs to be prohibited along with smoking and drinking. These activities increase the chance of spreading bacteria and other contaminants to the food that is being prepared. In some areas of your pizza shop it may be very hot and employees can have closed drink containers in those areas. It is miserably hot to tend deck ovens during the summer months.

Eyes, Nose, and Mouth

When you or your employees have a cold or even allergy problems, there will be sneezing and coughing. This can easily contaminate food, utensils, equipment, and linen. While employees are sick or sneezing, assign them to a duty where they don't come into contact with the food.

Hair Restraints

Customers are concerned about hair contamination in their food. All of us have experienced hair in our food at one time or another. Be aware of this common concern, and be sure your employees use caps or hairnets. It's a simple way to keep hair out of the food that is being prepared. The food can also be contaminated when employees touch their hair and then continue working.

Dishware

Even though your employees have been trained to wash their hands correctly, they still need to use care when handling dishware. These tips will help your employees handle dishware without contaminating the portions that will touch the customers' food or mouth.

- Use tongs, scoops, or food grade rubber gloves to pick up food items.

- Pick up glasses from the outside and hold cups from the handle or the bottom to avoid touching the rims or inside.

- Pick up forks and spoons by the handles.

- Carry plates by the bottoms or edges. Do not stack dishes, cups, and saucers to carry more.

- Wash your hands after handling soiled dishes.

- This may seem redundant, but always wash your hands before putting on gloves. Those gloves can be contaminated if you do something else while wearing them. When your gloves are

contaminated throw them away, wash your hands, and put on fresh gloves before returning to the food preparation.

• Don't use a utensil to taste more than one food item.

Gloves

Multiuse gloves can be a breeding ground for pathogens. These gloves must be washed, sanitized, and rinsed between uses. Hands must also be washed before putting gloves on. When gloves are soiled or the inside is contaminated, they should be discarded. Do not use slash-resistant gloves with ready-to-eat foods because they cannot be cleaned and sanitized very easily.

Natural Latex Rubber (NRL) Gloves – Natural rubber latex gloves can cause allergic reactions in some people. They can also cause reactions in people who eat the food being prepared with latex gloves. Keep this in mind when making a decision about the sort of gloves you will use in your pizza shop.

Each of these techniques are ways to protect your pizza shop and your customers from concerns about bacteria and contamination. There are many sources for additional information with the government and your local health department. While these tips involve more work and training, they will help you protect your business and your customers.

23

Leaving Your Business

No matter how much you enjoy your business, at some point in time, you will probably try to sell it. The alternatives are to go out of business or pass it on to your heirs. There is no way to know what will prompt you to sell. At that time, you will realize how important it was to build a saleable business to increase your return on investment. Since you are reading this book, you will know in the beginning that it is good to build your business with a possible sale in mind.

A profitable pizza shop with a loyal customer base and effective business systems can generate top dollar when you are ready to sell. This profit is a reward for those long, hard hours that went into developing the business.

Start building a valuable and profitable business from the start, and it will provide you with an excellent income. The right building blocks and a solid foundation will provide you with a valuable asset that can be sold in the future.

Atlantic Publishing offers a book titled *How to Buy and or Sell a Small Business for Maximum Profit – A Step-by-Step Guide* (**www.atlantic-pub.com**, Item # HBS-01). This one book offers many tips on how you can get the best price for your business when you are ready to sell. It explains the piles of paperwork and the laws which affect you when you sell or buy a business. You shouldn't begin the sales process before you read this book.

Your Exit Plan

You need to develop an exit plan. It doesn't need to be as detailed as your business plan, but you should review it annually to make any necessary changes. These changes are based on the condition of your business and your goals. Your plan should cover:

- **Best-case scenario** – When do you want to retire? Will you sell the business outright, or will your family manage it?

- **Current value** – What could you get if you liquidated or sold it?

- **Enhance business value** – Are there changes that would make the business more appealing to a buyer? Are there changes you didn't want to make, but that would increase the value? It's time to consider those.

- **Worst-case scenario** – What can be done in an emergency?

- **Prepare for the sale** – What are the tax implications of selling?

- **Bowing out** – How can you leave your business to others? How do you dissolve partnerships or corporations?

- **Secure your family's financial health** – Prepare your will. Can your family run the business without you? Do they have instructions for what to do if you are incapacitated?

You should meet with your attorney and accountant for invaluable advice about how to create your plan. You can see some examples of exit plans at:

- Principal Financial Group – **www.principal.com/bizprotection/ exitplan.htm**

- Family Business Experts – **www.family-business-experts.com/ exit-planning.html**

- American Express Small Business – **www.americanexpress.com/ smallbusiness**

Pass Your Business On

Millions of businesses are owned and operated by family members. Some of these are passed down through the generations, and some family members continue the family legacy. Another option is to have business partners or employees run your business.

If you plan to leave the business to your family, consider the tax implications. These issues and concerns include inheritance tax, trusts, and tax-free gifts. Each of these options is complicated and you should let the experts handle them. Talk with your banker, accountant, lawyer, and your estate planner. These professionals can ensure a smooth transition and minimize the tax burdens on your family.

- The U.S. Chamber of Commerce offers advice on passing your business on at **www.uschamber.com**.

- CCH Business Owner's Toolkit has helpful articles at **www.toolkit.cch.com**.

Groom Your Replacement

Depending on your plan, someone else may take over your position and responsibilities within the company. It's time-consuming to groom a replacement. When you hire people, you can consider whether they would

be a good successor to you. Also consider whether they would keep the best interests of your family in mind.

When you are at this point talk to the person you are considering. Share your vision for the future and develop a plan. Develop a plan to:

- Train him or her on the aspects of the business he doesn't understand.

- Increase his or her responsibilities to learn new aspects of the business.

- Review his or her decision-making abilities and skills.

- Listen to his or her needs and ideas and discuss ways to make them work.

- Share money-management goals and how you accomplish them.

- Set a timeline for transfer and stick to it unless there are major problems.

- Implement transition stages to lessen your duties and increase his.

- Set benchmarks and goals for each stage in the process.

- Examine and improve "problem" issues.

- Physically and mentally prepare yourself to leave the business.

Selling Your Business to Your Employees

If your family isn't interested in being involved without you, there is the option to sell to an employee or a group of employees. This has potential problems and risks unless they have sufficient financing. If you plan to sell to employees or friends, it's best to have your accountant or attorney act as a go-between to keep the transaction professional.

It's very easy to hurt one another in this situation. The potential buyers

will likely have ideas about how to change "your business" and "your way of doing things." You may also find it difficult to haggle over money with your friends.

Suggest that your employees talk to a professional in order to clearly understand what they are getting into. Business Law at **www.businesslaw. gov** discusses Employee-Owned Stock Plans (EOSP) as a way to transfer the business to your employees. You can also find advice from The National Center for Employee Ownership at **www.nceo.org**, and the Beyster Institute for Entrepreneurial Employee Ownership at **www.fed.org**.

Transferring your business to a worker co-op offers some advantages for everyone. Worker co-op structures are discussed at the National Cooperative Business Association at **www.ncba.org**. Transferring your ownership to employees (similar to family inheritance) can also be done.

Again, talk with professionals to ensure you have covered all the bases and things are being done in the best interest of the people involved. Talk to professionals you trust.

Say Goodbye

Saying goodbye to your pizza shop, the long hours and your dreams can be difficult. No matter how much you want to retire or to leave, actually leaving is hard. It is easier to say that final goodbye when you have planned for it. Knowing that your business will be taken care of will help you make the adjustment and changes that are necessary. You sacrificed and struggled to build a profitable and successful pizza shop—it is also your responsibility to preserve it!

Conclusion

We reviewed a lot of information within these pages. There are so many things to consider and expenses to evaluate, and I tried to cover all of these areas. The case studies I collected are from people who had personal experiences that I felt would be beneficial to you. Be sure to review the accompanying CD for forms and additional information you can print out.

Running a pizza and sub shop can be a lot of fun and very rewarding, but you also need a clear idea of the amount of work involved. Don't let it scare you away from your desire to own a pizza shop. Just go into this venture with your eyes wide open.

The tips were included to give you an insider's view of things that will give you an advantage over your competitors. Little alterations in the way you do business, design your menu, promote your business, control costs, and more will make the difference in whether you succeed or fail in business.

It's my sincere hope that you can benefit from the suggestions, information and my personal experiences included in the book. You could be the next big thing to hit the ever-growing pizza industry.

Manufacturer's Reference

Atlantic Publishing offers companies that provide relevant products and/or services the opportunity to be featured in their publications at no cost. Atlantic Publishing does not endorse the products offered by the manufacturers and was not compensated in any way to include photos or information in this reference manual. Submissions were voluntary. This is a comprehensive listing to help our readers find companies and products. Listings are alphabetical. We have provided Web sites and e-mail addresses if available. If you know some data that has changed or know of a company that should be listed, please use the form below and contact us via our toll free fax at **877-682-7819**.

Edit directory of manufacturers

❏ Please add a new listing
❏ Please edit/append my listing on page # _____

Your Name: _____

Organization Name: _____

Address: _____

_____

City: _____ State: _____ Zip: _____

Telephone: _____ Fax: _____

Web site URL: _____

E-mail Address: _____

Comments: _____

_____

_____

Please fax this form to 877-682-7819

Alto-Shaam, Inc
W164 N9221 Water Street
Menomonee Falls, WI 53052
1-800-558-8744
www.alto-shaam.com

Amana Commercial Products
2800 220th Trail
Amana, IA 52204
1-888-262-6271
www.amanacommercial.com

America Corporation
PO Box 91
13686 Red Arrow Highway
Harbert, MI 49115
1-800-621-5075
www.america-americabirchtrays.com

Aprons, Etc.
PO Box 1132
9 Ellwood Court
Mauldin, SC 29662
1-800-460-7836
www.apronsetc.com

Art Marble Furniture, Inc.
PO Box 413208
Kansas City, MO 64141
www.artmarblefurniture.com

Axim Equipment
4401 Blue Mound Road
Fort Worth, TX 76106
www.axiomequipment.com

Bakers Pride Oven Company
30 Pine Street
New Rochelle, NY 10801
1-914-576-0200
www.bakerspride.com

Banners Across America
6116 Camas Canyon Avenue
1-702-544-0699
Las Vegas, NV 89130
www.bestchangeablebanners.com

Berry Plastics Corporation
2330 Packer Road
Lawrence, KS 66049
1-812-424-2904
www.berryplastics.com

Biocorp
15301 140th Avenue
Becker, MN 55308
1-866-348-8348
www.biocorpaavc.com

Blodgett
44 Lakeside Avenue
Burlington, VT 05401
1-800-331-5842
www.blodgett.com

Browne-Halco, Inc.
2840 Morris Avenue
Union, NJ 07083
1-888-289-1005
www.halco.com

CAL-MIL Plastic Products
4079 Calle Platino
Oceanside, CA 92056
1-800-321-9069
www.calmil.com

California Milk Advisory Board
400 Oyster Point Boulevard,
Suite 220
South San Francisco, CA 94080
www.realcaliforniacheese.com

Campus Collection
PO Box 2904
Tuscaloosa, AL 35403
1-800-289-8744
www.campuscollection.net

Candle Lamp Company
1799 Rustin Avenue
Riverside, CA 92507
1-877-526-7748
www.candlelamp.com

CommLog
2509 E Darrel Road
Phoenix, AZ 85042
1-800-962-6564
www.commlog.com

DayMark Food Safety Systems
12830 South Dixie Highway
Bowling Green, OH 43402
1-800-847-0101
www.daymark.biz

Dexmet Corp
7 Great Hill Road
Naugatuck, CT 06770
1-877-4-Dri-Pie
www.dripie.com

Dur-A-Flex Inc.
95 Goodwin Street
East Hartford, CT 06108
1-860-528-9838
www.dura-a-flex.com

Duncan Industries
PO Box 802822
Santa Clarita, CA 91380
1-800-785-4449

www.kitchengrips.com

Effortless Innovations, Inc
107B Honeysuckle Lane
Largo, FL 33770
1-888-70-LUNCH
www.lunchandearn.com

Franklin Machine Products
101 Mt. Holly Bypass
Lumberton, NJ 08048
1-800-257-7737
www.fmponline.com

Front Line
95 16th Street SW
Barberton, OH   44203
1-877-776-1100
www.frontlineii.com

Gasser Chair Company
4136 Logan Way
Youngstown, OH 44505
1-330-759-2234
www.gasserchair.com

General Espresso Equipment Corporation
7912 Industrial Village Road
Greensboro, NC 27409
1-336-393-0224
www.geec.com

Genpak
PO Box 727
Glen Falls, NY 12801
1-518-798-9511
www.genpak.com

Global Cooking Systems
PO Box 75007
Wichita, KS 67275
1-866-681-2971
www.globalcookingsystems.com

Henny Penny Corporation
1219 U.S. 35 West
Eaton, OH 45320
1-800-417-8417
www.hennypenny.com

Hilden America, Inc.
1044 Commerce Lane
So. Boston, VA 24592
1-800-431-2514
www.hildenamerica.com

InTouch POS
1601 N California Boulevard
Walnut Creek, CA 94596
1-800-777-8202
www.intouchpos.com

Jones Soda
234 9th Avenue North
Seattle, WA 98109
www.jonessoda.com

Loyal Rewards
812 Chestnut Street
Perkasie, PA 18944
1-800-309-7228
www.loyalrewards.com

Moving Targets
812 Chestnut Street
Perkasie, PA 18944
1-800-926-2451
www.movingtargets.com

Pizza Equipment Supply, Inc.
1437 E. Franklin Boulevard
Suite 232
Gastonia, NC 28054
1-704-629-0000
www.pesi.us

Pizza Ovens.com
235B Industry Parkway
Nicholasville, KY 40356
1-877-FOR-OVEN
www.pizzaovens.com

Polar Ware Company
2806 North 15th Street
Sheboygan, WI 53083
1-800-237-3655
www.polarware.com

Postcard Press
1871 Broadwick Street
Rancho Dominguez, CA 90220
1-800-957-5787
www.postcardpress.com

Regal Ware, Inc.
1675 Reigle Drive
Kewaskum, WI 53040
1-262-626-2121
www.regalwarefoodservice.com

Rossetto
1822 Ridge Avenue
Evanston, IL 60201
www.rosseto.com

Rupari Food Services Inc.
15600 S Wentworth Avenue
South Holland, IL 60473
www.rupari.com

Sabert
879-899 Main Street
Sayreville, NJ 08872
1-800-722-3781
www.sabert.com

Sitram USA
4081 Calle Tesoro, Suite G
Camarillo, CA 93012
1-800-515-8585
www.sitramcookware.com

Slecta Corp dba Dickies Chef
13780 Benchmark Drive
Farmers Branch, TX 75234
1-866-262-6288
www.dickiechef.com

Speedline Solutions
1897-B Front Street
Lynden, WA 98264
1-888-400-9185
www.speedlinesolutions.com

Sportsblaster.com
122 N 1100 W
Farmington, UT 84025
1-877-529-8169
www.sportsblaster.com

Sunkist Foodservice Eq.
720 E Sunkist Street
Ontario, CA 91761
1-800-383-7141
www.sunkistfs.com/equipment

Tucel Industries
2014 Forestdale Road
Forestdale, VT 05745
1-800-558-8235
www.tucel.com

U.S. Cooler
325 Payson Avenue
Quincy, IL 62301
1-800-521-2665
www.uscooler.com

Vital Link POS
8567 Vinup Road
Lynden, WA 98264
1-877-448-5300
www.VitalLinkPOS.com

Wes-Pak, Inc.
9100 Frazier Pike
Little Rock, AR 72206
1-800-493-7725
www.wespakinc.com

WNA Comet
6 Stuart Road
Chelmsford, MA 01824
1-888-962-2877
www.wna-inc.com

Your Bag Lady
67 34th Street, 6th Floor
Brooklyn, NY 11232
1-888-569-9903
www.yourbaglady.com

Resources

Getting Your Slice of the Pie, Tracy Powell, Empowered Innovations, Jacksonville, Indiana

The Art of Pizza Making – Trade Secrets and Recipes, Dominick DeAngelis, The Creative Pizza Company, Plains, Pennsylvania

The Restaurant Manager's Handbook, Douglas R. Brown, Atlantic Publishing, Ocala, Florida

How to Open a Financially Successful Bed & Breakfast or Small Hotel, Atlantic Publishing, Ocala, Florida

Index

A

accident 427
accountant 80, 96, 115
actual food cost 219
advertising 20, 70, 77, 117, 358
air 435
alcohol 144
alfredo 131
allergies 143
American cheese 173
American Diabetes Association 141
American Heart Association 141
American Institute of Cancer Research 141
American Management Association 275
Americans with Disabilities Act 280
appearance 164
appetizers 159, 178, 236
appraisal 55
artwork 420
asiago cheese 173
auction 300

B

bacon 181
bacteria 440, 466
balance sheet 61
bankruptcy 79
beef 181
beer 152
Better Business Bureau 81
beverage dispensers 421
beverages 236
birthdays 386
Blood Alcohol Concentration 144
bookkeeping 354

booths 412
breakeven point 220
brochure 371, 374
Buddy LaRosa 28
budgets 109, 298
burns 428
business cards 370, 374
business license 89
business plan 59

C

calzone 185, 236
cannoli 205
canola oil 142
carbohydrates 141
carryout 399
cash 101
cash flow projections 73
ceiling 417
chairs 412
chamber of commerce 39
charity 391
check average 219
checks 105
cheddar 132, 173
cheese 132, 160, 173
chicken piccata 189
choking 433
colors 420
competition 43, 61, 69, 361
competitive pricing 227
computer 324
condiment 316
contamination 439
contributions 117
convection ovens 307
conveyor ovens 311

cook 257
cooking 453
cookware 303
cooperative purchasing 339
corporations 52, 64
coupons 103, 381
credit cards 104
critical control points 442
cross-contamination 464
cross-training 232, 257
customer recognition 386
customers 361, 385
cuts 429

D

daily specials 237
database 386
debit cards 106
debt 118
deck ovens 307, 309
deep chilling 449
delivery 259, 320, 340, 351, 399, 400
demographics 39
demo models 300
depreciation 114, 118
diabetes 141
disclaimer 254
discounts 365
disk-heated bags 405
displays 421
Domino's Pizza 29
dough 128, 142, 167
drive-thru 127
dry storage 353, 447

E

e-mail 367
e-mail marketing 359
East of Chicago Pizza 29
electricity 116
employee handbook 284

employees 113, 273
entertainment 117
entrees 236
equipment 298
equity funds 51
ergonomics 434
expenses 211
expiration dates 363, 446

F

falling 432
Federal Identification number 93
Federal Trade Commission 81
feta cheese 173
fettucine alfredo 190
fettunta 178
fiber 141
financial analysis 228
financial plan 109
financing 51
fire 426
first aid 426
flour 129
fontino cheese 173
food-borne illnesses 444
food allergies 143
food cost ratio 218
food costs 209
food safety 407
food service license 90
franchise 22, 29, 72, 75
freight 115
frozen storage 450
fruit 142
fryers 318

G

garlic 131
gas 116
gelato 207
gift cards 103

gift certificates 106, 382
gloves 474
gluten 130, 140
goat cheese 173
gourmet 136
grandfather clauses 47

H

HACCP 440
hair 473
hazardous chemicals 434
hazards 442
healthy eating 140
heat 116
hiring 276
holding 454
hot bag 404
hygiene 442, 466

I

income statement 73
induction heated bags 406
ingredients 127, 160, 164, 221, 317
inspection 55
insurance 20, 116, 274, 400
Internet 377
interview 277
intuitive pricing 227
inventory 20, 216, 332, 338
inventory costs 209
issuing 341
Italian sub 200

J

job descriptions 260

L

labor costs 113, 209

lasagna 195, 402
lawyer 81
layout 233
lease 20, 301
lease terms 46
legal fees 22
liability insurance 401
lighting 344, 418
limited liability company 64
liquor license 92, 144
loan 55
loan application 73
location 42, 60, 65
logo 357, 366, 369
low-carb 125

M

maintenance 20, 115
makeline 215
management plan 71
manager 258
manicotti 192
marinara sauce 176
marinate 452
market area research 38
marketing 209, 357
material safety data sheet 434
mayonnaise 142
meat 133
Medicare 100
menu 235, 367, 376
menu design 243
mixers 320
monterey jack cheese 173
mozzarella 132, 173

N

National Association of Pizzeria Operators 27
National Restaurant Association 122, 147, 216, 361

network 327
networking 27
no-carb 125
nutritional claims 254

O

office 354
olives 181
onions 131, 181
operating budget 72
operational costs 114
ordering 217
orientation 288
OSHA 426
ovens 307
overtime 113

P

packaging 304
pan 160
Papa John's 28
paper 373
parking 345
parmesan cheese 173
partnerships 52, 64
pasta primavera 193
patents 80
pay 283
payroll 97
pepperoni 181
peppers 132, 181
personal financial statement 62
personnel file 287
pesticides 433
pizza pans 313
plants 346
poison 433
population 39
pork 181
portion control 240
POS 327

press release 394
price 36, 69, 226
production 162
productivity 234
product mix 68
profit analysis 220
profits 209, 224
property taxes 116
protein 129
provolone 132, 173
psychological pricing 227
public relations 387
punch card 384
purchasing 212, 217, 221, 337, 444

Q

quality standards 164

R

rack ovens 307
ravioli 197, 198
real estate 45
rebuilt 300
receiving 213, 445
recipes 159, 167, 221, 241
reconditioned 300
reduced-calorie 142
reduced-fat 142
refrigerated food prep table 316
refrigerated storage 448
refrigerators 323
research 39, 60
restrooms 347, 464
resume 62
return on investment 297
reuben 201
revenue 110
revolving tray oven 307
ricotta cheese 173
royalties 76

S

safety 426
salaries 20, 113, 274
sales 111
sales mix 224
sales tax 89
sales volume 41
samples 162
sauce 130, 174
sausage 181
scales 318
scheduling 230, 290
screening 276
seafood 134
security 114
service contracts 306
serving 454
ServSafe 90
shipping 351
Small Business Administration 20, 53, 87
Small Business Development Center 50
smell 164
Social Security 100
sole proprietorship 64
sorbet 142
spaghetti 196
starch 141
storage 213, 350, 440, 446
store vouchers 103
substitutions 164
survey 55

T

tables 412
tagline 357
take-and-bake 127
taxes 20, 99
temperature 164
termination 294
texture 164
thaw 452
theft 228

thermal bags 405
toppings 131, 159
trademarks 80
training 274, 287, 439
trial-and-error pricing 227
turkey 181

U

uniforms 411
uniform system of accounts for restaurants 216
United States Census Bureau 39
utilities 20, 115

V

vegetables 133
vegetarian 141
vehicle 400
vendors 445
ventilation 463
venture capital 52

W

wages 20
waste 218, 353
water 322
Web site 375
whole grain 142
windows 346
wine 147
wood fire ovens 313
workstations 234

Z

ziti 402
zoning 91

Shri Henkel is from the Shenandoah Valley of Virginia. She had a strong desire to create and write for many years. Shri owns a management and marketing consulting business and is a freelance writer and marketing professional.

Her first three non-fiction books, which focus on business management, will be released in 2006.

Shri has 21 years of business management experience and 15 years of marketing experience. She uses the knowledge she gained in this work to create a helpful guidebook for business managers. These experiences include things that work and tips about things to avoid.

Shri worked as an assistant manager, marketing coordinator, and then a store manger for Domino's Pizza. This experience was invaluable when writing the pizza and sub shop book.

In addition to her non-fiction work, Shri has two novels that were released in early 2006. Her love of the coast, history, and lighthouses shows in her stories. On a trip to Cape Ann with her brother Chris, Shri discovered the area that is the setting for a series of books. The rugged land, hard-working people, and rich history were too compelling to ignore. Cape Ann and Gloucester, Massachusetts, are the setting for several of her books that focus on the "Stormy View" lighthouse.

For more information about Shri's work, visit her fiction Web site at **www.nikkileigh.com** or her business Web site at **www.sandcconsulting.com**.